THE DRAGON GIRL

THE BEGINNING

DARKHUNTER25

Printed in the United States of America.

ISBN	Paperback	978-1-68536-994-1
	Hardback	978-1-68536-995-8
	eBook	978-1-68536-996-5

Westwood Books Publishing LLC
Atlanta Financial Center
3343 Peachtree Rd NE Ste 145-725
Atlanta, GA 30326

www.westwoodbookspublishing.com

Chapter 1

"Help me, Crystal! I got stuck under a fallen tree, and I can't move it!" my sister shouted. Walking down the road, I was trying to find my younger sister, Sapphire.

"Where are you, little sis? I can hear your voice, but I can't see you!" I shouted worryingly.

"I'm over here! Under this big tree! I think it's an oak tree, but I'm not sure. . .Oh! I see you to my left!" She said quickly,

"Okay, I see the tree, and y-ooh, Sapphire! There you are! I'm coming. We will get you out of there." I said to her as I got closer to the tree.

"What do you think you are doing to her?" Said an angry voice. I looked over my shoulder, shocked to see the angry voice belonged to my best friend Laura and her friend Tasha.

"I'm saving my sister if you don't mind," I said.

"I do *not* think so! She broke into our house and stole some of our precious belongings that were not for her sticky fingers to touch," said Tasha.

"If you want her, you've got to get through me!" I said with anger.

"Okay, fine with us then," they said in unison. And then they did something unexpected.

"Then suffer the decision you made," Tasha said as she threw a crystal at me.

1

"Crystal, don't let it touch you, or it will kill you." Sapphire cried. But it was too late. By the time she said it, the crystal had already hit me.

"Aaaaaahhhhhh!"

I woke up covered in sweat and panting. I got up to go to the bathroom to wash my face. I went inside and turned on the light as I went in. I turned the faucet on, cupped my hands, and splashed water on my face to wake me up better. I looked in the mirror and saw a figure behind me, which scared me out of my socks. I turned around to see who it was. *Nothing was there.* I figured I saw things as usual, but it was there again when I looked back in the mirror. I started to walk backward out of the door when the figure shut with such force that it startled me.

"Where do you think you're going? We need to talk about you and your future." A voice said to me.

"Who are you?" I asked the figure.

"I'm Professor Keith. I'm from the future. I'm here to tell you some things you need to know. I need you to come with me to the future and see what it holds for you." He said.

"No way, I'm staying here. You can't make me go!" I said.

"Too late for that decision. You will come with me even by force." He said to me. Before I could do anything, a vortex came out of nowhere, taking me to an unknown place. When we stopped, I looked around to see if it was the same world, but a little.

"Okay, now follow me to my laboratory for your treatment." He spoke. I followed him. As I followed him, I noticed that not only did I not see his house, but also, I didn't see any houses. It was rolling hills as far as the night would let me see.

"Where is your laboratory?" I asked him.

"Right here under this tree, the front door is next to that big oak tree." He said to me.

Finally, I saw the door. We went into the professor's house and down to his laboratory. Inside, he had some of the weirdest things I had ever seen. I did not ask or want to know where they were or what they were doing. As we went deeper, I followed him to a machine that looked like something from a science fiction movie.

"This will tell me all about you with a single drop of blood. So, could you give me your arm? Don't force me to make you do as I ask unless you enjoy pain." He said when he saw the skeptical look on my face.

Slowly, I placed my arm in the machine, unaware of the pain I was about to feel. It was like a bullet piercing my skin. I had never felt such pain. To my surprise, the pain left as quickly as it came.

"All right, that's that. . .now let's take a look at the results. . .okay, looks like you are clear on that. . .and that too. . .and what is this I'm seeing here?" he said, though it seemed he was talking to his self rather than me. "Oh, looks like you are the right person we need for this testing we do here," he said, looking at me.

"What do you mean by that, professor?" I asked him, *puzzled*.

"It means you will be a lab rat for us for this new drug I've created." He said with a look of excitement in his eyes.

"And what if I say no? Because I disagree, and I'm leaving now. Bye!" I said quickly, slightly insulted by his answer.

"No, you don't," he said. I didn't realize anyone else was in there until someone suddenly grabbed me from behind. I broke free and ran for the door. I was five feet away, reaching for the handle when I suddenly hit the floor like a ton of bricks. I heard footsteps approaching from behind me. A foot rolled me hard onto my back; I was staring at the face that went to the hands that grabbed me from behind. He was young – maybe nineteen. He would have looked innocent except for the anger in his eyes. He was another lab rat of the professors. I didn't care; I just knew I didn't want to be his next subject. The next face I saw in my limited line of site was Professor Keith's. He smiled menacingly for a moment before speaking.

"Don't worry, dear; I promise you will be all right. We are not going to h. . .you a. . .so sle. . ." that is all I heard them say to me.

When I woke again, I got strapped to a lab bed surrounded by machines with wires attached. I kept looking around until I saw another figure strapped to another table to my left side. The female was about ten feet away. Looking at her, I thought I remembered her from somewhere around town, but I could not find her name at the time. Then I heard a door opening and closing and a shadow approaching behind me.

"Okay, let's see what treatment we need to use on you first. Ah, here we go. This one right here will do the trick. Now hold still." He said, walking towards me with a rather large needle.

"I don't think so! You're not sticking me with anything." I yelled.

"And how are you going to stop me." He said, smiling. And he was right. There was no way to stop him.

"With my help, you psycho." Said the girl next to me; she was awake now and angry.

"Now, shut up before I get rid of you for good," he said, glaring at her.

"Just try it." She said spitefully to him. He turned his attention to her as if going to inject her with the contents of the syringe. As he got close to the bed, lowering the needle towards her arm, she amazingly broke the straps holding her down and hit him with such force that it knocked him out.

After making sure he got knocked out, she untied me. We ran for the door. When we made it outside, I stopped to try and remember which way the professor had brought me. What took place next almost made me hit the floor again. The girl that helped me escape suddenly spawned a massive set of wings.

Before I could even process what I was seeing, she immediately grabbed me and took off into flight. I was terrified at first. I didn't know what to think.

"Relax, it's okay. I promise I'm helping you." She said, looking down and seeing how scared I was. Though her grasp around me was only holding me up, and we were flying frighteningly high, her voice was soothing when she spoke. *I believed her.*

I looked around and noticed that this world was almost like mine. I thought I must be dreaming. My thoughts were interrupted by my hero steering us toward the ground.

We landed in the woods, a tree that looked exactly like the one from my dream, to be exact; my sister wasn't there.

"Where are we?" I asked her to look around.

"Who are you," I said without giving her time to answer the first question. "What's going on here? How can you fly?! What are you? Who was that man at the lab? I want answers!" I spat the last part at her. I was glaring through tears. When did I start crying? I thought. But I didn't care. I was scared. I just wanted to know what was going on.

Slowly, she walked towards me. "We are in the same place you dreamed of when your sister got trapped under a tree. Do you recognize it?" I nodded my head.

"Okay, my name is Silverie. I've been waiting for you. You will need my help with the events that are about to take place in your life. You need to trust me. We only have a little time for me to explain what is going on with you, but we have little time. Explaining this would be a lot faster if you drink this." She said.

"Are you kidding me?! You want me to drink that after what just happened!? What do you mean, dragon girl? Is that how you can fly? None of this doesn't make sense." I said, still angry.

"Look, I know you're confused, but please trust me. I'm telling you the truth. Would I have just saved your life if I were here to hurt you? You must listen. They are still after us. By now, Professor Keith has gone to inform the twin sisters that he failed back there, and that's the last thing we need right now when you do not know what's happening. Please, drink this."

She was right. I had to trust her. "I might be crazy," I said as I swallowed the drink in one gulp. I didn't feel anything at first. Then like lighting, it hit me. My mind was flooding with the knowledge of previous dragon heroes. Where they come from and what they do. It was terrific, but still, it didn't seem real. Could I be one of these things?

I looked at Silverie. I was stunned as I had ever been. Calmly, she continued without asking anything about what I'd seen.

"Now, you aren't allowed to tell anybody about your powers. Nobody can know. Also, don't use your powers unless you need to." At that moment, three figures came out of the woods, walking towards us.

Silverie turned to me and said, "It's the *Twin Sisters*. Stay away from them." Before she could say anything else, she got surrounded by a force field she could not break out of alone.

"Well, well, well, what do we have here? The girl that got *Away from You*, Professor Dimwit!" said one of the sisters, "What should we do to her, sis?" turning to her sister.

"I don't know; the only thing that comes to my mind is to kill her." Said the other sister.

"I have an idea. Why don't you-" I didn't finish.

Instead, I turned to Silverie, thinking I needed to break the force field. As I reached for her, thinking maybe I could pull her out of it, a bright light shot out of my hand, breaking the force field.

Before I could even process what I had just done, Silverie rushed forward, attacking the sisters. But she was thrown back as quickly as she had run over there. It was as though the Twin Sisters were more robust than Silverie. If they were stronger than her, I knew they were stronger than me. What were we going to do? At that point, Silverie turned to me and said, "You need to get back to your time and change this before it gets too bad for me to handle."

"No, I want to help you," I said,

"No, you can't. For one, the Twin Sisters are too strong for both of us. Two, you are needed back in your time to prevent this from happening. I'll contact you, and if I make it, that will tell you what you need to do to help us in your time, understood?" Silverie said quickly. The Twin Sisters were getting ready to attack again.

"But," I started to say.

"No butts about it." She said, cutting me off and pulling some capsules out of her pocket. "You have got to get back to your time if you want to live and stop this madness from ever happening. It's the only way. Now, go before you get killed." She said.

At that moment, one of the sisters threw a crystal at Silverie. She let go of the capsule, ducking to avoid the crystal. When the tablet hit the ground, it made what looked like a portal. Silverie quickly pushed me into it, and everything around me dissolved. The capsule had created a portal. I was going back to my time. Everything around me was a blur, and my mind began racing. I couldn't focus on anything. I wanted to know what happened to Silverie. *Did she make it? Where am I going? What about all this dragon stuff?* Thousands of questions were running through my mind.

Then, just as fast as it started, everything began to slow down. I thought I must be almost home. That was good because I wanted to think things over slowly. However, as things slowed down more, unknown drowsiness overcame me. *I couldn't think at all.* As I somehow lay in my bed, I was trying to think about all that had happened, but now that I'd felt tired, I didn't want to. The last thing I knew, everything around me was still and quiet. I fell asleep.

Chapter 2

I woke up the following day to find myself covered in sweat and wondered what had happened during the night. *Was it all a dream? Did it happen? It had to be a dream; it just had to.* I looked at my clock. It was six o'clock in the morning. I needed to get ready for school. I got into the shower, still thinking about my dream. I just couldn't quit thinking about it. Not until I heard the familiar voices of my family that brought me back to reality.

"Kids, you need to come to eat before school starts." My Mom said. I rushed to get dressed and went downstairs to hear my fifteen-year-old sister complaining.

"Do we have to go to school today!? We just moved here a week ago. I miss my old school back in Bayview, New York." Sapphire said.

"Oh, quit your complaining, girl." said her twin brother, David.

"I didn't ask for your opinion on the subject." Said Sapphire.

"Okay, you two, stop the fighting." My Mom said, "Crystal, come down and eat. You'll have to take your brother and sister to school while I take Kevin and Susan to their school." My mother said to me as I walked down the stairs. Kevin is a twelve-year-old boy with nothing but games on his mind. Susan is the youngest of us at the age of nine. Her birthday is in about three months. "I have been to both the schools to do the paperwork so that you can go straight to class.

"Crystal, I have your parking sticker for your car, so you don't have to worry about that." Mom said again.

"Thanks, Mom, I appreciate that. Are we ready to go yet?" I asked David and Sapphire.

"No, because we don't want to go to school today."

"Well, you don't have a choice. I have to go so I can get to the practice field for football tryouts." I said to them.

"Why are you trying that dumb football stuff again? You know what happened last year." Susan said.

"Yes, I know, but this school has struggled in the past years to make it to the championship, yet they can't make it through the first playoff game, and I'll be able to teach them a few things. And as far as I know, the coach wants me back up there. But seeing as we moved and can't be there, I emailed him some pointers, and now they are doing very well. I'm only trying to help them out." I said to her.

"All right, that's fine by me. Just don't get hurt out there, okay? I don't want anything to happen to you." She said to me.

We finally got inside my car. A prize Mitsubishi Lancer Evolution VIII with a slick black paint job and a turbo kit to give me the feel of a fast but steady pace when I drive. As we got in, my brother asked me a question, "Can I drive your car when I turn sixteen?" he says

"No, because you will drive it as fast as you can and wreck it or get chased by the cops, put in jail, and the car impounded. I don't think so." I told him. I started the car, and we were off to school. As we got closer to the school, we noticed it was a busy place to be, with everybody trying to get to school on time.

"Man, there are many people at this school," said David.

"Yeah, and some girls to make friends with." Said Sapphire.

"That's right," I spoke.

I parked my car, and we headed to the office to pick up our schedule. When we got closer to the office, I saw guys staring at my sister as she passed them. They started to follow her, so I had to stop the situation.

"What do you think you are doing, buddy?" I asked him. "Do you have a problem with me looking?" he asked.

"Yes, I do have a problem with it," I told him,

"Well, I guess that's something for her to deal with you," he said. He was getting angry, so I stood in front of him. "You better get out of my way," he said.

"Or what?" I told him,

"You better, or you'll pay." He said. I wasn't going to move. This guy was a jerk. I wasn't about to let him near my sister. When he saw I wasn't going to move, he tried to push me out of the way. I immediately stepped aside, grabbed his arm, and pulled it behind him, making his face land first on the ground.

"Don't ever try to put your hands on me or my sister again," I told him, holding him on the ground while his friends watched, stunned.

I was so focused on making him realize he had made a mistake that I didn't see the teacher that walked up until she grabbed me by the arm, pulling me off him. She steered me straight towards the school building. I knew we were going to the office.

"I don't know who you are, young girl, but in this school, we fight firmly. Since you are new here, I will let you off with a warning this time, but if I catch you fighting again, we will put you in an alternative school," she said, leaving me at the school steps.

"Why did you do that for?" Sapphire asked.

"Because I'm not going to let a creep like that try to ask you out," I told her.

We went into the office and got our schedules without saying another word. As we headed to our separate classes, I told them to meet me in the car after school.

Then, I noted Sapphire to stay clear of that creep. I turned and walked to tryouts in the field house. I heard the bell ring just as I entered the room. They didn't want me there because they quickly put their pads in every empty seat I saw. "Football tryouts aren't for girls. Why don't you go find the cheerleaders?" The others laughed.

"I'm here for football tryouts," I told him. He stood up to intimidate me, but I didn't back down.

"Everyone, sit down now!" the coach said as he walked in the door. He walked by me, and he stopped. He looked at me for a second before he spoke. "Do you belong in this building? You know this is football tryouts, right?" he asked me. Without saying, I handed my schedule to him. He looked at it, handed it back to me, and kept walking to his office.

I just stood there. A few minutes later, the coach called another coach to his office. Suddenly, the door opened. the coach said, "Crystal, could you come into my office for a few minutes?" The coach asked.

"I told you girls don't belong here." said one of the players. I ignored him and walked to the coach's office, closing the door behind me.

"Crystal, I want to talk to you. Are you sure you want to do this? Football is a tough game." He asked me. I knew this was coming, so I reached into my backpack and pulled out some papers for him to look through.

"I've been playing since I was eight. When I got into middle school, I kept playing. Even in high school too. Most of the boys didn't like it until they saw me play. I'm good. Once they saw that, they accepted it, and we became good teammates. At my old school, we were a family. We took up for each other. Once these guys see that, they'll accept me too. I'm an excellent football player coach. It says in that stack of papers I gave you that I took my team to three state championships, and we won them. I have been offered scholarships to several colleges since tenth grade." I said. He looked at the paper and then paused before he spoke again.

"All right, now, I want to see what you can do on the field. Go ahead and wait for me," he said. When I went outside, I saw that the guys were warming up. The coach came out of the building and walked to the other coaches to tell them about me. After a few minutes, they waved me over there to talk with them.

"Crystal, are you sure you want to do this?" He asked me. I just looked at him and nodded. He knew that I was serious about my decision. "Okay, that's all I need to know. Most girls rarely stay long on this team. The guys are rough on them. So, we'll try you out as one of my receivers and see what you have for us this year." He said he called one of the guys off the field so I could get out there. I walked out, jogged onto the practice field, and took my place.

"Coach! Are you serious? We go through this every year, and not once has a girl ever made it past the first day of practice. It's a waste of time." Said the quarterback.

"Just make sure the ball makes it to me," I told him.

"Just stay out of the way of me," said another player.

"Make sure you throw the ball to Crystal, all right, Scott." said the coach. We huddled up to call the play, though none of them were talking to me. Then, as we broke up, I saw David standing on the sidelines watching.

"Hey, what are you doing here?" I asked him, "Just making sure you stay out of trouble. I've got study hall first period, and we were not doing anything, so I told the teacher I wanted to go to the library and snuck off down here." he said.

"All right," I said with a chuckle, and I turned back and ran onto the field for the play. The ball got snapped, and we were in motion. I ran down the field about ten yards, then turned to catch the ball. I looked up and noticed that the quarterback had thrown the ball too far to the right. I quickly changed direction and reached out, catching the ball by my fingertips only, pulled it close to me, and turned to run for the end zone.

"All right, that was good. Let's try running the play with the defense on the field this time and see if Crystal can avoid a few tackles," he told them. As the rest of the team ran to the huddle, Coach lowered his voice and told me, "You'll need to be careful. They will try and run you over hard, so you'll quit before you start. We try out at least one girl every year, and it gets annoying after listening to them fuss and talk about how they got hit too hard. These guys have to deal with this all the time, and it does get to them after a while, so they will be harder on you since you are new and the only one here. I just thought you might want to know that."

As I was heading back onto the field, I was thinking about what the coach had just told me and was shocked that he would say that to me. Well, whatever they were going to try to do to me, I was ready, and I was here to show them that.

I took my place in the line-up and waited for the ball to get snapped. The quarterback made the call, the center snapped the ball, and I took off down the field, zooming past the defensive linemen coming at me. I ducked out of the way of two players, found a hole, slipped through it without getting touched, and charged into a full sprint down the field to get the ball. Just as I got about twenty yards down, I caught the ball just in time to turn and run in for a touchdown without even getting touched. Maybe now I had shown them I could hack it in the game after all. As I ran down the field to meet the others, I didn't say anything.

As I walked up to the players and coaches, I noticed that some of them had smiles. Then Coach walked forward and said, "That was pretty amazing! You can squeeze through some tight spots with good speed. You might work out."

"Just because she ran one play without crying because she got hit doesn't mean she can hang in. That could have been pure luck." The quarterback spoke up, apparently not convinced. Then he turned to me and said, "Just because you convinced Coach doesn't mean you convinced the rest of us."

He then turned to the others and said, "Let's get back to practice. Let's run the play from the opposite side and see how well that goes." Without waiting for a word from the coaches, he and the team headed out onto the field.

"Don't worry about him; it's going to take a miracle to prove to him that you're on the team." The coach said to me. "He doesn't think girls belong on the football field unless they are in a skirt cheering the team on. He'll have to get used to it and get over it." Then he pointed me back on the field without saying anything else.

The rest of the practice went pretty well. I followed along with the plays and showed them that I could take a tackle without crying. As practice ended, Coach blew the whistle and called us in. "That was great for the first day. Crystal, you may work out after all. Go shower up and get ready for your next class." He said and turned to walk to his office. I headed for the girl's locker room, the only one in the gym by the field house where the girls' volleyball team was finishing up. I showered quickly and headed to get my bag to go to my next class. David was waiting with it outside the field house.

"Not bad! You sure showed them. Well, some of them, anyway. I would give anything to be on the varsity team this year." David was on the J.V. team and didn't have practice until the last period. He didn't like the idea of having to be put back down. David was on Varsity with me at our previous school and was upset that they wouldn't do it here. The school claims he must play with the J.V. until the coaches decide to put him on Varsity. We split our ways to go to our second period.

I headed to the elective building on the other side of campus. I walked into the classroom and noticed it wasn't like any shop class I had ever seen. They had just about everything, including changing rooms. I walked across the room and took an empty desk in the middle of the room. I was glad that I wasn't the only girl in this class.

As the course continued to fill up as it got closer to the bell, I overheard two boys talking behind me. I turned and looked behind me to see the clock, and one of them looked at me and smiled.

I didn't know whether I should smile back after what happened this morning, so I just turned around and faced the front. The guy smiling at me meant he wanted to talk to me because I felt a tap on my shoulder as soon as I turned around. I turned to see him still smiling. He looked at me for a moment before speaking, "Hi there, my name is Steve, and this guy behind me is Kyle. What's your name?" He said in a curious voice.

"Crystal," I said and turned back around. About that time, the only other girl in the class came and sat beside me.

"Don't let them bother you." She said, smiling at me. Just after she spoke, the bell rang, and the sound of students running to their seats was the only thing you could hear. The teacher came into the room, and he silenced everyone.

"My name is Mr. Ingram." He said in a lovely voice. "Now, I want you to consider what we discussed at the end of last year.

And for those who don't remember or weren't here, there is a big ag show coming up in about six months, and we want to make sure we do better this year. So, we will skip all the introductory stuff and get straight to work on your projects for this year, so we make sure you have enough time to finish them properly without being rushed." He spoke with enthusiasm in his voice. He seemed to be an excellent teacher. I could already tell I would like this class and this teacher.

"Now, I want you to take some time and figure out what you will do for your project this year if you haven't already. Write down your idea and what supplies you are going to need. Then, bring them up so I can sign off on it."

I spent about 5 minutes deciding to make a flatbed trailer for farming and hauling purposes, also with a removable BBQ pit. I thought carefully, wrote down what supplies I would need, and walked up to the teacher's desk for him to sign off on it. He looked at it for a moment and then looked at me. "Are you sure you can do this? You're biting off a big bite on this one. I know you're new, so why don't you start with something simpler?"

"I don't need to start with anything simpler. I built something like this last year at my old school. It wasn't this big, but it turned out nicely and sold for a great price there. And that was in New York. There are a lot more farmers around here. I'm sure this one will do even better." I said to him, smiling but not surprised by his asking that question.

"Well, alrighty then!" he said back with a chuckle and signed off on my project.

I spent the rest of class sketching out my idea and was proud of myself for the thought behind it. I gathered my stuff when the bell rang and headed out for the third period. The rest of the day went pretty well.

I breezed through the classes until lunch, when I got to sit down and relax. To my disappointment, my brother's and sister's lunch wasn't the same period as mine, so I had to eat alone, which didn't bother me that much. I had time to think about my day and remember some of the people I had seen and met today. I looked around and noticed that a few faces I saw were familiar. It was odd. There was no way I could know any of these people.

I thought back to classes so far. It suddenly hit me that some people in those classes were familiar too. The girl in my shop class was friendly, and the boy who talked to me was too. I seemed to know him from somewhere. I couldn't believe it. It was like deja vu looking at them for the rest of the day. I couldn't think of where I knew them.

"Do you mind if I sit here?" said a girl that walked up.

"No. Not at all. I wouldn't mind the company." I said, and she sat down across from me.

"So, are you new here?" She asked.

"I am; how could you tell that?" I asked her.

"Well, I have been going to these schools since the first grade, and I know everybody in them." She said.

"Okay, that's something new to hear from someone. By the way, what is your name?" I asked her.

"Oh, I'm sorry for not introducing myself. My name is Laura, and you are?" She asked.

"My name is Crystal, and I have a brother and a sister that goes here too," I said.

"I thought I saw someone like you earlier today, and she was you." She said.

"Yeah, I get that sometimes from people, and it's okay, so you know," I said. The bell rang for the lunch period to be over. "Oh, looks like our lunch is over. It was nice meeting you here." She said to me.

"The same to you also," I said and walked to my next class. When the final bell rang, I gathered my things and headed to meet my siblings at my car.

The car ride home was tranquil. David and Sapphire had a rough day because they didn't say anything. I was still too busy thinking about how odd it was that I somehow had seen those people and couldn't remember how. When we made it home, the two younger ones jumped out as soon as I stopped and headed for their rooms to drop off their things and do as they always do. I headed to my room to change clothes and think. After I put my things away and changed clothes, I headed back downstairs and told my Mom that I was going into town.

Even as I got in my car to go job hunting, I still couldn't understand where I had seen those faces. I knew I had to quit thinking about it, but I found it challenging. I knew I couldn't concentrate on finding a job with my mind off track, so I looked around and saw what this town had to offer.

It was the first day I'd had to get out of the house since we moved here. As I drove around, I noticed that there was little to do. I went into a nearby Mcdonalds', figuring I could at least satisfy my hunger. I made my way in and waited for the crowd to thin out before I went up and made my order.

I filled my drink, returned to the counter, paid for my food, and sat down. I watched the children playing and saw a couple of people from school come in. I chatted with a few of them for a few minutes and got up. I drove around a bit more, then turned to Walmart to look around. I walked through the clothes, picked up some more makeup, and headed to pay for it.

The next few days went by in a blur. Football practice was the only thing I was still struggling in. It wasn't the plays that were bothering me, however. It was the fact that there were still a few of the guys that didn't want me on the team. I didn't let them get to me; I kept my head down and worked hard to learn their plays and keep up with them. Finally, the first football game came after two weeks of hard training. The school was a blast on Football Friday.

The teachers didn't give us any homework, and we spent most of the class time finishing any work from earlier in the week. I was working on some last-minute ideas for my project in ag when an announcement came over the intercom saying, "All members of the football team and cheerleaders need to go to the gym for the pep rally."

I pulled my jersey over my clothes and headed to the fieldhouse. I walked inside and sat down with the other players. About ten minutes later, we could hear the sound of the students in the school heading towards the gym. That was our signal to get ready for our announcement.

We stood there for a few minutes before we heard what had to be the head cheerleader. She introduced the team, and the crowd went wild as we made our way onto the court and took our seats. At least the pep rally was good. The group enjoyed the whole thing. They cheered and shouted when the cheerleaders were doing their stunts. After it was over, we headed back to the fieldhouse and prepared to leave. Our first game was out of town. The bus ride was long and hot. We joked around a bit, and some even took a nap. Finally, after five hours of travel, we made it to the school and piled off the bus to change and stretch. We jogged out onto the field to run a couple of plays. After about an hour of warming up, we headed to the visitor's locker room. There were only about ten or fifteen minutes left before the game started; Coach came in with a grim look.

"Guys, I've got some bad news. One of our receivers didn't work hard enough to keep his grades up and can't play tonight due to a failing grade. We've been working hard, so I don't want you to let this get you down. I've found someone to replace him tonight, and I think it was a good move." At that moment, David walked in with a big grin.

"Coach, what's going on here? Who's this kid?" said Scott angrily.

"Team, this is David, Crystal's brother. I pulled him from the J.V. team. If he's half as good as she is, I'll know I made the right choice." Then he turned to David and said, "Sorry, you don't have time to practice with the team, kid. Suit up." Then he turned and walked out.

David, still smiling big, walked over and sat beside me. "This is so cool!" he said.

I looked at him, smiled, and asked, "How did this happen?"

"Well," he said, "we were finishing up practice when Coach ran out on the field and told my coach that he needed a fill-in player right now cause one of the varsity players couldn't play because of his grades and that all of you have just left and they didn't know yet. So, he called me up and told me to get in his truck. He drove me to the game. So, here I am." He grinned again and went to get dressed.

It was time to go out on the field and show my teammates what winning felt like for them. When our band started our school song, and the host announced our name over the speakers, we ran out onto the field. I felt even more confident with David running beside me. We made it to our sideline, and the team captains prepared to walk out of the field for the coin toss. The game was underway, and I was on the sidelines.

The coach said he wanted to allow everyone to play, so I was waiting my turn. David, being the only wide receiver, was on the field playing. He was doing well, too, but couldn't get the ball. It was apparent they would treat him the same way they treated me, not wanting to give him a chance. At the end of the second quarter, we all made our way into the locker room for halftime. We were losing 24 to 3. Everyone sat down, not saying much when Coach walked in, and we could tell he was not very happy.

"Can anyone tell me what the problem is?!" he snarled. "We had all this nailed in practice. David, do you need help keeping up with the plays?

"No, Coach. I'm having trouble getting Scott to throw me the ball." David said back to Coach, glaring at Scott as he said it.

"Look, Coach, I don't like playing with new players.

Why can't Tight End play? It's just a stupid grade." Said Scott. He sat there almost a pouty way and didn't say anything else. Coach just stared at him.

"Well, Coach, when will you put me out there? David and I play great together." I said to him. "You saw me in practice; you know I can play. Why are you holding me back? Are you afraid the other team might notice a girl on the field? Who cares? It is about winning!" I shot a meaningful look at him and didn't say anything else.

"I tell you what, Crystal, you're right. You'll be in the next half of the game. And as for this little situation about new players, Scott, you can take that up with Tight End; he is the one who didn't pass.

You will throw the ball to David or whoever else I tell you to when I call the play, or you're the next one out of here. I'm going into my office for the rest of half-time. You guys will work this out alone or get off the team." With that, he walked away.

We all sat there for a moment, then I finally got up, looked at them all, and said, "Look, we can do this. We all know the play. Scott, you know I know the plays, and David does too. Just trust us. I'm going out there; you guys figure out what you're going to do." And with that, I got up and left. Before I had made it ten steps out the door, David was running up behind me, smiling.

"I figured they ought to work it out on their own." He said simply

"What made you figure that?" I asked him back.

"When they told me to get out so they could talk." He said, now grinning broadly.

We walked together down the hall. We could hear the rest of the team's footsteps coming up behind us just before we got to the end to walk back out on the field. We turned and stopped to wait for them.

"Your right. We need to do this as a team. We can make this work. I'm sorry for acting like a jerk, guys." Scott said. I was shocked.

"All right then, let's get out there and win this," I said, pretending nothing had happened.

The second half went much better now that we were all on the same page. We didn't miss a step, drop a pass, or miss a field goal. By the end of the game, we had won 24 - 30. Our crowd was on their feet, cheering and yelling. The band was blaring the school song, and the cheerleaders were on the field with us, celebrating the great victory we had just taken. Things were finally going well. We headed into the field house, still celebrating the victory, waiting for the coach to give us a way-to-go speech, but it never came.

"Get changed so we can go, guys; it's late." That was all he said.

We changed and got onto the bus to get ready to go. As we were loading onto the bus, still celebrating, yelling, and cheering, I could have sworn I saw the girl from my dream, Silverie.

"No way!" I said quietly to myself and walked onto the bus without looking again.

David and I shared a seat on the bus on the way home. We were all still joking and talking about the second half of the game. After about two hours, we all started settling down and eventually fell asleep for the rest of the drive. The next thing I knew, David was waking me up.

"Hey, wake up, Crystal! We're back at school; let's go home." He said. I got up and walked to the car. I stopped at a soda machine on the way to the parking lot. I needed the caffeine to wake me up some more. David and I rode home. I was quiet during the trip. I turned up the radio so I wouldn't doze off and finally made it home. We walked into the house and to our rooms without even stopping for something to eat, which I knew we should have. I showered quickly and looked at the clock as I crawled into bed; it was 3:30 a.m. I was asleep before my head hit the pillow.

I kept dreaming of seeing Silverie at the game that night. I know it couldn't be confirmed.

Chapter 3

When I woke up, it was still dark, and though my body yearned for me to go back to sleep, my mind wouldn't let me. I looked at the clock and saw that it was only 5:30 a.m. I got up, headed downstairs for some coffee, and saw Mom was already up.

"Crystal, why are you up already?" She said to me.

"I couldn't sleep anymore. I guess I'm still excited about the game." I lied. I couldn't tell her the truth. She wouldn't believe me anyway.

"Well, I take you guys won then?" she said, smiling.

"Yeah," I said to her. She only asked a few more questions. We sat there drinking coffee and talking about how good things were going during our stay in this town. Before I knew it, the sun was up, and the mail carrier had just dropped off the mail. Mom checked it and returned with an assortment of what looked like bills and a massive package.

"Looks like you've got something, Crystal." She said to me and handed me the package. I didn't know what it was until I looked at it and couldn't believe what I saw.

It was from Silverie.

"Mom, I'm going to take this to my room, okay?" I said to her. I didn't want to open it in front of her.

"Okay, dear." She said it back and returned to looking at her mail.

I walked upstairs, not knowing what was in the package. I went into my room and locked my door. I needed to be alone and see what was in the box. Slowly and carefully, I opened the package and emptied everything onto my desk. There were only a few things inside, considering the envelope size. I looked at the items lying on my desk. They consisted of two different kinds of rings and bracelets, a book that seemed ancient saying read me, a letter that I'm sure was from Silverie, and some mirror. I didn't pay much attention to the mirror, but I immediately put on the rings and bracelet, opened the letter, and began to read it.

Dear Crystal,

Sorry, it took so long to contact you, but trying to avoid the psychotic professor and his assistant has been rough, and the Twin Sisters are furious that you got away. I had to ensure they weren't watching me when I contacted you. It took quite a few tricks, but I shook them off for a while. I hoped you remember the events two weeks ago. I hope you know you weren't dreaming. It would help if you had plenty of time to figure out your powers. I'm sharing two rings and two bracelets of power here for you. They belonged to ancient family members that long ago did the things you are about to encounter.

You must promise always to wear them. They will help your powers strengthen tenfold once you learn how to use them. Also, I have enclosed a two-way mirror. I also have a book explaining our race that you need to read. I expect to hear from you when you finish reading this letter. This mirror will allow us to talk to each other even though we are in different time frames.

Once you contact me, we can set up a time for me to meet you and continue your training. You must realize that this is real. Please, Crystal, pick up the mirror and say my name. That will open a small portal for us to communicate through. I'm not

joking, and you're not crazy. You must follow your designated
path before it's too late and they find and destroy you. I hope to
hear from you soon.

Sincerely,
Silverie

I sat there for a moment and stared at the letter. *Was this a dream*
too? Should I pick up that mirror and try to contact her? The truth is, I
have been thinking about it a lot, but I need to work on strengthening
my powers. How was I supposed to know how to do that? I sat there
again, not knowing what to do. I picked up the mirror and placed it up
about a foot from my face. I spoke the name "Silverie."

Nothing happened.

I sat there momentarily and realized how stupid I must look to
believe this. I put the mirror on my desk and laughed at myself. I had
just started to take the rings and bracelets off when I heard a not-too-
familiar voice say, "Hey, Crystal. I thought you would never use that
thing." I looked down and saw Silverie staring back at me, smiling.

"Oh my god, I can't believe that worked," I said, more to myself
than her.

"So, you finally got my package? It was tricky to send it back in
time. So, tell me, have you been working on using and controlling your
magic?" She asked me to get straight to the point.

"Are you serious? No, of course, I haven't. I woke up from what
I thought was a crazy dream. No proof that it was real. I didn't hear
anything for two weeks. You think I'm just going to assume that it was
real and believe what I thought was a dream was real, and suddenly, I
should know what to do? You can't be serious!" I said as I set the mirror
on my desk, leaning it against the wall to hold it up. "And even if I did
believe it," I continued. "How was I to know what to do? How to use
the powers? How to control them? You left me knowing nothing but
that someone wanted me dead."

"I know you're angry right now, but we don't have time for this
'feel sorry for me, I'm new' crap; you've got much ground to cover

to make up for what you don't know. I'm planning an extended trip to your time to help you learn your abilities. I'll pretend to be a new student at school or something. I don't know yet, but the important thing is that you start working on things until I get there. It will take about three days to get there and cover my tracks. So, I'll see you then." She said quickly.

"Hang on. Wait a minute. Are you serious? How am I going to do all this training and attend school at the same time? What about that? You are crazy. I can't believe this is real. Silverie, I don't know if I can do this." I said to her.

"You can. Have faith in yourself. That's the first rule. I'll help you through this process of understanding.

Now start working on your powers. Learn to control them. Use your mind. I'll see you in three days. Bye." She said with a smile and disappeared before I could say anything else.

"Silverie! wait! how do I. . .use my powers?" I finished quietly. I knew she couldn't hear me. "Great. Just great." I said out loud to myself.

I didn't give it much thought. I lay down on my bed and thought about what had just happened. The next thing I know, I'm being woken up by Sapphire telling me to come downstairs for dinner. Was it that late? I got up and looked at the clock, 6:30 p.m. I went downstairs and sat down at the table with my siblings.

"About time you got up." Teased David. "You only played half the game and slept longer than me." He said grinning

"I didn't sleep until 3:30 this morning, so shut up." I teased back. We continued our conversations throughout the dinner, cleared the table for Mom, and returned to our rooms. I spent the rest of the night finishing homework and looking in the Classifieds for a job. I thought about contacting Silverie again but decided against it. She would be here in three days; I could manage until then. But I decided it was too late tonight to worry about it, so I went to bed and slept.

I woke up Sunday morning and went for a morning jog to clear my head and get a chance to try and use my powers. However, it was too crowded to try today, so I jogged back home. I found it just as hard to work on it there with everyone in the house running around and being loud. So, I just decided to wait for Silverie.

I woke up Monday morning and got ready for school, wondering when I would run into Silverie. I grabbed the two-way mirror and headed to school. As we got there, I told Sapphire and David that I would see them after a while and went on to the field house early. While waiting there, I pulled out the mirror and tried to contact Silverie. She didn't answer. When the team entered the room, I put the mirror away and prepared for practice. Everything throughout the morning went as usual. I made a good start on my project; it was a quarter of the way done. I was on top of all my classes. Then at lunch, she showed up. "Hey girl, sorry I'm late." She said from behind me. "I had to make sure no one followed. So how are things going?" she asked me.

"Well, not so good. But we can't talk about this right now. There are too many people around. We will meet after school about it. For now, let's pretend you are an average new student and me and you became friends immediately." I said to her, looking around, hoping no one was listening. We ate lunch, talking about where she was staying and how long she would be here; the conversation we could have without worrying about anyone overhearing anything they shouldn't.

Lunch ended, and we went on to our classes. I found out that she would be having most of her classes with me, so we finished out the remaining time of the day doing homework and taking notes. Finally, the last bell rang, and we headed to my car.

I told David and Sapphire that I would be taking them home first and then going out with Silverie and asked them to tell Mom so I wouldn't have to go into much detail about what we would do. I dropped them off at the house. Silverie and I headed to a secluded place to practice. We found an old-looking turn off the road and went down until it reached the river access. It was a good-sized clearing and didn't look like anyone had camped there. I parked my car, and we got out. I wanted to know how this would work, but I thought it would be good to try. Maybe once she saw that I had no magical talent, she would leave me alone, and I could return to my everyday life.

"Okay, the first thing I want you to do is clear your mind. You must concentrate hard until you get the hang of it." She said as she walked around placing sticks, rocks, and other objects in a line on the ground. I noticed that things got more extensive. "Close your eyes and let all your thoughts fade away. Now, I want you to open your eyes and look straight ahead at the first and smallest object."

I opened my eyes and saw a small rock on the ground about ten feet in front of me. "Okay, now what?" I asked her.

"Now, I want you to concentrate on lifting that rock off the ground with your mind. I know it sounds crazy, but you can do it. Just concentrate on it rising off the ground as high as you can get it." She said to me calmly. "You can do it."

I needed to learn how to lift this thing off the ground, but I thought I could at least try. I stared hard at the rock, thinking that I wanted it to rise off the ground. Nothing happened. I tried harder. Before I knew it, I had beads of sweat on my face, but I didn't stop. I stared at the rock without blinking. My eyes were burning. I yelled in my thoughts, "Rise!" I couldn't believe what I was seeing, the rock started to shake slightly, and right before my eyes, the stone was rising off the ground. It was already two feet up. . .three feet up; I didn't stop concentrating.

Four feet, and five feet. . .

"Way to go, Crystal!" Silverie yelled. It broke my concentration, and the rock fell back to the ground with a soft thud. "That was great for a first try. Better than my first try, that's for sure."

"Really?" I said back to her, amazed at what I had done. "I didn't think that you were serious. I can't believe that just happened. Wow!"

"Now, I want you to work on the next object before you." She said encouragingly.

I looked at the next object, and it was an empty can. It was bigger but couldn't weigh more, so I needed to figure out how this would be more challenging. I closed my eyes and focused on it as I had done before. When I opened my eyes, it was almost instant! The rock was already three feet off the ground! I was doing it.

"Great job!" Silverie told me. "Now, let's keep going."

I worked my way down the line of objects, each time getting bigger, but it was easier and more accessible to lift each time. By the time I got to my last thing, my school bag, I had raised it without having to close my eyes and focus first. I had gotten the hang of small things in one afternoon. I didn't think it was possible. "I told you that you could do this on your own. You've mastered lifting small objects in just a few hours. It took me two days," Silverie said, blushing slightly at the end. "That's enough for today. It's getting late, and we have a different kind of homework now: school homework. It would help if you kept working on your levitation daily until we get it down. Come on, let's go."

We started walking to the car, and I had to try one more thing before calling it a day. I focused hard and opened my eyes to see that I had opened the car doors. I smiled at Silverie.

"All right, now you're just showing off." She said, laughing. We got in the car and headed home.

Silverie ended up being a great friend. We had much in common, not just our 'special abilities. We spent afternoons after school working on my levitation, which was coming along great. I could lift my car with my mind in less than a week. And we spent nights doing homework together for school. I had convinced my Mom to let Silverie stay with us, claiming that her parents were fighting a lot and she didn't want to be around it. It wasn't hard to talk Mom into it. She already liked Silverie. I was still having the same nightmare every night; I couldn't get it to stop coming. "It means the time is getting closer for you to fight them. They will eventually find us; I hope you've learned everything before then." Silverie explained to me.

The following week, Silverie told me that we were going to start working on my morphing, which, I had to say, scared me a little bit. After school, we drove to the same spot we had been using for a week to practice, but we weren't alone this time. Some of the kids from school had found it, and it just had to be the ones I didn't get along with them. That couldn't be a coincidence. They knew that we would be here. We continued to drive up to the end of the road, and I saw Laura and Tasha standing there smiling, guessing with their boyfriends. I stopped the car, and we got out but stayed close to the vehicle. Laura and Tasha started to walk a little closer, but I stopped them in their steps. "What are you doing here?" I asked them.

"What? Can't we come and see what's so interesting about this place? Don't you think we haven't noticed your car driving in and out of here every day for a week? Didn't you know? Does this access road go right past my house? Tasha and I have been watching you every day. What have you two been doing out here?" she said in a not-so-friendly tone.

"We don't have to tell you anything. What does it matter to you anyway?"

Silverie shot at her. Something about the way Silverie was talking to her didn't set right. It was almost like she knew her or something. Then I remembered that these two looked like the Twin Sisters from my dream, and my stomach immediately fell to my knees. If this was them, what were we going to do? I wasn't ready to fight them; I needed to learn more.

"We just wanted to know if we could join the party, that's all. You've got to be doing something out here that you don't want anyone else to know about you're doing. Why not come out here and ensure it wasn't illegal." Tasha said from behind Laura.

"Come on, Crystal, let's get out of here," Silverie said, turning to me and getting in the car.

"Aww. Are you going to run away? What's wrong? Are you scared? You don't seem to mind standing up to people at school; why back down now? No one to show off for?" Laura said to me.

"No, it isn't that. You're just not worth the time and effort." I said, and I got into the car, cranked it up, and started to leave. I thought they would follow us, but when I looked in my mirror, I saw them still standing there. It looked like the guys were digging into a cooler for something to drink, and I'm guessing it was a beer.

"I'm guessing even now they don't like you. What did you do to them?" Silverie asked me.

"What do you mean 'even now?'" I asked her.

"You didn't recognize them?" she said to me.

"Yeah, they looked like the Twin Sisters from my dream when I met you," I answered her back.

"That wasn't a dream, Crystal. Haven't you figured that out yet?" She said to me this time while looking at me.

"I know; I'm sorry. It's just hard to grasp that. When you sent me back to my time, I woke up suddenly like I had a dream. So, is that the Twin Sisters? have they found me?" I asked her, starting to worry.

"No, they're not the Twin Sisters. Well, not the ones that you have to worry about here. They are, however, related. Laura and Tasha from this time are just stuck-up teens who think they are better than everyone. Laura and Tasha, or Twin Sisters as we know them, want absolute power to be the best. To rule the world without stopping them, and let me tell you, girl, that would be bad for everyone in the future if we don't stop them now." She explained to me.

"So, you mean to tell me that those two drama queens can also change and do 'stuff.' Even now?" I asked her, suddenly worried.

"Well, yes, and no. Look, there is something you don't know. I came back in time to get you instead of waiting until it takes place thousands of years down the road because it has already happened. You see, the Crystal I am making you be now already existed in my time. She already fought the Twin Sisters, and I'm afraid to say she lost." Silverie paused for a moment before she continued. "I thought that maybe if I came back in time and trained you on your talents, you could defeat them before they could defeat you. It doesn't make sense, but I thought it could work." She said, seeing the look of disbelief on my face. I didn't know what to say to her. *How could I answer that?*

"So, you mean to tell me that I'm dead?" I asked her, finally finding my voice.

"In my time, yes, you died about two months ago. That's when I decided to come here and train you so you could come back with me to my time, catch them off guard because they think they've killed you, and I want you to kill them before they have a chance to see you straight. However, I didn't plan on them finding out what I was doing. That's why they came after you a couple of weeks ago when you thought you were dreaming." She explained this as though she was begging me to understand and not be mad. And to be honest, I did understand, and I wasn't angry, though I knew I should be. "This isn't how I planned on telling you this either, but you seem to be gaining strength in figuring things out and developing your powers. But now, you know. I hope you're not mad."

"No, I mean, this is just unreal. I can't believe you just told me I'm dead in another world, but I'm alive now; it's a lot to take in." I said to her in deep thought.

I didn't know what I was going to do. I just knew I was more determined now than ever to learn how to use the powers Silverie says I must stop them from killing me.

We didn't get to practice today. Instead, we went home, which was acceptable because I was still overthinking what Silverie had just told me. There was no way I would be able to concentrate on anything else.

The next day we spent all our time after school trying to find another place to practice, which we needed help finding. We decided it was now safe to practice my levitation at home in my room, but we would have to find another secluded place for everything else. Now that we had to run into Laura and Tasha at the campground, we seemed to be 'running into' them a lot at school too. Tasha was the worse of the two. She seemed to enjoy humiliating Silverie and me at her expense. Laura wasn't so bad. She mostly just stood back and laughed but never said too much. We would even have to evade them after school so they wouldn't follow us and find out where we were would be.

After a week of looking, we finally found an abandoned house. It looked like it could fall from the outside, but the inside wasn't so terrible. Plus, it had a huge backyard where I could park our car in, and we could practice everything else in. The first thing Silverie told me we would start as me learning how to morph. I was scared. Silverie said that she would go first to show me that it wouldn't hurt and so I would know what it looked like to turn entirely into "a dragon girl" warrior.

"Don't be scared. It isn't as bad as it sounds. The hardest part is learning to do it first and controlling when you change. It's all about mind control, just like levitating. You must know what you are and believe it. You're halfway there.

You know what you are now, believe it, and control it. I want you to think hard about it." She explained to me. "Now, just watch, and I'll show you."

She stood there for a moment, and then right before my eyes, she began to change. Her skin became rough-looking and scaly, and wings began to emerge from her back, massive wings, enormous beyond any point. Lastly, a tail formed from nowhere. A long tail with a large scale on the end of it with a very sharp-looking point. Even in this form, Silverie was beautiful. She stood there before me and smiled. Her face still looked the same, but the rest of her was like a science experiment, even her hair with a silvery look and blue eyes that go with it. Her skin was silver, with dragon-like scales on them, which also took the form of her clothes by their look. It looked as tough as dragon hide is said to be, but I knew I didn't want to find out. "Now, you see? It doesn't look that bad, huh?" She said, smiling. "Come on, try it."

I wasn't sure I was going to be able to do this. But I had to try. I closed my eyes and concentrated on what Silverie looked like in my head. Nothing happened. I tried again, thinking harder about changing. Suddenly, I felt an almost burning sensation in my stomach. My skin began to feel strange; I opened my eyes and saw that it was starting to look rough. A pulling sensation was coming from my shoulder. I turned my head to know that I, too, had massive wings emerging from my back. To my surprise, they weren't heavy as I thought. It was like they weren't there at all. Lastly, my tail formed, and that felt a little strange. It was very long, with a very sharp point. I looked at Silverie, and we both smiled. "See, I told you that you could do it." She said to me.

"Wow," I said breathlessly. "This is amazing."

"Okay, today, we are just going to work on changing into 'a dragon girl' and returning to normal. Now, think about being your average self to change back," as she said this, she was changing back into her human form. I followed her lead. In no time, I was back to myself. "Now, when you can control this all the way, you will be able to change without wasting time. It will become second nature to you. Our goal is for you to be able to change, fly and change back flawlessly. It will take some time, but it may be sooner at your pace than I think. So, let's do it again."

"Okay," I told her and changed again, this time, a little faster, but not fast enough. We spent the rest of the day working on morphing. By the time we got ready to leave, I still hadn't been able to change as quickly as Silverie, but I was doing better.

"That's it for today." She said, and we headed to the car. Once we were in the car and on our way home, she spoke again. "You are doing great. You're catching on quickly. Faster than I did. It took me three days before I could fully transform. The first day I couldn't even get my skin to change. You got the whole deal down on the first try. If you keep working at it, you could easily become better than the twins in no time. And I'm not just saying that to make you feel good; I mean it. I've seen them fight; you could be much better than them. It looked like it was natural to you. Like you've done it before."

"Well, I promise you I haven't," I said to her. "But I have to say that I like it. It's fun. I know it's not supposed to be fun. Saving the world isn't a game." I said, seeing the look on her face. "I can't help thinking I got chosen for something like this. I mean, surely there were others that you could have chosen. How did I become 'the lucky one'?" I asked her.

"The talent chooses whom it is born by the certain DNA. It can go on for generations without developing. It passes through the bloodline, so it may be another hundred years before you ever see it again. I don't want to tell you too much about the future because your time is here. I am only trying to save you in my time and defeat the twin sisters once and for all before they take over. With your death in my time, we don't think anyone can beat them. It was the only thing I could think of doing to defeat them. No matter how I say it, it still sounds like I'm using you, but I'm not." She explained to me.

"Well, whatever the reason, I'm glad I got chosen. I'll do my best." I said, looking at her thoughtfully.

By Saturday, I could morph and de-morph as smoothly as Silverie. Also, I had learned a new talent that seemed to develop with the rest of my powers, and without me having to practice, I had become a master of martial arts.

Silverie and I went through the moves smoothly and quickly because I didn't need any practice. Throughout the next week, I practiced with Silverie along with my schoolwork, shop project, and football games. I can multitask now too. I had no trouble managing any of this stuff.

The situation between Tasha, Laura, and myself hadn't improved either. Every chance we saw each other, there was a flash of rage within me. I guess I couldn't get over the fact that they were the ones who killed me, even though it is only about to happen hundreds of years from now. The sight of them just made me want to fight them here and now. But as Silverie explained, "You can't stop them before they get their powers. There's something you don't know about their abilities. Tasha and Laura weren't born to the descendants of the dragon girl ability. Professor Keith used them two to experiment to see if they could forcibly make dragon girls. I'm sad to say that it worked. Their bodies accepted the 'treatment' as he called it. Nothing like that has ever worked before. After they got injected with the elixir, the Twin

Sisters thought they could control the world if they could control who had the ability. And the only way to do that is to kill all the other dragon girls. That's why you fought them, and sadly, you lost."

"Where did the DNA come from that was injected into them to make them that way?" I asked her.

"It looks like I'm not going to get out of telling you all the details. I only hope you'll understand when I finish talking. I'll start over and tell you the story from the beginning. . .*the very beginning.*" She said, looking at me. She didn't want to tell me this, but it was too late; she had already dragged me into the middle. I was going to find out everything I could while she was talking. "Okay, so the dragon girl era goes back thousands of years. At one time, there were many of us.

"We took pride in keeping peace and calm in the land. We were terrific fighters and superb flyers and did very well in magic. You see, instead of casting spells, we had crystals. Those held the magic, but only a dragon girl could use it. Everything was great between everyone till one day, it all changed. A mysterious evil spread throughout the land.

"Everyone turned on each other, stealing, killing, raping, and doing anything they could. Eventually, the bands of 'Neanderthals' all joined together and somehow thought that we, the dragon girls were the bad ones, and decided to end that.

"By this time, the dragon warriors had hidden in caves and mountains. They were hoping that everything would fade in time. However, that didn't happen. Man hunted them down, killing them with fire, guns, swords, and anything they could get their hands on. The dragon warriors refused to fight them; instead, they cursed them, telling everyone that they would pay dearly for their greed and hatred. How were they going to survive without the dragon girls to protect them? How indeed? In the end, after every dragon girl was dead, the men and women of the land perished. Nothing was left but smoldering lands for miles. The curse had come true; their greed had led them to kill each other one by one until there were no more.

"However, there were five dragon warriors that they didn't find that had survived. Those five survivors were the ones that made sure the curse had come true. In a rage, the five remaining dragon girls annihilated the race of man throughout the land. It was a payment for the slaughter of the other warriors. Then the five warriors decided that it would be safest if they separated into other lands away from one another. For news of what happened would spread. They weren't safe together.

"For years, they lived at different ends of the earth, never contacting each other. They never wholly joined in with the human race either. How could they live with humans after what man had done to them? They lived alone, outside of any towns surviving on the land. As the years progressed, the Dragon Girls became a myth. They weren't born anymore to protect humans. The five remaining Dragon Girls sat back and watched as humanity took over.

"To this day, they are still in their hidden homes. They are now known as the elders, with powers beyond any means. We must visit each dragon elder first and persuade them to help us."

"Wait, how are we going to find them? When are we doing all this? And you still haven't explained how I died." I quickly cut in, asking questions.

"Let me finish. You see, if I hadn't intervened, then you never would have known about your powers. It would help if you got taught about these powers. Why do you think there haven't been any more reports of it? Nowadays, would people not have known about it if you could do it on your own without being shown? There have been others before you; they didn't know it. Now, we will skip you and your dream for a moment and skip about 400 years to my time. You've met Professor Keith and The Twin Sisters already. What you need to know is that this time has also already happened.

"You see, I brought you to that point with the intention that you would remember it. I am introducing this to you gradually, which has worked up until now. I sent you back and fought the twin sisters myself. Now you want to know how the Twin Sisters became what they are if they weren't born with it.

"Well, the answer is that they got their DNA sample from me. I worked with Professor Keith then, and he discovered what I was when he took a blood sample from me. I was unconscious then; otherwise, I wouldn't have let him. When he got it, he noticed the difference immediately because our blood is emerald green.

"When I came to, I had no choice but to explain it to him, or he would take it public and turn me into an experiment. Laura and Tasha also worked for him. He wanted to see what would happen if he injected them with it. I didn't like the idea much, but what choice did I have? I couldn't fight him, or he would go public, and I just couldn't let that happen. He injected Laura's body first to see how she would react, and Laura's body didn't reject it. Next, he injected Tasha. She also took it with no problem. Once they got the power, they used it. And they used it not for good. Professor Keith gave them the idea to create an army of us. However, the following subject didn't stand up to the injection. His body rejected it until it killed him. So, the idea was that Laura and Tasha would use the power to take over the world.

"You come into the picture two years after they get their powers. Things got worse after that. The world as you know it is gone. Instead, you led your life serving them. It's almost mid-evil all over again. I can imagine it's only worse with you gone. The fight that claimed you were the one that was going to end it all. The only bad thing is that they had a secret weapon that gave them an unfair advantage. Not only could they use my blood to make a dragon girl, but they could also use theirs to destroy a dragon girl. I couldn't believe it. They took you down by shooting you with a dart of 'the antidote,' and you lost your powers; then, they toyed with you, injuring you greatly. They made you suffer before they finally took your life. That's why I brought you back here. I wanted you to get them while they weren't looking like they did to you. Maybe even restore peace, where the life of the dragon girl flourishes like it once was.

"Now, I brought you where I did intentionally. I knew we would run into the sisters. I had already been to that particular time, but I was alone. I sent you back just before Laura hit you with the crystal. I was watching. It worked out perfectly until I discovered Professor Keith had been watching. He managed to sneak in and follow you back. The sisters caught me when I tried to stop him and sent me to the lab. A couple of hours later, to my regret, he showed up with you. He hadn't yet used the antidote on me, so we were able to get away. I sent you back that time knowing the only way this was going to work was for me to come and get you from your time, bring you to the battle and do it all over again, only this time, there would be two of us, and you know what is coming. As I said, it sounds like I am using you, but this is the only way to stop the terror of what is happening." She finished and didn't say another word.

"So, when is all this supposed to take place?" I asked her. She just looked at me for a moment and then smiled.

"We first must find the elders and ask for their help. Don't worry; I know where they are. We will leave in a week. That will give me enough time to get everything together." She said.

The rest of the ride was quiet. My mind was racing. I didn't know how this could be real. I just knew that I was going to do it. I wasn't going to let Laura and Tasha get the best of me. . .Past. . .Present. . .or future. . .

Chapter 4

We continued with everything usual that week. It was already getting close to the holidays. Halloween was coming up, so everyone was rushing around. We had won all our football games so far; I was ahead in all my classes and finished my shop project halfway. I took my free time to ensure that I was ready for what we were about to do. I still did not know how I would tell my Mom that I was leaving for a few days, especially since the holidays were coming.

When Silverie was at the school, she thought it was best to have her in all my classes to help, including football. It took a bit to get the coach to accept Silverie, but after a few plays, it was enough to convince him that Silverie on the team would help to win games.

We decided to tell her that the seniors were going on a trip for the fall holidays, and I wanted to go with them. I hoped she did not see anyone in town and ask about it, but Mom was usually good about staying out of my business, so I wasn't that worried. "Mom," I said to her, "the senior class is taking a trip for the fall holidays, and I want to go with them. We were all planning a trip to a resort that my friends used during the summer with their parents. It's perfect. Do you mind if I go with them, please?" She only looked at me for a moment.

"I guess, dear. You're doing so well in school. How can I say no? Will Silverie be going as well?" She asked me to smile.

"Yeah. We will be leaving this weekend, I know it's last minute, but I just found out the school does this. You don't mind?" I asked her to make sure she was not disappointed.

"I don't mind. Go have a good time." She said as she hugged me. Mom was always so understanding about wanting me to have friends. I knew that as long as I was doing well in school, she would not mind. With that task out of the way, I had to make it look like I was getting ready for a one-week trip. We packed all our clothes and decided to leave our luggage in my car. But as we were going to be traveling to places, I could not even imagine driving; now was an excellent time to ask Silverie how we would be searching for the elders. If they were scattered all over the world, how would we know where to

"I know where they are. Don't worry about that. We must fly some to get there, but I can time-warp us there for the most part. I have a few warp crystals left. That's why we are going to see the elders; to get your crystals and refresh mine. They are the only ones that make them. And each elder makes a different kind, so we must see them all." She said as she continued to get her things ready. Finally, she stood up and zipped up her bag, "You got everything ready?"

"Not yet," I said, waking up from my daydream. I had not realized I was staring off into space. I quickly began to finish throwing things in my backpack. I knew later I would regret not organizing it, but I did not care right now.

After another hour or so, I finally got done. We crawled into bed and went to sleep, ready for our road trip the next day.

I slept peacefully that night for the first time in months. No dreams woke me up.

I do not think I dreamed at all that night. We got up at about 4 a.m. and dressed for the trip. We picked casual clothes if Mom wanted to get up and see us off. She indeed did that. She was waiting for breakfast to go along with coffee and snacks. We left and drove for miles. Finally, we came to a small town that offered vehicle storage.

Silverie said it would be best to put my car in there so that no one would find it parked anywhere and start investigating where we were.

We paid for a one-week stay, we had to be back by then anyway, or my Mom would freak out. We headed off again, this time on foot. Silverie said walking allowed her to think better, and we did not have to hurry. I did not ask her out loud, but I wondered what she was thinking. That almost made me worry because she claimed she knew where we were going. I kept quiet and walked along with her, thinking about what it would be like on this trip. We walked down many streets; this town was small and not too crowded this early in the morning.

"Okay," she finally spoke, "here's what we are going to do; I want to wait until dark before we head out; it is harder to get seen that way. We will have to fly before we get close enough to walk. Don't worry; it will be all right; we can spend the day making sure we don't need anything else while we are somewhere we can shop for them."

We stopped in a few shops and found some small items we needed. I picked out a couple of heavy-duty flashlights, batteries, and other odds and ends for camping, paid for them, and threw them in my bag with everything else.

We found a small country café to eat in at lunch. It smelled great when we walked in. We sat at the table and ordered our drinks while picking our order from the menu. After we had ordered our food, I could no longer hold back my question. "Where are we going?" I whispered across the table.

She looked at me for a moment and then smiled. "You can't stand surprises, can you?" She questioned me back. "We are headed for Colorado. The closest elder is in the mountains. We'll have to change clothes when we get there. Her name is Dyna.

She's very cautious of visitors, so we must make our arrival safe. She's prone to attacks. Don't worry; she will only be trying to scare us. All we have to do is continue walking like nothing is happening."

I just stared at her with my eyes wide open. I did not know what to say. Was she crazy? Am I supposed to stand there while someone is trying to attack me?

"Just stand there?"

"She isn't going to hurt you. It's just her way of keeping unwanted guests away.

Don't worry." She said to me.

About that time, our lunch arrived, so the waitress cut off our conversation. After the waitress left, I asked another question "So what exactly are we getting from her?"

"Well, we must get you some crystals. That is why we are going to see all the elders. Each elder has their form of magic. Dyna will bless your crystals and then show you how to use them. It will take about two days to learn the basics, so you will have to work hard to ensure you get the hang of it quickly. Let's leave this conversation alone until we are in a less crowded area. We don't need someone to hear us. After lunch, we'll see if there are any rivers or lakes around where we can chill until it's dark."

We ate lunch and had small talk. It was all I could do not to ask questions about the task. After we finished eating, we paid our bill and left. We headed out to find somewhere secluded to wait until dark and fly out. I was excited; by the idea of flying, but at the same time, I was scared out of my mind. It took us another twenty minutes to get to where she was, but a fireball came out of the cave.

I was pushed back by Silverie, "Careful now; this lady is not very friendly to new dragons, so let me go first and wait for me to tell you to morph." She said; I nodded to what she said.

As we entered the cave, Silverie had morphed that way; the lady knew what she was, "Who's here in my home?" The elder asked,

"It's me, Madam Radiant, Silverie from the Valmore family," Silverie said,

"Why have you come here?" the elder asked,

"The prophecy has begun," Silverie said,

"You mean to tell me that it has started, right?" the elder said,

"Yes, it has, and this girl right here is the one to do it," Silverie said. The elder walked up to me and examined my whole body, which took her about ten minutes.

"Okay, morph for me." The elder said I didn't say anything, and I morphed. She watched as I did, and I was a complete dragon after about a minute, "Okay, now let me look at you again." The elder said, and she did. After examining everything about me, she returned to her chair and picked something up. "Okay, if you are the one, you should know what this is and how to use it." the elder said, and she handed me the crystal,

"I can tell that it's a fire crystal." I said, but I looked at it some more and spotted something else about it, "And there is also an engravement on it, and I know how to use it now." I said,

"Well then, show me how to use it." The elder said. I walked over to an object I could throw the crystal at for the test.

"All right, here we go for my test." I said to myself, "Macrofira," the crystal lit up in flames, and I tossed it to the object, which exploded into flames. "That's good for a first-timer." The elder said. After that, she walked away.

"That was good, girl; you did great for a first-timer," Silverie said. She returned after a few minutes, handing me a bag full of fire crystals.

"Here are your fire crystals; now you have enough to last awhile, but when you run out, come back here, and I will give you more." The elder said,

"Now, where can we find the others, Madam?" Silverie asked,

"I'm sorry, but I don't give that out to anybody; dragon law prevents that." The elder said.

"Then how are we to find the others?" Silverie asked,

"You will have to find them on your own." The elder said. After that, I don't remember anything that happened.

I was woken up by Silverie, "Hey Crystal, wake up. We got to go." Silverie said, which I did.

"Where are we?" I asked her,

"Well, we are about two hours from home, and for some reason, you have gotten injured from the blast," Silverie said,

"What are you talking about?" I asked,

"When the elder did her blast thing, you were not ready for it, and you went flying out of the cave, which you got some damage," Silverie said,

"Well, do my parents know about it?" I asked,

"Yeah, they do, and by the way, you have been in a coma for about two days. I also had someone play as a doctor so that it would match what happened to you. Don't need them knowing what happened, now do we." Silverie said,

"You mean I have been sleeping for that long?" I asked,

"Yes, you have been sleeping that long. Don't move too much, or you will do major damage." Silverie said to me.

Two hours passed, and I was at the house where Mom and Dad were waiting for me. "Hey, there, champ, how are you?" Mom asked me.

"Well, I have been better before," I said.

"She needs to be off her feet for some time now. That way, she heals up. That's what the doctor said." Silverie said,

"Yeah, that's what he told us, too, and thanks for getting her home to us." Mom said, and she helped me inside the house. I stayed in the house the rest of the day while everyone else did what they did best. "Crystal, are you okay, dear?" Mom asked,

"Well, not really. I think I'm going to go to bed to sleep this off." I said, and I headed up the stairs with her help. That night, I had that dream again, and it was getting on my nerve every time I had it.

"Okay, that's it. I'm going to win it this time." I said to myself and returned to bed when the dream came again. "Help me, sis," Sapphire said,

"Where are you?" I asked her,

"I'm over here," she replied, and that is when I spotted her and went to her side. It took me a few minutes to free her, but those girls showed up again on me as soon as I did.

"What do you think you're doing?" Tasha asked.

"I'm saving my sister," I told her.

"I don't think so." She said and came charging at me. Instead of me getting hit, my body somehow moved sideways in time; I grabbed her hair and spun her around. After that, I let her go to hit a tree.

"Oh, you are going to pay for that." said the other, and she came running to me. I did the same thing to her.

"What is going on here?" Tasha asked.

"This," I said, and I morphed into a dragon-like body that had three swords, two on my side and one big one behind my back,

"Oh no, she is complete in her transformation!" Laura said,

"Stop it! If you want to be afraid of something, be afraid of me." Tasha said to her. "Now go get her!" Laura morphed into the same body, but it was darker than mine.

She came to me with her swords drawn. So, I grabbed mine, and the swords clashed against each other for about five minutes. Suddenly, Laura knocked my blades out of my hand and pushed me to the ground. "This is the end for you," she said. And I felt my tail charging up, and I knew what was happening.

"I don't think so," I said and lunged my tail at her. The power in it sent her back approximately four hundred yards, and she didn't get back up.

"Laura, are you okay?" Tasha asked her, but she did not answer,

"You might have won this fight, but the war is what you can't win." She said, and Tasha grabbed Laura, and they went off.

"Thank you, Sis," Sapphire told me,

"No problem, I will always be here for you," I told her, and my dream seemed to disappear from nowhere, but I was still there.

"Excellent." someone said, and I knew that voice.

"Silverie, is that you?" I asked the person.

"Yes, and I was watching you in your dream, and you were finally able to save your sister and stop the evil twins." She said.

"You mean you have been watching my dreams?" I asked her.

"Yes, I was. That's why I told you to do that because when evil comes around your dragon soul, the crystal ball, will alert you about the sense of evil and will help you destroy evil," she said,

"How was I able to save my sister in this dream? I thought you said this was real; how is that possible? I need to ask-"

"Now is not a good time since you are still dreaming." she butted in on my sentence.

"Just wait until we are awake; I'll tell you more." She said. When she was gone, my alarm clock went off.

When I woke up and got to the edge of my bed, I noticed that I could feel my legs, and no pain was coming from them. "What is going on?" I asked myself.

So, I tried something; I stood on my feet and noticed that I could walk on them and felt no pain. I looked at the calendar and saw that it was Friday, and I knew they would need my help at the game, so I got ready for school as quickly as possible. After about twenty minutes, I could smell what got cooked for breakfast. So, I went downstairs to get some.

"Crystal, how are you walking today after what we saw last night?" Mom asked.

"I'm okay, I can walk fine now, and I don't feel any pain," I told her.

"I'm going to call the doctor about this," she said.

"About what, dear?" Dad asked.

"Well, Crystal should not be walking for another few days." She told him. So, he walked over to me.

"Do you have any pain in your legs?" He asked me.

"No, Dad, I feel fine, even better than before," I said, then he came over to look and feel my legs.

"Honey, come here." He told my Mom, and she came over and looked at my body together.

"Look, do you see any dislodge on her bones?" He asked her.

"No, there's nothing wrong with anything," she said.

"Well, young adults and kids can bounce back from stuff better than older people. Well, Crystal, go to the game tonight and kill them for us!" He said. Mom wanted to say something but did not say it before me. So I got something to eat and went into the dining room when everyone else was.

"Sis, you're back from your trip already? "David asked.

"Yeah, something came up, and we had to come home earlier," I told him, but David said nothing until I got to school and out of my car. The students were staring at me and watching me walk to the field house, wondering where I had been. The guys were not even happy to see me again when I arrived.

"Oh no, you're back already," Micah said.

"Yeah, and you got a problem with that little boy?" I said, and I got right in his face and stared at him to see what he would do.

"All right, let's break it up, you two." The coach but in. "Crystal." He said with surprise. "From what your parents told us, I thought you weren't to return for another few days." He said.

"How did you know about it, coach?" I asked him.

"Well, your Mom called to inform the principal and us about it. In turn, the whole school caught the wind of it too." He said.

"Well, something came up, and I had to come back early, and I didn't want to miss helping win another game," I said, and the coach told us to go outside for practice. This time, Silverie and I worked so well that the coach wanted us to go out together every time. We practiced for about forty minutes; then, we went to the next period. As the day went on, the students saw that I was back at school and wondered where I had been for the past week since I wasn't with the seniors on the trip.

During the seventh period, I had to leave to go down to the field house and meet up with the guys, but we had a sub today, and he still needs to get the memo about leaving early. "Excuse me, Mr. Soap, but I've got to go to the field house before the prep rally," I said.

"Yeah, I don't think so. So sit back down and wait for the class to finish." Mr. Soap said. "I'm not kidding, Sir; I am a player for the team," I told him.

"And since when do girls play football around here?" Mr. Soap asked.

"Since now." the door opened, and the coach entered the room.

"Come on, Crystal." The coach said. "You can't do that; she is not a player." Mr. Soap said.

"Well, talk to the principal about it and prove me wrong." The coach said, and he shut the door.

"What was that for?" I asked him,

"When I went by earlier, I saw you in there because most teachers around here don't believe that girls can play sports too, so I'm trying to find Silverie too." He said.

"Oh, she is in this room." I pointed to a door that was about ten feet in front of us, and he saw she was trying to get out, but the teacher never let her and the coach open the door.

"Silverie, come on," he told her.

"What do you think you're doing?" she asked him,

"I'm getting my two most valuable players for the prep rally," he said.

"You can't do that," she said.

"Well, talk to the principal about it and prove me wrong." He said and shut the door. We walked to the field house to get ready.

It was about fifteen minutes later when we were able to start the walk to the gym, and this time, Silverie and I were leading the pack just as the coach wanted, and if anybody objected to that, they were to do fifty big boy flips after the prep rally. "And here comes the lions." The cheerleader shouted. The band played, and we went inside the gym.

I heard some students calling out my name, and the other players did not seem to appreciate this. About ten minutes into the pep rally, they started to talk about me and what I did at the football game. "And can we have Crystal over here?" The cheerleader said. I walked over to her. "So, how does it feel to be a football player," she asked.

"Well, it feels good when the team is behind me to help at games," I said.

"So, you are saying they are not?" she asked.

"Yeah, that's what I'm saying, and if they help me sometimes, I will not have to work so hard," I said.

"Okay, well, is that what the team is doing out there on the field is not the" someone grabbed the microphone from her, which at second glance, I realized was another player on the team,

"You know, this prep rally is more than about some girl who cannot play football since she disappeared last week from school." He said.

"What is that supposed to mean?" She asked,

"Well, if you must know, girls cannot play any sports that guys play." He said that I was getting angry at him by this time.

"Well, what is your opinion about it?" she asked,

"Don't let her or the other girl play for this team." He said, and Silverie got tired of it, walked over to me, and stared him down.

"What? Do you girls think you can take me on? You're nothing but little wimps that aren't fit to play football." He said. He turned around, and I knew what he was about to do.

"Then, bring it on." He said, and he had his fist out coming for me. I caught it with my hand and pushed to apply pressure on his hand; therefore, he fell to his knees, and the girls cheered for me.

"Now you told me that I can't take you," I said,

"No, I didn't." He threw the other fist at me, which I also caught.

"Do you give up, or do I need to put you in more pain," I asked,

"No, I don't." He tried to use his legs, but I wasn't going to let him. So, I picked him up and let go of him, and he hit the ground.

"Now, have you had enough?" I asked, but he did not respond; I started walking back to the bleachers when he tackled me to the ground and started hitting me till I hit him in the back with my knee making him get off me. As I got up, he grabbed my throat and looked at me.

"Now, what are you going to do?" He asked. He started to squeeze, and when I kicked him right in between the legs, he let go of me and fell to the ground. Still, I got back up, pile-drove him into the wall at the other end of the place, and went to town with him. I did not stop until Silverie pulled me away, and she did and hit her in the face, and then I realized who it was.

"Oh, I'm sorry," I told her.

"That's okay; I knew you probably would have hit me. It was better than hitting a teacher, huh," she said.

"Yeah, I think so," I said, and the coach came over to me.

"Now, that's what it takes to get something done on a football team, folks, and at tonight's game, these two right here will bring back a victory for this town and bring us closer to a state championship," he said. The students went wild with it, and the coach went over to the guy and told him something I could not hear from where I was, but he wasn't happy with it. The cheerleader came over to Silverie and me, picked us up, and carried us outside the gym, which I enjoyed very much.

That night, we had to play against our rival, Kilgore, and they were a good team, from what I heard from the students. They saw them plow the lions into the ground, but that doesn't have to do anything with me.

We got to the Kilgore's base at about five-thirty. As I got off the bus, I saw that they had artificial turf instead of grass, like what we have. I know how to play on this stuff because my hometown had the same stuff, and I liked it. "Okay, let's go practice team." said the coach. I started walking, but the coach stopped me. "Hey Crystal, are you going to be able to play tonight?" He asked me.

"Sure, I'll be able to play for you, coach," I said.

"Okay, that's good because Kilgore can beat us without a problem." He said.

"Don't worry; you put me out there, and I'll make sure that we stay ahead of the game," I said, and I ran to catch up with Silverie.

"Hey, what's up with you and the coach?" She asked me.

"Oh. . . umm, he asked me if I could play tonight," I said.

"Uh-huh, yeah, sure, that's what you want me to think," she said.

"Well, that's what he asked me," I said.

"Whatever, girl," she said.

"Oh, you think me. I don't think so, girl; you better get that out of your head before I make you." I said, and we laughed. We continued walking down to the field to meet with the rest of the team.

We did our usual exercises and drills that we always did as the band showed up along with the Cheerleaders and Lionettes. Our fans started coming in. As they saw me, they started cheering for me. "Crystal." I turned around, and Sapphire was looking for me, so I took off my helmet and went to her.

"Yeah, what is it?" I asked. She pointed into the stands, and I saw that Mom and Dad were there as well as Kevin and Susan, waving at me, and I did the same to them.

"I saw them as they came in, and I was even surprised because of what happened to you a couple of years ago." She said.

"A player almost killed me in that football game, but I'm still here," I said,

"Yeah, well, I better return to my spot." She said and went back into the stands.

As I turned around to the other side, they saw that I was there on the field and was pointing at me and thought it was a joke, but they did not see Silverie because she still had her helmet on, and it was time for us to go in the locker room and have a talk with the coach.

After fifteen minutes, we walked back onto the field where the lion head was waiting for us. As the band started to play, we got in it; we ran out to our side of the field. When the coin toss was over, we had to kick the ball and be on the north side of the field, and I had to wait until we got the ball.

Kilgore did not take long to score a touchdown and get the extra point; it was our turn to get the ball. "Okay, Crystal, you and Silverie go out there." The coach said, and we were off to the field.

We had to start on our twenty-yard line, and the quarterback knew what to do, and I went to the line, and the guy in front of me saw me. "Oh, there you are, little girl; get ready to be pancaked to the ground." He said.

"Bring it on, little boy," I said. The ball got snapped, I ran down the field, and the guy was behind me. I looked back and saw the ball coming to me, but I couldn't see Silverie; I had no time for that; I got the ball and ran, and our side went wild and was cheering me on to the goal line.

"Come back here, girl." He said he was close to my feet, and I had about another forty yards to go, so I ran faster than I ever could, leaving the guy behind. But as I came to the goal line, I looked back and saw that he was still coming for me,

"Come on and get me," I said, and he jumped, but I sidestepped and got across the line for the touchdown. "Oh, I'm sorry! But did you miss me? Oh, too bad! Better luck next time." I said to him, and I went to look for Silverie, and I saw her on the ground about forty yards back and ran to her.

As I got there, she was still moving some. "Hey, are you going to be okay?" I asked, and she got up off the ground.

"Yeah, I'm fine. The guy blocking me took me to the ground, and I decided to lay here to catch my breath." She said.

"Okay, well, that's good! Because, the next time, you're going for the touchdown." I said, and she laughed. We got the extra point and then got off the field.

"Good job, Crystal!" The coach said.

"Thank you," I said and sat down on the bench.

As the game continued, the score was neck to neck until the fourth quarter, when Kilgore was up by seven, and the score was 35 to 28. We had the ball, but the clock had two minutes on it. "Okay, Crystal? Can you stall that clock long enough so the other team cannot get another touchdown on the board?" He asked. I shook my head and was off with Silverie.

We got out there, and we were on the thirty-yard line. Kilgore got fed up with Silverie and me, so Silverie and I had two to three guys on our side. As the minutes of the game wore down, Silverie and I got the ball down to the twenty-yard line, and the coach called for a time-out, leaving us about twenty seconds on the board.

He told us to make sure that Silverie or I got the ball and to keep the players off us while we got the touchdown, and then it was time to get back out there. As we got out of the line, the guy in front of me pointed to me and said something that I could not hear but knew was not good. Then the ball was snapped, and I ran down the field. But the player did a clothesline on me for some reason, and the officials saw it. They threw the yellow flag out, and Silverie came to my side. "Are you okay?" she asked.

"Yeah, that player just did a clothesline on me," I said.

"Okay, let's switch spots." She said, and I did.

Kilgore's penalty gave us another first down and put us on the ten-yard line. This time, when the ball got snapped, I ran behind the field to where the quarterback was, and he handed me the ball. I ran for the goal line, but I could not make it, and I saw that Silverie had no one near her, so I threw the ball at her. I went down as the players tackled me, and I heard the crowd erupting, but I did not know who won until I listened to our song and knew that Silverie got the touchdown.

I took the players some time to get off me, and then I got up. The team was praising Silverie, but they never did that to me. Then we went for the extra point and got it with ease, and the players picked up Silverie and carried her to the coach but left me out there to make me walk back to where they were. It was the same way as we were going home; everybody just sat there and talked to her as if I did not exist on that bus. The coach saw that and told me to sit with him. "Hey Crystal, it will be okay; they are just amazed at what she did tonight for the team." He said.

"Yeah, but I was the one who helped her," I said.

"Yes, and I'm very proud of you. I also saw how your family was amazed by your performance, and I would be grateful if you could stay on this team. Don't worry; give it time for the team to notice who helps them most at games." He said. I just sat there until we got back to Henderson.

When we got back to town, my family was waiting for us, and when they saw me get off, little Susan came running to me and gave me a big hug."

"Sis, don't do that again." She said, and I knew what she was saying.

"Okay, I won't." She ran off to see Sapphire and David. "Well, you did well out there, girl," Dad said.

"Yeah, but I didn't know if it would work on that last play. But it did, which was a good thing." I said.

"Yeah, it was. Let's get to the house," he said, and we got into the car and went home.

Chapter 5

As the school year pressed on, we won our games and became number one in our district, which the team had not done in a long time. By next week, they were going to do something special for me. I did not know what it would be because I was not supposed to know.

I went to school that week, and everybody was friendly to me because I had turned this school around quickly. However, Tasha refused to accept me for who I was, and whenever she saw me in the hallway, she would tap me on the shoulder and continue walking, which I did not mind then. When that Friday came around, I walked to the field house, and the people seemed happy to see me. When I got to the field house, the lights were out, "Uh, that's strange." I told Silverie she knew something was going on. *Is this what they had prepared for me?*

"Well, go on in!" she said, and I did, and the lights came on.

"Surprise!" The whole team was there and gave me a surprise party.

"Oh, my goodness." that was all I could say, and I saw Silverie laughing.

"You knew about this?" I asked her; she just shook her head.

"How come you couldn't tell me?" I asked.

"Because it is a surprise, and she couldn't tell you about it." the coach said.

"Well, I'm shocked and have no words to say," I said.

"How about saying hi to me, your little star?" someone said, but I did not know this voice. I turned around, and it was Emmett. I could not say anything to him but wave my hand. "Come here." He said, and he grabbed me and hugged me.

"What are you doing here?" I asked him; it had been about twenty minutes since I could talk again.

"Well, I was watching the news, and they said that a little town in Texas had a killer receiver, and I had to come to find out who it was and when I knew it was you, I just had to come to see you." He said.

"It has been a long time," I said.

"Yeah, five years since I saw you in the Dallas area playing against Texas's best team." He said.

"Yup, that's right," I said.

We just walked around for a bit and talked to each other until I had to go to my next class. I went all day wondering what would happen next, but I did not have to wait long. Laura stopped in the hallway to talk to me as I was heading for English. "Is it true that you are saying things about me that are not real?" She asked.

"No, I haven't, Laura," I said.

"Well, I'm being told differently, not just from one person, but about five. "She said.

"No, I couldn't do that to you," I said.

"And is it also true that you are not you but just someone who likes to use people's childhood problems and turn them around and doesn't care about that person's feelings?" She asked me.

"Laura, I would not do such things to hurt you or your feelings. I want to be your good friend because I want a friend to be next to me instead of against me." I said.

"Well, that won't be me, will it?" She just walked away from me, and I tried to go after her, but she never turned around when I called her name.

I walked into English class to find that Laura was not there as always, but her stuff was there. So, I just sat down in my spot, and she finally walked in and sat down but did not look at me at all. Laura did not talk to me for the whole day, even during lunch. She went and sat with Tasha and spoke to her. "Hey, what's wrong?" Steve asked.

"Oh, it's just that Laura believes everything Tasha tells her," I said.

"How can you tell?" He asked.

"I just know because Tasha does not like me one bit," I said, talked to him for a bit more, then just started walking to my next class.

Later that day, I was walking down to the field house for the prep rally, and the coach told me to stay in front of the group with him, and Silverie was to be right behind me the whole way up there. As we got there, the gym was packed, the band played our song, and one of the cheerleaders had the mic. "And here comes your Fighting Lions and Crystal, the killer receiver!" We walked into the gym and went to the bleacher to sit down.

The cheerleader had a little scene involving the enemy team, someone played my part, and at the end, everybody laughed when the mascot, who pretended to be me, just put the smackdown on them. "Now, we have a special guest with us today, and I would like him to come out and greet everybody," she said; it was Emmett and Troy.

The students were cheering for them as they walked to get the microphone. "Now, how is everybody doing today?" Troy asked, and everybody started yelling.

"Okay, you students are probably wondering why we are here today. Well, we are looking for a Crystal Dawlson." He said, and I stood up and started to walk to them, which then the students cheered for me too.

"Well, you're shorter than Emmett told me." He said.

"Well, anyways, I came here today to give you tickets for your team for a Dallas game. Wait, there's more. I also have a trip for your family to any place in the world for two weeks. There is also one for the team that is also to anywhere, but you can't go." He said, and I looked at him funny.

"Just kidding, you are to go with them as well, so don't hate me. For the school, I have in my pocket coming from the NFL giving this school a check for seven hundred thousand dollars so that they can give the players a better field and equipment and another check for Crystal here, but we can't tell how much it is for personal reasons. Now go tonight and take that win away from them," He said, and they stayed a little bit longer until the school bell rang, and everyone was trying to get out of the gym so they could get out and party.

I decided to get to the house to visit my family, but some guy stopped and wanted to talk to me. "Hey, I was wondering if you were seeing anybody?" He asked.

"Uh, no, not right now," I said.

"All right, how about me and you go to dinner, say Saturday night at eight o'clock, and let's meet at the Jalapeno Tree." He said.

"Okay, I'll meet you there," I said,

"Well, can I get a number from you?" He asked.

"I'm sorry, but I don't just give my number to anyone until I get to know them," I said and walked to my car,

"Okay, I'll see you there." He said and walked off.

As I got to the house, I wondered if that guy wanted to go out with me, but since he asked me out, I'll go up there and see if he showed up.

I only had about two hours to do what I had to do before I had to get back to school to get to the game, so I went home to see my younger siblings. They were happy that I came home and wanted me to stay, but I had to get back to the school, so I left there and went to the school and straight to the field house to wait on the team.

I waited for about twenty minutes before anybody finally showed up at the field house, and then the coach drove up,

"Hey Crystal, where is Silverie." He asked me.

"I don't know, coach; she said she might be running a few minutes late," I said.

"Well, I just got a word about the other team, and you may not like it, but they have not lost any games to anybody in the past five years, and I'm hoping you can win." He said.

"And who is it again?" I asked him.

"Well, they were the team that you beat about four years ago near Houston, and they are the Atlanta Wildcats." He said, and I was stunned.

"That's the team that almost killed me back then when I scored us the winning touchdown, and they fined the guy that did it and sent him to juvenile for four years and then finished it out in jail," I said.

"Is there going to be a problem with it?" He asked.

"Umm, there shouldn't be, but I'll be able to tell you when we play against them," I said, and Silverie just drove into the parking lot, where the coach pulled her aside and told her the same thing.

When the buses finally showed up, I hopped on the first one, and Silverie was right behind me and sat next to me. "Hey, did the coach talk to you about the team we are going against tonight?" she asked.

"Yeah, he did," I told her,

"Are you going to be okay with that?" she asked.

"Yeah, but I'm not sure, but I'll be able to tell when I get there," I told her; we did not talk for the rest of the time as we were to go to the SFA football field to meet the other team.

It took us about two hours to get there, and the other team was already there doing drills as we got off the bus, and as we walked out to the field, they saw me and knew who I was. "Hey chick, are you back for more?" said one of the players.

I did not pay attention and kept walking to where we were to do our drills and other things. We returned to the locker after about an hour, and one of the other players grabbed and pushed me against the wall, saying, "You made a big mistake when you first showed up about four years ago, and now you're back. When are you going to learn that you are no good?" He let go of me and walked away. I got up and went to our locker room, where Silverie was waiting for me.

"What was that about?" she asked, but I did not say anything about it. I just listened to the coach.

"Okay now, guys and girls, we have a team that is like us, but better, because they have been to the state championship and won a couple of them, but we can knock them out of the playoffs if we can keep our heads on straight here. Now let's go out there and win another one for Henderson," she said, and they walked out of the locker room, but he stopped me.

"I saw what happened. Now tell me what's going on?" the coach asked, "That player is an old boyfriend of mine. When I was a freshman in Bayview, when I got into football, he saw me there and wanted to go out with me, and I said yes. As the year went on, I became popular with the school because of my excellence in football, which he didn't like because a girl was better than him, and he ended the relationship. Then his family moved off to a different town, and then one night at a football game, he saw me and told me that he was going to end me."

"Which he did?" the coach asked.

"Yes. When I got us the win, my ex came charging towards me, picked me up, and carried me to the goalpost. My ex slammed me into it and then into the ground, where my ex beat me until I couldn't feel anything. Nobody stopped him from doing that until my coach came running with my pepper spray and called him. He looked up, got hit in the eyes by the mist, and then they took him down. They took him to the juvenile hall while I went to a hospital where I underwent five surgeries to be here today, but the recovery was slow. My heart stopped four times before I got to the hospital because he hit me in the chest so many times that he broke about seven ribs and fractured all the other ones. The only thing that kept me going was that my family needed me to be there for my little sister.

"When they finally got me to the hospital, they took me straight to surgery, where they cut me open to see the damage. My heart stopped three times, and the last time it stopped, I mean, they tried everything, but for about ten minutes, my heart was not beating until they stuck it with a little bit of shock. My heart started beating again, and that's when they decided to take my organs out of my body just so that they could let them heal some before they were to work on getting my bones back together. On the first surgery, it took them about twenty hours non-stop because they had to put my ribs back in the right spot, put my organs back in after they got out all of the blood I lost during that time, and then stitch me back up.

"My family was worried about me the whole time I was there. When they got the good news that I pulled through, they came into my room and just waited for me to wake up. When I did, I didn't know where I was until they told me what had happened and I couldn't believe what they were telling me, but it was true. I was in the hospital for about two months, and when I got out, I had to be wheelchaired to the car. A nurse came by the house to help me out during the day and carried me to my therapist every workday for about four months until I could walk, which was slow, but I survived.

"Then, I was able to go back to school. However, I had to use crutches for about another month so that I could walk normally, and after all that was said and done, they didn't do anything about my ex but put my ex away for three years which I can see that my ex is back." I said I was crying while telling the story, and Silverie was there. She handed me a tissue so that I could wipe my face.

"So, that's why you are afraid of him?" He asked.

"Yes, he is the only guy I fear the most in my life, and if he gets near me, I will just freeze right there and not move anywhere until someone makes me," I said.

"Okay, well, Silverie, do whatever you can to be there for her and ensure she doesn't get hurt." He said, and he walked out.

"So, why didn't you tell me about it?" She asked me. We were walking out the doors to where the guys were.

"Well, it's hard to tell anybody about it because I hate that every time I tell it, I have to live through it, and I hate to be snapping at you," I said.

"Oh no, that's okay! I asked for it whenever I did say anything about it," she said, and when the band played, we ran out of the head, and I went straight to the other side because I saw him walking a little bit too close for me, my comfort. We won the coin toss this time, and they handed the ball to us. After we brought it back to the fifteen-yard line, I went with the team.

As I got to the line, I did not see him, but I knew he was out there because I could feel him. When the ball got snapped, I ran down the field, and Silverie was beside me to ensure that nothing terrible happened to me. Then, I saw him running up behind me, and Silverie looked back and saw him. She also looked up and pointed at the ball, and I saw that I needed to move over on the field to get the ball. "You get the ball, and I'll handle him." She said, and I did just that.

I moved to where I was in a spot where the ball was going to land, and I got it and ran for the goal line. However, I looked behind me. He was charging and catching up to me. Silverie was right behind him and catching up to him. I kept running for the line, but he was catching me quickly, and I knew that if I did not do something, he would tackle me very roughly, which I could not handle right now since my family was watching. Sapphire saw who it was and told Mom and Dad it was him.

I knew I could make it as I passed the twenty-yard line, but he was only about seven yards behind me and gaining on me. So, I tried to run faster, but my legs would not let me go any quicker than I was going.

Then I got to the ten-yard line, and he was about four yards back, closing in on me. So, as soon as I got within two yards of the line, I jumped for it, hoping to make it, and he did the same thing, but he didn't catch me in time because I made it across the line for the touchdown, which I was happy for myself and the team came down to me.

As I got up, he was right there looking at me. Then, he walked towards me, and I backed away. However, he was still walking toward me and was not stopping. I turned around, and he was right there to tackle me from behind. The officials saw that and threw a flag. But he did not stop because he was at it again. This time, his team surrounded me so that no one could help me. He started punching me in the stomach and then in the head to knock me, but it didn't work.

The time stopped for only a few moments as I heard someone trying to talk to me. "Crystal, you can't see me, but there is a way you can beat him, and he would leave you alone forever; you just have got to confront your fear about him." The person said.

"But every time I see him, I freeze up and do nothing," I said.

"Listen, you have a dragon crystal that will help you not to be afraid of him. You've just got to let it tell your brain." The person said.

"But how do I do that?" I asked.

"Believe in it, and it will help you." Then, the time started moving again, and I did what the person said.

I thought about the crystal, and it started working because as I looked up, my mind told me that he was no longer a threat to me. So, I kicked him between the legs, and he fell off me. "What the hell was that?" he said as he got up.

"Me kicking your ass," I said, and I brought my leg around, did a three-sixty across his head, and made him spin and fall to the ground.

"You're not supposed to do that." He said. "Oh, I am now." I kicked him in the stomach and punched him a few times. Then, the last thing I did was kick him across the other side of his head to knock him out.

I looked at his team to see if anyone else wanted a piece of me. But they backed off from me and returned to their sideline while I returned to mine. The game went on, and we won it with a touchdown ahead of them. As we were going to the buses, I felt something was wrong. I looked up at the sky, and it was ripped, with two figures coming out of it, and I knew who they were. "There is Crystal." They said as I ran for the nearest hiding spot to escape, but I was unsuccessful because they had someone in their grasp; it was Susan.

"Susan," I said.

"If you want her, come and get her," Tasha said. If they want a battle, I'll give them one. I believed in the crystal; it transformed me into that same creature.

I charged at them with my swords drawn and had it out with Laura for a while. I knocked her to the ground and went after Tasha the same way. Tasha and I fought until I hit her right to knock little Susan out of her hand and catch her. I told her to return to her family and not tell anyone what happened. She nodded and ran to my Mom and Dad. I flew back over there to deal with Laura and Tasha.

Laura grabbed me and tossed me to the ground as I got over there. I hit pretty hard, and Tasha came in with a blow to my left side. Laura came in on the right side and beat me to where I could not fight back, and I let myself hit the ground.

As they drew near me, I came up with enough force to knock them off their feet, and I charged at them and hit them one at a time until one of them got behind me and was coming after me. I felt her coming fast, so I hit Tasha to stun her for a second. I got out of the way, and she hit Tasha, and they started to fall to the ground, and I would hit them as they were.

Then, Tasha did a blind blow to my face and put me out for a few seconds, and they would come after me and start hitting me. The fight continued until they hit me, and I flew backward toward where the fans were. I had no time to warn them, and I hit a car, and they saw that.

They started to scatter away from me while Laura came for the final punch but then, out of nowhere, Silverie joined in to help me out. "Need a hand?" She asked.

"Yeah, thanks for the help," I said.

"No problem." She said back.

She went after Laura while I chased after Tasha. She was trying to stay away from me. But every once in a while, I would get her and fight her. Then, she would take off again, and I would chase her down again. But this time, she hit me in the stomach. I fell to the ground next to my family, but they could not recognize me because of my white hair and lighter skin.

Tasha came down to get me by my feet and threw me into the car and the nearby building. Laura was also tossing Silverie around.

As I was heading for the ground, Tasha was coming for me. On our left, another dragon girl was coming to help us. She's here to put an end to this. Her appearance gave me time to get up and catch my breath. "Are you okay?" She asked. It was Susan.

"Yes, I'm fine now," I told her. I flew off again to help put the sisters back through the portal they opened.

As we flew up, they just went for it, and we chased after them. But by the time we got there, the portal was closed, and we couldn't get them. So, we flew back to where the people were to see if anybody was hurt. Luckily, no one was. Before I flew off, Susan grabbed my boot, "Where are you going?" she asked me.

"Why do you want to know?" I asked her.

"My big sister is still in the stadium, and I haven't seen her walk out yet. Could you go and get her?" She said it was so sad to hear her say that when her big sister was in front of her.

"Okay, I'll go see if I can find her," I told her and flew to the stadium.

When I touched the ground, I de-morphed and lost the strength to walk back out of the stadium to see my little sister, but the other two picked me up. They carried me to her so she could see that I was okay and was happy to see me, "Sis! Are you okay?" She asked.

"Yeah, I'm fine." Then, I passed out right there.

I woke up in my bed the next day wondering what had just happened the night before because I could not remember anything after the football game was over.

"Well, it's nice to see you are out of bed." A familiar voice said. It was my cousin from New York.

"Hey, Randall," I said. I went to hug her, then my door opened, and Silverie walked into the room.

"Well, Crystal, you finally get out of bed." She said.

"How did you know where I live at Randall?" I asked.

"Duh, someone in this room told me about it, and it wasn't you."
I looked at her, confused.

"Her, right there, told me where you are. She showed me," she said, and I looked at Silverie.

"Why don't you go ahead and tell her?"

"Well, umm. . . How do I put this? Don't freak out, but the dragon girl you saw last night was me." She said.

"How is that possible?" I asked.

"Well, she has been one for about two years," Silverie said.

"And you didn't tell me?" I asked her.

"Well, if I had told you, you would have thought I was crazy." She said.

"Well, if you put it that way, I probably would have," I said.

"See, in the future, we have to pick girls to play the role of dragon girl to keep our planet safe from bad things," Silverie said.

"Which would be Earth, right?" I asked,

"No, silly, have you read that book as I told you?"

"Oops, no."

"Like I mentioned when we first met about being here with humans, we were not born here but came here in search of a new world in case something happens to ours. We were in a war with another race that we came to know as the Squidiams, and we used the earth as a training ground for our new dragon girls, and yes there are boys in our race, but they are rare and don't fight, so they came here to train.

"However, as I said before, the humans slowly learned about us again and started hunting us. Have you ever heard of the mythical dragons from the old days? Those were a part of our planet. We brought them here for safety, but the humans killed them; this was after the war between humans and dragons as our world came under attack, and we had to return to earth.

"That brought us into another war with humans as they slowly tried to kill off us and others that were dragons. We retaliated by burning their villages and only hurting the ones trying to kill us. Still, we had to move our cities to unknown parts of the world so that the humans could never find them again by any means possible, including using magic to hide them, and so any history of the dragons that used to be here on earth was lost many years ago. We are still here today because the Squidiams will not stop till all dragon girls get destroyed, and in my time working with the professor, he is the scientist that works for the king of the Squidiams, so that's how we got the Twin Sisters." She said.

"Okay, but that doesn't explain everything to me since I'm one, and Randall is too. How come we are not on your planet helping? Also, how am I part of a prophecy? Why did the elder need to look me over?" I asked.

"Well, for one, you're not a real dragon girl. Only through that crystal ball you became one. Our elders had a prophecy written thousands of years ago that an unknown species would help us win our fight against the Squidiams. The prophecy never mentions the species, but their body can maintain a crystal ball in their chest that gives them power, and each ball is unique to their body. That's stuff I had you drink before forming it inside your body. The prophecy said that the right mix of species and crystal ball would make an unstoppable dragon girl once they became a full dragon girl. Only when you pass on in this body will your soul and the dragon girl become one. You will face the Squidiams and be able to take them down, we have been in this fight for a century and have not found her until now, or so the elder thinks we have from what she told me; she said to keep you safe cause you might be our savior ." She said.

"And how old are you?" I asked her.

"Here, I'm eighteen. But I'm two hundred and three years old in my dragon life." She said.

"Oh my, you don't look like it," I said.

"That's because our race can live for about seven to nine hundred years before dying." She said.

"Wow, that's amazing. Is there anything else that I should know about?" I asked,

"Not right now," she said, and the door opened. Susan came running and hugged me.

"Hi, sis." She said.

"Hi, did you have fun last night?" I asked.

"Yeah, I sure did, and another thing happened also. I saw this lady dressed in a dragon outfit, and she saved me from these two girls that picked me up." She said.

"Well, that sounds like a good night, doesn't it?" I asked. She shook her head and ran back out of the door.

"Wow, that was weird to hear from her, but I guess it was a surprise for her to see," I said.

Later that day, I saw Laura's car pulling up, so I went downstairs to greet her, but when I opened the door, she didn't look pleased. "What's wrong?" I asked.

"Come outside so that we can talk about something." She said, and I walked outside.

"What does this look like?" She showed me a picture on her phone, and I saw what she was talking about when I looked at it. The image was her future self, with Tasha's future self next to her and me falling to the ground.

"Now I need to know why I saw myself in the sky last night and where you were hiding when these two showed up at the stadium." She said.

"There is an explanation for all of this," I said.

"Oh, there is, huh? Well, guess what? I felt that Tasha was right about being the person you are and hurting other people. After all, you are someone that is messing with people's lives and stuff, which I cannot have now, so don't call me anymore because we are no longer friends now." She said and walked back to her car, and drove off.

I walked back into the house where Silverie was watching the whole thing from inside the house and just held me while I tried to regain my composure. As the day wore on, I had to get ready to go out that night with the guy that asked me Friday, so I told my Mom that I was going out for the night and did not know when I would return.

I arrived at about seven thirty and waited in the car for about ten minutes, but I decided to head inside the restaurant. When I got in there, I thought I had seen him for a second, but I couldn't tell. "Can I help you?" The hostess asked.

"I'm waiting for somebody," I told her, and she walked off. I waited until 8:10, and the guy still didn't show up, but the guy that looked like him was still there, and a girl was sitting with him. So, I decided to walk to the restroom to see if it was him. As I passed by their table, it was him. I kept walking to the bathroom.

When I returned, I saw that he was still there, and I walked up to the table. "What are you doing?" I asked him.

"Uh oh." He said.

"Yeah, uh-huh. I thought it was you. I could see that you played me." I said.

"You asked her out to dinner?" The girl asked.

"Well, honey, it was a joke. The guys at school pushed me to do that. He said.

"And you just had to do it, huh? I can't trust you enough, and this relationship is over." She said and walked out the door.

"Man, why did you have to do this to me?" He asked.

"Why me? You're the one that did what your boys told you to do. So don't blame this on me, boy." I said.

"Well, do you still want to do that date?" He asked.

"No, because if you can't trust your girlfriend enough, how can I trust you?" I said and went to my car.

I headed straight for Walmart to calm myself down and see if anybody was there. But when I got there, there was no one. So, I just got out of the car and leaned against my car. I kept thinking about what that guy just did to me. Suddenly, a car was driving fast toward me.

A guy hung out the window, and it was him. "Here, wear this." He said and threw a pie with whipped topping on it at me. I couldn't move in time, it hit me right in the chest area, and they took a picture of me.

"How do you like that girl?" He said, and they drove off. I just stood there covered in pumpkin pie with whipped topping and no way to clean it off. As I was trying to get it off, another car drove up, but this person stopped, got out, and had a towel in his hands. "Here you go." He said.

"Thank you," I said, wiping off the stuff.

When I got it off, I handed him the towel. "Thanks, now I just got to get it home and clean it now." He said.

"Let me guess, you saw what happened to me, and you're going to laugh about it, right?" I asked.

"Yes, to seeing what happened to you, but I'm not going to laugh at you." He said.

"You mean that you're not like that?" I asked.

"Well, when I saw what happened, I knew it was childish for them to do that. I just came up here to help you and try to talk to you about who they were." He said.

"Well, the guy that threw it was someone that asked me for dinner yesterday, then I found out that he had a girlfriend. She didn't even know about it, so we were even. I said.

"Yep, that sounds like my brother." He said.

"Your brother?" I asked.

"Yeah, well, you can say that. See, my brother likes to ask girls out, and then he won't show up or disappoint them when they appear." He said.

"Now, how about that girl that he is with?" I asked.

"Oh her, yeah, she was in it too because she asked me about it just like my brother and I told them that one day you're going to do that to the wrong person, and they are going to get you in the long run." He said.

"Well, that is true," I said,

"I just have a question for you, and I know it would be true but are you seeing anyone now?" He asked.

"Um, no. Why? Do you want to go out with me?" I asked.

"No, I'm not asking. Just want to know if you are." He said.

"Well, no, I'm not," I said.

"Well, that's a plus in my book, how about you and I go out next week in Tyler? We're going to get my brother back for that." He said.

"Oh, by the way, what is your name, or have you already told me?" He asked.

"No, I didn't, but I'm Crystal, and you?" I asked.

"Well, I'm Brandon, and it was a pleasure talking to you. Here's my number; call me when you need to talk to someone." He said.

"Hey Brandon, is this number right? I've gotten numbers before, and they were wrong." I said.

"Why would I want to do that to you? Yes, it's the right number, give me a call tomorrow, and I'll see you at school." He said, and I looked at him, confused. "I'm a senior at school." He said.

"Then how come I don't see you at school?" I asked.

"Because I'm a lone wolf and tend to hang out by myself around the school. Plus, I have work, so I don't stay at school often but for only half the day. Anyway, I do see you every day in the hallway. Just keep looking, and you'll find me." He said and drove off. That time, Steve entered the parking lot, saw me sitting by my car, and drove up.

"Hey, what's up?" He asked.

"Oh, nothing," I said.

"Yeah, I heard Laura talking about you, and I'm wondering what is going on." He said.

"Oh, nothing; she believes a bunch of lies that Tasha is telling her. Supposedly, I said something about that to other people, and it's just a big mess." I said.

"Well, do you want to come to Tyler with me tonight?" He asked.

"I don't know because I just got a pie thrown at me, a guy asked me to dinner next week, and Laura is acting odd. I mean, I don't know anymore." I said, sounding frustrated.

"Well, you don't have to if you don't want to." He said.

I'll stay in town tonight. I told Steve.

"All right, don't do anything crazy without me now." He said. I smiled then he drove off.

I stayed at Walmart for about three more hours, then drove home to sleep and waited until Monday to see what Laura would do.

When I got to school on Monday, I walked down to the field house, and people laughed at me. I wondered why and walked past a picture of me last Saturday night. I got mad, tore it down, ripped it up, and ran to the field house as fast as possible.

When I got there, the team even laughed at me because the picture was also there. So again, I took that one down and ripped it up. I looked around and saw more of the images and just forgot them. "All right, now what's going on here?" The coach said as he looked at the walls. He wasn't very delighted about it.

"All right, who put these up here?" He asked, but no one answered him.

"If no one answers me, I will make you run laps the rest of the week, and nobody will play football." He said. Micah and about four other boys stepped up.

"We did it," Micah said.

"Well, that's better, now go out there and do laps until I tell you to stop. But before that, I want all these pictures disposed of around this field house. I will get the one that is responsible for all of this." He said, and the boys went to work.

"Now, let's go outside." He said. As we got outside, he pulled me aside to talk to me.

"Hey Crystal, at last week's game, how could you stop that guy?" He asked.

"I just confronted my fears with him," I said.

"Well, that's good; now I need your help to get this team in shape for this week's game because we are going against a tougher team than the one we just beat." He said.

"Okay, and what do they need help with?" I asked.

"Well, their teamwork, for one thing, and whatever else needs to be worked on because I'm going to make you the team captain." He said.

"Why is that?" I asked.

"Because last week, he was supposed to get this team into shape, but he failed to do any of that. I told him a while ago that he is no longer the team captain. He got mad, so be careful because he can get a hothead about it." He said.

"Oh, don't worry about it. I'll get this team ready for the next game." I said, and I knew just what to do.

That day, I was able to make the team run some tests and things to see what they needed to work on for the games. By the end of the day, I discovered their teamwork was too low even to put on a board. That was one thing; the other was the trust in everyone. Even I knew that. I told the coach what I would need tomorrow, and he said he would get right on it.

As I was heading for the next period, the students were laughing at me as I walked down the hall until I got to ag and walked in. Micah walked and laughed at me. "Oh my, I can't believe you thought somebody would go out with you, and you fell for it." He said and then laughed.

"Why you-" I said. I hit Micah right in the face and made him fall.

"Say something else, and I will make it hurt big time," I said. Micah got up and went to his chair. "That's what I thought," I said and sat down in my chair.

When the bell rang, Mr. Ingram told us to go outside and work on the projects. When I got out there, I saw that I needed to order some more metal and get my tires and axle in order so they would be in about a month. I work on getting the trailer ready for the tires, finish up on the sides and get the neck of it welded out so I can get the hitch in there, which I already had there just waiting to do that so I can get it in there.

After about forty minutes, I had everything I wanted to do done and told Mr. Ingram about the tires and metal I would need. He said that he would get right on that. The bell rang again for the next period, and the students were still laughing. So, I walked out the door to the right of the classroom and the other building so I would not hear the laughter.

I made it to my next class without worrying about students laughing at me, but some of them in the class were snickering a little bit. Laura did not say a word to me as she sat down in her seat.

The teacher told us that we had a group project to do and that she had already picked the groups. The students did not like it, but I did not mind it until she mentioned that Laura and I were to be in the same group. I looked at Laura, and she just gave me an evil look.

As we worked on it, she would not say a word to me, just to the people we got grouped with for the class. "All right now, what are we going to do about this book that we need to work on?" Brian asked.

"Well, you can do the main part since you are a whiz at figuring it out," Keely said.

"Okay, and you can do what you do best in a book." He told her.

"And I guess me and Laura can do the other part," I said, which I should not have because that set her off.

"I don't think so." She said she just got up, lunged for me, knocked me out of my chair, and started hitting me.

"All right, you want to be that way, huh," I said and hit her right in the face to knock her off, but she came back for me, and this time she drove her shoulder into my stomach and took me to the ground. I did the same thing again but harder, and she got back up. By this time, the teacher had two male teachers come into the classroom to break us up.

They finally got in between us, pulled us off each other, and took us to the office. The teacher told someone to bring our things to the office. In the hallway, they kept us separated to keep us from hitting each other again, but Laura somehow got away from the guy holding her and pulled me out of the hands of the other teacher.

She threw me away from him and came after me, so we fought in the hallway for about five minutes. Every time one of the teachers got in between us, they would get hit in the face. They called the security guard, and he had some pepper spray. I saw it and tried to stop what I was doing, but Laura insisted on fighting me.

The guard called for his backup to see if they could pull us apart. They did by grabbing me, throwing me to the ground, and putting handcuffs on me, but I fought them, as did Laura. The guards had enough of it and sprayed us in the face. We stopped moving while they put the cuffs on us and took us to the office. I was tearing up because of the pepper spray in my eyes and mouth.

My parents told me I was allergic to some peppers and would break out from them, "It's burning my eyes." I said.

"Well, you should not have been fighting." He said and sat me down in a chair in the office, and they put Laura on the other side.

She also complained about the burning sensation in her eyeballs, but they did nothing. We sat there for about five minutes, and I did not feel so good, so I tried to get the guard's attention. "Sir, I'm not feeling so well right now. I need to get some water." I said.

"Oh, stop the complaining about the spray because I've heard it all before." He said.

"Well, I need to tell you that I'm allergic to some peppers, and I think a few were in that bottle," I said.

"I don't listen to kidders." He said.

"But I never kid. . .around. . .sir. . .so. . .need. . .wat-." that was all I could say because I started to tremble in the chair. I fell to the floor and started breaking out all over my face. The nurse came in to see what was happening and saw me on the floor.

"What is wrong with her?" She asked.

"I don't know; she complained about the pepper spray used on her." He said.

"And you didn't wash it off?" She asked.

"Uh, no, I didn't think she was serious."

"Well, you better hope she survives this attack because I don't have the stuff with me now." She said, and she ran off to get it.

After a while, she came back with no luck; then I tried to say something,

"My bag. . .has. . . the. . .stuff. . .front pock-." and I went back into shock once again. The nurse went to my bag, found the stuff, took the cap off it, and stuck it in my arm, and I felt it enter my body. About two minutes later, I stopped shaking, and my face went back to its original state, and then they helped me up, and by that time, the principal walked in,

"What happened to her?" Laura asked.

"Well, she went into shock thanks to some pepper spray." The nurse said.

"Is this true?" she was looking at the guard.

"Yes, ma'am," he said.

"And you didn't do anything to help her in any way?" She asked.

"No, ma'am." He said.

"Well, you better be glad that she carries that stuff around, or she would be dead by now, or close it at that. Now get her out of the handcuffs but keep her in here. I just finished talking to the teacher, and she is the one that started it so that she can go back to her classes." She said and took Laura back to her office while the guard took off the cuffs.

"Go on to class." He said, and I headed back to English class. When I walked by a classroom and saw Brandon in there, I noticed that the bell would ring in about thirty seconds, so I just waited until it rang. Then the door opened, and Brandon walked out.

"Hey there, good looking," I said, and he turned around.

"Hey there, what are you doing out here before the bell?" He asked.

"Well, I got into a fight with Laura, and we went to the office, and they found out that she had started it, so they let me go," I said.

"Well, that seems like a wild thing to do on a day like this," he said, and we walked to our next class together, talking. When I got to the classroom, Brandon told me he would meet me at my car after school, and I said, "Okay."

When I got to my car, he was waiting for me like he said he would.

"Where are you heading?" He asked.

"Well, I'm going to head home and then go back to Walmart," I said.

"How about I follow you to your house to meet your folks?" He asked,

"Whoa, buddy, slow down there, Brandon; I don't know you that well just yet," I said.

"Well, I just want to see who your parents are because they are going to want to meet me Friday anyways; I just might as well come over," he said, and he was right because my parents do like to meet boys that I go out with to see if they are okay.

"Yeah, I guess you are right about that, so just follow me," I said, and David and Sapphire showed up at that time. We headed home with him behind us. He got out of his car and walked over to me when I got there. "Wow, I like the house." He said.

"Well, thank you," I said, and we walked into the house to where Mom and Dad were.

"Hi, there! and who might you be?" Dad asked, and my Mom looked up to see what was happening.

"Oh, my name is Brandon, and I'm going to take Crystal out on Friday. I wanted to meet her parents so that they would know who she is with." He said.

"Okay, well, that is good that you did come by for my wife and me to get to know you before you take out our daughter," Dad said.

"Yeah, well, I'm a good person and will take care of her in some bad situations if they come around her." He said. My parents talked to him for about five minutes until Susan came in, and he played with her.

My Dad saw that and liked how he was getting along with her. "Well, it seems you like kids, huh?" My Dad asked.

"Yes, I do because I had to care for my little brother," Brandon said.

"Okay, that's another check mark in my book for you. It seems you can date my daughter; just don't hurt her feelings; she would hurt you very badly." Dad said.

"Yeah, I would, and you know why?" I asked.

"Yeah, now go have some fun this Friday, and please show her a good time Brandon. Is that right?" Dad asked.

"Yes, sir, that is." He said and shook my Dad's hand, and followed me to my room for a little bit. When we got in there, everybody was in my room, "What is everybody doing in my room?" I asked.

"Oh, we're just wondering whom this guy is and hoping he won't do anything here to you," David said.

"Get out, all of you!" I said, and they got out of the room. We were in there for about ten minutes when David walked in and handed me the phone. "Hello?" I said.

"Sis, I need you to come to get me," Sapphire said.

"Okay, where are you?" I asked.

"Well, I'm at some guy's house, and they are taking me to Walmart so that I can meet up with someone with a van, and they're going to do something to me in there. We're leaving right now." I didn't hear anything else after that.

"What's going on?" Brandon asked.

"Sapphire is in trouble, and I've got about four minutes to get to Walmart, or something bad will happen," I said.

"All right, let's take my car, it's faster than yours, and I know my way around this town." He said.

"Okay," I said and followed him out to his car.

He was not kidding when he said that his car was faster because we got there with about two minutes to spare. "There she is, but I don't see a van," I said as we pulled in.

"Stop here and let me out," I told him, so he stopped, and I got out. I ran up to where Sapphire was and noticed that she was unharmed, "Sapphire, are you okay?" I asked her.

"Look out! Behind you!" she said, and by that time, the van was coming down the parking lot, and two guys had just walked around the corner and saw me.

"Hey! who are you?" They asked.

"Time to split!" I said, picking her up off her feet and running with her. The van made the corner as I ran up an aisle to escape. By this time, Sapphire had managed to untie herself, so I put her down, held her hand, and started running.

As the van drew closer, I pulled her in between some cars. Just as the vehicle passed us, we ran back to Brandon's car, but we got cut off before we got there because the van's door opened, and they grabbed Sapphire and me. Then they shut the door, and Brandon came after them. "Oh, we picked up a stray." I looked up just in time to see that it was Tasha and Laura from the future.

"Oh no, not you again," I said.

"Oh yes, and be proud of it," Laura said, kicking me to the side while someone else tied Sapphire up.

"What are you going to do with her?" I asked as I got back up.

"We're going to use her against you," Laura said and kicked me again this time; she didn't stop but just kept hitting me until I couldn't get back up; then she opened the van's back doors.

"Now, here's your stop," she said; she reached for me, but I pulled her towards me, knocked her to the side, and started hitting her and trying to get my sister out. But the girl that tied her knocked me back, and Laura got back up and picked me up by my neck.

"Nice try; better luck next time." She let go of me, kicked me right in the chest, and knocked me out of the van. I could not grab the vehicle and headed head-first for the pavement. I knew it would hurt when I hit the pavement, and I was right about; I slid about two hundred feet, rolled, and bounced until I stopped.

When I did stop, I saw that I was in the middle of the road and could not see the van anywhere. Brandon pulled behind me and came to help me, but I didn't want to.

"No, I couldn't do that." I said, I just sat there and cried until Brandon got help from some people and tried to get me in the car, but I refused to, "No, I don't want to." I said.

"Hold her. Crystal, I have to do this," he said, and I felt pressure in my neck and went to sleep.

Chapter 6

I woke up in my bed later that night at about two o'clock in the morning. I wondered how I got to my room if I only remembered where I was being put in a car and taken home. I went to the bathroom to see how I looked and when I turned on the light, I was shocked.

When I saw my face, I noticed a cut down on my left cheek and another on the other side but just a little bit higher, and my chin was cut open. I looked at my chest, and I got bruised on the left, and right side of my chest and stomach, some more cuts on the stomach, and my legs had it worst. They got cut up very badly, and my right foot hurt every time I pushed it out as it got sprained in my little incident on the highway.

When I got done there, I just went to the kitchen to get something to drink, and as I passed through the living room, someone was in there sleeping; it was Brandon. He must have stayed here to ensure I was okay. I just smiled and continued to the kitchen.

As I was in there, I felt someone coming into the kitchen. I turned around, and it was Brandon who had followed me into the kitchen. "I see you are up very early." He said.

"What happened to me?" I asked.

"Well, I had to knock you out to get you home because I knew you wanted to go after your sister." He said.

"Ohhh, okay, where is she?" I said.

"We don't know; the van that got her just picked her up and disappeared because I got the license plate number, and the police ran it, and nothing showed up around it." He said.

"I should know why it can't get traced because it is my fault that she is gone," I said and started crying, and he held me.

"Don't worry about it; we will find her," he said, and I walked back to my room to go back to sleep and try to forget what happened to Sapphire.

Brandon decided to take me to school that day because of how my legs looked, and I didn't feel like driving either, so it worked out just right for me. David got his car, so we didn't have to worry about him unless his vehicle was to break down.

When I got there, I went straight to the field house because I didn't want to hear anybody talking about my sister or me because I would fight with them, and that's the last thing I needed now. As I walked in, everybody stopped talking, looked at me, and then went back to talking while I made my way back to my locker and got ready to change.

I realized my legs would be showing; I didn't want the boys to see them, so I just put on some leggings, went outside, and walked to the coach. "Well, are we ready to train the team?" He asked me.

"Sure am," I said and waited for the team to get out before I began the practice. "All right, team, let's work on our teamwork to beat the next team at this Saturday's game and move on," I said, and they groaned about it but did as I said.

I watched them through the whole time, and they were not progressing. I told them how a team works like a car would when all the parts work in unison, and the car would work better than one with pieces that were messed up all the time and couldn't get right, but no matter, they still did as they pleased.

"Okay, I'll take today as a bad day, but it better not happen tomorrow, or we will not make it to the final game. That's it for the day." I said, and Silverie came up to me.

"You'd better be on your toes with Laura." She said.

"Why is that?" I asked; it didn't take me long to figure that out because I saw her coming down the walkway, and she looked mad.

"Run, girl," Silverie told me and opened the door and went down the hallway, and about five seconds later, Laura came through the door.

"Come back here, Crystal," she said, but I didn't stop for her, but then Tasha came out of the hallway down a little way and saw me.

"There you are," she said as she came after me. I took the hallway to my right and then took a left. I knew where I was going. I was making it to the A.G. shop so I could cut through and not deal with them. As I went past an intersection, Tasha ran out to crush me against the wall, but I stopped. She then hit the wall at full blast, which knocked her to the floor.

I kept on going; the teacher had unlocked the door earlier, and I locked it back as I went through. When they finally reached the door, they couldn't get in.

"Don't worry, Crystal; we'll get you later," Tasha said, and they walked off. I walked to A.G. class.

"Crystal, what are you doing walking through the shop?" Mr. Ingram asked.

"I'm sorry, but two girls chased me down the hall," I said.

"How can we believe you?" Michael said.

"Shut up, boy; you weren't there when it happened," Silverie said.

"You mean the two girls were chasing her?" He asked her.

"Yes, sir, because if it weren't for me, she would not be in this class right now." She said, and he sat back down.

We worked on our project during class, but since I kept thinking about Sapphire, I only got a little far into it because I needed to get her out of my head longer to do anything. Then it was time for the next class period, and Laura was going to be in there, which could not have been a better combination now.

When I got to class, the teacher looked right at me and did not say a single word, so I walked in. I noticed that the teacher assigned us seating because the teacher put our names on the desk.

I had found my seat, but Laura was right beside me to my left. I groaned at the idea. She walked in and discovered that she was sitting by me. She put a big, ugly grin on her face as if she liked the idea of me sitting next to her. I started feeling sick.

I told the teacher that I was not feeling so hot, and she told me to go to the restroom. I ran down the hallway. When I got to the bathroom, I stayed there until I felt better. I did not feel like returning to the classroom, so I walked to the office to see the nurse, "Excuse me, but is the nurse in?" I asked.

"Umm. . .I don't know, let me look for you," the nurse said. I nodded and leaned against the desk counter.

I started to feel weak in my knees and was losing eyesight quickly. As the nurse came down the hall, my hands lost feeling, and I let go of the counter and fell straight to the ground. I could not get up for anything. Suddenly, I passed out. I woke up in the nurse's office. "Oh, you finally woke up," said the nurse.

"How long have I been out?" I asked her.

"For about an hour," she said.

"Oh man, now I have a headache," I said, and the nurse gave me some medicine.

"Here you go, take them, and it will go away. I figured your head would be throbbing with pain when you woke up. You had hit your head hard on the floor, and luckily enough, you didn't damage it by the fall." She said.

"Well, am I able to go to my next class?" I asked her.

"Yeah, I think you're well enough to go," she said, and I left her office. When I looked at my watch, I saw that my class would let out for lunch in about ten minutes, so I just went outside to wait for the bell. I also needed some fresh air. The students headed back inside when the bell rang as others came out of the building to go to lunch.

I saw Brandon come out of the building, and I went and gave him a big hug. "What are we doing out here so early?" He asked.

"Well, I felt sick, so I went to the office and fainted; I had just recovered from the fall," I said.

"Hopefully, you don't plan on kissing me." He said.

"No way, man, I don't do that until the third date, and I wouldn't even kiss you if I was sick because one guy did that to me, and it was nasty enough to tell him goodbye," I said.

"Oh okay, well there's some good news," he said, and I saw Laura, who had seen me.

"Protect me from her?" I asked him.

"Why is that for?" he asked, and I looked at him.

"Oh, that's why. Okay, well, tell me how long to, and I'll be there for you," Brandon said, and we walked into the lunchroom while he got something to eat. "Are you getting something?" He asked.

"No, I still feel a little bit sick," I said, and he insisted on me getting something to eat and said he would pay for it. I just got some fruit and water; then we ate outside.

We went to sit down with Steve and Kyle. "Hey, where were you today?" Steve asked.

"I was in the nurse's office," I said.

"Oh, that, huh?" He said.

"Where did you hear that?" I asked.

"From me," Brandon said.

"He and I share the first period," Steve said.

"Oh, okay, that would explain it," I said; I looked up and saw Tasha looking at me.

She started walking towards me with her fist curled up into a ball as she would hit me, and I nudged Brandon. He also saw her, "What are you doing over here, huh?" She asked me.

"I'm eating," I told her.

"Well, I want to talk to you in private." She said and pointed to an area unoccupied by other students eating lunch.

"If you have anything to say, you can say it here," Brandon said.

"Oh really? And what are you going to do? Because you know you can't hit a girl." She said.

"No, but I can." I looked and saw that Randall was beside me. Silverie showed up too.

"That's not fair!" She said.

"Oh, but I think it is," Silverie said as she lunged at her. Tasha turned around, without looking, and hit a tree dead on, then fell to the ground. Everyone laughed, including me. That made me feel a lot better.

I took out my mirror and saw that my face was starting to heal. "Thank you, guys, you just made my day," I said. "Crystal, your face, looks beautiful," Steve said.

"Hey," Brandon said.

"Sorry, it's just a compliment," Steve replied.

"Well, that's all it better be," Brandon said. "Hey babe, he has a girlfriend already from Tyler, is that right?" I asked Steve.

"Yes, I asked her about a week ago, and she said yes to it, and I couldn't be any happier." He said.

"And neither can I," I said, and we walked to our next class.

I felt so well that I just wanted to kiss Brandon, but it did not go right the last time I did. "Are we ready?" He asked.

"Yup, let's go," I said. I got in his car, and we drove to my house to drop me off.

"Now, are you able to take care of yourself?" He asked.

"Yes, I can; thank you for caring," I said, and he drove off. I walked inside to greet my sister, Mom, and Dad.

When I got home, my parents asked if I had seen Sapphire, and I told them that someone had taken her last night in a van and that Brandon couldn't find it in the system, so they called the police to do a missing person report in hopes the cops find her.

After about an hour, my phone started to ring.

"Hello?" I answered.

"Hey girl, are you doing anything right now?" It was Angel.

"No, why?" I said.

"Well, I'm wondering if you don't mind coming to Tyler, and you and I can talk for a little bit." She asked.

"No problem; I'll be there in about forty minutes," I said and hung up the phone.

"Who was that, honey?" Mom asked.

"Oh, a friend wants me to come to her house," I said.

"Okay, but don't be out too late now." She said,

"Okay, Mom," I said, walked out the door, got into my car, and then went to Tyler.

Like I told her, I got to Angel's house in about thirty minutes instead of forty. I went to the door and knocked. Angel opened it and saw me, "Hey there, come on in, silly girl." She said, and I walked in and sat down. "Would you like something to drink?" she asked,

"No, I'm okay," I said.

"Well, what's been going on, girl?" She asked.

"Oh, you know, just trying to get my team a championship, but it's just getting them to do what I need them to do," I told her.

"Well, did you hear about Steve and me?" She asked.

"Yeah, I heard you two were going out now, which is good," I said.

"Yeah, and I heard about you being with somebody." She said.

"Oh no, we're not dating," I said.

"Oh, come on now, don't be shy. You can tell me about Brandon." She insisted.

"Well, he came to me after some boys did something stupid one night, we started talking, and I started to like him right off hand. He was easy to talk to and wasn't in any hurry to get me to his house. He is just an amazing guy to be with, and he likes and l chicks like me." I said.

"Did he say that?" She asked.

"No, I just threw that in to see if you knew me better," I said.

"Well, Steve is the same way you described your boyfriend because he likes to hang out with friends, and he has no problem with coming over here to sit down and watch T.V. for a while. Then, he would kiss me and go home." She said.

"Yeah, that would be my buddy. I haven't got that far yet in my relationship with Brandon." I said.

"So, he does have a name. I was starting to wonder if he was real." She said and started laughing.

"Oh, why you little fuss. How could you say that about Brandon?" I asked.

"Well, you're the one who told me his name after telling me about him." She said, and we kept talking for about an hour; then I looked at the clock.

"Oh man, look at the time. It was good talking to you." I said.

"Yeah, you are too. Hey, Steve was saying you were having some problems with a couple of girls." She said.

"Yeah, they are giving me many problems," I said.

"Well, I'll tell you what to do. Use the girls' weakness against themselves." She said.

"Yeah, but I don't know what that could be. Oh, wait, I know the girls are afraid of bugs. Two, they don't like to get dirty, and three, they hate geeks like Steve." I said.

"Hey, don't you put my boyfriend in this." She said.

"I'm just using him as an example," I reassured her.

"Well, there you go. Use those things, and they will stop messing with you for good, and maybe Laura will be your friend when you do because she will stop believing what Tasha says and become your friend again." She said. I told her bye, went to my car, and drove home.

The rest of the week went okay; aside from that, Laura and Tasha still followed me at school. When I got to school that Friday, I hoped to see improvement in the football team.

Halfway through practice, they were still doing the same as they did that Monday, and I told the coach to call them in so I could talk to them. "Guys, what the hell is that I'm seeing out there? To me, it looks like a bunch of idiots trying to hump a football, and the thing is, the game is tomorrow. And from what I see, we will lose by ten miles on the board if this team cannot be better than this." I said.

"Yeah, but you suck as a Team Captain," I heard very faintly but very clearly, and it came from Michael, "You boy. Why don't you show us why you will lose tomorrow?" I asked him

"Why do you just pick on me all the time?" He said.

"Because you need to keep that mouth shut and not speak because I can hear clearly, boy. No, you know what? Run some laps for your rudeness since I suck as a Team Captain; charming remark, by the way. Get moving!" I sternly told him and resumed the team running, "You guys have to understand that I took a school to three straight championships, and trust me, there were games where I thought we were going to lose, but we somehow managed to beat the other teams, and I know if they could win, then you can too. The team that we play tomorrow is far better than last week's, and I want you to dream about that because I'm going to make sure that this team wins, even if I'm carried on a stretcher back out of the stadium." I said as I told them to get back to work.

The talk did not do any good, and I told the coach to try anything he could to get them to realize the seriousness of the championship and what it would do to this school. At our next period, Mr. Ingram told me we were going outside to help the other A.G. classes kill, boil, de-feather, and clean up some chickens. I was all up for it, and as we walked outside, I saw Tasha and Laura standing to the side of the tables, having nothing to do with the chickens.

It was my opportunity to turn things around. I grabbed a dead chicken and dunked it in hot water for about twenty seconds to loosen up the feathers and took it to the table right in front of them. After a few minutes, they finally noticed me plucking the chicken. "Hey, why don't you two grab a chicken and help for once?" I asked them.

"Eww, no, I have expensive clothes, and I don't want to ruin them," Tasha said.

"Oh, you baby, these are nice clothes, and I'm still working here," I said.

"Because you're disgusting, and that's just wrong!" Tasha said.

"Well, how else do you expect to eat?" I asked.

"Well, I'm a vegetarian, and I don't kill things to eat them," Tasha said.

"Well, I'm afraid to tell you, but fruit and veggies are living things, and you kill them just to eat them," I said.

"Well, you know what I mean." She said.

"Why are you lying, Tasha? You know you eat pizza and burgers and stuff in the cafeteria." Laura said.

"Well, I've changed some." She said.

"Well, you said that you wouldn't lie to me, and now you're telling her something different than what you've been doing," Laura said and walked off, then Tasha walked over to me.

"Now, what are you going to do, huh?" She said, and I grabbed a handful of feathers.

"This," I said, threw the feathers at her, and got her shirt covered.

"Oh no, my shirt is ruined!" She said.

"Oh, I'm so sorry, but you know, that stuff comes right out in the wash," I told her.

"Oh, you're just a nasty girl." She said and walked off to find Laura.

"Why thank you for the compliment," I said, and we returned to work on the chickens.

"You know what you did was just something I have wanted to do for a long time but could never get her close enough for me to do anything." Someone said, and I turned around, but I didn't recognize her.

"Who are you?" I asked her.

"Oh, I'm Leslie, and Tasha has been picking on me ever since middle school." She said.

"Oh, well, I'm someone you can talk to about it, and I'll see if I can do something for you," I told her.

"You sure about that?" She said.

"Hey, it doesn't hurt to try now, does it?" I told her, and we worked there together.

She told me everything that Tasha had done to her since middle school and how she treated her just so wrong. It made me want to batter her to feel the pain she had put Leslie through ever since. I told Leslie I would do something for her to make Tasha pay for it. She was happy and hugged me.

As I walked to the classroom to clean off the chicken stuff, Laura walked out of the doorway, but Tasha was nowhere near her. "I'm sorry for how I've treated you, and I would like your forgiveness because Tasha told me about what you said. I didn't believe her until I saw myself in the sky that night and came to you about it. Somehow, you seemed to be the person you had done it, but when I saw you get carried out of the stadium, I wondered if you were telling me the truth. I didn't know until Tasha lied before me and told me she never did that to her friends and family. I just told her that she is no longer my friend, no matter if something happens to our friendship." She said, and I just looked at her.

"Well, do you forgive me?" She asked me.

"Well, I don't know now. Let me see, since you have finally come to your senses about me, then yes, I do forgive you." I said and hugged her. Then, we walked back to our classes.

At lunch, Laura was sitting with us this time, and we did not see Tasha at all. I was happy because I did not have to worry about her for the rest of the day.

I did neither worry about my date with Brandon nor wonder what I would wear to go out because I got rid of many things that reminded me of the last guy that gave me something.

So, when I got home, I went to my closet to look for a dress. Instead, I found a cute skirt and a low-cut shirt to go with it. My Mom must have got it for me during the week and did not tell me about it.

"Oh, you found my gift! I was going to leave it on your bed before I got home, but I just got busy around the house and forgot about it. Go and put it on; silly to see if it fits. Since you didn't go with me, I had to guess your size." She said.

I took off my clothes and put on the new clothes that my Mom had bought me, which fit pretty well. "Oh, just perfect; my big girl looks very beautiful for tonight." She said.

"Thank you, Mom, for this," I hugged her.

"Oh, you deserve it; you needed to find a nice guy for a change." She said.

"Mom." I just looked at her.

"Well, it's always nice to have a nice companion around every once in a while."

She said. "Don't worry, Mom; I'm sure I'll find Mr. Right someday." She walked out of my room so that I could get ready.

After about two hours, someone rang the doorbell as I got out of the shower. Mom opened the door, and I heard Brandon's voice from downstairs. I threw a towel over my body and hair to see him. "Hey there, still getting ready?" He asked.

"Yeah, I still am. Give me about twenty minutes, and I'll be back down." I dashed up the stairs, went to my mirror to put some makeup on, and then put on the outfit.

I was ready in about twenty-five minutes because my hair was giving me problems, but I managed to get it fixed as I wanted to.

When I walked downstairs, he looked at me and was amazed at how I looked. "Wow, um, I mean, I don't know what to say, but you are gorgeous, and with that outfit, it just makes you stand out." He said.

"Thank you," I said politely.

"Now, how come when you wear your usual clothes, you're not as polite as you are now?" Dad asked.

"Because Dad, you are the one that taught me how to act when I'm going out with friends. Isn't that right, Mom?" I asked.

"Yes, that sure is." She said.

"Well, just be careful now and have a wonderful time," Dad said. We walked out of the house, got into his car, and drove off to Tyler.

We talked about things that happened during the year and what he and I did as kids. We talked, and I didn't realize we were in Tyler about to pull into the restaurant parking lot. It was then that I saw where we were. "Oh my, I've never been here before," I said.

He took me to Red Lobster. We did have one in Bayview, but I never went in for particular reasons that I won't share with anybody, only those very close to me that I can trust. "You mean you've never been in a Red Lobster, and you said you live near New York City." He said.

"Yes, but there were reasons I didn't go, and I won't tell you about them," I said.

"But would you tell me later?" He asked.

"When I can trust you enough," I said. Brandon did not say anything after that.

As we walked in, the place was busy, and we waited for about five minutes before we could get a table. When the host turned to us, he saw me in my outfit, and I guess I had taken his breath away because he did not speak right away, but he finally caught his breath after a minute.

"Hello there, two for you, and will that be smoking or nonsmoking?" He asked. "Smok-"

"Whoa, buddy," I cut Brandon off before he could finish the word, "Nonsmoking."

"Okay, right this way." The host said, and we followed close behind him. He sat us right next to an aquarium. It had beautiful fish in it. "Okay, there you are, and your waiter with be with you in a jiffy." He said and walked off.

"How come you cut me off back there? I said it because the T.V. was over in the smoking section, and I wanted to watch it." He said.

"Well, if you haven't noticed, my family doesn't smoke for one reason; my sisters and I are allergic to certain chemicals in cigarettes. We don't know why, but the boys are okay. They found out when they brought me home that my uncle was smoking like a train right before me. I started to break out, and I've been that way ever since.

"That made my Dad stop cold turkey, and he's been smoke-free for eighteen years. They found out my sister had the same problem when somebody did the same to Sapphire. So, they knew Susan would have it when they found out she was to be a girl. Come to find out; she did; that's why I prefer nonsmoking." I said.

"Okay, if that is true, how come you did not break out the other night when we were around some people smoking?" He asked.

"Because I carry around an inhaler with a special formula, that way, all I have to do is use it, and I'll be okay for about eight hours or so. I don't have it tonight because I figured we would be in the non-smoking section. Now, did you get all of that?" I asked him.

"Yes, I didn't know. All you had to do is tell me, and I would have gotten us sitting over here." He said.

"Well, I won't say much about my problems. It is our first date; I do have to get to know you before I tell you more about me." I said. At that time, the waiter showed up.

"Hi there, my name is Alex. I'll be your waiter this evening. Can I have your drink order?" He asked.

"I'll have a Dr. Pepper, and what would you like?" Brandon asked me.

"Oh, I'll have tea." The waiter walked off to fetch our drinks.

After a while, he returned with the drinks and asked if we were ready to order. We told him what we wanted, and he was gone for a time. When we got done eating, Brandon drove us to a park and told me to follow him. I followed but was hoping it would not lead to a bad situation. "Okay, tell me more about yourself." He said as he grabbed my hand and sat down on a bench.

"Like, what do you mean?" I asked.

"Like how you became a football star; I mean, most girls would call you crazy for being one, Crystal." He said.

"Well, I like to be different from other girls. I hate it when people look at me differently because I am a football star." I said.

I talked some more about my life, and so did him, and we sat there and talked for about thirty minutes. "But you know, telling me your story might have brought us closer together." He said

"Yeah, I believe so too," I said and leaned up to kiss him, which was very romantic.

"Oh girl, you kiss very well." He said.

"Thank you, and so do you," I said; we stayed in the park and talked some more until we got home so I could be ready for tomorrow.

When I woke up, I went straight to the bathroom to prepare for the game. I wanted us to move on in the playoffs so the boys could feel victorious when we got the trophy. It did not take me long, but my brother was dragging that morning, "Boy, what did you do last night?" I asked him.

"I just party too much, that's all," he said,

"Well, do you know today is the game?" I asked.

"Yeah, that's right. Well, I'll get ready in no time," David said and went to his room. My parents came into the living room and were ready to go.

"Well, Crystal, how was your night?" Mom asked.

"Well, I would like to do it again sometime. It was the best time I have had in a long while with a guy." I said.

"So, what did you do?" She asked.

"Well, we went out to eat and then went to the park and just talked for about an hour, and then he brought me home."

"Uh-huh," Dad said.

"What? It's true. I wouldn't lie to you."

"You have before." Mom said,

"Yeah, but that was my wilder side, Mom. I have grown out of that because I got in trouble a bit back then. I want to be a better example for my siblings."

"Okay, well, are you ready?" she asked; I nodded. "Now, where is your brother at?" She asked.

"Right here." He said while coming around the corner. He had somehow slipped and hit the wall, which made me laugh. "What are you laughing for?" he asked, then started to tickle me for laughing,

"Well, you're the one that slipped on the floor, and I couldn't help it," I said.

"Yeah, right." He helped me up off the floor.

"Well, let's get going before you become late," Dad said. We got into the van and went on to the school. We arrived on time; David and I got out and went to the field house.

Silverie was already there. "Where were you last night?" She asked.

"I went out with somebody," I said.

"Well, I was looking for you. You could have given me a call."

"Well, I just forgot to call because we had a wonderful time. I'm hoping to do it again." The coach told us to get on the bus, and Silverie and I kept talking. "Well, tell me what it was like." She said.

"Oh, better than a dream I had ever dreamt before because he asked me about my past, and I told him. When I did, I felt a lot better now than before. The only people that knew about my past were my close family, and that was it, and I believe he is the first friend I talked about." I said.

"Oh, you told him, but you can't tell your best friend about it?"

"Well, not on the bus. It will have to wait until we are alone."

"Okay, but don't forget, all right?"

"Okay." We kept talking because it would take about two hours to get there, which was a long time away for anybody.

Finally, we arrived at our destination. We then got off the bus and started walking to the field to prepare for practice. The other team, who was already there, saw me. The guys that were not looking got nudged so that they saw me. "What? Do you have a problem with a girl, or are you afraid I'll run you into the ground?" I said.

"You don't belong out here! You're not part of that team!" One of them yelled.

"Yes, she is, and she is going to run right over you on this field and make you go home, so we will go on to win the championship." I turned around and saw that Scott, the quarterback, was saying it.

"Hey, thanks," I said.

"Yeah, no problem." He said.

"I'm sorry for the way I treated you in the past. I'm just not used to a girl playing football, and it took me some time to accept that. Some of the guys are starting to do the same."

"No problem. The team that I played with before was the same way, and it took them some time too. But I know someone won't like me at all."

"Yeah, don't worry about him. He's just in it for the popularity, for some stupid reason that it doesn't remember."

"Well, am I going to have help today, or am I alone?"

"No, today you have the team behind you, and we will help you all the way." He said. I was glad to hear that from him.

We went on to practice for about forty minutes until everyone started to show up for the game. With about ten minutes left, both teams walked off the field and into the locker rooms.

The coach talked to us about the other team and how they were undefeated this year. After the coach talked, we headed back outside. The stands were full of both teams' fans, and I saw my Mom and Dad in the crowd, cheering for me. I had to get with the rest of the team.

The school song got played, and we ran out of the lion head and to the sidelines to wait for the coin toss; I was going to be the one to do it all. As I walked out there, the ref saw me. It took him a second to finally said anything.

"Call it." He told the other team. "Heads." The coin hit the ground, and it was tails.

"Kick or receive?" He asked me. "Receive." The other team took the North side of the field, and I ran back to the sidelines to wait for the offensive players to get out.

Then, the coach walked up to me, "Crystal, I want you to be on the receiving team and to run the ball as far as you can." He said. I was off onto the field and waiting for the kick.

I saw the ball getting kicked and followed it all the way. I got into position to get the ball, but it fell right on the five-yard line. The other team got in front of me and blocked them. They knocked players out of the way left and right as they went forward until they reached mid-field and ran into thicker traffic. I had to move around because the ones we passed were after me and catching up to me.

They finally got me at the forty-yard line, and the coach was pleased. I stayed out on the field and waited for the offense to come out. It did not take us long to get closer to the goal line. As David was going for the touchdown, he was stopped right at the one-yard line, and we knew it was going to be tough to get through to get the touchdown.

I told Scott to give me the ball, and I'll get it in for us. He agreed, so I got ready, and Scott snapped the ball. The team held the other right where they stood, and he handed me the ball. I ran for the bunch and jumped over them. They did not even touch me, and I got the touchdown for us. The fans went crazy over it.

The score was still very close as the first quarter ended, but we were ahead by a touchdown. The other team was going for another touchdown fast. The other team was almost at the goal line, and the defense couldn't stop the offense.

They got the touchdown right before the quarter ended, scoring 21-21, and for the rest of the half, it stayed that way. It was not until about one minute left, and we had the ball, and I told Scott to give me the ball, and I'll get the touchdown again. He said yes.

When he got the ball, I ran down the field and got ready for the ball to be thrown, which I did not see for about a second or two until I saw it right behind me. I stopped to catch it, and the other players were after me, so I darted for the end zone.

I crossed the line to get us a touchdown as time ran out. Our team kicked the extra point as I walked off the field with the coach. "That was impressive to watch. You are doing good so far." He said.

"What do you mean by that?" I asked.

"Well, if we keep this up, we will probably take a trip to the capital to see someone."

"Okay, coach, just let me know when it will happen," I said, and I walked into the locker room so the coach could talk to us more about how we needed to keep them guessing what we would do next. I could barely hear some fans calling my name as we walked back out. I put my hands up, and they were going wild for me.

I got ready for the second half to go underway. As the third quarter went on, the other team scored on us, and we tried to get a touchdown. This team knew how to play and would not let us take the win easily.

When we got the ball back, the coach told Scott to hand me the ball, so I could run for a touchdown and try to keep us ahead.

As the ball got snapped, he threw me the ball right there, and I ran down the field. As I did, the players were after me. I did not look ahead quickly enough, and one of them power-drove me in the stomach and took me to the ground. Somehow, I managed to hold onto the ball. When he got off, I could not move all that much, and the referee came over there to see if I was okay. "Are you hurt anywhere?" They asked.

"I don't think so; I just got the wind knocked out of me, that's all," I said. The referee helped me up. I walked off the field under my power and sat on the bench. We managed to get the touchdown with Silverie's help, but the other team got one, which kept them one touchdown ahead of us.

The third quarter ended, and we were on the fourth. Both teams were not making any progress on the field, and time was running out. I saw we would not get the touchdown we needed, but I could not do anything just yet.

We had about one minute on the clock to make the touchdown, and we were at a standstill. I walked up to the coach. "Hey, coach, let me in. I'll get us that last touchdown." I said.

"Are you sure? You took a big hit out there before."

"Coach, if I wasn't sure I couldn't get us the touchdown, do you think I would be up here telling you to put me in?"

"All right, go in there and get us that touchdown!" He said. I got my helmet, and the fans called out my name as I walked there.

This time you could hear it as clear as day, and the other team was not looking good. "What are you doing out here?" Scott said.

"Just hand me the ball, and I'll take care of the rest," I said.

"Okay, I'll do that." He said and broke the huddle. We got to the line, and the clock started counting from one minute.

He snapped the ball, and I ran down the field and waited for the ball. I saw it coming my way, caught it, and ran down the field as fast as possible. Then, I heard a voice in my head say. "Crystal, throw me the ball when you can't go anywhere; I'm about five yards away to your left." I looked over for a second and saw that it was Silverie. So, I kept running until someone grabbed my feet, which made me throw the ball over to her. She ran for it, and the player got up and thought he had me. "Yes, I told you a girl can't play football." He said.

"Umm, I wouldn't be talking if I were you," I said and showed him my hands.

"Oh man, got the wrong one!" He went after Silverie, but it was too late because she had already got a touchdown. We went for the two-point conversion, and I went in, made the catch, and got us the win.

The fans went wild and were chanting for my name. Everyone on the team was doing the same, and I could not be happier.

As the fans were leaving and I started to walk out. I felt something terrible coming, as did Silverie and Randall. She was our water girl for the rest of the season, and we got together to talk about it. "Hey, do you feel that?" I asked them.

"Yeah, I can, but it feels like three of them instead of two," Randall said.

"Here they come," Silverie said, and I looked behind me.

They were topping the stadium and starting to scare the fans. We would not have that, so we found a place to morph into the dragon form and went after them. "Oh, look, Laura, they're back for more," Tasha said, and I saw who the third one was.

"Sapphire," I said, but she acted as if she did not know me.

"Back away, or I'll kill you!" She said.

"Now that's a good girl. See? she doesn't know you because we made her like one of us." Tasha said.

"Let her go!" I spoke.

"Oh, let me think, no. Not until you give yourself up and join us will we let Sapphire go." She said.

"Don't do it, Crystal!" Silverie said.

"Oh, you shut up," Laura said, and she attacked her.

"Come on, Crystal, what are you afraid of?" Tasha asked. I knew she was up to something.

"Nothing," I spoke.

"Oh well. You better be." She said as she charged at me. She had something in her hand, and I saw it. I moved just right of where it just barely missed me, and we fought. Randall had sought to fight Sapphire.

Tasha was trying to touch me with the item she held in her hand for some reason, and I knew it wasn't good. I did not know what it was, so I kept my distance.

I kicked her out of the stadium and followed her to ensure she would not hurt anybody while I was looking for her.

I found her knocked out, lying by a car, or so I thought. I drew my sword out and poked her with it, she launched for me, but I backed up. She drew out her sword, and we fought for about five minutes.

People were trying to get to safety, but one of them was getting closer to us, and I had to break away to push him back. Tasha jabbed me in the back with her sword, and I felt it as it dug into my skin, but it did not go far. As I kicked her, the sword came out, and I felt blood trickling down my back.

The blood had stopped gushing out of my wound after a few seconds, and I went back to fighting Tasha. We brutally fought for a little while until I knocked her out of my way.

Sapphire was charging at me with her sword drawn. She attacked me, and I had no choice but to fight back, but I did not want to. We continued the brutal fight until Tasha knocked Sapphire out of the way.

I swung to hit Tasha, but she ducked, and I hit Sapphire right smack dab in the chest with my sword, and she fell to the ground. I had sprung into complete shock at what I had just done and tried to help her, but I knew I could not because she was the enemy. "Crystal, look out!" Randall said, but it was too late.

Tasha had snuck up behind me, stabbed her sword through my chest, and then stuck in what she had hidden in her hand. I felt it sink in as it encountered my skin, creating a horrific sting.

It was already too late to get it out because it got buried underneath my skin. Tasha then pulled her sword out, wiped off the blood, and put it back up. Silverie and Randall came to my side to assist in my aid, but they realized there was nothing they could do to stop her.

I felt that my dragon ball was starting to fail on me and that my morphed body had just disappeared, and I was back to myself again. "What did you do to her?" Silverie said to Tasha.

"Oh, I just disabled that crystal of hers, and now she can't get it back for nothing because the painite has made her unable to support one," Tasha said.

"Why you no good bi-" Randall was struck by Laura before she could finish.

"Oh no, we have kids present," she said.

"And now, back to our business of taking over the future," Tasha said, and they were gone.

"I'm sorry for what happened," I said.

"Oh, don't worry, we'll somehow get that thing out of you soon," Silverie said.

"Crystal." I heard someone say.

"Oh no, that's my Mom, and she won't be happy about this," I said.

"What was that I saw you doing?" Mom asked as I was getting up.

"I thought you weren't going to lie to me, yet you did."

"I'm sorry for not telling you, but you would not have believed me even if I told you." That did not work because her anger got worse.

"When you get home, you will tell us everything about what happened tonight." She said and walked off.

"Let me get back with the team. At least the team didn't see me de-morphed." I spoke.

I walked to the buses with Silverie, who somehow had stopped time, as did Randall, and they sat near me to keep me safe. I kept thinking about what had just happened to me and wondered how I would reverse the effects of the painite that Tasha had placed into my body.

As we traveled the road, I examined the part where Tasha's sword had gone through me but did not see any scar. It made me wonder if the painite stripped my powers from me or if the painite did not work right. I pulled out a knife, cut my arm, and waited for it to heal.

I did not see anything happen, but blood came out of my arm, and I put a towel over it and held it there for sixty seconds. When I pulled it off, I saw that the cut was not visible. I knew that I still had my healing powers but not anything else, and after a while, I grew tired. My eyes slowly started to close, and I fell asleep.

Chapter Z

That following week, I was out of school for Thanksgiving. I knew my Mom would need my help preparing for the occasion because every year, she invites all the family over to stay for about three days. She needed me to go to the store with her and help with the stuff we would need for the feast.

As we got there, she still did not say a word about last night, and I was hoping she had forgotten about it. I would not have to tell her about the dragon bird stuff. We walked around and debated on what to get. "What do you want this year for the main course?" she asked.

"Well, I was thinking about a turkey," I said.

"We had one last year. I was thinking of a ham." She said, and we looked at the hams, but they were expensive.

"Okay, we will just stick with the turkey, and you go pick out what you know we need," she said.

"All right, be back with it," I said, and I wandered off to pick up the items we always get yearly.

We have stuffing, canned cranberries, cornbread, green beans, English peas, and other things. I found my Mom in an aisle down from me and put all the stuff in the buggy. "Good eye, Crystal," she said.

"Hey, when I go shopping with you every Thanksgiving, I always know what you get. Now, I know without asking what you get." I said, and we walked to the front to check out.

I happened to see Steve walking with Kyle in Walmart. "I'll be right back," I told my Mom, and I ran to catch up with them. "Hey, what's up, guys?"

"Oh, hey, Crystal. What are you doing up here?" Steve asked.

"Oh, I'm just here with my Mom shopping."

"Where are your sisters?"

"Oh, um, they are over there with her," I said, but by that time, my sister showed up happy to see Steve and Kyle.

"What's up, Stevie?" Susan asked.

"Oh, did you teach her that?" He asked me.

"No, she learned that by listening to me, and she just picked up on it and stuff like that."

"Well, what are you doing tonight?" He asked.

"Umm, nothing. Why?" I said.

"Because I was going to Tyler, and I would like to take you and Kyle here to play some pool," Steve said.

"Yeah, I could. I would be bored at my house all night anyway." I said.

"Okay, I'll come by to get you later." He said, and they walked off. I went back over to my Mom.

"What are you doing tonight?" She asked.

"Just going out with Steve and Kyle," I said.

"Okay, what about Brandon? Would he get mad that you are going out with them?" She asked; by this time, we were walking out to the car.

"No, they have girlfriends and wouldn't want to cheat on them," I said.

"Okay, just making sure," Mom said.

"Mom, don't be like that," I said.

"Like what?" She said.

"You know what I mean," I said.

"Not really," Mom said.

"Mom!" I said.

"I'm kidding, girl. Go out and have fun before you get to be my age." She said. I just stared at her with a shocked look, and she laughed. Then we went home.

Later that night, Steve came by to get me, and Kyle was already in the car. We then headed to Tyler. "Who's all going to be there tonight?" I asked Steve.

"I don't know, but a guy told me to expect a big crowd up there."

"Well, that's good news for us. More people for me to beat at pool," I said. We kept talking until we got to the pool hall. As I walked in, I saw Angel working; she saw Steve, so she ran to him and hugged him. She walked with him to the back while I looked at the wall.

There was a picture of me and something about me being a hero for the club owner. I must have done something for him and do not remember it. I kept walking, and I saw someone that looked just like me. I went up to talk to her. "Hey there," I said, and she turned around.

"Do I know you from somewhere?" She asked.

"No, I don't think so."

"Because we look a"

"Lot alike and think-"

"Alike also." We said. "Well, I'm Crystal," I said.

That's strange because mine is close to yours. It's Kristen," She said.

"Wow, that is weird how our names are so close. Do you know who your Mom is?" I asked.

"No, I was adopted when I was little, but they told me they didn't change my name from my birth name," Kristen said.

"And what would your middle name be?" I asked.

"Well, it would be Rose." I had the most startled look on my face. "That is very close to mine. It's Ruby." I said I was starting to feel I had a twin, but I did not know for sure. "Is there anything else that you can remember?" I asked her.

"Yes, I have had this locket since I was born. My parents gave it to me when I was about six, and I keep it around my neck and never take it off." She said, and she showed me the locket.

Surprisingly, it was the same as mine, and mine was also around my neck. "I have one just like that, and my Mom had it with her. She gave it to me and told me to hang on to it. I always wondered what it was for, and now I know. I have a twin, and I will talk to my Mom about it and see if it's true." I spoke.

"Hey Crystal, let's play some pool," Steve said, but he went to the wrong one.

"I'm sorry, but I'm not Crystal," Kristen said.

"Yeah, but you look like her," Steve said.

"That's because she's my twin, and we just found that out," I said, turning around to face him.

"Whoa, you are twins. Man, you know you can get somebody confused by doing that." He said.

"Yeah, twins can do that to people that they know." She spoke.

"Hey, why don't you join us in some pool?" I asked her.

"Sure. That would pass the time quicker." We walked over to the pool tables to play some games.

After a while, it was Kristen's and my turn to play. As we did, I noticed that she was as good as me at pool, and in the end, she beat me, but just barely by knocking the eight ball in before, I did. "Now we can say that someone is better than you," Steve said.

"And you are talking to someone that beat you at pool," I said.

"Well, I was having a bad day."

"Right." Kristen and I had said at the same time. After we played pool, we headed home, but I wanted to talk to Kristen some more. "Hey, what are you doing this week?" I asked Kristen.

"Well, my parents left on a cruise they won, and they couldn't invite me, so I got stuck at the house for the week," Kristen said.

"Well, why don't you come home with me and find out if we are twins? My Mom is still up because she is getting ready for Thanksgiving." I said.

"I don't know if she could take the shock of seeing me," Kristen said.

"Well, it doesn't hurt to try," I said.

"Okay, I guess I can go with you," Kristen said.

"All right, let me just tell the boys I'm going to ride with you," I said and went off to tell them.

Kristen walked out beside me, and they said, "Okay," and drove off. Then, we hopped into her car, which was in okay shape, but she could use another one.

As we made it home, I saw that the kitchen light was still on, which meant that Mom was still up trying to get stuff ready to cook for tomorrow. "Hey, Mom," I said as I walked in.

"Well, there you are. Did you have fun?" She asked me.

"Yeah, I made a new friend," I said.

"Oh, you did, and who is this friend?" Mom asked.

"Well, she is right here," Kristen walked in.

"Oh, my goodness, Kristen, is that you, or am I just seeing things?" Mom asked,

"Yes, it is; how do you know me?" she asked,

"I remember you from when we adopted your sister Crystal here."

"Was there a reason you couldn't take us both?" Kristen asked; Mom gave her a big hug and cried. So was Kristen,

"Why was Kristen left behind, and I'm also adopted? why didn't anyone tell me?" I asked.

"Well, we couldn't support both of you. At the time, we had issues with having kids, so we decided to adopt instead; we wanted you both, but due to income and expenses, I didn't expect you two to meet each other this soon."

"Well, you could have told me about it," I said.

"Well, if I did that, you would have done anything to find her. That's why you had to find out on your own." Said Mom, and she walked back into the kitchen.

I followed her into the kitchen to ask more questions, "Why wasn't I told about this sooner than now?" I asked,

"Well, we didn't know how to say it to you and when to, but I'm guessing now is the best time to do so. I will let you know that you were adopted right at birth; from what we know, your mother was very young and couldn't care for you two. Her best option was to give you up for adoption, we don't know who she is, and those files have gotten sealed, but she loved you both very much and wanted the best. Hope that we have been the best parents for you; I will let your Dad know that we talked about this." she said,

It was a lot to take in because all this time, I didn't know I was adopted and didn't know how or if my siblings knew about it, but I wouldn't let that let me down; I walked over to her and hugged her,

"You have been the best Mom I have known, and I'm happy that I'm part of this family, but I have one question. Do the others know about me, and are they your kids." I asked her,

"No, they do not, and yes, they are our kids, but we still love you all the same; just because you were adopted doesn't change how we love you all," she said,

"Hey, Mom, I was wondering about this locket around my neck. Kristen has the same one also now. If I was adopted, then how do we both have one." I asked,

"Oh, the locket is the last gift from your Mom. They never told us much about it, but she had them made before she decided to give you two up. But maybe since you both have found each other, you two can figure out what they are for." she said,

We talked a bit more as I helped her with a few things; Kristen walked into the kitchen and helped with dinner.

"Well, I guess we'll go to my room," I said, and Kristen followed me up the stairs and to my room. She liked my room.

"Oh wow, I like the color," she said.

"Thank you, it reminds me of my childhood and young teenage years before I got terrible," I said.

"Oh, okay. Hey, who is this?" She had picked up a picture and was examining it.

"Oh, that's my sister Sapphire, which she is missing right now; that's David, that's Kevin, and that's little Susan. She is attached to me." I said. She walked around the room, picked up a book, and read it. Then, she walked over to the bed with it and showed it to me.

"Do you know anything about this?" She asked, and I noticed that it was my dragon book.

"Umm, no, I don't know where it came from," I said, and I grabbed the book. My face was telling me off.

"Yes, you do. Don't try to hide it because I'm one too." Kristen said. I looked at her,

"Prove it," I said,

"Okay, get ready." She morphed right at that moment, and then she morphed back.

"My, well, I am one, but I can't morph because of some painite that this girl threw in me, and now it's not working," I said.

"Oh, I know what that is. I knew that I was going to need this." She said, and she handed me a bottle.

"Here, drink this, and you will be back to normal in about five minutes. Then I started to feel a burning sensation where Tasha stuck the painite inside my body as it slowly forced its way out and cut through my skin. I wanted to scream, but Kristen put her hand over my mouth. It only took about 30 seconds before it fell onto the floor; as my skin healed back up, I felt the ball coming back to life and could morph again.

"How did you know what to do?" I asked her.

"Because I also experienced it with some girl too. I studied up on the book and read about it. You are reading this book, right?" Kristen said.

"Uhh, no," I said.

"Well, you might find some of this information useful someday, you also might know that painite is deadly to dragon girls too, and tomorrow would be a good day to start. You can read it in a day, and you will know all about the dragons and how they are here to save the world now and in the future." She threw me the book. "Read it tomorrow, and I'll take care of what Mom needs to do, okay?" I nodded. She then turned the light out, and I went to bed.

The following day, I did not hesitate to read the book. It talked about how I could stop time, turn it back to save the past, and contain a semi from hurting anyone. The best part was about my powers, how to use them, the healing process, and how I can use them on others.

I finished reading the book in about four hours and walked downstairs. I saw Kristen talking with everybody, and Susan ran to me. "Sis, we thought she was you," Susan said.

"Oh, yeah, I know she looks like me and everything," I said.

"Did you read the book?" Kristen asked me.

"Yeah, I sure did, and it was good," I said.

"Well, how about we go for a walk and talk about it?" Kristen said.

"Hey, I'll come along," Silverie said.

"I will, too," Randall said.

"Hey, what if I want to go?" David said.

"Sorry, but only girls can go," I said; he got mad.

"Don't worry; we'll be back in no time." We walked outside.

Kristen led us to a place where no one could see us.

"All right, now try to stop time," Kristen told me.

"Okay, here we go," I said. I had to concentrate on making time stop, but I needed to do it better. It took me about four tries, but I finally did it. After that, I had to go through all the other things, which I did well according to Silverie's standpoint, but then I had to use my powers. I morphed and used them perfectly like they wanted me to, and everything else fell into place like it should have been.

"All right, not bad for a beginner," Randall said.

"Hey!" I said.

"Well, you're doing better than me on my first try. Now, draw out your swords and see how good you are at them." Kristen said. I got them out, and we practiced.

Every time that I would fight, she would somehow beat me. I was frustrated and wanted to quit, but she told me not to.

"I can't do it," I said.

"Hey, you're trying too hard. Believe in the crystal, and it will help you beat me. That's the only way to beat Tasha and Laura. Just do that, and then attack me." I did, but something was coming through the sky, and I had no time to do anything when Tasha came rushing through with her sword drawn at me.

I believed in the crystal to help me win, and it blocked her from hitting me. I pushed her back.

"Impressive move, Crystal. Let's see how good you are against me," Tasha said, and we swung our swords. They rattled every time they hit. I tried to get a blade close to her, but she would knock it away. Then she pushed me into the wall and came at me with a sword. I moved just in time, and she missed me. I swung at her, but she blocked it, and we kept fighting.

I threw her to the ground and tried to stab Tasha, but she moved out of the way and swung at me. She had missed also but managed to knock the sword out of my hand, then the other one, and pushed me to the ground. "Now, what are you going to do?" Tasha asked.

I truly believed in the crystal, and it told me to grab my big sword and pull it out, which I did, and move out of the way. "This," I said. I swung my sword, knocked her swords out of her hands, and pushed her to the ground. I had the blade right at her throat. She then looked horrified. "Now, what are you going to do?" I asked her.

"I was just leaving," she said. I had let her go.

She got her stuff and started to leave when she went to Susan, "No, don't take her." I said, but she had grabbed her and was taking off, and I chased after her and didn't care if the others followed me.

I was on her tail the whole time and was catching up to her fast until I got right beside her, "Give me her back now." I said,

"You have to fight for her," she said, and I chased her until she stopped and put Susan into a sphere that looked connected to her; we fought again with our swords, and the others finally made it there, Kristen wanted to help, but Silverie held her back.

We continued our fight until she hit me in the face. Tasha tried to stick me, but I moved out of the way and managed to stab her with my sword. She screamed, a bloody scream when I did. She got me in the stomach, then in the arm, and I happened to strike Tasha right across the chest, and we kept throwing blows back and forth. We had cuts all over our bodies. Tasha was getting weak because of the way she was fighting me, and I was starting to do the same. Then, she tried one last time to strike me with her sword.

My tail was starting to tingle as if it was telling something. I brought it around to block the sword. When Tasha struck my rear, her blade broke right in half, and she was in awe that my tail had destroyed her sword. My tail's end grew bright red, I felt the power growing, and she pulled out the other blade and tried the same approach. It, too, broke on her, and she did not know what to do because she did not have a tail. "Let my sister go, or I will make you. Take your pick." I said.

"You can't have her." She said.

"Then, you are going down," I said, and we went into a fistfight right there; we took more pounding and started to make each other bleed. All the time, my tail was growing stronger as we kept fighting until Tasha kicked me. I started falling, but my wings brought me back up in the sky, and I hit her.

She fell to the ground, and I followed her all the way to finish her, but she managed to kick me right before I took her to the ground. When she hit the ground, I saw that she was not coming back up, so I came full blast toward her with my tail in front of me. She couldn't move, and as I drew closer, she looked scared by the second until I hit her right in the chest with it. Blood seeped out the wound, and she didn't move after that.

So, I went and got my sister. I told Randall to take her home and keep them safe while I returned to Tasha, which was in bad shape. "Excellent, Crystal. You stopped Tasha from taking anything from you. Now, it's time for you to send her back to the future. See if she has something on her to make a portal." Silverie said.

When I looked back at Tasha, I was sad about almost killing her to get my sister back. I searched her body and finally came across some dark crystal Silverie saw,

"That might be what they are using. Throw it and see. Does Tasha have another one?" Silverie asked; I looked some more but came up empty,

"No, it's her only one," I said,

"Okay, well, throw it and send her back, Crystal." she said; as we walked back toward the house, Silverie turned to me, "You did a good job, Crystal, and I'm proud of you for stopping Tasha from trying to take you, sister," Silverie said.

"Yeah, but was there any other way to stop her from doing that?" I asked, but before she could answer, I investigated the distance and thought I saw Sapphire; however, it was just an image that looked like her,

"No, and if you hadn't stopped her, she would have taken your sister. I know you don't want that to happen," She said.

"Yeah, it's just that I couldn't stop them from taking Sapphire that night," I said.

"Don't worry; we will get her back. It will take time and some more to break the hold on her to get her back to our world." She said,

"Oh, Silverie, why didn't my mother ask about what happened last night?" I asked,

"Oh, no need to worry about that. I took care of it for you." Silverie said, and I wondered what she did as she looked at me again, "Oh silly, I might have made her forget about that issue last night. I do have magic remember." she said as we walked back inside, where Susan greeted me with a big hug. I was so happy to see her.

"I'm sorry, sis. I just wanted to see you." She said.

"That's okay, at least now you are safe in my hands, and nothing will happen to you anytime soon, I promise you that," I told her, and

I played with her in the living room, and she was having fun with me and everyone else there.

After a while, I walked outside and thought about Sapphire. I wondered what she was doing now and if she knew she was being brainwashed and did not even realize it. "Don't worry, Sapphire; I'll find you and rescue you from the future. I will bring you back home to me so you can enjoy life again with your family." I walked back inside the house.

The next day, Brandon came over and did not know about my twin sister yet. He was surprised about it. "Hey, when he rings the bell, you answer the door because he will think you are me," I told Kristen.

She went to the door and answered it. "Hey, there, baby," she said.

"Well, how are you doing today?" Brandon asked.

"I'm doing okay now," she said, and he leaned in to kiss her. She turned away.

"Whoa, you know better than that."

"What? I thought the last time we went out. It would be okay. What's wrong with you? You never talked like that, and you are acting differently. Are you sure you're Crystal?"

"Uh, no, I'm Kristen. I think you got the wrong person." She said.

"But you look just like Crystal," Brandon said.

"That's because she's my twin, silly," I said, and I came around the corner.

"Well, that would explain a lot." He said.

"Yeah, we just wanted to prank you a little bit to see what you would do," I said.

"And you never told me you had a sister, let alone your twin," he said.

"Well, I didn't know until a few nights ago when Laura took me out, and we met at a club," I said.

"Why were you at the club?" Brandon asked

"Because Laura asked me if I wanted to go," I said.

"You know better than to go to clubs without me." He said.

"Hey, does my body have anything written about me being your property? No, it doesn't, and besides, it was a girl's night out. I don't cheat on guys; they cheat on me. I don't know why." I said.

"Well, let me know what you are doing next time," Brandon said.

"What if I can't remember next time?" I said.

"Oh, why do you always do that?" he said.

"To keep your mind guessing about who I am," I said. After that, he did not say anything else, and I walked to my room.

He followed right behind me. When he walked into my room, he shut the door. "Uh, no, keep the door open, please," I said.

"What? We're not going to do anything," He said.

"Not my rule, my Dad's. He is very strict on it about us. If we have a friend over that's of the other sex, we are to keep the door open at all times." I said.

"Well, that's crazy," Brandon said.

"Ask my brother; he's the one that made it happen. He had his girlfriend over, and Dad didn't know that, so he went into his room. You can figure out the rest." I said.

"And how long ago was this?" I looked at the calendar to see how long it had been.

"Umm, I want to say about a year next month, and as long as I live in this house, I have to go by it."

"Man, that's rough. Well, I can't say much because my Dad is the same way about me."

"Hey, sis, what are you doing right now?" Kristen asked.

"Um, nothing at the moment; why?" I asked.

"Because Mom needs your help." She said. I walked down to the kitchen and saw that she was having problems there.

"Hey, Mom, why don't you go sit down? Kristen and I will take care of this for you," I said, and she sat down.

"You want to do it?" Kristen asked. I knew she meant to use our powers to get things back in order.

"Yeah." I got busy with the turkey getting it ready, along with anything else to be cooked on the stove before the feast. After thirty minutes, Kristen and I have everything in order. Then, Mom walked in there. "Oh my! You did a wonderful job. How could I have managed all this when you two are working together to get it done?"

"Well, Mom, you can help us out," Kristen said.

"Oh, you don't have to call me Mom if you don't want to." Mom said.

"Well, you are my real Mom, so that's what I'll call you when I visit and when I can move in with my sister," Kristen said.

"Oh, well, that's good to hear," she said. She started to help us out so we could get it done faster and for it to be ready tomorrow before the guests showed up to stay for a few days.

When we got done cooking, I went to find Brandon, who was playing with the girls outside. "Oh, please tell me it's you," he said.

"Don't worry; we won't do that to you again, babe. That was not my idea in the first place, okay, so don't hate me," I said.

"So, what's going to happen tomorrow?" he asked.

"Oh umm, we have about fifteen to twenty people showing up; they will leave on Saturday or maybe even Sunday. We do this yearly, and the crowd grows because my cousins have kids or new friends they want to invite. You are welcome to stay here tonight; you must stay in the spare bedroom. Don't try anything sneaky, and try to get into my room," I said.

"What would make you think that?" Brandon asked.

"No, I don't mean it that way; my Dad sometimes gets up at night. I don't know when, but he will get up and walk to each bedroom every night to ensure we are okay. The times always vary on when he has to use the bathroom," I said.

"Oh, so your Dad does that?" he asked.

"Yeah, ever since I was born, he's been doing that. He wants us to be safe and protect us. He can use some things if he has to." I said,

We were outside watching Kevin and Susan playing in the sand with a friend,

"Now, that would be a good picture right there." He said.

"Yeah, they like their friends because they are not far from the same age."

"And you say I have a tough time with my memory." He said and laughed.

"Hey, that was mean to say," I said, and I lightly punched him,

"Oh, I'll get you for that," he said, and he started to tickle me, and I got away, and then he hugged me from behind and watched Kevin and Susan play outside until Kristen came out.

"All right, you two, get a room," Kristen said.

"And who asked you to watch?" I asked.

"I'm your twin, I know about what you do, so you can't hide it from me." She said.

"Man, I hate that sometimes because there are things that you think of that are crazy," I said.

"Well, don't think about them then," Kristen said.

"Well, I can't help that," I said.

"Well, what are you going to do later?" Kristen asked.

"I don't have anything in mind right now," I said.

"Good, because you are going with me somewhere, and I can't tell you, or it would not surprise you." She walked back into the house.

I decided to go inside to see if I had any e-mails from Laura or Silverie. Silverie returned to her time to spend with her family and would be back at the end of the week. Randall was on a cruise to the Bahamas with her parents, and Laura was at the house.

They said they would try to keep in touch with me by e-mail, but when I checked it, I did not have anything in there. I wrote them a letter and sent it to all of them, then just waited for their reply. As I walked out, an instant message came up on my computer. When I went to check it out, I found it was Laura.

She asked how I was doing, and I told her everything was okay. It's just that I was getting ready for tomorrow because our place will be busy with my family and relatives. She said that she was glad she was not me and that it was wrong to her. She laughed about it and had to go after that, but she told me she would talk to me after ten o'clock. I said okay and walked back down to the living room. I told everyone that I was going for a walk. Brandon said that he would go with me. We then both left the house.

When I returned from my walk, I went to my room. Someone had left me a message, and it was from Laura. I read it. She told me her Thanksgiving plans and what her family was doing, which was not as much as my family. I sent her an instant message to see if she was still at her computer.

About two minutes went by, and she finally responded. While I was looking at some sites that Kristen told me about for games, she had been taking a shower when I sent it and said she would be free tomorrow, so she would come by and meet the family. I said I would see her then, and Silverie popped on the screen.

She told me that her family wanted to see me, but I said there would be no way I could. I probably could, but I did not want to right now. She was okay with that and would be back in a few days.

She mentioned that I am going with her during Christmas and that I cannot get out of this one. I was thinking, "oh no," to it, but instead, I said, "okay." Then, she got off, and Laura said she had to go to bed, so she was gone. Then, I was all alone in my room.

After ten minutes, I got off the computer and watched TV for a while. I tried to lie down, but Kristen came into the room. "Hey, can I talk to you?" She asked.

"Yeah, what's the matter?" I asked.

"Well, my other parents are still on vacation, and they just called me and told me that they got held up and to find a way to school. I told them about us moving here and wondered if they had gotten me going to Henderson or Tyler school. They said I was to start in Henderson next week and find someone to stay with until they got back. So, I would like to stay with you until they return."

"Yeah, I don't mind; just don't take my man," I said.

"Who said I would?" Kristen asked.

"I'm just telling you. Don't try it, or I'll get you for it," I said.

"Don't worry, girl; I already have someone, so your man is safe with me." She walked out of the room, and I went to bed.

The following day, I went downstairs and saw that it was about nine o'clock and the family should be showing up in about an hour. I heard some clanging coming from the kitchen, and I went in there and saw Mom doing some things. "Mom, what are you doing?" I asked.

"Hi Crystal, you're up early on Thanksgiving." She said.

"Well, I couldn't get much sleep last night. I kept waking up for about ten minutes to try to sleep again." I said.

"Well, why don't you make sure your father is up also?" She asked.

"No need to worry; I'm right here," Dad said as he walked into the kitchen,

"Well, Crystal, why are you up so early?" He asked. "Well, I couldn't get any sleep last night; I guess I have a lot on my mind right now," I said and walked outside to see what was going on today.

A car drove up, and I saw that my family was starting to show up. I went out to greet them. They were happy to see me, then the rest of the family began to drive up as we headed into the house. Laura then drove up, and I went to her car, "Hey, girl." I said.

"Hey there. Wow! you have many visitors." She said.

"Yeah, well, I have my grandparents, aunts and uncle, and my cousins, and you can come in too," I said.

"Hey, grandpa wants to see you," Randall said, and I went inside to see what they needed me to do.

When I got inside, I saw grandpa sitting in Dad's chair, "Well, there's my football star. I heard you are still in the playoffs and have three games before you go national. Then, go for four more to win the championship." He said.

"Yup, you heard it right," I said.

"Now, what will we do when we get out?" He said.

"I'm thinking of going to college to get a career," I said.

"Do you know what yet?" He asked.

"No, not yet, but I'll think about that," I said. Grandpa saw Laura behind me.

"And who is this behind you?" He asked, and I got out of the way.

"Oh, my name is Laura, I'm a good friend of hers, and this is April." She said. I knew her from school because she would always be looking at Brandon. I would not like it one bit, which he knew, and then he walked in, and she saw him, "Hey, Brandon." she said.

"Hey, April. Hey honey, I need to talk to you quickly." He told me, and so I followed him outside.

"Yeah, what's up?" I asked,

"Hey, do you mind if I go back home to spend some time with my family?" He asked.

"Yeah, I don't mind. You go on; I'll be fine here." I said.

"No, it won't be for a few hours from now because they are out of town and won't be back until tonight." He said.

"Okay, that's not a problem," I said.

"All right, thanks." He said and walked back inside the house, and I followed him.

After talking to my family for a few hours, we decided to eat, and I looked for Brandon but could not find him. I still saw his car out there and wondered where he could be. "Hey Laura, have you seen Brandon anywhere?" I asked.

"No, I haven't," she said, so I asked Kristen.

"Hey Kristen, do you know where Brandon is?" I asked.

"I don't remember where I saw him, but I think he is upstairs." She said, so I bolted to my room and opened the door, but he was not there.

I went into the guest room and saw him watching TV on the bed. "Boy, you know it's time to eat," I said.

"Oh, it is; let's get downstairs then." He said, and so we went to the dining room to eat. It seemed packed in there. Some of us had to sit in the den and the living room to eat. After we got done, Brandon walked up to me, "Hey, I'm going to the house. Do you want to come along? I'll bring you back." he said,

"Yeah, sure, I'll go," I said.

"Hey Crystal, me and April are going to tag along in my car," Laura said. I nodded my head, and we headed out of the house.

When we got there, his family had a much smaller party than ours. Brandon introduced me to his folks and went into the living room to talk to them as we walked in. "Well, buddy, you know how to pick them, don't you." said his older brother, whom I didn't know.

"Well, we just started talking one day, and that was it." He said I told him I had to go to the restroom. Then, he told me where to go. When I got into the bathroom, I looked in the mirror and looked like a ghost. But I felt a little bit sick, so I washed my face.

When I returned, I noticed that Brandon was not sitting in the living room, and April was not there either. "Hey Crystal, he went upstairs." his brother said, and he told me where his room was. I went up there, and when I did, someone shut his door, so I opened the door.

"Hey, Brandon." but when I investigated his room, I saw him in his chair with April in his lap kissing him,

"Oh man, April get off of me," he said when he noticed me, and she just sat there.

"You know whom you want, boy, and that's me." She said.

"I think I'm going to be sick," I said. I ran down the stairs and out the door. As I made my way out the door, my dinner was all over the ground, causing some people to walk away. The others laughed at me when I did it because my clothes got some of it.

He came out after a minute, and by then, I got done losing my thanksgiving dinner,

"Honey, I'm sorry, but she came on to me," he said, trying to hold me, but I pushed him away.

"But you couldn't tell her no. Was that it, or was I not that attractive for you to say that?" I asked.

"No, that's not it; she just came into the room, hopped on me, and started kissing me." He said.

"Stop saying that; you're just making me sick again," I said. April came out of the house, and she knew I was mad at her.

"Come here, you," I said, got a hold of her hair, and pulled her to me. "What made you think you could just walk into Brandon's room with his girlfriend in the house?" I asked her, but Brandon came over there and grabbed my hand, and made me let go of her.

"You're not going to hurt her like that." He said, and I was hoping he was not taking her side.

"Why are you protecting her? "I asked.

"Well, I saw your little action back at the game the other night, and when I saw it was you, I knew you had been lying to me." He said.

"What are you talking about?" I asked him, and he showed me a picture of me as a dragon girl and another one when I was de-morphing,

"Now, explain to me about this." He said.

"Well, it's hard to say because it's a very hidden secret and hard to explain," I said.

"Well, how can I believe everything you told me?" He asked.

"You just have to," I said.

"No, that's not going to cut it. So, let me tell you, like I've told all the rest, get off the property and don't come back." He said he walked back inside with April, and I fell to the ground crying.

"Come on, let's get you home," Laura said. I got into her car, and we went back to my house.

As we got there, I could hear the party from outside the house, but it still didn't cheer me up. When I walked in, everyone saw that I was sad, and the talking came to a stop as I walked past them and went to my room,

"Go check on her." My grandpa told Kristen, and she followed me upstairs to my room.

"What happened with him?" She asked, and I looked at her. "Yes, I know you two split up tonight." She said.

"How did you know?" I asked her.

"Duh, we're twins, so basically, we share the same brain, so I know what happens to you most of the time. This time, you got me sad about something. That's how much we are connected." She said.

"Well, he saw me the other night at the game," I said.

"Shit, pardon my French, but that's going to spread all around the school in no time." She said. Laura walked in, and I was mad at her too.

"What do you want?" I asked.

"Hey now, it's not my fault for what happened tonight, I swear." She said.

"Like I'm going to believe that," I said.

"She would not stop bugging me about coming with me tonight. Then follow you two to Brandon's house. I had nothing to do with that; I swear to you that much." She said.

"I don't know what to do anymore," I said. I started crying again, and Kristen held me, and Laura got beside me.

My mother came in there to see what the problem was. "What's wrong, honey?" She asked.

"Oh, Brandon dumped her, and she took it hard," Kristen said.

"Oh, okay I will tell the others to give her space for now." She said and walked back outside.

"Are you going to be okay to go back downstairs with everybody?" Kristen asked.

"I think so, as long as no one asks about it," I said, still crying a little bit.

"Okay, let's go." She said, and we walked downstairs.

When we went down, everybody was sitting here and there talking to each other, and when they saw me, they kept talking to everybody else and left me alone. So, I decided to walk outside to think about what just happened to me and how Brandon could do that to me besides seeing me at the game, which shouldn't have done anything about our relationship, but it did.

My phone started vibrating, which scared me a little. I looked at it, and it was Steve.

"Hello?" I answered.

"Hey girl, what are you doing right now?" He asked.

"I'm in my backyard thinking, why?" I said.

"Well, I'm about to be at your house in five minutes, and I need to talk to you about something." He said.

"Okay, I'll wait outside to meet you," I said and hung up the phone. I walked around the house to the front.

He got there in five minutes and didn't look happy either. "Hey, what's up?" I asked him as he was getting out of the car,

"Well, Angel and I broke up," He said.

"Why is that?" I asked.

"Well, let me ask you something. If a guy came up to you and asked if you were single, what would you say?" He asked.

"Well, I would tell the truth no matter what," I said.

"Well, when I got to her apartment and opened the door, I saw a guy in the living room kissing her. When she saw me, she just looked stunned that I was there." He said.

"Then, what did you say?" I asked.

"I told her to stay with him because I would not return. Since then, she has called me ten times, and I haven't answered the phone yet." He said.

"Well, I'm in the same boat as you; I'm single also. Brandon played me the whole time he was with me, and I couldn't handle it." I said.

"Well, that's some interesting stuff to hear on Thanksgiving from you." He said.

"Yeah, you can say that again, but don't," I said.

"Well, what's going on inside the house?" He asked.

"We have a party that's going to happen for about three days," I said and brought him inside the house. Kristen saw him walk in.

"Hey Steve, what are you doing here?" She asked.

"Um, I'll tell you later." He said and walked into the living room, where my family saw him.

"Crystal, who is this?" grandpa asked,

"Well, gramps, this is Steve. I've told you he's a friend about being there when I needed him most." I said, and Steve shook his hand.

"Well, that's a mighty fine handshake you got, son. Just keep her safe for me." He told him.

"I sure will, sir," Steve said and pulled me to the side to talk.

"Hey, um, are you going to be busy this weekend?" He asked.

"Um, no, I don't think I will; why?" I asked him

"Well, I would like to take you to dinner as friends. At least that way, our weekend will end well." He said.

"Yeah, that might help out a lot." I said, and he said he had to go, so I said, "Okay," and he left.

The next day came by quickly. When I got up Saturday morning, my phone rang. "Hello?" I answered.

"Oh, I'm sorry. Were you sleeping?" It was Steve.

"Yeah, I was. But I need to get up, and it's good that you called me." I said.

"Well, I'll be at your house in about an hour. So be ready to go to Tyler and have some fun." He said and hung up the phone. I got ready in about thirty minutes and waited on him.

When he showed up, I told Mom I was going out with a friend and would be back later; they said, "Okay," and I went to his car. We talked the whole way to Tyler; it was just things that happened over the holidays and what Christmas would be like for us.

As we made it to the mall, he parked the car, and we walked in. He stayed close to me the whole time. It was beautiful to walk into the mall with a guy because I could find out what they do alone. He walked me right to the leather store.

I fell in love with one of them, and the price was a little high for me, but I didn't care because it had to do with NASCAR. When he saw it, he looked at me, "Oh come on now, are you a Gordon fan or what?" He asked.

"Oh no, I'm a Jr. fan. I don't like Gordon much, but I don't mind Johnson." I said.

"Now you know that's not right." He said.

"Well, he did help Jr. out some," I said.

"Yeah, well, until I'm convinced about him otherwise." He said.

"Well, my pick is Jr. next year because he showed so much promise this past year," I said; then I heard a gunshot from outside the store and saw people running,

"What's going on?" Steve asked, and I looked toward the jewelry stores. One of them was getting robbed.

"Look over there," I said, and he saw them.

"Okay, let's try to get out of here." He said, but one guy was watching.

"No, we can't because that guy will kill us if he sees us," I said, and we stayed there. I looked at them closely, but I didn't recognize them. I knew someone needed to stop them. I also know that I could. "I'll be back," I told him.

"Where are you going?" He asked.

"To the restroom," I said.

"Okay, but be careful." He said, and I strolled until they could no longer see me. I ran to the restroom so I could morph.

When I did, I ran back down the hall to the opening and saw they were still there. The cops had the place surrounded. They could not go anywhere fast and were looking for any exits but needed help finding one. They finally saw me.

"Oh no, not you. Man, I thought you said those dragon things were phonies." He said.

"I did." The other one said.

"Well, look over there." He said, and he saw me.

"Well, you know how to take care of that, don't you?" He said and pulled out his gun. He started shooting at me. I dodged the bullets easily, and everybody screamed whenever they heard a shot go off. I pulled out my sword and hit a cable that dropped a sign right in front of him so he could not see me.

I tore right through it, took him to the ground, and knocked him out cold. "Ralph, oh, you're going to pay for that." He said he started fighting me, which he was good at but not good enough. I took him out in no time.

Then, the third came at me. I took the guy out quickly, and there were still two left. They ran for the front of the place, so I flew after them.

"Oh, shit, man, she can fly." He said.

"Well, take her out!" The other said, and he began shooting at me. He got me in the leg, which left a blood trail. Then, another got me in the arm and cracked the bone. I fell to the floor but got back up and went after him.

He tried to shoot me, but I came too fast, nailed him in the chest, and took him to the ground. The last one went out the door, where the cops were nowhere around. He managed to get to his car and tried to escape, but I was hot on his tail.

I smashed right into his back window, which shattered. After that, he stopped the car, got out, pointed his gun right at me, and began shooting again. He only shot three rounds, and the gun was out of bullets, so I pulled my sword back out and taught him with it.

He finally went to the ground giving up. The cops finally showed up to see what was going on. They saw me and started pulling their guns on me instead of the robber as they took the guy into a car.

"All right, miss, put the weapon down and give yourself up, or we'll shoot you." The officer said, but I didn't listen.

I flew off into the sky. The cops started shooting me, and they were missing me. Some of them were getting me, and I knew I didn't have long to make it back into the mall where Steve was still.

The cops stayed right behind me, and they were still shooting. I used my tail to create a barrier and to stop them from following me. I de-morphed down the hall and cleaned myself up.' There were officers in the hallway, so I went in another direction and came up empty-handed. I flew around until I had no cops on my tail wherever I went. However, it was kind of hard to do that. Luckily, I saw a door and the end of the hall.

I ran to it with the cops on my tail, closed it, and locked it so they could not get to me. When I turned around, I saw that I was in a storage room in the leather store, so I de-morphed and walked out the front door.

I came around the corner to see Steve outside the store.

"Oh, there you are. I thought something might have happened to you." He said.

"No, I'm fine now. Thank you." I said.

"I saw that dragon girl again; she stopped those robbers." He said.

"Yeah, I saw her pass by," I said, and he noticed my leg bleeding.

"Hey, what happened here?" He asked, and I looked.

"Oh, I guess one of the bullets got me, but I'll be fine. Now, let's get out of here." I said, and by that time, the cops came back around the corner and ran looking for me. They came up empty-handed to find me because they were looking for the dragon, but she was gone for now.

"Hey, I got you something." He said and handed me a leather purse with the number eight on it.

"Oh, you shouldn't have," I told him and hugged him.

"Well, I did it for our friendship and because you don't have a boyfriend to spend Christmas with." He said."

"Are you asking me out?" I asked.

"Well, yes, I am. But you don't have to say anything right now. I'll leave myself open for you whenever you are ready." He said.

"Oh, you are so kind; why didn't I decide to be with you instead of, never mind." I shook my head. "I don't know; I'm getting hungry here," I said.

"Yeah, me too; let's get something to eat, and then I'll take you home." After we ate, he took me to my house, and as he dropped me off, he told me something.

"Remember, if you need a friend, I'm there for you, but if you need a boyfriend, come to me." He said.

"Okay, I'll keep that in mind when I think about it," I said, and he drove off. I walked into the house feeling happy about myself. I felt so pleased that I wanted everybody to know what I did today before they were to leave to go back home.

They were happy for me, and I went to my room, and Kristen was already up there, "Hey, I heard the good news about you. I'm so happy that you finally be the right guy this time, and I know he will be good to you." She said,

"And that is very true," I said and kept talking until we went to bed.

Chapter 8

As I went to school that following Monday, I thought about what Steve had said at the mall. I will tell him my answer today because Kristen and I discussed it over the weekend. She rode with me that day to the school to see what everyone would say about it.

When I parked the car, and we got out, students stopped and stared at us because they never knew I had a twin. Scott saw me and thought I was Kristen, "Hey Crystal, umm, I need to talk to you." He said to her.

"Um, well, I won't be able to help you with that," she said, and I turned to him.

"Scott, I'm over here," I said.

"Oh wow, I didn't know you had a twin. Anyways, I need to talk to you about this week's game. The guys want to know how we are to beat this team." He said.

"Tell them I'll be right down to help them with that," I said.

"By the way, is she playing football too?" He asked.

"No, I don't play football. I'll be a cheerleader. I don't do what my sister does, which I don't see how she can do that." She said.

"Well, my Dad got me started, and I just stayed with it," I said.

"Well, see you down at the field house." He said, and he walked off.

"Hey, where can I get my classes at?" She asked.

"I am about to show you; follow me," I said, taking her to the office.

The principal saw us, and I didn't know what to say, "Well, they told me that your sister was starting here today; I just didn't expect her to look like you." She said.

"Yeah, the teachers will react the same way about it," I said, and she got her classes. I looked at them; we had about the same ones except for her first period.

"Okay, I'll see you at the next period." She said.

"Okay," I said and walked off to the field house.

When I got there, I talked to the players about the next team we played on Friday. I told them they would be challenging, and we were to work on teamwork and trust.

As they did, I saw them improve from last week's mess. I liked it. Every time they did something right, I would tell them they would get better at it, and the coach walked over to me. "Hey Crystal, good job on getting this team back on track. I have never seen them work this hard for anything in all my years handling them," he said.

"Well, for some reason, it seems that a female motivates guys if they like the girl a lot, which I think they are starting to like me. I'm starting to see that I can take this team to the championship game, and if I got them behind me, then we will be unstoppable to anybody that goes against us." I said.

"Well, this week, we fight a rival that is only about a ten-minute drive from here, and I heard that they have a strong offensive and good defense. Are you going to be able to get this team ready for that?" the coach asked.

"If they keep doing what they are, we can beat them with no problem," I said, and I didn't realize that the bell was about to ring in five minutes. I told the guys that they could change and start back up tomorrow. I went to get my stuff and headed for my next class to meet with Kristen.

As I made my way down the hall, I saw her right in front of me, and I ran to catch up with her. I finally did, as she was about ten feet from the door. "Hey, Kristen," I said.

"Oh, there you are. I was beginning to wonder where you were." She said.

"Well, let me go in first, then you come in behind me, so they don't think you are me," I said, and we did just that.

As I walked in and she came in behind me, Michael saw her and was starting to drool on himself, "Oh man, it seems every time you see some hot girl, you just can't keep to yourself." Steve said.

"Man, shut up! I wasn't even looking at you. I'm looking at her." He said while pointing at Kristen.

"Oh, boy, why don't you get a life? And stop staring at me because you are not my type. Besides, I have a boyfriend." She said.

"Well, if you break up, you want to go out with me?" he asked, which was so stupid to say.

"Umm, let me think, um, no, and don't ask again, or I'll pound your face in and make you not go out with a girl for a while," she said. He turned away and gave the birdie, and she saw it.

"Oh, you're mine," she said and hopped out of her chair. I reached out in time to get her shirt so she could not beat Micah up and pulled her back. "You're lucky my sister is in here with me." She said.

"I was right; you are twins. I might have thought you were. Is it true that you can read each other's minds?" Allie asked.

"Yeah, we can. Crystal can write something down, and I can say what she wrote without looking at it." Kristen said.

"Wow, that's awesome! I wish that I had a twin." Allie said. The teacher walked in and saw Kristen behind me.

"Is it me, or am I seeing two Crystals in my classroom simultaneously?" He asked.

"You are Mr. Ingram. She is my sister Kristen, and she will finish her studies here. She also might want to help me with my project." I said.

"Would you like to do that?" He asked her.

"Yeah, sure, I've been in a shop class before and know how to do things." She said.

"Good looks like you can do that pit on the trailer, Crystal since you got your sister to help you with it." He said and told us to work on them. Kristen was right behind me.

"Pit! On what?" she asked.

"On this gooseneck trailer right here," I said.

"Oh my, you picked a good one to do. My biggest contribution is a ten-foot trailer, and I made the sale on it." She said.

"Well, I've done one of these last years, and I decided to do something different on it. I placed a pit on the front that is removable when you need to haul something that would need the whole trailer." I said.

"Well, what do you need me to do?" she asked. I looked at the trailer and saw that my brackets needed welding.

"Okay, the brackets need some welding, and I'm going to try to get the axles on the trailer. I may need your help with them." I said, and she welded them.

I got the first one on with no problem. However, the second one didn't go as planned, and the jack slipped. The axle fell on me. Kristen saw it and stopped what she was doing to get it off of me.

"Oh, Crystal, are you okay?" She asked.

"Yeah, this axle just' doesn't fit in. Then the jacks failed on me. Can you help me? I'm going to push it up, and you get the jacks back under it." I said, and she nodded.

"One, two, three," I said and lifted them. They were heavy. Kristen worked quickly to get the jacks in line to hold the weight.

"Okay, this is starting to get heavy here," I said.

"All right, you can set it down." She said, and as I did, they slipped again. This time, the axle was on my neck and was choking me. Mr. Ingram saw it and got Kyle and Steve to help while Micah laughed.

After a minute, I could get out from underneath it, and they put it back on the ground.

"Are you good now?" Kristen asked.

"Yeah, I'm good now. Thanks for helping me." I said.

"Hey, that's what sisters are for." She said, and Micah was still laughing.

"Oh, you think it's funny to see me getting choked, huh? The next time you need help, I won't be there to give you a hand. I'll let you know how it feels to have a three-hundred-pound object on your neck." I said.

"Oh please, I can lift three hundred pounds with no problem; it's just hard for you because you are a girl, a wimp, and too chicken to say it's true," he said, and I stared, walking towards him.

"Wimp! Boy, I bet you fifty dollars that I can bench press more than you could do." I said.

"I'm sorry, I don't take bets from girls." He said.

"What, are you chicken?" I said.

"Your call; tell me when and where. I'll be there to see you cry." He said.

"Today at three-thirty in the field house. You better be there, or you lose the bet." I said while I was bleeding from my neck. I went to the restroom to clean it up. However, there were no mirrors, so I poked my head to get Steve to look at me. "Hey Steve, can you come to give me a hand to get this cleaned up?" I asked, and he came into the restroom,

"Oh, I see why you needed me in here for." He said.

"Yeah, there's no mirror here, so I can't see what I'm doing. Hey, I thought about what you said last Saturday. I want to go out with you if you still want to." I said.

"Oh, I was joking about that." He said.

"But you told me to think about it and even gave me a gift. I thought you want-" I said, but Steve butted in.

"Oh, I was kidding. Yes, I would love to go out with you, girl, but don't be too quick to judge me, okay." He said, and he got finished with the cut.

"There, that should do it," He said and walked back out of the restroom while I was right behind him.

I looked at my watch and saw it was time for the next period. Silverie stopped me. "Hey, what did you and Steve do in the restroom?" she asked.

"Oh, I had a cut from the axle that fell on me, and the restroom had no mirrors. So, I got Steve to help me out." I said.

"Uh huh, you did something more than that; talk to your sister because she told me," she said, and I looked at Kristen.

"What can I do? We share the same mind, so I know what you sometimes do," she said.

"Yeah, but you don't have to tell the whole about it," I said, and we headed back into the classroom.

The rest of the day went okay until it was time to head to the field house to prove someone wrong. We got there simultaneously, and a few students were there to watch it.

"Okay, now we will find out how much each of you can bench press and whoever does the most weight wins and has bragging rights about it. Now, here are the rules: One, you cannot wimp one rep. It must be a complete rep, and you must do ten of them to keep your title up. Now, if you only complete a certain number, the other person can do all ten or do one more than you did and win it. No cheating whatsoever, or you will get disqualified. The opponent will then have an easy win. We'll start you two at one-fifty. Don't take your time on them; get ready and go." the coach said. I started to do them, and Micah was right behind me with his also, which we finished at the same time,

"Okay, now increase it to one-sixty," he said. We both completed that also. The coach got the weight up to two-sixty, and it was doing a number on my arms, and I could see it in Michael's face as he strained to get the last one done.

"All right, the next weight will be two-seventy," he said, taking me longer than before. But I finished before Micah got to his seventh rep, which gave me some break time.

Then, they topped the weight at three-ten. As we started, my arms began to feel the pain, but I pressed through them but got held up on number seven, and Michael saw that. He took advantage of it, pushed his arms to the limit, and finished before I did.

I had just finished the seventh one, which he was starting to celebrate as he would win, but his celebration slowly faded as I got closer to finishing mine. He was getting mad. He grabbed a weight and was going to hit me with it, but the coach stopped him.

"Hey, if you do that, then you're just a sore loser," he said, and I got it done.

"Hey Crystal, do you want to give up?" Kristen asked; she knew I was in much pain, but I wouldn't quit that easily.

"No, I don't," I said, and they added more weight until it topped out at four-hundred-eighty, which my own body weighed one-sixty, which meant I was going to hold three times my body weight above my chest.

When the coach gave the go, Michael went to work putting reps up, but then, he started to slow down extremely fast and stopped at eight while I went through the third rep. I saw he wasn't doing it anymore and got one of the guys to help him get it off.

He watched me as I finished the fourth, fifth, sixth, and seventh until I got to number eight. I tricked him into thinking I couldn't do anymore, and he was getting happy and came over to me. "See, I told you, you're not better than me," he said.

"Oh yeah, well then, watch her," Kristen said for me, and I completed number eight, then I went on to do nine, then ten, and did about four more after that. I got so tired that I needed Kristen to help get it off me.

I got off the bench and celebrated. "There's no way you could have beaten me; you cheated somehow," he said.

"How could I have cheated? You were right beside me the whole time." I said.

"So? That doesn't mean you two could have switched spots when I wasn't looking." He said.

"I'm sorry, but if that was true, shouldn't we both be sweating right now?" Kristen asked. He shut his mouth and walked off.

"Well, that proves I'm better than him," I said.

"Dang girl, I didn't know you could lift that much," Steve said.

"Oh, I could have lifted more, but I don't want to see him cry," I said.

"Well, you should have done that." He said.

"Okay, you do that and tell me if you would have gone any higher on the weight to prove yourself," I said, and he did not say anything. "Yeah, that's what I thought. Come on, let's go home, Kristen. See you later, Steve." I said, and I kissed him on the cheek.

"All right," he said and went to his car. I went to mine and drove home.

When I got home, Kristen ran into the house to tell Mom about what just happened at school. When I walked in the door, she came up to me. "Well, Kristen just told me that you lifted to four hundred and eighty pounds at school. I don't see how you could have done that without any help. Are you taking anything to do stuff like that?" she asked.

"No, Mom, I wouldn't do that! I'm a strong girl, and you should be proud of me." I said.

"Yes, I'm very proud of you because you showed the guys that girls are not as weak as they think. Well, I have supper ready if you feel like eating." She said.

"All right, I'll be in there in a minute," I said, and I went to my room to talk to Kristen.

"Why did you tell Mom that?" I asked.

"Hey, I'm just trying to get you in a good mood since Thanksgiving," she said.

"Yeah, but you didn't have to do it like that. I'm happy for my team; the team has finally got a brain to use in the games and is noticing how much I'm doing for them." I said.

"Well, I'm just looking out for you because you're the only person I care about right now, and I don't want anything to happen to you." She said.

"Hey, I thought your boyfriend was the only person you cared about?" I asked.

"Oh well, I'm just dating him because he asked me to go out, so I did. He doesn't talk to me except around his friends, whom I think is weird." She said.

"Hey, how about you and I switch on him and see what he would say to that," I said.

"Are you sure about that?" she asked.

"Yeah, I'll bet you that I'll get him to feel so sorry about you and that he would show you more attention than what he is doing now," I said.

"I don't know if I want to do that to him," she said.

"Oh! come on; I would like to do this to him to see what will happen in the end." I said.

"Not right now. Let me see if I can do something before we put your plan into action," Kristen said.

"Okay, but I'm telling you, you'll need my help with this one," I said.

"Well, you might be right, but I'm getting hungry here, and the food is downstairs," she said.

"Okay, let's go eat before you bite my head off," I said, and we went downstairs to eat.

After a while, I heard my phone ring, and I ran to pick it up and answered it. "Hello," I said. "Crystal, is that you?" A familiar voice asked.

"Who is this?" I asked.

"It's me, sis, Sapphire. I need your help. I'm trapped, and I can't get out because there are these girls that are surrounding me." she said.

"Oh my god Sapphire, it's you! Where are you? Can you tell me exactly where you are?" I asked.

"Umm, well, I can't tell. But I think I'm near an old building with a fallen tree near it. It looks like people are walking, but I can't tell." she said.

"All right, I'm coming to get you; just stay there and don't move." I placed the phone down, and Silverie walked towards me.

"Who was that?" she asked.

"It was Sapphire," I said.

"What did she say?" she asked.

"Um, no, but she told me where she was, though," I said, and as I walked out the door, she grabbed my arm and pulled me back.

"It's a trap, I know it!" she said.

"How do you k-"

"I know how people are in this world, and if I'm correct, the twins are behind it, and you are going to need help in this one if you are to get her back," she said.

"Yeah, but I can do this myself," I said.

"I know you can, but I'm coming no matter what, and so is Kristen," she said, and Kristen was right behind her.

"Okay, let's go," I said, and we headed out.

As we looked for her, she kept us updated about where she was, but we couldn't find her. That was until I looked and saw her next to a building she had told me she had seen.

"There she is," I told Kristen, and she turned the car around and drove to her. I hopped out of the car and ran to her to see if she was all right. "Are you okay, sis?" I asked.

"Yes. I'm fine now, but not for long," Sapphire said, and then Tasha showed up behind her.

"Thank you, Sapphire; you have been a big help to us now that we have Crystal here," she said.

"Let her go!" I said.

"Yeah, sure, after we destroy you," she said, and Laura came into the picture with Sapphire right behind her, but she was right in front of me.

"But if this is Sapphire, then who is that?" I asked.

"Oh, let me introduce you to her clone. You like it, don't you?" Tasha asked.

"Why would you do that?" I asked.

"Well, since I got her, I decided to make a clone so that I could weaken you when I want to fight you," she said, and I cut the lines that held her. She ran behind me, and then another girl came out. Randall was with us, and she saw her.

"Amy, there you are!" she said.

"That's your sister?" I asked.

"Yes, that is her, but she doesn't know me," she said.

"I'll make her," I said and ran to her.

"No!" Randall said, but I was already on her. I grabbed her, pulled her away from Tasha, and brought her back to us. She was fighting me the whole time until I had Kirsten hold her as I dug into the pouch given to me by the elder and grabbed a bottle, forcing Amy to drink it.

After a few minutes, she got off the ground. She saw Randall and ran to her. "Sis, I missed you so much," she said.

"I know, but you're back now," Randall said.

"Ohh, enough of this," Tasha said, and she flew towards Randall. She struck them, which sent them flying.

"No! Oh, you're going to pay for that." I said, and I morphed. I pulled my swords out and attacked her, and she did the same thing.

Kristen got Sapphire away from the fight, so they could not get her again, but she did not want to.

"No, I want to be with my sis," she said.

"Sapphire, you have to get to safety. I don't want to lose you again, so go." I said, and she looked at me. "I'll be okay," I said, and she went off with Kristen. Silverie joined me in the fight with Tasha and Laura.

Sapphire's clone got involved, and I stopped fighting when she got in front of me. That was what Tasha wanted. She flogged me and knocked me to the ground. I would get back up and fight her, but she would get back into the picture every time, and I couldn't do anything.

Then finally, when she came around the last time, it didn't phase me. I was able to hit her, and she went to the ground. "Oh no, you are not supposed to do that," she said.

"Well, I just did," I said, hitting her some more until Tasha told her to get out of there and come to her.

"This is not the end. We will get you one day Crystal," she said, and they disappeared into thin air.

After what happened, we went to Walmart to talk about it. "Sis, why did you do that to me?" Sapphire asked.

"I did that to ensure you would be safe and not get hurt," I said.

"Well, thank you for saving me from the Twin Sisters, but I don't think you'll be able to kill her because she is my clone." She said.

"I'll figure a way," I said.

"Oh, and I won't tell anybody about your dragon body," she said.

"How can I make sure of that?" I asked.

"You have to, sis. By the way, you looked dangerous in that outfit that you were wearing. Can I get one?" she asked.

"I don't know about that," I said.

"Oh please, I'll make sure it won't get out of the house," she said, and I looked at her.

"Just kidding, can you think about it," she said and hugged me. Randall walked up to me with Amy beside her.

"Thank you for helping me get my sister back," she said.

"Oh, no problem; besides, you helped me before. So call it that we are even for now." I said.

"Yeah, I'll say that too," she said.

"How old is she?" I asked.

"Well, she is only about ten months younger than me, and she is in the same grade as us," she said, and then Steve drove up.

"I got a call that you were doing something, and I came to see if we're okay," he said.

"Yeah, I'm okay now; thanks for asking me," I said.

"Well, I see that Sapphire is back with you." He said.

"Yeah, and so is Amy, my sister," Randall said.

"Oh, you didn't tell me about her." He said.

"Because you didn't ask me," she said.

"Well, I have to get home with Sapphire. I'll see you guys at school tomorrow." I said, and I got into my car and drove home.

When we arrived, mom saw Sapphire and gave her a big hug.

"Oh! Sapphire, there you are, sweetie. I thought we lost you there for a while." she said in a worried voice.

"Thank Crystal here. She's the one who saved me tonight," she said.

"Well, I'm thankful for your help in getting her back," she told me.

"Thanks, Mom," I said and headed to my room. I was getting ready for bed when Sapphire walked into my room.

"Hey, I'm sorry for how I acted when I was with those idiots. I didn't know what I was doing because they brainwashed me into fighting with them. Could you ever forgive me, sis?" she asked and looked at me with those sad eyes.

"Oh Sapphire, I forgive you because it's also my fault for not showing you the attention you wanted from your big sister. From now on, I'll do anything for you but to a certain extent, okay?" I asked her.

"Deal," she said and hugged me. She returned to her room. After I shut my door, I went to my desk and took out a book I was reading. It was a good book because Randall told me about it.

The book was sci-fi, and the author was good at writing it. One day, I could write a book that people would like and make a movie out of it in my way, or I wouldn't let them.

For the rest of the week, I got the team ready for the big game that Friday, and we had a pep rally. I was to be the big talk about it, and the coach wanted me to be ready. So he told me to be at the field house a little earlier than usual.

When it was time to go to the field house, the teacher did not allow me.

"Sorry, Miss, but I'm not going to take your story about you playing football seriously." He said.

"But I'm part of the team," I said.

"Still, I would need proof that you are a football player," he said.

"Oh, I can't believe this. I'm not going to wait for that proof for you, so I'm just going to leave whether you like it." I said.

"You do that, miss. I'll just let your teacher know about this," he said.

"Go ahead and see what she says about it because she knows I'm a football player," I said. I walked out the door and headed for the field house.

The coach was waiting for me. "Where have you been?" he asked.

"Oh, our teacher wouldn't let me out because he thinks I was lying about being a football player," I said.

"Oh, okay. We need to prepare you for your speech for the prep rally. Are you ready?" He asked.

"Ready as I will ever be," I said, and he helped me as much as possible.

When it was time for the rally, we headed out, and as I walked in, the students were calling my name nonstop. The team was doing the same as we headed for the bleachers. After everyone settled down, the cheerleader got the mic and talked to the students until she called me to come up.

"Okay, Crystal, just talk to them," She said, handing me the mic.

"All right! who's going to win tonight?" I asked the crowd, and they said we would.

"Okay, now you know that we are only a few games away from getting the state championship in our hands, and I won't stop until we do," I said, and they cheered.

"Now, the cheerleaders have prepared together a little something for us to enjoy, so here you go," I said; the cheerleaders performed something involving the opposing team and us. It was funny. After their performance, I talked for a little bit more. "For tonight's game, I will need your help to get us through it because this team we play is adamant in the league. But with me to help the lions out, I know that we will come out on top of the game and continue to next week's game." I said, and the students went wild.

I gave the mic to the cheerleader and returned to my spot in the bleachers. I waited for the prep rally to be over so I could get home before we had to leave for the game.

After about an hour, I had to return to school so that we could go to the game. I hopped on the bus with Silverie and sat down when I got there. She talked to me until we got to the field, and the other team saw me.

They did not like that I was playing football because they had heard about me on the news for the past few weeks. They knew that they were to be beaten by me if I was nonstop during the game. I knew that also.

After about forty minutes, the coach called us in to talk to us while the fans filled the grandstand. Mom and Dad were near the bottom, and I was towards the middle of them. They waved to me, and I did the same.

The coach told the team to make sure nothing serious would happen to me because if they had been watching the news, they would know how good I was at the games we played. They knew I would need extra support to keep the other team off me. After that, we headed for the locker room to get ready.

After ten minutes, we returned to the field, and the crowd was chanting my name. The other side heard it as they walked to the center of the field. They won the coin toss and decided to kick the ball instead of catching it. I had a bad feeling about that, but I couldn't do anything. I waited until the offense went onto the field to get us on the scoreboard.

During the first couple of plays, I managed to get us about thirty yards; then, I barely gained ten yards here and there until we got to about fifteen yards from the end zone.

"All right, Crystal, I'll fake it for you. I want you to run to the end zone, turn around, catch the ball, and break." Scott said, and we headed for the line.

When he snapped the ball, he faked it to me, and I ran for the end zone as I had planned. But they knew he would throw it at me. I got hit before I even got to the ten-yard line, and the ref called a penalty on it as I got back on my feet,

"Defense number 67 pass interference, ten-yard penalty first down," he said, and the opposing team's fans booed about it as they moved the ball ten yards.

This time, Scott handed me the ball, and I ran for the line, but I got stopped short of about one yard. The next time I ran the ball, I made it and put us up the scoreboard 7-0. Then, I walked back to the sidelines.

As I got there, my side was hurting slightly, but not that much. "Are you okay, girl?" Silverie asked.

"Yeah, I was just shaken up a little from that blow earlier," I said,

"Yeah, I saw what he did to you. Man, that was rough to see from here," she said,

"Well, hopefully, the defense can hold them back for a little while. I try to rest up here," I said, but I was wrong.

The other team made a touchdown in no time, and I had to get back onto the field and rerun the ball. It was a game of staying ahead of the other team or trying. By the end of the half, the teams tied the score at 27-27. I was hurting all across the chest; the coach could see it in my face.

"Are you going to be able to play the second half?" he asked me.

"Yeah, I just need to rest for a few minutes before I get back out there and get us the win," I said, and he talked to the team about how I was doing. He told them to do their best to keep me out of harm.

When we got out onto the field, the fans repeated my name. Every time they do that, I gain strength. I ran to Randall.

"Hey Randall, can you get the crowd to do that as I'm running the ball so I can do better than what I am doing?" I asked.

"Yeah, I think I can do that for you," she said, and I thanked her. I went back to the sidelines with the rest of the team.

This time, the other team got the ball first and ran it back like it was nothing. I was back on the field trying to get tied with the other team, and we were only yards away from the goal line.

When the ball got snapped, one of the players hit me hard again, and it was the same guy from before. But this time, I stayed on the ground, and the referee came running to me.

"Miss, are you okay?" he asked.

"Yeah, I think so. The wind just knocked me out. I said, but I wasn't telling the referee everything. I got up and returned to the game, where we got the touchdown.

I was feeling the pain around my waist, and the coach walked up to me,

"Crystal, you don't have to keep getting hit by that guy. Just take about ten minutes off and rest," he said.

"If I do that, this team will lose. The team is not strong enough to play without me. I must return to ensure we still have a fighting chance in this game." I said, sat down on the bench, and waited for the offense to get back onto the field.

As I watched the team make their way to the other side, they got slowed down by our defense. On a play where they threw a pass, one of our players caught the ball and ran with it for about twenty yards until he got tackled. I saw that this team was finally coming together, and the coach liked that move. I went out onto the field.

This time, when I ran the ball, I had help getting a little further than before, thanks to the team blocking the other team from reaching me. We were ahead by a touchdown during the third quarter, and it looked good for us until the fourth quarter.

They got ahead of us by a touchdown, and I tried to tie us with them, but they would get back ahead every time. The quarter was running out, and I saw I had enough time to make one more touchdown and then go for the two-point conversion to win the game.

Scott knew what to do, so we went for the win. It was getting more challenging as we slowly made our way down the field to the other side. As we got to the twenty-yard line, Scott handed me the ball. I went about six yards when the guy from before nailed me so hard. I almost lost the ball, but my grip was more substantial.

I fell to the ground. This time, I could not move very much, or I would feel the pain.

"Miss, are you all right?" the referee asked.

"I'm in some pain," I said as I tried to get up, but every time I moved, the pain got heavier for me to take. I told the ref that I was staying in the game. The player that did that to me got pulled out of the game. They should have done that earlier.

"Are you going to be able to run the ball into the end zone?" Scott asked me,

"Yes, I'm going to be able to with the fan's help. Just signal to the cheerleader for them to get the fans to chant for me, and I should make it." I told him, and I went to my spot.

He waved to the cheerleaders, and they got the fans to yell my name. I felt my power grow with every chant they did. Scott snapped the ball, and I was off.

As the crowds got louder, I got stronger and ran faster. Scott threw the ball to me. I caught it, and the other team was right on me, trying to take me down. However, they could not do that because the crowd kept me going until I made the touchdown.

They were cheering, and the team ran to hug me. But they knew it wasn't over with because we still had to make two points to win the game. So, we had to plan for it, and it was simple.

Scott was going to hand me the ball while he went into the end zone and waited for me to throw the ball. It did not go as planned because they took him down as soon as Scott got the ball. I had to run it in, but the other team was closing on me until the crowd chanted my name, and I managed to duck and dodge the players. I run for the end zone to win the game.

I fell to the ground, and Scott ran up to me. "Are you okay?" he asked.

"Yeah, I'm just in pain right now, and I'm going to need help getting off the field," I said.

"Well, how about Scott and me carry you off the field?" Steve asked.

"Yeah, that would be nice," I said. Scott and Steve picked me up and carried me off the field. The crowd was cheering and shouting my name, and the team was doing the same.

The coach gave me a thumbs-up, and they took me to the bus. I got in a seat and fell asleep; I tried to sleep off the pain. Silverie woke me up as we made it back home. As I got off the bus, the coach pulled me to the side to talk to me.

"Crystal, I would like to thank you for all the help you have done for this team, and I know that you will take this team to state," he said.

"Yes, I sure will, coach. I'll see you next week and talk about the game for next week." I said, and I jumped into Randall's car. She took me home.

The next day, I stayed in the house because I was in much pain when I got up. I tried to walk to the kitchen, but I had to sit in the living room to rest, and Dad saw me.

"Hey princess, are you still hurting from last night?" he asked.

"Yeah, just a little bit. I need to get the wrap and get my stomach wrapped to lessen the pain. "I said.

"Here, let me get it for you, and I'll get it on you," he said and walked into the kitchen to get it.

About a minute later, he walked back into the living room with it. "All right, stand up and pull your shirt up above your stomach," he said, and I did. He saw how nasty the bruise was.

"Oh, my god, hon, they got you pretty good. Okay, hold still while I put this on," Dad said, putting the wrap around my waist. Kristen walked in.

"Whoa, Dad, do you have to do that in the living room?" she asked.

"What? I'm certainly not going to do this in the bathroom now. It will only be a few more minutes." he said, and then Mom walked in.

"Honey, what are you doing to her?" she asked.

"Well, I'm putting this wrap on her because she has got a good-sized bruise on her stomach," he said, and she looked at it.

"Oh my, you're right about that. Well, you better get that on before little Susan comes down the hall," she said.

"Yeah, I know what you mean by that, honey," he said and finished up. I put my shirt down when Susan walked into the room and saw me. "Hey, sis," she said, and she hugged me.

"Hey there," I said to her.

"Are you okay now?" she asked.

"Yes, I'm fine now. Thanks for your care." I said.

"Well, you're my big sister, and I don't want anything to happen to you," she said, and I just held her again for saying that.

After a while, there was a knock at the door. I answered it, and it was Laura.

"Hey, girl," I said.

"Hey there, are you busy right now?" she asked.

"Not at the moment. Why?" I asked.

"Well, I just got a call saying that someone special is coming to town. Some guy would like to meet you at Walmart," she said.

"How do you know this?" I asked her.

"Because Steve is down there right now talking to him. He told him that he knew you and wants to see you," she said.

"All right, I'll take my car and bring Kristen along," I said.

"Okay, but hurry though; I want to get back down there to see him too," she said and got into her car. I called Kristen to go with me, and we left for Walmart.

When we got there, I saw a trailer parked near the doors. I saw the number eight on the side. I knew who it was. I drove quickly through the parking lot to get to meet him. When I parked, some idiots went too fast by me, and I saw Brandon.

I knew he was looking for trouble in the wrong place. I dashed to the trailer to see if it was Jr. who had seen me.

"Well, if it isn't Crystal, the girl I've heard so much about," he said. The car came in too close this time. He moved out of the way and struck me, sending me backward. I hit the pavement, and I started bleeding from my stomach. I felt the pain again. The car revved its engine up and came towards me, but Jr. got my arm and pulled me out of the way just before it hit me again.

"Are you all right now?" he asked.

"Not really. I'm in pain, and I know that guy." I said, and he called the cops to report him. They arrived in no time. We told them what had happened and said that they would find them. Their assurance made me feel better.

I stayed to talk to him because he wanted me to come to the track later that year to serve as grand marshal for the day. I said I would love to go, and he was delighted because I was establishing a reputation in the football world.

He wanted me to be there so that I could drive a car and raise money for kids that have cancers. I agreed to it because I care for kids. I love them because I take care of little Susan. I told him that I was coming. It was getting late.

I told him that I had to go. He gave me his number and told me to call him if anything came up, and I couldn't make it, so I got into my car and drove off. I waited at the light for it to change, and I was talking to Kristen.

"Man, that was cool to meet him," she said.

"Yeah, I know," I said. Then out of nowhere, someone hits me from behind and sends me into the middle of the highway where two diesel trailers were coming down the road, and Kristen was screaming.

"Hold on," I said, and I gunned it. I moved out of the way just in time and drove down the road as the car followed.

"Who is that?" she asked.

"I don't know, but I don't want to find out anytime soon," I said and continued driving.

Then he hits me again. I almost lost control of my car. He struck me on the corner and made me do a fishtail. I turned around to face him, threw the car in reverse, and then drove backward. When I did that, I saw that it was Brandon again.

Then, I turned my car back around and drove as fast as possible, but he stayed on my tail.

"I'm going to see what this car can do," I told Kristen as I hit the gas pedal to kick in the turbo. When it did, the car went faster. I had lost him, but he did the same thing. There was no way to get rid of him. I managed to get the cops involved in the chase as we continued passing cars left and right down the road. Sometimes, I tried going into other lanes to get rid of him, but it was no use because he was as good as me.

The cops laid back to see what would happen. He hit me again, and I started to lose control. I got it back and kept going, then took a side street. He missed the turn but caught back up with me in no time. Then, he hit me again, spun me into someone's yard, and stopped my car. He stopped his car and was about to get out when my car returned to life, and I went on again. He got back into his car and came after me.

The cops finally found us, and they ran after him again as we got back onto the highway. Kristen didn't know what to do at this point but to hang on for the ride. My car could no longer go as fast as it did from all the damage it got. The same goes for Brandon's car, but that did not stop him from trying to hit me whenever he got the chance.

Then we got to the point where five highways intersected, and I tried to avoid getting wrecked, but Brandon hit me from behind. I was launched toward a sizable big rig, bouncing off and hitting another. The big rigs stopped my car then, and he came over to me while I was still moving inside, but only just.

"This will remind you how not to play games with me." He said.

"Wha-" He cut me off, got hit in the mouth, and walked off. After that, some people came over to help me out, but since the car was severely damaged, they couldn't open the door.

A car pulled up, and it was Steve. "Crystal, I'm coming. Hold on!" he said and ran to me with Laura.

"Oh Crystal, are you okay?" he asked while he was about to cry on me.

"Not really, but now that you are here, I feel better," I said. Then, the cops entered the picture, saw my car's situation, and came to my attention.

"Excuse me, son, but I need her." said the officer. "Okay, ma'am, are you hurt?" he asked me.

"Yes, I can't move my legs, and they are in pain," I said.

"Okay. We'll get the ambulance and the jaws of life to get you out." He told another officer to get them while he went to the other side to check on Kristen. She was just in bad shape like me. But she was not as stuck as I was, and they wanted to get me out of the car first.

After about thirty minutes, with the jaws, they managed to cut away the car just enough to get me out and lay me on the ground. Then, they went to the other side and got Kristen out immediately. They got her onto a stretcher, and I was right behind her on one also. They placed us in different ambulances and took us to the hospital. The cops came up there to talk to me about what happened, but the doctors would not let them in to see me, and I was glad about that.

My sister and I were in the same room. Mom and Dad came by the hospital after Steve told them where we were. They cried when they saw us on the beds with bruises.

"Oh, girls, are you okay?" Mom asked.

"Yes, Mom." We said together.

"Well, thanks to Steve here, they got the guy who did this to you, and he is going to jail as we speak. The cops won't be up here to bug you about what happened because the doctor said you two must rest for the night without disturbance. We are going to be here all night to make sure that they don't come in." Dad said.

"Okay, thanks," I told him. I fell asleep, and so did Kristen. I could still hear Mom crying for about five minutes until I could not listen to her anymore.

When I woke up the following day, Dad was asleep in the chair, and Mom was on the other side of the room watching TV with Kristen. She was already up, and she noticed that I was up.

"Well, it's about time you wake up," she said.

"Very funny; what time is it?" I asked.

"Oh, let's see, I got nine fifteen," Kristen said, and at that time, the doctor came into the room.

"Hello, how is everybody doing?" he asked, and Dad woke up.

"Oh, we're doing okay," Kristen said.

"Well, that's good news. You are good to be discharged today since there are no signs of complications that we could find. I'll have the nurse come in here and get you two set to go home." he said and walked back out of the room. The nurses walked in. Mom and Dad walked out to get us ready to go home.

After about forty minutes, they got us into wheelchairs, and the doctor gave Dad a paper so he could get us some pain relievers. Then, he let us go down the hall and out to the car sitting right out front.

Sapphire got out of the car to help me get in. Randall helped Kristen in the van, and Dad drove home. As we got there, the cops were waiting to talk to us.

"Crystal, we want to know what happened last night during the race you had with Brandon," he said.

"Race? We were not racing; he was chasing us because he tried to run me over earlier that day at Walmart, and I have proof he did that." I said.

"And who else saw it happen?" He asked.

"I did," Kristen said.

"And so did I," said Jr., who just drove in. "I was there watching the whole thing unfold. She almost got run over by him if I didn't grab her hand and pull her out of his way," he said. "And I saw the same thing happened too," said Steve and came to my side.

"Well, it seems that you were not at fault, and Mr. Brandon will be paying for your medical bills and getting you a new car." the officer said. After the talk, he got back into his car and left.

"Dale, what are you still doing in Henderson?" I asked.

"Well, when I heard you got hurt, I decided to stick around and make sure that you wouldn't get into trouble." He said. "Thank you," I said,

"Well, I got to go. Just let me know if you can't make it in the spring." He said and went to his car and left.

"What did he mean by that?" Steve asked. "Oh, he wants me to come to the Texas Motor Speedway this year to be a grand marshal for the day," I said.

"Well, that sounds fun," he said.

"Yeah, it sure does," I said, and I headed into the house with Steve. Our family had a fun night until I had to go to bed and prepare for the semifinal football game later in the week.

Chapter 9

When I got to school the next day, people looked at me and wondered how I could walk after what had happened last Saturday.

"Oh, Crystal, are you okay?" Scott said as he caught up to me.

"Yeah, I'm fine. Did you hear about the wreck?" I asked.

"Yeah, I heard it on the news after it happened. I saw you put on a stretcher while being taken to the hospital." He said.

"Well, I'm feeling better now. Don't worry; I'll be playing this weekend. I also have something to tell the team when today. So, gather the players together so I can talk to them." I told him and ran down the fieldhouse to talk to the coach about how the team did last Friday.

"Well, Crystal, how did the team do for you?" he asked.

"It took them a while, but I saw them being a team rather than acting like one. I was impressed by what they did because the defense stopped them a few times, which is hard to do for a team like that." I said.

"Well, are you going prepare them for the next one?" He asked.

"Yeah, sure; whom are we playing?" I asked.

"Well, they are coming from the northern part of Texas, and they have beaten every team that they have faced with at least two to three touchdowns; they are the Charlotte Wildcats," he said, and I looked at him.

"The Wildcats? are you sure?" I asked.

"Yeah, why?" he asked.

"Because I heard they are the best team in the country, and they have rarely lost a game in the last six years, and we have to go against them? Okay, Crystal get it together; you can get this team ready for that game." I said.

"Crystal, this team will be able to beat them this coming Saturday," he said. "If they do as I say and no other way. They will cream us." I said, and by that time, the team had come out onto the field where I was standing.

"Hey guys, I'm impressed by what you did last Friday. By that, I mean that the defense did a good job stopping the Bulldogs a few times and making them punt the ball, but the offense still needs a little work, but not much. Just stay open and whoever gets the ball, protect them from the other team as much as possible. I got word about our next opponent, who is a tough team. If you do as I say, we can beat them without problems, and we will win the game." I said.

"And who is this other team?" Scott asked. "The Wildcats from Charlotte, Texas. They are a tough team; in the past six years, they have lost only four games, which was the state championship game. I know because I did a paper on them for my old school last year." I said.

Yeah, I heard about them. This year, they have destroyed every team they have come against and won about two or three touchdowns." Scott said.

"Yeah, I need this team to put the game together this week. Let's get that teamwork top-notch for the game because I don't plan on losing now since we have gotten this far. Come on, let's get to work." I said, and they did what they needed to do.

I planned to prepare them for the game, run a few plays on Friday, and see if they could do a great job on those. If I like them, then we will win the game.

Thirty minutes passed, and it was time to go to AG mechanics to work on my project. As I got in there, the teacher wasn't there. So, I sat down in front of Steve. Kristen entered the door and saw Micah look at me with an evil look.

"What? you got a problem with me?" I asked him, but he just turned his head and looked away. The bell rang, and the teacher came from the restroom and told us to go outside and work on our projects, and we did. As I made it out, Kristen was right behind me and went to work on the top while I was on the bottom looking at the welds. As I looked at the beams, something didn't look right. They seemed bent, and I know I didn't do it. I walked to where the bend was and saw someone had taken a sledgehammer and hit the trailer side because I could see the impression in the metal. I know Kristen didn't do it.

"Damn it," I said.

"What?" Kristen asked.

"Look." I pointed to the impression.

"Damn it, man." She said.

"Who could have done this?" I said, and she looked toward Micah. He was laughing about it.

"I'll give two guesses, but you're only going to need one," she said.

"Let me say; it was him," I said.

"Yup, you're right," she said.

"Mr. Ingram, could you come over here right quick?" I asked and showed him the dent in the metal.

"Whoa, girls, where did this come from right here? It was straight the last time I saw it," he said.

"Someone hit it with a hammer because you can see where someone hit it," I said, and he looked closer.

"Yeah, I see it now. Well, the only thing I can tell you to do is try to get it out or replace the part of the beam. However, it would take a while, and I know you don't want to be up here during the holiday working on it." Mr. Ingram said.

"Yeah, you're right. I'll try to get it out as much as possible." I said. I grabbed a torch, lit it, and placed the flame on the metal. I was getting the metal cherry red so I could hit it, knock it back into place, and try to get it just like it was, but it took me all period to get it back halfway because I had Kristen look at it from the top and bottom. She commanded me about what to do. My arms got tired of swinging that hammer during the whole period. Stop here

"Well, Crystal, you almost got it, but we may have to fix the rest tomorrow. Come look at it and see what we need to do," she said, and it got where she was. I got one of the big ones out, but it still looked terrible enough to notice.

"Yeah, it's going to take a few more days to get it right. Let's call it a day and see what we can do next week." I said. "Well, we still need to get that last axle on the trailer," she said.

"True, we also need to get the neck going on it and start on the pit for the top. Let us also figure out a way to get it on and off the trailer." I said.

"Yeah, let me work on that, and I'll let you know what I come up with. Okay? But don't make any crazy idea that would not work. Think of something that will be easy for us to do." I said.

"All right, no problem. Well, that was the bell. See you at lunch." she said and walked off to her class while I headed for English. Laura talked to me before we got into the classroom.

"Hey, I heard what happened the other night, and the guy that did it is in jail, right?" she asked.

"Yeah, they picked him up right before he could get away from the cops. He is also paying for my next car." I said.

"Well, I'm glad you are okay now," she said.

"Yeah, I am, too," I said, and the bell rang.

The teacher walked back into the classroom and talked to us about our tasks for the next few weeks because she knew some of us would be going next door to the other teacher, and I was one of them. We worked on some things together, and when the bell rang, I headed for my next class. It was boring. We had a sub-teacher, and he made us work by ourselves. He told us to be quiet and reminded us that we couldn't go to the restroom even if we needed to. However, he didn't care much because he was reading a book. I needed to use the bathroom, but he denied me two times and didn't care. I went out the door, and he came after me. He got me before I got to the restroom by grabbing my arm. I yelled because he pulled it so hard. A door opened, and another teacher walked out to see what was happening.

"What in the world do you think you are doing to her?" she asked him.

"I'm taking her back to the classroom because she has no business here," he said.

"And why not?" she asked. "Because I need to use the restroom badly, but he won't let me," I said.

"Let her go in. Let her do her business, and then she can return to the class when she is done," she said.

"No, because she didn't ask permission," he said.

"Well, I'm telling you to let her go, or I'll tell the principal. I know you don't want that now," she said, and he released me. I went into the restroom as quickly as possible. When I was done, he was waiting for me to come out.

"Now, let's get back to the classroom," he said and grabbed my arm again. But I pulled it away.

"Hey, I don't need help getting back to the classroom. I think I can go there on my own, thank you." I said, walking beside him the whole way down the hall. As I got into the classroom and returned to my seat, he read his book as if nothing had happened just a few minutes ago.

We went to the cafeteria for lunch. Laura talked to me about what had happened in the hall when we got our food.

"Hey, what did he do to you in the hallway?" she asked.

"Oh, he grabbed me by my arm and pulled me back to him. I yelled from it, and another teacher came out and told him to let me go. Then, he tried to do it again, and this time, I pulled my arm away and told him I didn't need help back to the classroom. He probably thought I would wander the building after using the restroom." I said.

"You know, you can get him in trouble for that," Randall said.

"Yeah, that's true. He is not supposed to touch you like that. People could see that as something that doesn't look right." Steve said.

"Yeah, I'll let the principal know about it and see if she will do anything," I said.

"Hey, did any of you get to take those semester exams?" Kristen asked.

"I got exempted from all of mine," I said.

"And so did I," said Steve.

"I know I did, but Amy got to take them," Randall said.

"Yeah, Sapphire has to take all of hers because of all the days she missed this year," I said.

"Well, I know I'm staying at home during then," Kyle said.

"Oh, by the way, Kyle. How is Miranda doing?" I asked.

"She's doing fine. She's in the first lunch, and I only see her during the last period. She is also exempted from them, and she will be eating lunch with us next year." he said.

"Well, lucky for you, sis, I have to take them," Kristen said.

"Hey Kristen, you don't have to take them all. Remember, you have an identical twin right before you who can help you out." I said.

"Hey! that's cheating!" Laura exclaimed.

"Not if they know it's me instead of her. That will be hard to tell now that we talk and act the same way." I said.

"Yeah, I will need the help to get through them. So, I'll need help with some of them," she said.

"Okay, just let me know which ones, and I'll be there for those. Don't tell anybody because they won't know the difference between us except Mom. I don't know how she can because whenever Kristen and I dress the same, she can still recognize us." I said.

"Well, that's not fair," Laura said.

"Hey, Mom knows best, right?" I said.

"Well, that's true. Hey, what are you doing for the holidays' Crystal?" she asked.

"Oh, Mom has some big celebration, and the family is coming back to visit. I told her I was going to be busy, but she said I was not going anyway until after the party, which lasted for four to five days. I get New Year's Eve alone, and I plan on bringing it in with a big bang. I will get many fireworks and pop them with all my friends." I said.

"Will everyone be there with us?" Kristen asked everyone.

"Yeah, why not?" Laura said, and the bell rang. I went on to my next class.

That week, I decided to ride home with Laura because I knew how my brother drove his car. Even Sapphire, who rode with him one day, told me she wouldn't ride with him anymore. Sapphire is getting her car soon, as well as I am after my car got totaled by my idiot ex-boyfriend.

When I got home, Susan came running to me, talking to me about how school was, and told me she didn't want to go back anymore because there was a boy that was being mean to her. I told her to use their personalities against him and make him scared of her. She ran off and played.

"You know, that's not a good way to teach." Mom said.

"What? well, if I remember correctly, you also did the same to me." I said.

"Yes, I remember how I raised you," she said.

"And look how I turned out being a good adult now. But I did have a rough time, though." I said.

"Yeah, I do miss the old you, where you would just stay up in your room and be gone half the night to who knows where," she said.

"You seriously don't mean that," I said.

"No, honey, I'm just teasing you. I like you the way you are. By the way, when is that boy buying you a new car?" she asked.

"Oh, the cops told me I'll be getting it sometime this week, but I don't know exactly when. It's going to be the same but a new one." I said.

"And who is paying for this one?" she asked.

"Brandon will since he destroyed my last one for no reason," I said.

"Okay, I'm just making sure about that," she said.

"What do you mean by that?" I asked.

"I don't know, it's just that he does what he did to you a few weeks back, and now he does this," she said.

"Well, I kind of got into a fight with the girl here during thanksgiving, and he didn't like it very well," I said.

"Now you know by doing that, you get nowhere," she said.

"Yeah, I just wanted to pay her back for what she did to me. That's why Brandon went to me for it." I said.

"Well, you'll learn one of these days that fighting gets you nowhere in life," she said.

"Yeah, one of these days when I'm older, I guess," I said and helped her with supper that night because she needed help in the kitchen on some nights since we have numerous guests all the time, and we don't know if they will stay to eat or not. Most of the time, they would wait to eat and talk for a while and then go on their way.

When I finished dinner, I decided to go to my room to see if anything new was on my computer. But I still need to write for a couple of days.

Sapphire walked in. "Hey, sis, are you in the mood to talk?" she asked, and I turned around to see her.

"Yeah, just shut the door," I said. Sapphire closed the door; she sat on my bed while I was typing up some things on my computer.

"I'm having a problem with someone at school," she said.

"And who would that be?" I asked.

"Well, it's my boyfriend. He won't do much of anything with me at school but talk to his friends. I want to know what he's doing aside from talking with them because he has kept a distance from me since I've been with him. It seems that something is getting in between us, and I would like to know." she said.

"Well, I would tell you to end the relationship with him. But before that, I would like to meet him myself, and maybe I could give you an idea about his business, and if you can get a hold of his cell phone, I could see if any number is on there besides yours." I said.

"Well, he's supposed to come by during the holidays and spend some time with me, but I don't know if he'll be here because of how the relationship is going right now," she said.

"Well, bring when I am here for us to meet. I'll let you know when I want to meet your boyfriend in person." I said.

"Okay, sis, I'll do that." She said and walked out of the room.

I went back to typing. After that, I notice that I should be in bed by now. So, I rushed to get my nightclothes and get into bed to prepare for tomorrow.

As the week passed, the only thing that happened was my team getting better at what they were working at and in AG mechanics. I managed to get the bend out of the metal, and Mr. Ingram said that it would be okay and, hopefully, no one else would hit it because it was not going to take me three days to get it, just like it was because that is much work to do.

When Friday came, I went to the field house to talk with the coach about tomorrow and what would happen at the game. As the team did what I needed them to do, I liked how they came together.

"All right, let's huddle up." said the coach.

"I like what I'm seeing out on the field here. The team became one instead of ten, which was not good for trying to win games. Come tomorrow, and that will decide if we continue into the playoffs and go for the championship game. With the help of Crystal in preparing the team, I believe she deserves something special," he said, and out of nowhere, a few players got a five-gallon water jug and dumped cold water on me.

Everyone laughed at it, and so did I.

"Oh, that was wrong, coach; now I'm freezing here," I said.

"Well, I'm sorry, but the guys wanted to do it, so I let them. Thanks for the help and support for this team. I don't know where we would be without you here to keep these boys on their game. Let's win tomorrow's game and go for the championship game," he said, and everyone agreed. I went to change out of my damp clothes, and it was good to keep a spare change of clothes up there in case I needed them.

The bell rang for the next period as I got them, so I headed out, but the coach stopped me.

"Hey, they are going to talk to you today. So, I need you to be here about the same time as last Friday. Okay?" he said.

"Got it," I said and headed out. As the day went on, the only thing good was the prep rally. Then, I would walk into the gym and see posters of me on the wall holding the championship trophy.

After a while, the students wanted me to talk to them about it, so I walked to the mic and told them how I did it. It took me about ten minutes to tell them how the team was going to win the state championship and was going to win tomorrow's game.

One student asked a question. "Hey Crystal, what do you plan on doing after you finish here?"

"Well, I would like to start my career, but I'm going to see if I make the pros and take the team to the Super Bowl. Then, be the first female to play and win one." I said, and they cheered. Another student asked a question. "Now, you know that the pros may not use a female on their team. How would you deal with that?" he asked.

"Well, I'll have to prove them as I did with this team and show them how good I am and even better with them behind me. I'll show them during college football because I've already received letters from about ten colleges to attend their school and play football for them. So, I'll make the team in the pros one way or another." I said, "Let's beat the Wildcats and go to the championship game," and the gym went crazy. I returned to the bleachers and waited until the prep rally was over.

As it ended, the students were leaving the gym. As I got to my car, Steve came up to me to ask me something.

"Hey Crystal, what are you doing tonight?" he asked.

"Well, I don't plan on doing anything fun," I said.

"That's good because I would like to take you out to eat and then go to a club to have some fun," he said.

"Well, that will be okay with me. Just come by the house and pick me up." I said, and I ran to Laura's car. She took me home because Sapphire went home early, and I needed to find out why because she rarely does that. When I got to the house, I went to her room, and she had her door shut. As I walked in, she looked at her face in her mirror, and I wondered why.

"Why are you here?" she asked.

"I'm just wondering why you left early and are staring at the mirror," I said.

"Well, it's none of your business," she said, and then I saw her face as she turned back to the mirror.

"What happened to your face? Yes, it's my business because no one will hit my little sister and get away with it." I said, and she turned back to face me.

"Promise me you won't tell Mom about it?" she asked.

"Yes, I promise," I said.

"Okay, well, my boyfriend wants me to hang out with his friends now, and he won't let me hang out with mine unless he is there to listen. But the girls walk off when he shows up to see what is going on, and in the past few days, he came over and pulled me away from them and told me to stop talking to them because he heard that rumors were going around the school. He told me that it was them. So today, he saw us when I was talking with the girls. He pulled me to the side where no one could see us and slapped me across the cheek. He said that it was a warning and the next time will be a harder slap." she said.

"Ohh man, why are you still with him if he likes that?" I asked.

"Well, I thought he was a good guy. I never got to meet his other side," she said. "Well, try to get away from him," I said.

"I'll try this Monday," she said.

"Thank you, and if you can't, call me. By the way, how is he compared to me?" I asked.

"Well, he's about two inches taller and eighty pounds more than you," she said.

"So, that would put him at six foot and weighs about two ten. Well, I can still take him down, no matter." I said.

"You should because you have tackled bigger guys than that, and please, don't tell Mom, okay?" she said.

"I won't tell her anything about it; just keep that covered, girl," I said, referring to her face. I walked out the door and went downstairs to see what Mom was doing. I found her in the kitchen making supper for the family.

"What do you want, Crystal?" she asked as she saw me in the doorway.

"Oh, let's see here," I said, and she looked at me.

"I'm kidding, Mom. Just checking what you are doing. That's all." I said.

"Uh huh, now how can I believe that?" she said.

"Well, you just have to," I said.

"Okay, I'll believe you this one time," she said.

"Yeah, you know that you will believe me as long as I tell you the truth about anything, right?" I said.

"Yes, that would be the right answer I was looking for," she said.

"Yeah, I thought so. Where's Dad? he should be home by now."

"Well, he called and told me that he was staying late just for tonight to cover for someone because they had a family problem and couldn't make it in," she said. "Hopefully, that's what he is doing and nothing else," I said.

"That's not nice to say about your father now. I'm going to tell him that when he gets home. Since we've been together, he has never cheated on me once, and neither have I. So, I know that he is working late. He can also assure you that it's true because he believes everyone has a soulmate. You must find them." she said.

"Oh, well, I haven't found mine yet," I said.

"Don't worry, you will find one day," she said.

"I know I will, but would I have to deal with him arguing all the time?" I asked.

"Honey, all relationships have their ups and downs. There's no perfect relationship in this world. When your father and I got together, we had our differences here and there, but we sorted them out. Now, we rarely argue about anything, and that's how it should be, and you'll be just fine." she said.

"Well, I'm going out tonight; that's why I was wondering," I said.

"Oh, and who are you going out with?" she asked.

"Oh, Steve asked me to go out and eat with him. Then, go to a club and have some fun. Is that going to be a problem?" I asked.

"Oh no, honey, just be careful whom you go out with because some people are very different when they are away from school and their family," she said.

"Oh, Steve should be no problem to be with," I said.

"Okay, have fun," she said and went back to cooking.

When Steve came by the house, I told Mom I was leaving and headed out the door. I got into his car, and we went for Tyler. As he drove, he talked to me about anything that he could think of, and I was doing the same thing to him. As time passed by, I discovered that he was a funny guy to be around. Even though I wanted him to ask me out because it felt like I had known him for a long time and wanted to be with him every minute, I knew I couldn't do that. I wanted to, but he may not like it very much. As we headed to the restaurant and parked, I saw that he had taken me to T.G.I.F. When I entered, I saw that it was a nice place to eat.

The hostess sat us in the non-smoking area that Steve picked, and I needed to find out why. As we sat down, she handed us menus and said that the waitress would be with us momentarily, and she walked off.

"Hey, why did you pick the non-smoking for?" I asked.

"Well, since I'm not a smoker, I don't want to be near people who smoke because of the second-hand smoke, and I don't like smoking myself makes me cough," he said.

"It's a good thing because I'm allergic to some chemicals in cigarettes, and so is the rest of my sisters. But my brothers are fine with it, and we don't know why." I said.

"Well, it might be something that you and your sister have in common; it runs in most families like that," he said.

"Oh, okay, the doctors have looked for anything pointing to how I'm allergic to cigarettes. They still haven't found out why, but they are getting close, though," I said, and the waitress walked to the table.

"Hi there, my name is Tessa, and I'll be your waitress for the evening. What would you like to drink?" she asked.

"I will have tea. What about you, Crystal?" Steve asked.

"Oh, I'll take the same," I said.

"Okay. Are you ready to order?" Tessa asked, and Steve looked at me.

"Not just yet," he said.

"Okay, I'll be back with the drinks and then see if you are ready by then," she said and walked off.

She was gone for about five minutes, and then she came back. We were also ready to order, and I got the same thing that Steve ordered. The waiter went to process our orders. Steve looked a little bit strange to me, and it seemed he was hiding something from me.

"Are you hiding something from me by chance?" I asked.

"No, I'm just delighted you decided to come with me tonight," he said, and we talked a little bit more about each other. We discovered things we didn't know, like events I did not expect to happen to him, and I was amazed by them.

After a while, the food arrived, and we ate. The food was delicious, and we talked some more. We finished in about fifteen minutes, then sat there for a bit longer. I saw him looking like he was hiding something again, and this time, he reached into his pocket for something.

"What are you doing?" I asked.

"Well, I have something here for you, and I was wondering if you would take it for me," he said and pulled out a small box. He handed it to me, and I opened it. There was a ring inside that had a green stone in it.

"Oh my, this is beautiful," I said.

"Yeah, I figured you would like it. I want to ask you something. Would you like to go out with me to prom this year?" Steve said? I wore the ring.

"Oh, it fits my finger perfectly and is also my birthstone. How did you know that?" I asked. I was so happy.

"Well, your sister told me about it and said to get you that ring," he said.

"She did, huh? Well, I've been eyeing it for a while at Walmart. She must have noticed me." I said.

"So, would you like to go out?" he asked again.

"Oh, I'm sorry I didn't answer you. Yes, I want to go out with you, and I will go to prom this year." I said. He looked delighted, and we hugged each other. I was happy too.

After that, he paid the bill. As he said, we walked out of the restaurant and went to the club.

After about four hours at the club, he was tired and wanted to go home. I had a game the next day, and so did he. He grabbed my hand when we arrived at my house and dropped me off.

"Hey, what are you doing for Christmas?" he asked.

"Well, my family is having a big feast, and I need to be here for it," I said.

"Okay, I'll come over and join the feast, too," he said.

"You mean that?" I asked.

"Yes, why not? Since we are going out, I wouldn't miss spending time with you during the Christmas holiday," he said.

"Ohh, I appreciate that. I would love you to come by. Maybe I'll also come by your house and meet your parents during that time." I said.

"They would love to see you. So, I'll see you tomorrow at the game. Play hard and win for the town." He said and smiled. I smiled back.

I shut the door, and he drove off into the distance. I was never as happy in my life as I was right at that moment. When I walked in the door, my Dad was still up watching T.V. and saw me come in the house.

"Hey, sport, how was it?" he asked.

"Ohh, it was lovely, Dad. I think Steve will treat me better than any other guy I have known." I said.

"I hope so because I hate to see you sad around here. By the way, your mother told me what you said about me," he said, and I just looked at him.

"I will tell you that I would never hurt your mother in any way that I wouldn't want to be hurt. I'm talking about cheating. I know these days that most relationships don't last as long as they did back then. But if you find the right person and you two connect as we did, you will have a healthy relationship for the rest of your lives. Now off to bed; you have a big game tomorrow." he said.

"That was long, Dad. Okay, I'm off. Good night." I said and went to my room. I saw that Kristen was in bed and had room for me to sleep. So, I just got under the cover and went to bed.

When my alarm went off, I noticed Kristen had her arm over my body and was still asleep until I nudged her. She finally opened her eyes and saw me.

"What time is it?" she asked and yawned.

"It's about eight o'clock, and we need to get up for the game. Come on and get out of bed." I said as I got up slowly and stretched.

"You know, it's too early to get up for a game," she said.

"That might be true, but I don't want to be late for the bus. Now, get out of bed." I said, pulling her to make her sit in bed. After about a minute, she was finally out of bed.

"Now, we have to get ready because we need to leave here at about nine so we can be there on time for the bus," I said and went to the bathroom to take a shower so that I would not have makeup on my face and the boys might notice.

After about thirty minutes, I heard that everybody was up. It sounded like they were in the living room talking about how the game would turn out today. We are going to win it by a field goal.

As we made it to the school, the coach pulled me aside and told me something. "Hey Crystal, Scott has a problem with his arm. We may have to use someone else to take his place. The only other person who could play for him couldn't play football because of his grades. What do you suggest we do?" he asked me, and I looked at him, puzzled about whom to replace Scott. Most of these guys never played as a quarterback. Then, I thought of someone.

"How about me?" I asked.

"You? but you are my best receiver. I can't put you in Scott's spot," he said.

"I know, but I'm the only person who knows the plays, and I can get Silverie to help me out sometime, or you can use her," I said.

"Use who? Me? Whoa! I'm not just going to be the quarterback because you want me to." she said.

"Hey, this is the perfect chance to get into better colleges and things like that, girl," I said.

"Well, if you put it that way, then okay, I'll be one also," she said.

"All right, you two will be swapping it out throughout the game," he said.

I got on the bus with Silverie right behind me. We talked about the plays so that when the time came to run them, we wouldn't be trying to figure out what to do during the run.

We were heading out to Dallas again, going to the same stadium we were at last when the twins showed up. This time, they won't be showing up. I was praying they would stay away because I couldn't be sure about that.

The other team saw me when we arrived and just stared at me. The other team started moving away from me when I turned toward the other team. It seemed like the other team feared me.

"It looks like they are scared of you, Crystal," Scott said.

"Yeah, I've been in the news a lot lately. They might have heard about me from New York State, but I couldn't tell if they knew me that way." I said.

"Well, I'll tell you this much, I have been on the news before you came here because they talked about you a lot and how you were very good at football. You were also on some shows talking about it," he said.

"Well, I hope you will also be in the news one day to see what it feels like on tv. That's nothing against you or anything, just to let you know." I said, and I walked over to where the coach was. He was saying some things for us to remember and not to let up when we get ahead.

After he finished talking, he came up to me and told me to throw some footballs to see if I could do some throw, and he wanted Silverie to do the same to see what she could do. As I threw for about ten minutes, the coach noticed I could be a quarterback backup if needed. The team was catching most of the passes Silverie, and I did. Then, he called me over to him and told me something.

"Crystal, I need you to get us on the board and stay ahead. Can you do that." he asked, "I sure will coach." I said and walked back over to Silverie and told her the same thing. After she nodded, the coach knew we would do our best to stay ahead of the other team.

After the crowd started to come in, it was time for us to head into the locker rooms and wait for them to wait for our appearance on the field to show off what we had learned. After ten minutes, we headed outside and saw a stand full of people from both schools. Henderson's side had posters with my name on them, and they cheered when they saw me walk out onto the field. When the other team saw that, they looked more nervous about me, and I loved it.

As we made our way onto the field for the coin toss, the other team had a perfect look at me, but I didn't care about it. We won the coin toss, and we were to receive the ball. We took the south end of the field, and I got back off the field while the special team went out onto the field to get ready to run the football around for us.

"Are you ready for this girl?" Scott asked.

"Yeah, I think so. Hopefully, I don't mess up." I said.

"As long as you keep your mind open, you'll be fine. Just avoid getting hit by a player, all right?" he said, and I had to head out onto the field to run the football. As I got ready to get the ball, the other team saw where I was, and I knew what they would do. I snapped the ball, stepped back about five yards, and looked for an opening, but everyone was covered, and the defense broke through and was coming for me. I thought I would get sacked, but Silverie opened at the last second, and I threw it at her. After about a minute, I went down and heard our crowd go wild. I knew she had caught it, but I didn't realize it after that because the player was still on me.

When they got off, I saw that she ran for about forty yards and then got tackled. However, after the next few drives, I ran the ball, but we barely got yards in those two drives. So, I threw the ball and managed to get us down to the ten-yard line. I told Silverie to stay open because I could throw her the ball better, and she agreed. When I got to the ball and snapped it, she bolted for the end zone waiting on me to throw the ball. But before I could, I was sacked from behind and was thrown back about five yards. I still hung onto the football, and I tried it again. This time, I kept an eye out for that play. When I got the ball and Silverie was open, I threw the ball at her. She was able to catch it and made a touchdown. I was happy, and so was the crowd. As we went for the extra point, I got the ball. Silverie ran into the end zone, and I threw the ball to her for two points. That puts us up eight points ahead for us to have a chance in the game if they try to tie it up.

As the game continued in the second half, we were ahead by two touchdowns, and in the fourth quarter. Silver took over at the third because I was getting tired, and I got sacked about six times, and it gets harder and harder every time it hits. So I told her to take my spot while I rested and ran the ball. She did a little better than me, but I didn't care because I ensured we were ahead of the other team.

In the fourth quarter, they caught up to us and passed us up on the board, and when we got the ball back, we had only fifteen seconds with no timeouts to use. The coach didn't know what to do, but I suddenly had an idea.

"Hey Silverie, how far can you throw the football?" I asked.

"I don't know, maybe about sixty yards if I know where I'm throwing it at," she said.

"Well, I'm going to run down the field to get to it. Give yourself enough time to toss it without being sacked, and I'll get it in the end zone." I said.

"I'll do my best," she said, and we headed out onto the field for the game's final drive.

As we got ready, and she gave me the signal that she was getting the ball, I bolted out of my spot and ran down the field as she grabbed the ball in her hands. Looking back to see where she was, I noticed that she just threw the ball. No one was coming after me until they noticed me down the field. They came after me, but I was already about twenty yards from them, and I finally saw the football as I crossed the fifty-yard line. It was going to hit at the thirty, which meant I had to get there in the next five seconds to catch it, or that would be the end of the game.

So, I ran faster and got there just as it came into my hands. I grabbed it and ran for the end zone, with the other team dragging to keep up with me. But they never caught up with me, and I scored the winning touchdown. The crowd went wild, and my team came running for the end zone to carry me on their shoulders. The lion fans went crazy about the win and chanted my name as loud as they could. I couldn't be happier than getting my team into the finals and winning that game. The coach made his way to me, and they put me down so that I could talk to him.

"That was amazing, Crystal. I don't have any words to tell you but to do that at the championship game and get us the win. Thank you ." he said, hugged me, and so did the rest of the team.

"All right, everyone in the bus," he said, and they took off their padding. We were headed for the bus when Sapphire came up to me. "Hey, girl, good game. Um, Mom and Dad want to see you before you get onto the bus," she said, and I went up to them.

"Hey Crystal, that was a great play right there. Just make sure you do that at the championship game, which would make you the first female in football history to win state four years in a row," he said, and they said they would meet me in Henderson to pick me up when the buses stop. I agreed and headed out with Silverie to the bus.

After the game, the Christmas Holidays out of school started. The team will play the championship game next year after we return to school. I wanted to spend time with my family and friends during this beautiful time of the year and try to start the new year with goodness.

When I got up the next day, my sister was already up and was moving around in the room. She saw that I was awake.

"Hey, sis, I didn't mean to wake you up," she said.

"That's all right. Besides, I don't need to sleep too late because I would get used to it too quickly, which I'm bad at doing. You can ask Mom." I said.

"Well, anyways, when I got up and walked out of the room, I saw that Sapphire was in the bathroom doing something, but I couldn't find out what. When I asked her, she got mad and told me to leave her alone," she said.

"I'll talk to her and see what's going on. Then, I'll let you know." I said, and I walked out of the room. Sapphire was back in her room, so I went inside and saw her sitting at her desk, looking at something. I walked towards her.

"Hey there, what are we up to this morning?" I asked, and she turned to me. I saw a mark on her neck and right cheek. I was shocked.

"Sapphire, why are you letting him control you?" I asked.

"I don't know; I can't get away from him. Every time I say that I'm leaving him, he keeps saying something that draws me back to him," Sapphire said and started crying.

"It's okay; big sister is here to hear you out. I want to meet him so I can give him something to talk about." I said.

"Sis, don't do anything to hurt him, please," she said.

"I'm sorry, but he will not push you around anymore. I have been through it. I don't want you to make the same mistake that I made because you are not like me. I don't want you to fall before him and have difficulty getting away for good." I said, and the doorbell rang.

"That's him, I'm certain," she said.

"How do you know?" I asked.

"Because he just called me and told me that he is coming over this morning to take me to Tyler and have some time alone," she said.

"Well, that's going to change right now," I said, walking downstairs with Sapphire.

He tried to enter the house without hesitation when I opened the door.

"Hey, what do you think you are doing?" I asked.

"I'm trying to get her; why don't you just get out of my way?" he said harshly.

"I'm sorry, but I didn't invite you into the house, and you can wait outside until she comes out," I said.

"No, you don't get it. No one tells me what to do." Get out of my way so I can get to my girl," he said.

"You are not coming in," I said.

"Girl, you are making me mad, get out my way, or I'll make you," he said.

"Well, at least someone can resist the so-called love you showed my sister here," I said. He got mad and looked right at my sister.

"I told you to shut your mouth about our relationship, but you told your sister here, and I'm going to make you regret that." He said and shoved me out of the way. He slapped Sapphire across the cheek and then on the other side. When he tried again, I caught his arm, and he turned to me.

"No male will hit my sister, including you, boy," I said and hit him right in the face. He fell to the floor.

"You slut! You broke my nose!" he exclaimed and swung for me, but he missed. So, I grabbed the back of his neck and walked him to the door.

"Nobody calls me a slut!" I shouted and tossed him out the door.

"If you ever mess with my sister again, I will make you feel her pain three times as bad, and I mean it," I retorted. I walked back into the house.

"If he messes with you again, don't stop me from hurting him," I told Sapphire and walked past her. I went to the living room, where Kristen was watching the whole thing.

That whole week, that guy never messed with her again because I was with her everywhere. She also feels safer that her big sister is watching over her.

As the next week started, Steve came over to see what I was doing for the holiday, and my family was slowly coming in for the party we had prepared for Christmas. He told me he would pick me up on New Year's Eve and pop some fireworks out in the woods. I told him the only way for that was for him to come to the party and have a good time with my family. He agreed to it.

The party was going to be on a Friday, and New Year's Eve was only four days away. The day that I told him was on Monday, and it is already Thursday today. He has yet to call or come over since then. I was worried about him because he would call me every day to check on me. I would also call him, but I've been busy these past few days because my mother needed help in the kitchen.

"Crystal, did you ask Steve to come over tomorrow and meet us?" Mom asked.

"Yeah, I did. But I haven't heard from Steve for a few days, and I'm worried about Steve." I said.

"Oh, don't be; besides, he should be here for it. I mean, he's part of the family around here," she said.

"Should I call him?" I asked.

"I would tell you, yes, but I wouldn't know if he would talk to you," she said.

"Well, I'll call him just to see if he would answer his phone," I said.

But when I called him, he was not there. His parents told me that he was out with some of his friends and didn't know when he was coming back. I asked them to tell him that I called to see if he was still coming over tomorrow, and they said they would. I hung up the phone and waited. After about four hours, the phone rang.

Mom told me to answer it, and so I did.

"Hello?" I answered.

"Hey girl, what are you doing?" Steve asked.

"Oh, nothing; I was just wondering if you were still coming over tomorrow to meet my family?" I asked.

"Oh yeah, I meant to call you about that. I have some changes to tell," Steve said.

"What do you mean? you can't make it?" I asked.

"Oh no, I'm still going to be there. I will be a little later than I said the other day. But don't worry, it will be before four o'clock. I must watch my little sister while my parents are gone to town. They'll be back by three, and I'll be over there. When I make a promise, I mean it. I don't want people to lose their trust in me. Okay?" he said.

"Okay, well, I guess I'll see you tomorrow, huh," I said.

"Yeah, you will," he said, and we hung up the phone. My little sister walked into my room after that, so I spent some time with her.

The next day afternoon, our family started to arrive, and they were coming one at a time. They would stay until New Year and return home so that we would spend one week with them. I was not in the mood for that because I had some cousins I didn't like. However, I have little choice in the situation.

As time passed and four o'clock was nearing, I looked for Steve to show, but I didn't see his car. I started to wonder where he was.

"Who are you waiting for, Sis?" Kristen asked.

"I'm waiting for Steve to show up, but I haven't seen him yet," I said.

"Well, if I know him as you do, he will be here. I'm sure of it," Kristen said at that time, he drove up to my house, and I ran to his car to meet him.

"Hey, sweetheart," he said.

"Hey there, I was starting to wonder about you," I said.

"Yeah, I thought you might since it's after four. My parents were shopping, and they didn't realize the time. They arrived home late." he said.

"Well, I'm hoping that is true, buddy, because I don't want to take up for my sister here," Kristen said.

"Well, how about you call my folks right now and ask them if I'm cheating on her because they would know," he said to her.

"I'm just kidding; besides, I know when a guy is cheating on a girl because of how they act, and you don't act that way," she said and walked off.

"Well, do you want to meet my family inside?" I asked.

"Yeah, might as well get used to them before we get any further in our relationship," he said, and we walked into the house. My parents saw Steve walk in.

"Hello there, Steve. Are you still taking good care of my daughter?" Dad asked.

"Yes, sir. I will take care of her through anything and make sure she is safe sir," he said.

"Well, just making sure. Now, make yourself at home and meet the family." Dad said and walked with me. I introduced him to all the family members, and he talked to some of them. I walked outside where all my cousins were playing, and Steve was out there about ten minutes later and saw me talking to them.

"Hey there," he said as he walked up.

"My goodness, Crystal, who is that? and what is he doing here?" Rachael asked.

"This would be my boyfriend, and I invited him here," I said.

"Well, you could have picked a better one than him. There are boys out there far more handsome than him. Besides, he has freckles all over his face and arms, girl, you know that I can hook you up with one of those guys I'm with and can treat you better." she said.

"You know, that's what makes us different from one another. You see people for their looks, while I look at people's personalities. You need to realize that you cannot judge a person for their appearance because they might look like angels from heaven, but they can be snotty, uptight, and preppy. I don't want that because that's how the guy I was with was until Steve asked me out. I realized how different he was from the guys I used to date. Steve doesn't tell me what I can or not do. I can talk to whomever I want as long as he can get along with them. I don't have to worry about him cheating because he says it's immature. He will also not lay a hand on me if I make him mad, which is not that often." I said.

"Well, I just don't like him," she said.

"Why? because I'm not a prep like you? I'm not sorry for the way you are judging me because it's in a preps nature not to like ugly people. After all, if they hang out with one another, their friends will talk badly about them, and they will blame it on the ugly people. Well, let me ask you something else, who does your household chores? Because I know you don't do any of it because a maid does all of it. What will happen when you get out and have your place? Are you going to hire a maid to do all your chores? Or make your roommate do all of it? I'm telling you right now; I would not pick up someone that can't. I bet you can't even clean up a room properly. Man, it must be nice to have a maid and not worry about doing it yourself, or does your Mom do that for you?" Steve asked. *Wow, that was long.*

Rachael didn't have anything to say to that and walked off.

"My goodness, sweetie, I never heard you talk that way to someone," I said.

"Well, that's how I am, and I won't change it for the world. Besides, why should I change just because someone that doesn't like me?" Steve said.

"I don't like her much anyways because of how she is. Sometimes, she can be a brat, and I don't like it." I said.

"Well, I think she will leave you alone for good right now since I'm here," he said, and we sat down in the grass. We looked up at the sky until it was time to eat.

As Christmas passed and New Year's Eve drew near, I was getting ready to bring in the new year by going out and buying fireworks because Steve couldn't buy them. So, I volunteered. I kept them in a safe place until New Year's Eve. On New Year's Eve, Steve came by the house and picked me up to meet his folks and find a place in the country to light the fireworks.

As we arrived at his house and made our way to the door, I saw his parents in the living room.

"Hey, Mom, I'm back," Steve said as he walked in.

"Oh, that was quick," she said as she walked into the kitchen.

"Hello, you must be Crystal," she said.

"Yes, I am," I said.

"I have heard so much about you, and you look like a good girl for my baby boy here," she said.

"Mother," Steve said.

"What? You haven't told her that you are my youngest boy in the family?" she asked.

"I don't think he did," I said.

"Well, he has two younger sisters in their room right now. Steve, why don't you introduce Crystal to them and check what they are doing," she said.

"Okay, Mom, I'll see if they are up because they were still sleeping before I left," he said.

"They should be because I heard noises coming from their room," she said, and we walked to their room. Steve knocked on the door, and the door opened.

"What do you want?" one of them said.

"Can I bring in Crystal so you two can meet her?" he asked.

"All right, come on in," she said, and she let us in.

"All right, Crystal, the older one is Sara, she is sixteen, and the other one is Keely, and she is fourteen," he said.

"Nice to meet you," I said.

"Well, are you done here, brother?" Sara asked.

"Yes, sis, I'll leave you alone until you come out of this room," he said, and I followed him, but Sara grabbed my hand and pulled me back into the room.

"Hey, don't judge me by how I treat my brother sometimes. That's how we react to each other sometimes. There are also times that we play games with each other; Keely does that too. She is closer to him than me because he has taken care of her longer than I have, and I'm just not that close with him, but I would like to change that." she said.

"Well, I could help you if you want me to," I said.

"No, I don't want to bother you with my problems," she said.

"It's okay, my family was that way until someone from the outside came in, and now, we are closer than ever. Just let me help you." I said.

"Okay, I'll let you do that," she said, and I agreed. We walked out of the room and went to where Steve was. As the clock was nearing ten o'clock, Steve and I were heading out until Sara and Keely came running out and hopped into the car with us.

"I thought you were staying here?" Steve asked.

"I decided to come and have some fun," Sara said, and Steve drove on to the place we picked out to pop the fireworks and count down the minutes until the new year was here.

As we were popping fireworks, Kyle and the rest of the gang drove to where we were and brought some fireworks too. We popped as many as possible until I brought out the big boy. I was going to shoot it off as the final second went by. I had Steve watch the clock and count me down until he got to four seconds. I lit it, and when it hit zero, the firework shot out and burst into a beautiful flower. Then, it went away, and everybody said happy new year to each other, and I turned to Steve.

"Well, happy new year to you, and I am happy to spend it with you," he said.

"Ditto," I said, and we kissed, and everybody started whopping.

"Now, you know we have kids out here," Silverie said, and everyone laughed. We stayed out and decided to sleep in the cars because I didn't want this moment to end too soon, so Steve agreed. Everyone did the same, and I passed out about an hour after the new year started.

Chapter 10

That following week after the new year started, we returned to school. I dreaded it because the holidays didn't last long, and I wanted to stay home another week, but Mom ensured that I was at school that Monday.

When Sapphire stopped her car and parked it, I got out. I headed for my fourth-period class last semester to pick up my schedule. Then, I headed to the field house because we still had to take the off-season part of the class even though that football season was about over. When I arrived, the coach pulled me to the side to talk to me.

"Crystal, there is some good news about the last game of the season," he said.

"Yeah, go ahead," I said.

"Well, we won't play for about a week or two until they can find a stadium we can go to, and the other team can. So that would give us time to get ready for it because they are as good as us in beating the other teams by four to five touchdowns on most of their games, making us look bad," the coach said.

"Well, you are there anyways," I asked.

"Now, don't freak out, Crystal, but they are from New York, and the town would be Bayview. Your hometown," he said, and I looked shocked at him.

"What?! That cannot be right, coach. Are you sure?" I asked.

"Yes, that's whom we are playing against," he said.

"Oh man, they are going to see me. Since I've played games with them, they know all my ways, which will be my weakness. Coach, is there any way of changing our opponent?" I asked.

"There is no way to change it, Crystal. We must play the team, or we give up on getting the championship cup, and I know you don't want that," he said.

"Yeah, you are right about that. Well, I better get the team ready for the game because my old team might know me, but my old team doesn't know all my tricks." I said and walked over to the team. I gave them the laydown of what would come on the last game, whom we were playing, and the nature of things.

After I talked to them, the coach made them run some plays to see if they had gotten better than before. From what I saw on the field, they were doing excellent, and I am delighted to see it working as it should. After about thirty minutes, I told the team to huddle up around me so I could tell them something.

"All right, team, you are doing an excellent job out there with all the plays, and you are running them as they should, and that's how we need to do come the last game. I would like to see this team beat my old school to see if this team has enough teamwork in their blood to stop them and run them over and score as many points as we can. I know they are my old school, but I will show them no mercy regarding my scoring. They are just another team for me to put into the ground, and we can prove it as a team should. Let's win that final game and become champions for the first time in ten years." I said, and they were yelling. We placed our hands in the middle for a minute and then split for the locker room to change and prepare for our next class.

As I made my way to AG and sat down in my chair, Michael was his usual self and would not stop staring at me for some reason, so I turned to him.

"What do you want?" I asked.

"Oh, I was wondering if you would like to go to prom with me this year?" he asked.

"Sorry, but no, I already have somebody taking me," I said.

"Oh, I see how you are going to be a stuck-up little girl that only wants cute boys to go out with," he said.

"You know, for your information, Steve asked me to go with him, and now, we are also dating. So, I don't want to hear what you say about me." I said.

"Oh, so you'll go out with him but not me," he said.

"Well, if you can grow up, I might consider a friendship with you, but I would be wasting my time anyway," I said, and he didn't say anything after that.

When the teacher walked in, he told us to go ahead and head out to work on our projects and get them finished because we had only two months to go before the show started. I still had a long way to go yet.

Kristen and I were coming up with ideas on how to get the pit to work on the trailer. I told her how I thought it should go.

"Hey, sis, what if we made it to where it would come off the side somehow," I said.

"Yeah, I was thinking that, but how would it be taken off because I know that it's going to be heavy to move," she said.

"Well, we could make a ramp where it can slide off on a rail system and put it back on the same way," I said.

"You know, that might work. All we need to do is put two down the center and make the ramp the same way, but how to get it back up is what I'm wondering," she said.

"How about a whence to pull it back up and let it off the back because we can put rail wheels on it, as well as heavy-duty wheels for when you have to run it on the ground," I said.

"That would be the best way to do it," she said.

"All right then, let's get started on it," I said, and we began putting down lines to where the pit was to sit and where the rail system would be. Then, I went to Mr. Ingram with the idea, and he said that it just might work that way, and I told him what I was going to need. He told me that he would have the stuff there in about two days, and I agreed and began measuring how much wood we would need for the trailer's floor. Kristen finished up on what she needed to do and saw that the last axle was still not on, and she was going to do that right quickly before something happened to it.

After I finished what I was doing, I went to where she was and helped her get it in. Still, it took us about ten minutes to place it where it should be and bolted it in place, and then I finished some welding that needed completion before we had to get cleaned up and ready for next period class.

Then, Steve came by. "Hey there. Wow! It looks like you're going to finish that up before the show." he said.

"Yeah, I should finish it about two weeks before the show," I said.

"Well, Kyle and I should be done with ours in about a month from now," he said.

"You two are doing that picnic table back there?" I asked.

"Yeah, that would be ours, and we are going to make it shine," he said and walked on to the classroom while I stayed there, put the stuff away, and walked in afterward.

As the week passed, it was already Friday. The team was starting to get better by the day, and the coach told me that we were playing Panthers next Friday at SFA, and the other group was going to fly here because it would be better down here than going up there.

Then, I went to AG and sat down in my chair. I saw a note on my desk and opened it. It was from Micah asking me to go out with him and take me to prom. I already rejected him first, and Steve won't like it if he saw that note. But he is already at my back reading the letter as well.

"Hey boy, what makes you think you can go out with my girlfriend?" he asked.

"Because I want to be the one to date her," he said.

"Well, for one, she doesn't like you, and two, she is going out with me, and I don't like you," he said.

"I don't care what you say. I'm taking Crystal to prom," he said firmly.

"Well, you try to do that, and I'll make sure you remember not to do it again," Steve said, and Micah turned to talk to Allie; she slapped him, and he turned to the front of the room and said nothing else to anybody.

When the teacher came in and told us to head out, he called me to his desk.

"Crystal, your project is getting attention from the kids, which is good. But some of them have destroyed some builds because they want theirs to be the best overall. Now, I can keep an eye on it and make sure nothing happens to it. But, if anything happens to it, like that dent that wasn't there when you saw it last time, let me know right away then I'll find out who did it. Your metal came in today, sitting right outside whenever you need it. Ask for help if you need to.

Now go out and work some." he said, and I went outside to where my sister was, looked over the trailer, and saw nothing wrong with it. So, I headed out and saw my metal sitting on the ground. I called Kristen over, and we picked up a beam, walked back in, and laid it next to the trailer.

When we sat down, everyone watched us the whole time, but I didn't care and walked back outside to grab the other one and bring it inside to get it measured and cut to the length of the trailer. As Kristen did that, I started working on the pit. Mr. Ingram had brought me two pipes; one was about seven inches in diameter, and the other was about twenty-four inches. I had to weld them together, so I put them on a table with Kristen's help, made some marks to where they needed to be, and started welding.

At the end of class, Kristen had the beams cut and had one sitting on the trailer, but she didn't set it yet, and I got the two pipes welding and was working on cleaning them up when Mr. Ingram told us that it was time to stop and get back into the classroom.

During the rest of the day, I was thinking about next week's game and wondered what my team would say about me going against them and how they would win it instead of us.

While I was doing that, Laura was trying to get my attention about something, but I didn't even know she was until she hit me in the arm, and I looked at her.

"Crystal, are you back now?" she asked.

"Oh, I'm sorry, I was thinking about something. What are we doing again?" I asked.

"Well, we are in the library, and Mr. Propes wants us to do this paper right here, and we need your help on it," she said.

"Okay, let me see what it is," I said, but it didn't take me long to lose my concentration on it and started thinking about the game, and Laura snapped me back out of it.

"Girl, you have some serious issue that we need to know," she said.

"Oh, it's nothing. Now let me look here." I said.

"Oh no, you are going to tell us what is bothering you right now so you can get your mind off it," Laura said.

"Can't it wait?" I asked,

"Nope. You are going to tell us now," she said.

"Okay, well, it's about next week's game. I can't stop thinking about what my old team will say when the other players see me on the team they are against and what they will do about it." I said.

"So, that's what your problem is. Girl, why didn't you tell us in the first place?" she asked.

"Well, I don't want you to stress my problem with me because you have other things to worry about," I said.

"Like what?" she asked.

"Well, I don't know what you have to deal with, but there must be something," I said.

"Well, as far as I can tell you, you are my friend, and friends help each other with problems no matter what. Now, let's talk about this so you can help us out here," she said.

"Okay," I told her about the whole thing, and it seemed to get off my mind slowly. After about ten minutes, we worked on the paper and almost finished it before the bell rang. We had to go to lunch and meet up with the guys to see what they did with their writing.

When we finally sat down outside with the guys after getting our lunch, we asked them about it, and they told us what they did.

"Well, I never thought of it that way, but it might work out in the end," Laura said.

"Yeah, but you need to do it that way, or it just won't work," I said.

"What are you talking about, Crystal?" Steve asked.

"I don't know, just don't pay attention to me," I said.

"She is having problems with the game next week against her old team, and it's getting to her," Laura said.

"Laura, you are supposed to keep that on the down low," I said.

"Well, he does need to know, don't you?" she asked Steve.

"Well, she could have told me about it when she wanted to. But I'm not mad at you for saying something about it." Steve said.

"Well, I think I have got it behind me now. So, what are you doing this weekend, Laura?" I asked.

"Ohh, I'm supposed to watch after my neighbor's kid, which can be a pain sometimes," she said.

"Well, are all kids like that?" Kyle asked.

"Yeah, you don't have to tell me that; I should know," I said.

"That's why I plan on having just one, and that's it for me," Laura said.

"Oh, come on now, why not more?" Sapphire asked.

"Because one would be enough for me," she said.

"Well, Amy and I plan on having about two to three," Randall said.

"Well, what about you, Kristen?" Laura asked.

"Who? Me? Well, I don't want any. Taking care of my siblings is enough to drive me insane." she said.

"Hey now, Susan is not that bad," I said.

"Well, when you are not around, she goes off the wall, and she stays that way until about ten o'clock, and she gets tired, and I put her to bed. So, I don't want to have kids," she said.

"Yeah, but what if your boyfriend asks you to have one?" I asked.

"Well, he would just have to find someone else for some, and that's final," she said, and the bell rang for lunch to be over.

"Well, it's time for us to head to class," Steve said as he was heading with Kyle back onto the building.

"Okay, I'll see you after school," I said, kissed him on the cheek, and walked on to my class at the other end of the school grounds.

As Sapphire was driving on our road to the house, I noticed that a car I didn't know was out in front, and I saw that Mom and Dad were out there with it, and as soon as the car stopped, I hopped out and went to them.

"Well, there you are, sport. What do you think?" Dad asked.

"Is this my new car?" I asked.

"It sure is, honey, just what you wanted, I guess." Mom said, it was a 2020 Honda Civic EX with four doors, and it was black like my old car. As I looked inside, I saw that it was a stick shift and black on the inside.

"Oh, thank you so much for the car," I hugged them.

"Well, you can thank that boy for finally paying for this car here because he was found guilty of the whole thing. They made him pay for everything, and you didn't have to. Here are the keys, have fun." He handed me the keys. I got into the driver's seat and sat there thinking about how I would look in the car when I drove it.

As I was thinking, I decided to see what was under the hood, so I popped the hood and opened it to see that it was still stock, and I knew that was going to change, but I didn't know what I could put on it because it was different from the Lancer that I had.

So, I went inside the house and went to my computer to look up on the internet to see what I could do to it and how much it would be. Kristen came in there to see what I was doing as I did. "Hey there, what are you looking up there?" she asked.

"Well, I'm just checking what I can buy at a store for my car out there," I said.

"Oh, so you got the Honda. I wondered who owned it because I knew Sapphire and David had a car, and yours got wrecked. I figured it was yours just by a guess." she said.

"Hey Kristen, you drive a Honda, don't you?" I asked.

"Yeah, what are you getting at now?" she asked.

"Well, I was hoping you know what would be good for my car because you have one almost like mine," I said.

"Well, okay, I'll show you what to get at a store, and it won't hurt your car that I have been wanting to get for me for a long time now," she said.

"Well, you know I can get it for you, and you don't have to worry about paying me." I said, "You would do that for me." she asked.

"Yeah, because you are my sister, I'll help you with just about anything." I said, "All right, you can get the stuff that I have been wanting." she said, and she pulled up a chair, and we looked at all the parts and things that can go on our cars, and she showed me something that I like, and we wrote down what they were and where to find them. We had surfed the net for an hour when I heard a knock on my door. When I opened it, Steve was standing there.

"Hey there," he said.

"Hey, babe," I hugged him and walked back to my computer.

"What are we doing to the new car?" he asked.

"Ohh, just going to get it upgraded a lot, but I need to be careful and not void the warranty," I said.

"Yeah, you don't want to do that," he said.

"Yeah, that's why we are writing it down so that I can talk to my parents about what I want to do to the car and help Kristen out with her car," I said.

"Well, I would like something for my car," he said, and I looked at him.

"Just kidding, don't take that seriously," he said.

"Well, your birthday is coming up, and I'll get you something, but I don't know yet until later," I said.

"Anyway, I'm here because I want to know if you would like to go to the movies, and Kristen can come too," he said.

"Okay, but I only do that if we take my car," I said.

"That sounds like a winner to me," he said, and as I went downstairs, I told Mom and Dad that I was leaving for a little while and be back later. They approved, and we left the house. That weekend was the best one I have had in about six months because it went as perfectly as I expected. I didn't want it to end, but it had to.

Monday came in a rush, and I drove to school that day. No one knew who was in it until I stopped the car. As I got out, some students walked up to me and asked about it and how I got it, and I told them how it came into my hands. When I got to the field house, the coach motioned me into his office to talk to me.

"Yeah, what's up, coach," I asked.

"Well, we have a problem, your brother doesn't seem to be doing well in his third-period class, and somehow he has ended up in SOS and won't be out until next week, and we will need him for the game," he said.

"Well, okay, but what does that mean?" I asked.

"Well, if you are in SOS on a day that your team plays a game, you cannot be in it," he said.

"Ohh, man, he's my backup on the field. What are we going to do?" I said.

"Well, how about your sister? Would she play in his spot?" he asked.

"No, she wouldn't want to, and besides, she is a cheerleader," I said.

"Ohh, that's right. Well, the only one left would be Silverie or your cousin Randall," he said.

"Well, Silverie has lost a little of her play in the past couple of games, and Randall is not as good," I said.

"I guess you need to figure out something," he said.

"Okay, let me talk to them and see what they want to do, and I guess you start them out in David's spot and tell them where to go," I said and walked off to find them.

I found them outside waiting for me.

"Hey girls, I need to talk to you. am going to need to put one of you in David's spot and get you trained on what he does." I said.

"Well, I'll do it, Crystal, because I know his spot better than anyone else," Silverie said.

"Are you sure you can do it?" I asked.

"Yeah, over the past few weeks, I just had something on my mind, and I've gotten over it now," she said.

"Okay, I guess you can go ahead and take care of that," I said.

Then, the coach approached me again and told me some more bad news.

"Hey Crystal, I just got word that Scott was in a wreck just down the road, and he was hurt fairly badly, and it doesn't look like he will not be able to play this Friday. I need you to take his spot while Randall takes yours," he said.

"Okay, that puts a whole new meaning in what will happen this Friday," I said.

"Well, I would put someone else in there, but he doesn't really like you right now," he said. I knew he was talking about Micah, and I didn't want him to be the quarterback because he would lose the game.

"Well, Randall, it looks like you are to take my spot, and I'm going to be the quarterback for the last game of the year," I said, and I walked with them to the rest of the team, and we did a few plays to see how the girls would do one their drives.

As we did those, it looked like they were going to do good at the game this Friday, but it was me that needed to get better at my spot because it was a lot to learn for me in only five days, but I knew that I could make it as a quarterback.

As the period was ending, I headed to the coach to talk to him about what needed to be done with the team to ensure we would win the game because they needed to block the defense and keep the players off me. He said he would talk to them about it, and I walked on to AG.

During the walk to AG., Kristen came up from behind and startled me a little.

"Hey, girl," she said.

"Ohh my, Kristen, you almost gave me a heart attack," I said.

"Well, I was going to ask you how you were doing on the pit," she said.

"Well, I still have much work to do. I need to get the legs on, put the doors on there, and try to see how to get it on the rail system." I said.

"Well, I got that out on the trailer and tacked on for the time being, so I guess I'll help you with the pit, and then after we get that done, we work on the trailer part," she said.

"Okay, but it will still take about three weeks to get it together and get it on the trailer, which would give us a month to get the wood on the trailer and then paint," I said.

"I meant to ask you what you were going to paint it," she asked. "Well, I was going for red, then I switched it to black and put some white lines on there to just bring out some of the features," I said.

"Well, that's okay with me," she said, and we walked into the classroom, sat down, and waited for the teacher to walk into the room and say some things to us. After he talked to us, we walked outside, and Kristen and I started working.

As we worked on getting to pit together and Mr. Ingram was standing there seeing how we were doing and talked to us about it, and we told him how we were going to put the rail but didn't know if it was going to work; just yet and he told us just try and see what would happen and he walked off.

As we were working on the pit, somehow, one of the leg's welds broke, and the pipe landed on my left foot, bounced off, and hit the ground right by my right foot.

"Oh, man," I said as I limped over to the side to look at my foot, and Kristen came over to see how my foot looked.

"What happened, Crystal?!" Mr. Ingram asked in panic as he walked back over to see what had happened.

"Well, the leg pipe somehow came off the pit, landed right on my foot, and then just missed my other foot," I said, and as I took off my sock, I saw some blood on the front of my foot. I took it off to see that my first two toes were bleeding, and the teacher went to get the first aid kit.

"Well, it could be worse," Kristen said, and I looked at her.

"Hey, at least you still got your toes there," she said.

"Yeah, that's always a good thing," I said, and by that time, the teacher was back with the kit and was treating my toes. For the rest of the class, I had to ensure that nothing hit my toes for a while until they healed up, which wouldn't take long. As the teacher told us it was time to come into the classroom, Micah laughed at me and mocked me about what had happened to my foot.

"Ahh, is the little girl going to cry about her foot," he said, and I turned to look at him.

"Ohh, what are you going to do? Are you going to try and hurt me because I can take more pain than you could," he said.

"Keep talking and see what happens," I said and stood there to see what he would say next.

"Well, you better tell your sister to get an icepack because you just might need it since you cry at the littlest of pain," he said, and I just hit him right in the face with my fist. He fell back about four feet and looked at me.

"I told you to shut your mouth, but it seems you can't understand," I said and walked back into the classroom. Micah walked in, and his nose was bleeding, and the teacher saw it.

"What happened to you?" he asked.

"Well, Crystal hit me in the face on purpose," he said.

"Now, how can I believe that when I know for a fact that you have bothered her on many occasions and you don't know how to keep your mouth shut about certain things," he said.

"You mean you are not going to do anything about it?" he asked.

"Well, I do have to see it to write her up, which I didn't, so better luck next time," he said.

"Man, that is not fair," he said.

"Oh, it's fair enough to me," I said.

"Shut up, little girl," he said.

"Do you want the other fist too?" I asked, and he hushed up and waited for the bell to ring to get away from me. I have never seen him run so fast to stay just far enough away. Steve and the gang were laughing about it, and he got mad but didn't do anything because I was there, so we just walked to our next class.

As the week passed, and I was playing the quarterback, I was getting better at it, and the coach liked what he saw. He believed us to win the game this Friday in SFA Stadium. The school was going to let out early today just so that we could get down there in time for the game and get tons of practice in about the field because we hadn't been there since our first playoff game, and he wanted us to be ready for it.

"Okay, Crystal, I like what you are doing, and I hope that the other team doesn't know what is coming for them this Friday because they only know you as a receiver, not a quarterback, so it just might give us an edge to win," he said.

"Well, that's always good to hear, coach," I told him.

"Later on, we are having a prep rally today, but I've heard that it is supposed to be special, and I don't think you want to miss it for anything. I just wished that your brother didn't get dumb and end up in SOS on the championship week," he said.

"Don't worry, coach, we are doing fine with the girls helping out," Scott said.

"Thank you for saying that, Scott," I said.

"Well, I can see that you can easily replace me as the quarterback," he said.

"I don't think I'm that good yet, buddy," I said.

"Well, you never know what a college school would say if they saw you as a quarterback. They might get you to come to their school and play for them," he said.

"I'm sorry, but I've already had one picked out, and it's in Tyler. They have accepted me into their school and will let me play football; even though the boys may not like it, they can get over it," I said. The team kept practicing on a few more runs until it was time to get ready to go when the bell rang.

"Oh man, I didn't realize the time had gone that fast," I said and dashed to change into my clothes and run to AG before I was late. I made it there with only seconds to spare. I sat down as the teacher made his way back into the classroom.

"Okay, students, you only have one month to prepare your projects for the show, or you won't show anything. So, if you are trying to do two projects in one, try to get one done first, then if you get time, come back and do the other but don't put yourself in a bind as the days wear on and you don't get done with any of them," he said, and he didn't talk for a few minutes. Then, he told us to head outside to work on what we needed to do.

As I got to the trailer, I still had about half of the pit to finish up before it was ready to test to see if the rail system would work. Kristen had a little more work to do before she finished her part. Then, she would help me out with mine as much as she could. But when I noticed that the trailer didn't look right, I saw that someone had messed with it again. This time, the axles, and one of them was barely hanging onto the trailers under the frame. I pointed it out to Kristen, and she wasn't happy either. So, I had to get down there to see the damage. Mr. Ingram came over just a few minutes later to see what was happening.

"Hey there, what's wrong?" He asked.

"Well, someone has messed with the axles, and now one is just hanging by threads, and it's about to let go, and I need to get it fixed," I said.

"Well, can you get it, or are you going to need help?" he asked.

"The only help I would need is Kristen, and that's about it for the time being," I said.

"Okay, call if you need any help," he said and walked off the trailer while Kristen held the axle. I put the bolts back in, and this time I decided to weld them to the trailer to ensure that no one could do it again.

As we left the classroom, my phone was vibrating, and when I looked at it, I saw Sapphire's message saying that she was in trouble and was in the first-year hall heading out the door and going to the practice field. So, I ran out of the building and saw her running from her boyfriend; he was chasing her down. Before she could cross the street, he grabbed her, threw her to the ground, and started slapping and hitting her in the face.

"That's it," I told myself and ran up to him, and just power drove him off her, and as he got up to see what happened, he was mad.

"You are going to pay for that," he said.

"No one hits my little sister, including you," I said.

"I can do whatever I want to her because she is mine," he said.

"She is no one's property and never will be," I said.

"Get behind me," I told her.

"What are you going to do, huh? Protect her from me?" he asked.

"I will do whatever I need to keep you away from her," I said and looked to my side and saw that Steve and Laura were beside me.

"Well then, I'll just take you out for good," he said.

"If you feel froggy, then jump for me, boy," I said. He ran for me and saw that he would do a power drive on me. So, as he got in range, I put my foot right in his stomach, making him stop and fall to his knees and start coughing, and he looked up at me.

"Hey, you are not supposed to do that," he groaned.

"Oh, I'm sorry. How about this?" I asked, hitting him right in the temple, putting him out cold.

"Thank you, sis," Sapphire said.

"That's why I'm here, girl," I said, and we left him there and walked on to our classroom before we were late.

As the day moved on, and we went to lunch, that guy was there also and was not very happy with me for kicking him and then knocking him out, which I thought was funny.

"Hey, there's that guy you knocked out for Sapphire," Laura said.

"Crystal, you mean to tell me that you took out that guy?" Kristen asked.

"Yep, I mean, he was too controlling with Sapphire. He wouldn't let her talk to her friend or hang out with them; the only ones she could were his friends, which she didn't like because of how they acted, and I just got tired of it and gave him a taste of his own medicine." I said.

"Yeah, but did you have to do it that way?" she asked.

"Well, what would you have done?" I asked.

"Well, I mean…I don't know, but I wouldn't kick his butt," she said.

"Oh, come on now, you know you would have done it. That's our sister that I'm talking about, Kristen. How would you feel if somebody was doing that to me?" I asked.

"Well, I guess you have a point about it," she said.

"Yeah, and then I did the right thing. Besides, Sapphire doesn't need a guy that goes violent on females because if he is dumb enough to do that, then he is not a man in my book." I said.

"Yeah, that's very true, babe," Steve said.

"See, Steve knows what I talk about is right," I said.

"Sometimes, girl, sometimes," he said.

"What do you mean abo-oh okay, I'll shut up about it," I said, realizing what he meant while I was saying.

"Now you know what I mean," he said, and the bell ranged for lunch to be over.

"Well, I guess it's time for us to head to class," Randall said, and we headed off in different directions.

As the seventh period started, I told the teacher that I was to leave at two forty-five so I could go to the field house.

"What do you mean by that?" he asked.

"Well, I'm a football player," I said.

"Well, I have never seen you on the team," he said.

"Well, when that time comes, sir, I'll assure you I'm walking out that door and going to the field," I said and sat down in my assigned seat.

My last-period class had none of my friends in it because it was a class my Mom wanted me to take, and I couldn't change it because it was in my file not to take me out of the course. It was a landscaping class, and I was not fond of landscaping that much, but my mother wanted me to be like her. However, I like to build things out of metal and wood and wanted to be like my Dad. What he does for a living is that he is a supervisor over a crew that builds portable buildings and other small things like that.

"All right, let's get started here." the teacher said.

"Now, today, what we need to do. . ." After that, I lost interest in what he was saying, but after about ten minutes of talking, he called my name.

"Crystal, could you tell me what this is?" he said, and I looked at the board and saw the same thing my Mom had taught me. It was a sloping incline, but a landscaper would tell you its angle.

"It's a slope at fifteen degrees," I said.

"Very good! How did you know that?" he asked.

"Easy, someone taught me," I said.

"Yes, I know that, but you wouldn't have known the angle of that slope without being taught by a landscaping expert," he said.

"My mother taught me," I said.

"And who would that be?" he asked.

"Her name is Mary Dawlson," I said.

"You mean, you are her daughter?" he asked.

"Yes, I would be her daughter," I said.

"Oh, I can't believe I didn't see it before. I have seen you in some pictures of the houses your mother did. I have always liked her designs and how they would be so beautiful when she would use them on some houses." he said.

"Yeah, she is very popular in New York State," I said.

"Yes, that's where she would do some of her shows. I want to ask you, could you see if she would help with my lawn to make it look beautiful?" the teacher asked.

"I don't know about that; she is married and has kids," I said.

"Well then, come with her. And another thing, ask her if she is going to do any more shows because I would like to see them," the teacher said.

"Okay, I'll see what she would say to that," I said, and it was time for me to leave and go to the field house.

I just got up and walked out the door, but he didn't say anything to me and just allowed me to go. I told him that the person he liked so much was my mother and he must have forgotten what we talked about at first of the class.

As I made my way to the field house, the coach pulled me aside and talked.

"Hey, Crystal. Now, they will be asking all kinds of things about you tonight, so be ready," he said, but I wasn't ready.

At the prep rally, after about ten minutes of other things happened, the cheerleader called me over to her and handed me the mic.

"How's the Henderson Loins doing today?!" I asked, and they cheered.

"You know the last game of the season happens tonight, and I know everyone in this room wants us to bring home the championship cup, but I'm going to need all of the loin fan's support to overcome the game and get it. You may not know, but the team we are playing has never lost a game in the past four years, and they will do anything to win. So, be at the game and help me with your support, and we'll be successful in getting the win." I said, and the students were yelling, whopping, and doing anything else they could do. Afterward, I handed the mic back to the cheerleader, sat down, and waited for it to be over.

After the prep rally, I had about forty minutes to get home to do what I needed to do and get David and my sisters back to the school for the bus, but only after I talked to my mother about something.

"Hey dear, what's wrong with you?" she asked because I was not very happy about something.

"Did someone do something to you?" she asked.

"Yeah, and they are right in front of me," I said

"What did I do wrong to you?" she asked.

"You put me in a landscaping class when I didn't want it in the first place," I said.

"Well, I figured you could be like me when you get my age," she said.

"You couldn't have asked me first before you did it. Mom, I'm not like you about the landscaping stuff. I'm not too fond of it and can't get out of the class because the principal said that my file had a note saying that I could not get out of it, and it was in your handwriting. Sometimes, I wish you would just let me do what I want to do when I want to and not have to ask. Okay? because I'm about to be eighteen soon." I said.

"Also, your Dad wanted it too, so it looks like you are stuck in that class for the rest of the year," she said.

"Well, that's just great. Now I will have to listen to a guy who has seen your work and won't leave me alone." I said and just walked out of the kitchen and headed to my room and waited on the others so that I could leave the house.

After about ten minutes, David came into my room and told me they were waiting for me downstairs, so I went down there. When I arrived, mother sat in her chair looking at a magazine, and Dad watched his show. I just walked out the door with David and Sapphire behind me, and we got into my car and drove to the school.

When we got there, I parked the car and headed straight for the buses because I didn't want to talk to anyone the whole time while we were on the bus, and I didn't want anybody sitting next to me, so I just put my legs in the seat, and everyone just kept on walking to the back of the bus. We left the school and headed for the stadium when everybody got on.

It took us less time because the school got us charter buses. They could go beyond the speed limit, and we had a sheriff in front of us to ensure nothing wrong happened to us.

"Hey Crystal, what's the matter?" Randall asked.

"I don't want to talk right now," I said.

"Hey, listen now, you can't talk to me that way because I'm not that kind of person. You can tell me," she said.

"I prefer not to; I just want to be left alone until we get to the stadium so I can see what kind of team we are going against," I said, and she left me alone after that.

It didn't take long to get there; we arrived about two hours. As we got there, the other team was doing their usual routine out on the field, and as I made my way to the area, and saw me. As each one of them got the attention of the guy next to him and made him look up, they didn't like seeing me.

"There she is; I told you she would keep playing football." someone said, and their coach saw me.

"Oh my, there's where she went to, and look how far she got that team to go," he said.

"Hey Crystal, did you come here to prove that you are still the best in the league? Or are you going to tell that team of yours about your past?" the quarterback said.

"Hey, get back to practicing." another coach said.

"What was that about?" my coach asked.

"Don't worry about what they say; they are just trying to get in my head, that's all," I said, and we went to practice, and our stuff was the same as theirs, which they didn't like.

After about an hour of practice, the fans started to show up then our cheerleaders, drill team, and the band was getting ready for the game as well. As it got closer to game time, both teams entered the locker rooms to prepare for the game. The coach talked to us and told them that no matter what happened out there, we were still winners to him, and after that, we headed back out to the field, and the other team was already out there waiting for us.

As I looked around the stadium, I saw the whole place had no seats left as people stood next to the fence trying to see the game. Then, the band played our song, and we ran through the loin head and onto the field and to the sidelines waiting for the coin toss.

After everything was said and done, we were to kick the ball and take the north end of the field. I got back off the field, waiting to get back out there; as the other team was getting to the ball closer to the end zone, the defense was slipping, and in about two minutes, they had a touchdown.

"Damn, they have gotten better since last year. Well, here I go." I said as I headed for the fifteen-yard line. I was going to do a pass to Randall but faked it and went for Silverie, but it didn't go as planned. The defense knew my plays very well because I had to be the quarterback for them for a year, and before they could get far enough, a player sacked me about five yards back, the coach was not happy, and neither was I at my team.

I tried to do it again, but this time, they knew what was happening, but I was ready. When they came in to sack me, I ducked and got back up to see Randall open and threw her the ball, and she caught it and ran for about twenty yards before she got taken down, and the fans were cheering.

After about two minutes, we made it to the fifteen-yard line. I wanted to throw it, but I knew the other team would know that, so I ran it. As I snapped the ball, I faked it to Randall and then pretended to Silverie to throw off the defense, and it worked because they went after them while I ran for the end zone. It took them about a second to realize that I had the ball, and they tried to tackle me, but they missed the whole time. I made a touchdown, put us on the board, and tied it with the extra point, that's when I realized that this was going to be a tough team to beat, but I knew that I could.

After the first quarter, the teams still tied the score at fourteen to fourteen, and we had the ball since they had to punt it to us. So, I passed the ball here and there and got us back to the twenty-yard line. While waiting for some players to change out, one of them told me to do a particular play: throw a pass to Randall. She threw it to Silverie and went for the end zone, so I went ahead and went with the plan, but it didn't go as it needed to. A player almost tackled me, So before it happened, I threw the ball to Silverie instead. She was able to get us a touchdown and get us ahead in the game, but the other team answered back and somehow got a fourteen-point lead on us before the first half was up, making the score thirty-five to twenty-one.

As we made our way back to the locker room, the team was not talking at all, and the coach was not there to speak to us, so someone just said something.

"You know, when this season started, I said that we were good without Crystal here, but she proved me wrong after she ran back the ball from the five-yard line to make a touchdown," he said.

"Yeah, and another time she managed to make her way around the defense to make one." another said.

"And there was also a time she tackled that one dude and made him lose the ball, and she picked it up and ran it into the end zone also." said another one.

"Now, she has her old team out there making her lose her focus, but we are going to stop that and as a team, let's come together to help her," said Scott. He still had his arm in a cast but wanted to be there.

"Now, let's go out there and win this thing," I said.

"For Crystal!" they all said and ran out the doors and onto the field. The fans were cheering with them.

"Well, Crystal, are you ready to win this thing?" the coach asked.

"I sure am," I said and headed out to the field with the rest of the team. I could hear the fans yelling my name, and the other side was trying to overpower it, but they didn't have enough to overcome it. With the remarkable team on the other side kicking the ball to start the next half, and after they ran it to the thirty-yard line, I ran out onto the field to see what I could do.

During the first half, we got back one of the touchdowns, but the other one couldn't have gotten which the other team didn't score because our defense kept them from doing anything, so it would give me a chance to do something.

As the fourth quarter was starting, we had the ball, and I had the get the ball across the field. I had a play that could work right here.

"All right, we have fifteen minutes to get two touchdowns, so here's the play. All we need to do is keep the ball moving and make it to the end zone, which I know we can do; now, let's go for it." I said, and we broke the huddle and went to the ball.

As I snapped the ball and tossed it to Silverie, she ran down the field, and before she got tackled, she handed the ball off to someone else. He ran down the area, and they kept tossing the ball until it got to Randall. I was beside her until she threw me the ball, and I had no one near me, and I ran full speed to the end zone while the crowd was getting louder as I got closer. I had someone catching up to me, but when he leaped for me, I sidestepped, and he fell to the ground. I went across the line for a touchdown. The team ran up to me, cheering and patting me on the back as I made my way to the sidelines. Still, before I was able to get off the field, one of the other players hit me right in the back and took me down hard; the ref was right there, and he threw the flag, and that player was not to be back on the field for the rest of the game.

As he walked away from me, I was not moving that much. When I got on my back, I felt a pop, and I hurt like a bullet hitting me, and it was my leg. I looked at it a saw that it was out of place, and I could not move it, and Kristen came over there.

"Did your leg just pop out of place?" she asked.

"How do you know what's wrong with her?" the coach asked.

"Because I'm her twin, and I can feel the pain in my leg, and I can help her," she said and pulled my leg out so that she could put it back in place and then looked back at me.

"Are you ready?" she asked.

"Go for it," I said, and she pushed my leg back the other way, and I felt the pop again. This time, it hurts more than when it went out.

"Damn it, that hurts," I said.

"Yeah, I know," Kristen said, and she was laughing.

"What are you laughing about, huh? you want me to do that to you?" I said.

"Here, let me help you up," she said and took my hand and pulled me up off the ground; the crowd clapped their hands as I sat down on the bench.

"Are you going to be able to finish the game?" the coach asked.

"Yeah, just tell the defense to wear that clock down so we can win the game," I said, and he did.

When I got back out on the field, the clock had two minutes left, and both teams tied the score. I had to wear that clock down even more, so I did by throwing some passes and then running the ball.

As the clock neared twenty seconds, I called our last timeout to stop it and get the team together.

"All right, we need to make this twenty-yard run to make a touchdown and win the game. Let's make it happen; no matter what happens, we are still winners." I said and headed back out on the field.

The play was for me to run the ball to the end zone while the other team would tackle other players that they thought had the ball, and it would work just like that.

When I snapped the ball and faked it to Randall, the players went after her and held it to where they couldn't see it. The ref knew I still had the ball, but the other team didn't, and when they finally tackled Randall and saw that she didn't have the ball, they came after me.

"And this is when I start running," I said and bolted for the end zone as the clock read ten seconds left. I couldn't go as fast as I wanted to because of my leg, but I still managed to make it to the line, but the other team tackled me, and I saw that I was going over the line, but I had about ten players all over me as the clock ran out.

As the players were slowly getting off me, the ref saw that I was across the line, and the ball was too. He called it a touchdown, and my team came running to me and picked me off the ground. They carried me on their shoulders, and I saw some of them pouring water on the coach, and when they sat me back down, they did the same to me. The fans cheered me for the win, and the refs handed me the cup. I held it high to show the fans that we won the game.

As the fans slowly emerged from the stands, I felt a strange wind. So, I headed around the corner to change morph to my dragon form because I knew it would be Tasha and her bunch by now. I was right because as soon as I transformed, they appeared.

They went after the fans and flew around them when they came out of their time warp. They were making them run into each other as I approached.

"Leave them alone," I said.

"Oh well, now there's the girl who ruined my plan last time. You are going to pay for it now," she said and threw something at me, but I dodged it.

"You must be quicker than that if you want to get me," I said, and she tried it again. She kept missing every time, and by this time, Randall, Silverie, and Kristen joined the fight.

"All right, let's get them," Randall said, and we went after them with our swords drawn, and we went to fighting. Randall went after Laura, Silverie went after Sapphire's clone, and Kristen and I went after Tasha, and she managed to make another clone of herself somehow. I fought her clone, but this battle was the toughest one so far.

Randall and Silverie were getting hit more than they were hitting Laura. Sapphire and Kristen weren't doing any better, and I was having a rough time too. However, I was able to knock out Tasha's clone, but as soon as I went to help out one of the girls, she would hit me, and I would go back at her and knock her back out, and this time I threw her to the ground, and Tasha saw it.

"I'm going to get you for that," she said and did some magic spells on Kristen. She fell right out of the sky, came after me, and hit me right in the face. The other girls lost their battle as we fought and moved around in the sky with our swords striking one another. Mine was still going strong, and as Tasha swung her sword, I ducked and hit her in the side of the head, knocking her out, but before I could get away, she somehow still did a spell on me, and it hit me, making me lose my flying ability. I was going headfirst to the ground. I hit the ground hard, and Tasha landed next to me. She watched as I got up from the fall.

"This will be the last time you can fight me, girl," she said and threw a black crystal. I tried to move, but I couldn't. It seemed a spell she used on me had made it to where I couldn't move, and the crystal was coming my way. So, I closed my eyes, but it never did hit me. I heard someone else scream in pain, and when I opened my eyes, I saw that Kristen had taken the crystal, and she had de-morphed in front of me.

Tasha was unhappy because Kristen freed me from my statue, and I flew up into the sky. I was trying to help the others, but it was too late because the same thing that happened to Kristen also happened to them. Then, they surrounded me, and Tasha had one more in her hands.

"Now I will give you a choice, you either power down and not try to do any hero stuff, or I'll throw this at you, making you powerless. Your choice," she said, and I thought about it and came up with an answer.

"Okay, I guess I'll power down," I said and felt my crystal make me look at Tasha because she had the main black crystal inside her. Then, I knew what I had to do.

"But not before I do this," I said. I got my sword and went for the crystal to destroy it. She cried in pain as the black crystal that she was holding just vaporized into thin air. She fell back, and I flew away, but

I didn't get far from them when Tasha came up behind me and hit me with her magic sending shock waves through my body, deactivating my crystal making and me de-morph right in the air over the fans. I fell straight to the ground right in front of everybody, and the others came to my side to see if I was okay.

"I'll get up next time, girls," Tasha said, and they flew back into the time portal and disappeared soon after that.

As I got onto my feet, everyone saw who I was, and they just turned and started walking away from me.

"How could you not tell us?" I turned around and saw that my mother was right behind me.

"I would have, but it's complicated," I said.

"I told you to never lie to me about anything. Do you remember me saying that?" Mom asked.

"Yes, but I-"

"You heard what I said," she said and walked past me.

"How could you hurt your friends?" I knew that it was Laura and I turned to her.

"I'm sorry I couldn't tell you the truth about me," I said.

"Well, since you are all about secrets, then I guess we can't be friends," she said and walked off. Then, Steve came into the picture.

"Oh, don't be mad at me, babe. I'm sorry that I kept it a secret from you too." I said, but when I went to hug him, he pushed me off.

"I'm sorry, but I don't talk to people who play games and not tell them what they need to know about ahead of time. I can't date a girl who cannot tell their boyfriend everything. Bye." he said and walked off. He left me there, and the rain started to pour. Everybody ran to their cars while I walked back to the bus. As I got on the bus, everyone stared at me like I was a terrible person. So, I just sat down in the front and started crying. I couldn't remember when I stopped because I fell asleep shortly after that.

Chapter 11

The following day when I got up, I thought about what had happened the night before. I was going to dread going downstairs to see my mother not talk to me. So, when I headed into the living room and saw her sitting in her chair, she saw me. She looked right back at the newspaper and didn't say anything. Dad did the same thing as well. So, I headed out to the backyard to see what Kristen was doing.

"Hey, there, sleepy head. It's about time you get up," she said.

"Is Mom and Dad mad at me?" I asked.

"Yep, they sure are. They asked me if I knew anything about it, but I told them no. Why, of all places, would they show up there?" Kristen asked.

"They wanted my friends to see who I was and make them not like me," I said.

"Oh, so that's why." Steve came by earlier this morning," she said.

"And what did he want?" I asked.

"He told me to tell you not to speak to him at school and to give him a ring back that is on your hand," she said, and it was still there.

"Oh, okay, anything else happened?" I asked.

"Nope, that's about it. I'm just trying to keep the siblings outside because Dad and Mom told me they don't need to hear them talking to you in about ten minutes," she said.

"What do you mean?" I asked, but she didn't have time to tell me. My Dad grabbed my arm, pulled me inside, and sat me down on the couch, and my Mom looked mad.

"Now, I want to know why this book is in your room." Dad said and laid a book on the table. It was the book that Silverie had given me.

"I got it from the library," I said.

"Don't play dumb with me, I know where it came from, and it wasn't the library.

Your sister out there told us about it last night because we saw her too. So, where did it come from?" he asked.

"A friend gave it to me," I said.

"Okay, which one? and you better tell me the right answer," he said, getting mad every time he said something.

"It came from Silverie," I said. "Well, that answers one question of mine. Now, here's another one. Is Silverie from this time, or is she from the future?" he asked.

"From the future," I said.

"And how did you end up being a dragon thing in the first place?" he asked, but I didn't know how to tell him.

"I was given this bottle with a potion inside to take, and I just became one in minutes," I said, and by this time, I was on the verge of crying.

"Okay, now, was there any way of telling her no to it," he asked.

"No, there wasn't," I said in a teary voice.

"Well, here is what will happen, you are grounded, you are only allowed to go to school and give the keys to your mother when you get home. Next, no cell phone until I can trust you again, and the only people you can talk to are the one that calls the home phone, and even then, you are not to answer the phone. Lastly, you are not to go out with anybody unless your mother or I go with you. Lastly, you can go out with family members only. If any of these get broken, you will get punished big time. Silverie and Randall cannot enter the house, and you cannot open the door for them." he said and looked at my mother.

"You have anything to add?" he asked.

"Not at the moment, but I'll think of something later," she said.

"Now, give me your phone and keys," he said, and I handed him both.

"Now, you may go do what you want to," he said, and I ran up to my room crying the whole way and slammed the door shut. I fell on my bed and just moped.

About a minute later, Dad came into the room. "Oh, I forgot, no internet and computer," he said. Then, Dad got the phone line and the power cords and took my cable box. "And no box, but I'll let you have what stations you can pick up with your tv," he said and walked out of the room.

The whole weekend went to hell because of what happened that Friday, but going to school on Monday was going to be any better. The students that did like me didn't even bother to tell me hi or anything to me, which I wasn't expecting them to do anyways.

So, I walked down to the field house to see what the guys would say. When I walked into the building, not even one talked to me about what happened the other night. They came up and just spoke to me, happy about the championship game. Then, Scott came to talk to me.

"Hey girl, a good game you played out there," he said.

"Aren't you mad at me?" I asked.

"About what? Oh, that? No, I'm not mad at you about that. I don't see why anybody would be. Everyone has a dark secret that they can't tell anybody. Heck! Everyone on this team has something like that and won't tell anybody unless they know you are not going to tell anybody else about it." he said.

"Oh, the students would not say anything to me out there," I said.

"Hey, don't worry about them. Just know that you helped this team get what they have been for this season." Scott said.

"Yeah, I guess your right about that," I said. I saw Randall sitting on the bench, and I sat down beside her.

"Hey there," I said.

"Hey," she said.

"What? did your parents ground you, too," I asked.

"Yup, they sure did. They took away everything from me but my clothes and make-up," she said.

"Hey, the same thing happened to me, so don't feel down because I don't like to see you this way," I said.

"Well, did you hear about Silverie," she asked.

"No, I didn't." I said, "Well, I heard that some guys took her away and are looking at her and stuff, but she managed to get away from them, and now I don't know where she could be at now." she said.

"Don't worry; she'll return to school when she can. You must understand that she is a full-blood dragon girl, and it's hard to hide it from anybody." I said.

"Yeah, well, don't let me pull you down," she said.

"Who said anything about pulling me down? I'm pulling you up." I said, grabbed her arm, and got her to stand up and have fun.

After about ten minutes, the coach walked up to me.

"That was a good season that you played, Crystal; I have been getting calls from schools from all over the US wanting you to play at their college and the university also," he said.

"Well, I'm trendy, but I think I'm going to stay with the one in Tyler, coach," I said.

"They also called and want you to come to their college to talk to the football team," he said.

"I'm not talking about Tyler Junior College; I'm talking about the University of Texas in Tyler," I said.

"Oh okay, well they haven't called me yet," he said.

"What do you mean by that, coach?" I asked.

"Well, it seems they don't want you to play for them," he said.

"That can't be right," I said.

"Well, you can give them a call yourself, but they may just say no," he said, and I went to call them. After I talked to them, they told me why they didn't want me because of what happened after the game, and that was why they said no to me. "Well, there goes to that school;

I'll just go to the other one and prove that I can play there," I said, and the bell rang. I knocked on the door and went to AG class.

As I walked into the class, I saw that everyone looked at me but didn't say anything. So, I just sat down in a chair away from Steve because he still looked mad at me, and then Kristen walked in and sat next to me.

"Hey there," she said.

"Hey." I said, "Man, you wouldn't believe what people say about you.

They're saying that you are the best player that the football team has had in ten years. They are also going to do something, but they thought I was you, so they didn't say it in front of me." she said.

"That's about right, huh? They thought you were me. It seems they still can't tell us apart from one another." I said the teacher had walked in then, and the bell rang.

"All right, class, you have six weeks before the AG show. I won't be here late from here on out like last year. So, let's get out there and get busy." he said, and I headed out the door and went to the trailer. As I made my way to it, I noticed we still had a way before we were even ready to paint it. The pit was almost ready to go; I just had to finish up on a few things. As I looked at the trailer, I saw that the rail system was in place. So, I had to measure how far apart they were and ensured it was the same up the front so the pit won't have any problems getting up there. After checking, I returned to the BBQ pit, measured it, and saw that it would be a close fit, but I could make it work.

"What's wrong, Crystal?" Kristen asked.

"Ohh, I was trying to see if this pit would go all the way up on the trailer. I think it will until about two-thirds of the way up. It seems it's knocked in about a quarter inch, and that will be hell getting that out." I said.

"Well, you work on the pit while I take it out," Kristen said as she grabbed a sledgehammer and went to work while I did some finishing touches on the legs of the pit and then put on the wheels that would make it go up and down on the trailer.

After about twenty minutes of banging, Kristen got it straight. I looked up, and it was just right, but I wouldn't be sure until I tested the pit. Then, she came to help me out on the BBQ pit the get it ready to go on there. The BBQ pit weighed about three hundred pounds, and I couldn't pick it up three feet off the ground. So, earlier in the month, I put together pull-out ramps extending about five feet out, making it easier for the winch to pull up there.

As the winch was linked up to it and began pushing the pit up the ramp and onto the trailer, it was doing good so far, but to ensure that it would not fall off, I stepped behind it and prepared in case the cable on the winch snapped.

Then came the big test, where the bend was, would the pit continue, or would it get stuck and not go anywhere? As it went over the spot, it kept going until it got to the front and stopped.

"Well, that is a good thing," I said.

"Yep, we can work on something to make it much more stable up there," Kristen said.

"Yeah, but that can wait until tomorrow because I think it's time to get ready for the next period," I said, and I was right because when I looked at my watch, it was already time. We headed inside the classroom.

As the bell rang, I headed out. Steve never said a word to me as I passed his sight and went to the fourth-year hall to attend English class and to see if Laura was going to be in a better mood than she was. Unfortunately, she was not happy to see me. She didn't say a word to me the whole time we were in class. The teacher told us to do something that day, so I didn't have to worry about being partnered up with her.

During the class, I wondered how Silverie was doing and if she would ever return. Also, if my friends would accept me for who I am without judgment. As the class ended, the bell rang for us to head to the next class, Economics class. Steve and Kyle were in there, and so was Laura, and I just sat somewhere away from them. Kristen was in there, and she sat next to me to keep me company so I wouldn't feel left out of the class.

During that class, the teacher made us work with another person in the room. However, there needed to be more for that. So, one group needs to have three, but Steve's group got that, so I partnered up with Kristen, and we worked better together than anyone else because we share the same mind. Hence, we can do things faster than by ourselves.

The bell rang after forty minutes. Kristen and I headed out to lunch. They had banners with me holding the cup as we entered the cafeteria. They clapped their hands and called my sister and me to go to the front line and get our food first. No one treated me this way back at my old school because the team was always good no matter what.

So, when we got our food and walked outside, more students were doing the same. When we sat at a different table, they came flocking over there and sat down with us or just stood there talking to us while my ex-friends were staring, maybe wondering how this could be happening right in front of their eyes. I didn't let it bother me because I would enjoy this if I could until they lost interest in me.

As the day went on, they threw a special prep rally for the team to win the championship game.

At the prep rally, I walked in front of the whole student body and had to talk to them.

"You know, this would not be happening if it wasn't for all of your support out last Friday. The team has come a long way from what they were, and I'm pleased about it. When I arrived, and the team saw me in their field house, I knew it was not usual to see a female play football around here. Still, after a while, when they saw me helping them win game after game, they started thinking differently about me and accepting me as their teammate rather than as an outcast. It has been something seeing this team like they are now. They have gotten the teamwork down, and they can go on into college, take the stuff they have learned, and use it for the next team they will play for." I said and handed the mic to the principal.

"Now, Crystal, the student body wanted to do something special for you today, so they put what they could in a donation to get you this right here," she said and pointed behind the stage. I saw someone covered up and when I turned to see who it was, it was Kelly Clarkson!

"Oh, my goodness, it's my favorite singer. How did you find out?" I asked. "Your sister, of course," Kelly said.

"Oh my, this must be the best day of my life; I've always wanted to meet you live," I said.

"Well, why don't you and your sister come up here on the stage with me, and we can see a few songs you should know. Do you know them by heart?" she asked.

"Ohh yeah, every one of them," I said, and Kristen got up on the stage, and all of the students came running, and that's when her security guards blocked the stage off so that no one else could get up there. Then, we sang all the songs she had on the radio, and no one could tell the difference in whose voice she was singing.

As we finished the last song, I saw a bright light hit my eye and saw that someone in the school had a gun and was pointed right at Kelly.

"Look out, Kelly!" I shouted and knocked her to the ground. The gun went off and missed her by inches away as it hit the wall behind her.

"Whoa, that was close. Thank you for doing that," Kelly said.

"Anytime, now if you excuse me, I'm going to stop that man," I said, and I hopped off the stage while everyone was running to get out of the doors. I was also trying to do the same thing.

By the time I got out to see where he had gone, I had heard a bullet had reflected off the building right next to me, and I looked to my left and saw him running down the driveway. Then, I went after him. The run only lasted about a minute when he hopped into a car and came after me. I had no choice but to go the other direction and run into the trees next to the road so that if he was to shoot at me, they might miss me and hit one of the trees.

As I came out on the other side and looked behind me, I saw that it was Brandon with his friends. They had guns, and I saw that I was only about ten feet away from my car, so I ran to it.

As I did, I unlocked it, and the door opened so I could hop right in and get out of there to keep Kelly safe from these guys. They were behind me in their car and shooting their guns at me as I drove out.

As the chase continued, I tried my best to get some cops involved so they could stop him and put him back behind bars. However, I was having no luck until, out of nowhere, one almost pulled out in front of me while doing one hundred and ten on a highway with Brandon right behind me doing the same. Then, the cop followed with his lights until Brandon took him out, and he spun out into the grass. I had to do something to make him flip his car. I slowed down just enough to make it on-ramp and hit it, going about sixty. When I finished the turn, I got back up to speed and looked back to see that he was still hot on my tail. So, I sped up again and went around the loop to where the dead end was. I knew that this was where one of us would get hurt, and hopefully, it would be him. As I got to the end of the road, I just kept it in full throttle and closed my eyes. Then, I hit the brakes and hoped I would make it out. When I finally came to a stop, I heard someone crashing, and when I opened my eyes, I saw that Brandon's car was flying in the air and landed about twenty feet away from me while I was safely sitting in a field of grass with no scratches on my vehicle. Then, I heard sirens coming down the road, and I got out of my car to check on Brandon.

As I made my way up to him, I saw that he was hurt badly and his buddies. He smiled when he saw me.

"You know, you are one tough person to hurt, but I will say, I have never seen anyone drive like you. If you were seconds late, you might not be alive now because that truck missed your back end by inches. That's why I'm the one who hits him." he said.

"Why are you doing this to me?" I asked.

"Well, I wanted my revenge on you for what you did back then, but it looks like I won't be able to do it now," he said, and the cops arrived. Then, they came over to the car and opened the door to get Brandon out, but he had internal bleeding.

"Sir, are you okay?" they asked him.

"I don't think so," he said.

"Where are you hurt?" the officer asked.

"He has internal bleeding near his stomach. He is losing blood and only has about an hour to live unless you can get him to a hospital now." I said.

"How do you know that?" the officer asked. "I'm just that good, sir." I said, "Well, can you tell me about these other two also." he asked, "Well, this one is suffering from a head injury, and he should live with minor brain problems, and this one has some internal bleeding but not as bad as him but still needs to be treated in Tyler also." I said, and when the ambulance showed up to see what was wrong, they didn't believe what I said. They didn't know that with my powers, I could somehow sense injuries in their bodies, but with Silverie not being there, I couldn't ask her.

"Well, why don't you check his arms and legs and see if you see any veins popping out," I said, and they couldn't see any. "Okay, well, I guess you are better than us, and we will get him to Tyler right now," they said, putting him in the ambulance and getting him out of there. Then, they worked on the other two boys and put them into the other one. By that time, Kristen showed up with Kelly riding with her.

"See? I told you she can drive extremely well." Kristen said.

"Oh, stop it; you're making me blush," I said.

"Well, it's nice to see that you are all right and if there's anything I can do, just let me know," she said.

"There is," I said.

"And what would that be?" she asked.

"You will find out," I said, and then the officer pulled me to the side to find out what happened. I told him everything, and I walked back up to her.

"I would like you to come to my house because my Dad has wanted to see you for the longest time," I said.

"You would have to say that, wouldn't you? Okay, let's go to your house and meet them," she said and got into my car. Then, we headed there with her crew right behind Kristen. I parked the car and ran to the door as we got to the house. Dad and Mom were sitting in the living room watching TV.

"Hey, Dad, I have someone you've wanted to meet," I said, and he looked my way. Then, when the door opened, he saw it was Kelly Clarkson. His eyes looked happy. He got up out of his chair and went up to her to shake her hand.

"I'm so happy to meet you in person, Kelly, finally," he said.

"Well, thank you for that. Crystal told me you always wanted to meet me," she said.

"Yeah, and so are my wife and the kids," he said and motioned to Mom. Then, the kids came running in to see what was happening.

After about an hour of talking and stuff, Kelly had to get going on the road and bid everyone goodbye. Then, I followed her out to the bus.

"How will I stay in contact with you?" I asked.

"Well, here is my number. You can give me a call whenever you feel like you need to talk to someone," Kelly said.

"Okay, I sure will," I said and started walking off until she said something else. "Crystal, if you ever need a job and are out of school, give me a call, and I'll put you as one of my singers," she said.

"All right, I'll keep that in mind," I said, and she hugged me.

"Take care now," she said.

"You too," I said, and she got on the bus and left just like that.

As the week went by, and the news of me being a superstar for the football team slowly started to fade, the students began to not come around me anymore, which I already expected to happen. My old friends didn't say hi or anything to me for that matter, and I figured by now they would at least wave to me, but every time I see them, they look away.

When I made my way to A.G. class that Friday, I wanted to know if the rest of my project would be there so that I could finish it and get it ready for the show. But when I walked in, the teacher was sitting at his desk, and he called me to talk.

"Hey Crystal, you know you only have about three weeks to get that ready. Are you sure you will finish it on time?" he asked.

"Yeah, I should be able to if I can get the wood by Monday next week," I said. "Okay, well, they said they would be here today to drop it off, but it hasn't arrived yet. I'll let you know when it does," he said, and I walked back to my seat and waited for Kristen to arrive.

She was almost late when the bell rang. She was running in the doorway and sat down.

"It's a mad house out there in the hallway today. It seems like everybody is trying to stop and talk to me, asking about you and what happened the other day," she said.

"Well, read the newspaper and find out," I said.

"They wanted me to ask you how one hundred and ten feels like," she said. "If they want to know that, they should try it themselves and see what it's like," I said, and then the teacher told us to go outside and work on the projects to prepare them for the show.

When I got into the shop, some of the small trailers were not there, and some picnic tables were getting loaded on some trucks to take them home and take care of them until the show. Mine was still there and needed work; I only had five weeks to complete it. I had about another week on it before it was ready to be painted, and still, it would take about another week to get in there to get the paint. It took me about four days to prepare it, which would leave me about one week to ensure everything was complete before we showed it to the judges.

So, I told Kristen what we needed to do to prepare it. We started working on the pit to ensure that attachments would secure it to the trailer by putting bars around the front and attaching a heavy lock on it, which took about twenty minutes when Mr. Ingram came in there to tell us something.

"Hey girls, come on out here. I have something that belongs to you," he said. So, we got off the trailer and followed him.

As we got out there, I saw that the wood had finally arrived, and he was going to put it as close as he could to the doors so that we didn't have to walk far to carry it.

"Good, it's about time it shows up. Now, we can work on getting it on the trailer." I said. Then, I carried it two at a time and set it on the trailer until it was all completed. After that, I went to work putting the floor in until it was time to get ready. I had about half of the foundation laid out but still needed to nail it down, which I would have to worry about next week.

As February was starting, Valentine's Day was special for me because I would receive something every year from a guy who had a crush on me or some friend who was pleasant to me. Still, the guys I have dated in the past always gave me the same thing every year, but as the week of the fourteenth started, they were handing out roses to some girls for the first two days. I was waiting for mine to come from Steve, but his rose never appeared. I was hoping he didn't call it quits on me just because of a little problem that happened almost a month ago. However, it seems like he did. So, I was going to talk to him during lunch to see what was happening. That next day when I got to AG class, I saw Steve talking to Kyle. I sat right before him to see what he would say, but when he turned to me, he just turned right back the other way, which I had about had with him.

"Steve, what's your problem?" I asked, and he turned around.

"Well, I don't like people lying to me, especially from someone I'm dating," he said.

"Oh, so you are talking about that thing. Well, it's hard to tell someone when it doesn't need to know because I might share it with the wrong person, and I would end up being some scientist's special project to see what my limits are and see if scientists can improve on them." I said.

"Well, you could have a least told me that," he said.

"I just couldn't," I said.

"Well then, I don't think we need to be dating anymore because I can't trust you to tell me the truth about you," he said.

"What? you are breaking up with me?" I asked.

"You didn't hear me the first time when I said it? It is over between us. Also, don't bother talking to Laura or any of my friends, for that matter." He turned back around to continue talking with Kyle.

Afterward, I returned to my seat and put my head on my desk while waiting outside to work on the project. Then, Kristen saw me with my head down and sat beside me.

"Hey girl, what's wrong?" she asked.

"Steve just broke up with me," I said in a low crying voice.

"Oh no, please tell me that's not true," she said.

"We just did right before you walked in, and not only that. I also can't talk to any of Steve's friends either." I said.

"Oh no, I don't think so. Let me talk to Steve," she said and walked over to Steve. I watched the whole thing, and, in the end, Steve just told her to butt out of his business and didn't say anything else to him. She walked back over to me and sat back down.

"Well, he wants to be a no-good person to my sister. So be it. I know what drives him out there, and I'm going to make him pay for it." she said.

"No, don't do anything that would make you regret it," I said.

"Oh, don't worry about that. I'm just going to do some markings on Steve's car that would make him think twice about hurting you again or any girl for that matter," she said, and then the teacher walked in for told us to head outside to work on our projects.

As I went out to see what was still in there, I noticed that my trailer was the only one left. I need to get all the wood nailed down to make it shine by applying varnish. But I was not really in the mood to do that because Steve just kicked me to the curb due to the situation. I'll find out later what will happen. Right now, my priority is to finish my trailer and get it done before the final week so that I can put up the tired on it and get it outside the paint room.

As Kristen worked on one side, while I was working on the other side of the trailer, we were going down every five feet and putting nails in, which we were doing good timing on it, but before we got about to have way, I heard Mr. Ingram calling for me and so I got off the trailer and went to him.

"All right, Crystal, how much more do you need to finish?" he asked.

"Well, I still need to put some varnish on, put the tires on, and get it out here," I said.

"So, that would put you at about two weeks before it gets out here. Okay, I'm just checking because students would completely paint these trailers by the time they get out here, so you can start on it as soon as you get it out here," he said and told me that I could go back to my work.

When I got back in there, I saw Kristen finished with her side, so I went to work my side to catch up with her. It took me another ten minutes with her help. But I finished it before class was over. Tomorrow, we were going to start applying varnish. When the bell rang, I made my way out of the room and headed to English class. I saw that Laura was right in front of me. I wanted to talk to her, but she didn't give a damn when I called her.

So, when we entered the classroom, I confronted her. "Hey Laura, what is going on here with us?" I asked, and again, she turned away.

"It's not me; you can't tell your friends the truth," she said.

"So, you're saying I should have told you about the Dragon thing?" I asked.

"Yeah, that might have something to do with it," she said.

"Well, I can't tell anybody about it because it's supposed to be a secret between the other dragon girls and me," I said.

"And who are these others?" she asked.

"I'm not going to tell their names to you," I said.

"Well, if you can't tell me who they are. How can I trust you again? We are no longer friends." she said and turned away. Then, the bell rang, and the teacher walked back in to start teaching. However, I lost interest and started daydreaming.

During class, I saw that Laura looked mad at me every time I look at her way. I couldn't help myself because I wanted to know the real reason behind all of this, which I told her, and that caused her to snap and fight me. She leaped out of her chair and knocked me right out of my chair. Then, she started hitting me until I knocked her off and went for the door.

Still, she pushed me, and I hit the door hard. I fell backward onto the floor, and she pulled me up by my hair and hit me right in the face. The doorknob turned to open when I flew out the door making the person behind it hit the wall and fall to the floor.

As I was trying to get up, Laura came after me again. However, this time, I moved, and she smacked right into the wall and knocked herself out. Then, the teacher came out to see what had happened. They wanted to take me to the office, but I told them that she had started it, but still, they wanted to take me instead. I had no choice in the matter. This time when they took us both, they knew to keep us separated because she would try her best to get me again, but somehow, she managed to get away from the teacher and then came after me again. The teacher released me so I could run through the hall to escape her. After a while, the teacher came out to see where she was and when she saw them, she ran from them, still looking for me, but Laura didn't know that I was behind some cars until she arrived around the corner and saw me. She crouched there and came after me. Then, I got up and ran the other way. Then, the teachers were right behind her to stop her. I kept running for a while and tried to lose her in the building, but it was no use, she was always right behind me, and everyone classroom noticed it.

After a few minutes of running, I was tired and wanted to take a break, but I couldn't because she was right behind me. Then I saw she was getting tired as well, but that didn't stop her from doing anything until she had me in her hands. I won't let that happen. When I arrived at the corner, I was unaware of the wet floor, so I slipped and slid about ten feet. Then, Laura came around and did the same thing, but she hit the wall instead of me. She did not move for a while, which gave me a chance to get out.

I was in a restroom hiding from Laura and trying to calm myself down before I walked back there. After a while, I didn't hear anything. So, I walked over to the door and opened it to see the teacher carrying her right there. I stayed there to ensure they didn't see me, which they didn't. So, I walked out of the restroom and went down the hall.

As I returned to the classroom, I heard something strange, but it wasn't the girls. I heard some guys talking, and I looked out the door to see about ten guys dressed in back holding AK-49 guns, and they looked inside to see me, and then I ran with bullets going off behind me.

"Oh man, this is not my day," I said as I ran down the hall, trying to escape the guys.

"Come back here, little girl," one of the guys said, and I just kept running until I turned the corner, saw a door open, and ran inside to find out that there was an ongoing class. Then, the teacher caught me.

"Who are you?" she asked.

"Don't worry about that, miss," I said and saw a door in the back of the room and ran to it. When I looked back, I saw the guys looking in and had their guns raised as I ran into the next room with them following and shooting at me. As I made my way, I saw a door and went in it. Then, I locked it, hoping they wouldn't find me.

"Crystal, wake up. It's time for you to go to your next class." said the teacher. I somehow fell asleep in the classroom because the class was empty.

"What happened?" I asked.

"You just fell asleep; I saw that you were tired, so I just let you catch up on some sleep," she said.

"I had the craziest dream ever," I said.

"I bet you did." Go ahead and get to your next class before you are late," the teacher said. I got up, walked out the door, and went to my next class. Kristen was waiting for me.

"Hey girl, what happened in there?" she asked.

"I just fell asleep, that's all," I said.

"Well, it's good that you didn't have to watch that dream in your head like I had to," she said.

"You mean that you saw the whole thing?" I asked.

"Yep, every bit of it. You were starting to scare me there for a second. I thought you were not going to wake up before those guys got you." she said.

"Well, I didn't know that I fell asleep in there. I just got woken up by the teacher." I said.

"Well, don't do that again," she said.

"All right, I'll try not to," I said, and the teacher gave us by-partner activities that would take about four weeks. We stayed there for about forty minutes until it was time to go to lunch. When I got my food and went back outside to sit down at a table, I saw that Steve and Laura were nowhere near me and the only other person that was sitting with me was my sister, which I knew would always be there for me like I'm also there for her no matter what happens.

"Hey Kristen, what are you going to do for prom? You know it's only about six weeks away." I asked.

"Well, I would like to go with someone, but he has someone, so I think I will go by myself," she said.

"What happened to the last guy that you were dating?" I asked.

"Oh, he broke up with me about three days ago. He said we were not going anywhere with the relationship," Kristen said.

"Oh, well, we are in the same boat, are we not?" I asked.

"You can say that," she said, and out of nowhere, someone threw some plastic and hit me in the head. I looked at where it came from, and some guy was laughing.

"Oh, you think that's funny, huh?" I said.

"Hey now, come on. Don't let people get on your nerves," Kristen said.

"Well, I hate it when people do that to me," I said.

"Well, just pretend that he is not here and continue with your life, girl," she said, and I did. He left me alone after that. As lunch ended, the students moved around, and I walked to my next class. Kristen was walking beside me.

"Is your class this way?" I asked.

"Of course, silly. I stayed behind to talk to some friends, but they were not around. So, I'm just walking beside you to make sure no one else bothers you for the time being." she said.

"Thank you, Kristen," I said.

"Hey, I will always be here beside you when you need me," she said, and we kept talking the rest of the way until she had to go inside her class while I still had to walk more before I got to mine.

Over the next two weeks of school, the trailer was almost ready to go. All we needed to do was put the paint on it and inspect it one last time. That Friday was the time to put it in the paint shop, put on the primer, and then come back with black paint. Then, finish it with pin strips down the side and make symbols down simultaneously.

I made my way into the class, and the teacher told us to head outside. I waited for him to come out, used a forklift, picked up the front of it, moved it out there, and got in the shop.

"Okay, Kristen, are you ready to do this?" I asked.

"I don't know if I can. I never painted before, and I don't want to mess it up," Kristen said.

"Don't worry. This paint is just the primer that we are putting on. It doesn't matter if you do it wrong here. When we put the black on next is what you need to be careful with." I said.

"All right, but you may have to help me with it," she said.

"I'll show you how to use this, all right," I told her to put on her mask and check to ensure that she could breathe through it before we started. Then, I showed her how to put the paint in the sprayer and onto the trailer. I made a few side-to-side motions then and gave them to her. She learned in about five minutes and was doing a great job. I started on the other side, and we worked down the trailer until we got all the outsides done, but we still had the inside part of doing the trailer. I told her I would do it because teaching somebody how to paint while on their back is difficult.

After we finished all the white, we had about ten minutes to go, so I told her to stop and go ahead. I also told her to take off her mask and not breathe until she is outside, or she can wait until she is outside, then she can take off her cover.

As we got out there, we started walking back to the classroom, and she talked to me about it.

"Man, that was easy to do," she said.

"Yeah, that part is, but wait until we start putting on the black paint on Monday if no one messes with it before," I said.

"What do you mean by that?" she said.

"Well, the paint is going to take almost one whole day to dry, and during that time, that trailer cannot have any wind on it, or it would make the paint run making me go back over it again to try and get it out," I said.

"Oh, okay. I didn't know all about this painting stuff," Kristen said.

"Don't worry. I'll teach you everything you need to learn." I said, and by that time, we were already in the classroom waiting for the bell to ring. Suddenly, Kristen went to the restroom. I couldn't figure out why until I felt sick to my stomach. So, I went in there to see what was going on.

When I got in there, I saw that she was in the last stall, and when I opened the door, I noticed that she was sick, which was also making me sick.

"Hey, are you okay?" I asked.

"Not really. I think I have the flu," Kristen said, and she got sick again.

"Come on, let's get you to the office and get you home," I said, putting one of her arms on my shoulder and helping walk her out of the restroom. We went straight to the office while Allie was carrying our stuff.

When we got there, I told Allie, "thank you," and she said, no problem and went to her next class. A teacher came to us and asked, "What can we do for you?"

"My sister has the flu and needs to get home," I said.

"Well, she seems to be too sick to drive home. Is there anybody that can come and get her?" she asked.

"You can try our Mom; she might be home now," I said,

"Okay, I'll go check on that, and I'll get back to you," she said and walked off.

"Where is she going?" Kristen asked.

"She's going to see if Mom is home and if she is, then she'll get her to come and get you," I said.

"Okay," she said and leaned against me. We waited for the teacher to get back. It didn't take long before she came back to tell us that Mom was on her way and would arrive in about ten minutes.

"Okay, thank you," I said. "Also, you can go back to class. We got Kristen from here," she said.

"Oh no, I will stay with my sister until our mother arrives," I said.

"I told you we've got it from here," she said.

"And I told you I'm not leaving until our mother shows up, and that's the last time I'll say it," I said.

"Miss, just let her stay with me. I'm doing better with her here by my side." Kristen said.

"Okay, I'll just let you be, and I'll just write you a note telling you where you are for your teacher," she said.

"Thank you," I said, and she walked off. After about ten minutes, mother walked into the building and saw us in the office.

"Oh, there you are, Kristen," she said as she walked in.

"Thank you, Crystal, for being here with her," she said.

"It's my life to ensure that nothing bad happens to her," I said.

"Okay, I'll meet you at the house, and we need to talk about something. It's nothing bad," she said.

"Okay, Mom, bye," I said, and she hugged me and walked out with Kristen. "Here's your note, Crystal." said the teacher.

"Thank you," I said, walked out of the office, and went to my next class. As I walked down the hall and entered the classroom, I felt a little lonelier without Kristen, but I knew there was a reason. I didn't let it get to me until lunch came, and that guy was doing the same thing, but I never gave him any attention while I was eating my lunch.

When lunch was over, and I was walking down to my next class, some students were walking behind me, still throwing some things at me. I was tired of it, but I kept walking like they were not there.

As the day was ending, the same students were behind me, and this time, they were not throwing anything but just making rude comments about me. I could hear every word they were saying, which was slowly getting to me. So, I turned around to confront them.

"What's your problem with me?" I asked.

"Oh, nothing; we were not talking about you," he said.

"Oh yeah, then what were you saying?" I asked.

"It's for me to know and for you to find out whenever you can," he said and walked off. So, I just headed to my car and drove off to the house.

Over the weekend, it seemed that Kristen's condition worsened as the days went by until she had to be rushed to the hospital and found out that she got Strep throat along with bronchitis and still had the flu, but it was going away. However, it needed to be faster. That means that she cannot attend school the following week.

As the week went on and the trailer was nearing completion, it was due to be done that Friday, which would give me about one week to run it through some tests and see if it was ready for the show. When I got there and saw that it was outside and the paint was dry, Mr. Ingram came up to me.

"Well, I'll say it has got to be the most difficult project so far," he said.

"Yeah, I'm done with the paint. All I need to do now is put the final touches on it and see if it will be good to go for the show." I said.

"Well, you know what you need to do," he said.

"I'm on it." Then, I continued to work on the trailer. I was putting on the pinstripes. I was only paying little attention when the teacher updated me.

"By the way, how is your sister doing?" he asked.

"Oh, she's doing a little better than last Friday," I said.

"Well, I hope she will be well enough to be at the show," he said.

"Oh, she will be, Mr. Ingram," I said as we walked into the classroom.

That day was different from how I wanted it to go because after I left there, I went to my following classes and went to lunch; about five minutes later, I got my food and walked outside to sit down; some guy called my name.

"Hey Crystal. Think fast," he said, and when I looked up, a piece of food flew to me and hit me right in the chest area, then fell into my lap. I looked back up to see him laughing at me, and everyone that saw it was doing the same thing. Then, someone else throws something at me again, hitting me in the side and then in the head. So, I just got up and grabbed my stuff, then ran down to my next class about fifteen minutes before I was supposed to be there. Before I went in, I saw Steve looking at me, and I saw in his eyes that what they did to me was wrong, but he didn't do anything to stop it from happening. So, that night, I was going to do the stupidest thing I could think of, which was to end my life one way or another.

Later, I paid a guy to get me three cases of beer, a bottle of crown royal, and a gun. I gave him five hundred dollars, and he gladly did it. Then, he gave it to me.

That day, my mother never saw me come home because I was too upset to be there to talk to her. I just wanted to find a place where no one could ever find me, and I just started drinking away. I listen to music while thinking about what the people around me feel about me and how they treat me.

After about one hour, I was getting drunk, and I knew because I used to do this all the time when I was younger, and I only had about twelve beers, which I didn't care about. I just kept popping them open and continued drinking.

The drunker I got, the more I drank until I didn't know how many I had, and I was starting to see funny things appearing in the field. Then, I see myself out there with Steve and a little girl playing with him, and we are having so much fun, and that's when I realized that I needed to hurry up on what I was doing and end all of this.

When I looked at the time, I saw that it was only midnight, and I still hadn't touched the gun. I wanted to do this but couldn't pull the trigger when I pointed it at my head. Then, I threw it away from me, grabbed the crown royal bottle, and only downed three shots when I just passed out on the side of my car and figured I was dead.

Chapter 12

"Crystal, wake up," someone said, and I thought I was dreaming, but when I opened my eyes and saw that Steve was standing by my side, holding my hand.

"There you are. It's about time you wake up. You had Steve and me worried about you for about three hours." Laura said. I saw her standing right beside Steve.

"Where am I at?" I asked. "Well, you are in the hospital; your stomach is getting pumped to get the alcohol out of your system," Kristen said.

"How did you guys find me?" I asked.

"Your sister over there could see where you were after she put her mind to it," Laura said.

"Oh, okay. I thought you were mad at me." I said to Steve.

"At first, I was, but during lunch, I was watching those guys throwing that food at you, and I told myself that was being too mean to you, and after you walked off, Laura and I took care of them, and they won't be bothering you for the rest of the school year," he said.

"But you guys were so mean to me. Why care now about me? I was better off without you guys in my life," I said,

"Well, we were mad at the secret you kept from us. We didn't know what to think, but if it's a part of you, we will accept or not be friends. But seeing how you almost claimed your life, I don't think we can do that, so do you forgive us, Crystal." He said,

I lay there looking at both of them, wondering if I could forgive them for what they did but also I had kept a big secret from my friends and family that I should have never kept from them, to begin with,

"Well, we should start over as friends and not have secrets like this. As far as forgiving you both, I can accept it but let's start over as friends, and I will still go to prom with you, Steve, just as friends; for now, it can change later." I said.

They both looked at me as Steve spoke, "I think we can do that and work back to where we were, and I'm sorry for judging you and not being there when you needed us." as Laura put her hand on mine,

"And I'm sorry for what I did to you, Crystal; you are a good friend, and I don't want to lose that," Laura said. Then, the doctor came in.

"Well, it seems you are finally up and alert, but that was not the case about three hours ago when you came in. The alcohol in your blood reading was .47, which is only about three hundred from death, and with the alcohol in your stomach, you would have put it at .55 or more which is a good thing that you got in here before that happened," he said.

"Will she be okay?" Steve asked.

"Well, from here on out, she might want to watch that alcohol, or she won't be as lucky the next time," he said and walked back outside the room.

Mother was walking down the hall, saw me, and ran into the room.

"Oh, Crystal baby, why did you do that? You know you could have killed yourself," she said.

"I know, but at the time, I didn't care about my life because everyone at school treated me like trash, so I decided to end my life," I said.

"Well, it's a good thing that you have a twin, or you would have been left out there and died," she said in a worried voice.

"I know, Mom, but I had to do that or use a gun. But I was not strong enough to pull the trigger. So, I threw the gun away and just stuck to the drinking part." I said.

"Well, at least you have learned your lesson," she said, hugged me, and walked out of the room.

After they finished getting all the alcohol out of my stomach, they said that I could get discharged to go home and get some rest which I plan on doing and play by ear on what I do during the next few weeks until the show is over.

When I came home with my parents, we talked about what all went down and asked how this happened to me, and I explained to them that I was somehow part of something big that could save the world. At first, they didn't understand, but as I talked and with Kristen's help, they slowly started to get it. We also told them that Sapphire knows about it, but no one else does, and they said it's best to stay safe and always know that someone will hurt you in one way or another. My Dad put his hands on my shoulders and said, "With great power will always have a great responsibility to control it. Just keep that in mind."

As the final week of getting things ready for the show, I was back at school that next week and Steve was being a friend again. Kristen, there with me; I would like to see those boys mess with me now that I'm back to my old self and my parents are allowing me to do what kept me happy because they didn't want the incident to happen again. When I came home after that night, they told me I was ungrounded, so I just hugged them and thanked them for caring about me.

When I arrived at AG class that Tuesday, Mr. Ingram walked up to me and asked me something important, "Crystal, is the trailer ready to go? Because if it is, we need to get it to the show by Thursday and get it in a spot that it can fit in."

"Let me look at it quickly, and I'll let you know," I said and walked out. I saw that the pinstripe was just like it should look, and the paint was also good. Then, I walked back to Mr. Ingram.

"Yes, it's ready to go to the show from here," I said.

"Well, good job on making the trailer, and the best of luck to you on making the sell because since it has a pit on it, the judge may like it more now than if it wasn't on there," he said, walking off.

I walked around the trailer and enjoyed its outcome. Kristen and I amazingly did it. Then, someone came to me.

"Wow, this is a beautiful trailer." It was Laura.

"Thank you, Laura," I said as I approached where she was.

"Oh, I didn't know it was your trailer," she said.

"Yep, well, it's Kristen's, too," I said.

"Well, you did a good job on it. I'm out here to give my goat a haircut and get the goat ready for the show." Laura said.

"Oh, which one is he?" I asked.

"Oh, that one right there," she said and pointed to the one that was solid white.

"Now, that is a cute goat for you to have," I said.

"Yeah, my Mom wanted me to do something in AG, so I decided to raise a goat because it would be the easiest thing for me to take care of," she said.

"So, what else are you doing at the show this weekend?" I asked.

"Oh, I plan on going out with my boyfriend and having fun after that," she said.

"Oh well, that sounds like fun for you. Steve has to be at the show also, so I'll be able to see him a lot, and I don't plan on doing much but that." I said.

"Why not?" she asked.

"Remember what happened over the weekend?" I said.

"Oh, you just want to spend some time with him, right," she said.

"Yeah, that's all I want to do because I don't want to lose him again as I did before because of some stupid reason," I said.

"Yeah, I know what you mean by that." I have a goat to take care of," Laura said, leaving me by my trailer.

"Guess who it is?" someone came behind me and covered my eyes.

"That would have to be Steve because I know his voice," I said.

"Well, you are good at knowing who is talking, but it's not me," he said, and someone took their hands off, and I saw him in front of me.

"Oh, so who was it?" I asked.

"Me silly, what you can't tell when your sister is behind you," Kristen said.

"Now you know I'm not that good at saying that," I said, and Steve got beside me. "So, are you ready for the show?" he asked.

"Ready as I'll ever be," I said, and we walked around the place until it was time to leave the class and head to our next one.

As Thursday came around, there were no classes because it was the start of our spring break and the show was to go on for four days. I was up early waiting for Kristen to get out of bed because we were to ride with Dad to pick the trailer up and carry it to the corral where the show was supposed to be.

"Come on, Kristen, we've got to go," I said as she dragged herself out of bed.

"No more late nights for you," I said.

"What time is it?" she asked.

"It's half past my butt. No, come on, let's get going." I said.

"Oh, you would have to joke this early in the morning," she said.

"When it comes to getting up on time, I have to joke to make you laugh and have some fun," I said.

"Well, I guess I'll get my butt out of bed," she said, and finally got out and stood up to the bathroom. We left about twenty minutes later, and Dad was asking questions about the trailer, "Okay, now what kind of trailer are we picking up from your school?"

"A gooseneck trailer about forty feet long with a pit on it," I said.

"Well, that might prove to be a problem because you see, I don't have a hitch in my truck for that," he said.

"You mean that you can't get it? but Crystal said that you had one." Kristen said.

"Don't let him fool you about that. Just look in the back, and you will see it." I said, and when she did, she saw it and turned back around.

"Oh, okay, then why did he say that?" she asked.

"He has to be that way sometimes; you have to get used to it," I said.

"Well, it took you about seven years to realize that I joke more than being serious about things, so why should you be talking?" he asked.

"Well, I knew you had one because the last trailer was a gooseneck," I said.

"Yeah, but not as long as this one because that was your first one to build, and you almost didn't get it done in time. You wasted more time than work on it," Dad said.

"Yeah, I know, but I did much better this time," I said.

"Huh yeah," he said funnily.

"Well, wait until you see it," I said.

"I don't know if I want to. I might scare it away," Dad said.

"Let's hope you don't, Dad," Kristen said.

"Well, she caught on quicker than you did sport, and she hasn't known me that long," he said.

"Well, I'm a quick learner," she said, and we kept talking until we finally got to the school and saw it around back, and Dad was impressed by it.

"Wow, girl, you did a good job on it," he said as he backed up and hooked it up to the truck. He got out to hook up the light wires and tested them to ensure they worked, and when he checked them out, we drove off to the AG barn to find a spot for it.

As we made our way to the AG barn, we had to come in the back part of the barn because that's where the shop project was, and as we pulled in the place, I looked around and saw that they were some other gooseneck trailers, but they were not as long as mine. One of them saw mine and was staring at it as we pulled right beside him, and I hopped out of the truck. Then, I put down the stands, and Dad pulled out and told us that he would be back after he went and got Mom and the rest of the family.

As he pulled out of the barn, Kristen and I were dusting off the trailer and making it shine with some polish and Windex to make it stand out a little more. Then, I saw Steve coming into the barn with his project, which I had never paid any attention to the whole time I was there.

Steve and Kyle built an eight-foot-long picnic table with backs to it, and it had little stand-out pieces of wood on the side of it, making it look good if you were born in Texas, which I wasn't.

"Hey Crystal, how are you doing today?" Kyle asked.

"Oh, I'm doing just fine; how about you?" I asked back.

"Never been better. Hey Steve, where's the Windex at?" he asked.

"Oh, it should be in the truck. I hope that I didn't leave it," Steve said.

"Hey, don't worry, babe. I've got some that you can use," I said and gave him a bottle.

"Thank you, hon," he said and went to work getting it wiped down and making it shine. I told Kristen I would walk around and see the other projects to check if we had anybody to worry about later. Then, she said that she was going to do the same thing. So, I walked off and looked at the other goosenecks and saw they were not as big as mine. However, they still had a chance of taking the top spot.

One of the guys walked towards me and said, "Hey did you build that trailer yourself? Or did a guy help you with it? I doubt it was done all by you."

"How about you ask my sister then and see what she has to say to you because I know you are not trying to size up your trailer against mine now, are you?" I asked.

"Well, I may not have the length, but I am a guy, and the judges see that as a plus because girls cannot do what guys can do," he said.

"All right then, how about we make a challenge then? If I can pick up your trailer's front end off the ground, hold it one foot high, and hold it there for ten seconds, then you have to take back what you said about me." I said.

"And if you lose, you have to go out with me for the night and do whatever I say," he said.

"Okay, but you are going to eat those words," I said and got into position. Then, my sister came over there to count me off.

"All right, in three, two, one, and lift," she said, and I lifted on the trailer. It was heavy but not as much as ours, and I am sure of it because I did that about two weeks ago to fix one of the stands.

As Kristen was counting, she kept a measure of how high it was, and when she counted to ten, I sat it back down and looked at him.

"Now, take these words back," I said.

"You cheated, you had your sister do the count, and she didn't measure right because that was not a foot off the ground," he said.

"Yeah, I said, a foot high off the ground. I didn't mean in inches, either. You should have heard me better than that boy." I said.

"She right, because that's what I heard." said the guy standing next to him.

"Man, that's not right because I wanted to have some fun with you," he said.

"I'm sorry, but I already have a boyfriend, and he's right over there, so see you later," I said, and I left him figuring out what just happened.

For the rest of the day, I walked around the place to see what everyone brought to the show, and as I walked towards the front, I saw that they had rabbits on one side and chickens on the other, but I didn't see anybody that I knew that was showing them. So, I kept going until I started to see goats and sheep in the same area, and then I spotted Laura putting hers away and giving it some food and water when she noticed me.

"Hey Crystal, how are you doing today?" she asked.

"Oh, I'm doing okay, for the most part. How about you?" I asked.

"I'm doing okay myself," she said.

"Have you seen Randall around here? she told me she had an animal but didn't tell me." I asked.

"Oh, she has a pig, and I think she just showed up about ten minutes ago, and they are right up there," she said.

"Okay, I'm going to go and see," I said, and I walked off to where the pigs were and saw Randall taking care of her two pigs.

"Hey Randall, what are you doing with your two pigs?" I asked.

"Well, my Dad wanted me to get two, but all I wanted was one, but I may have luck getting one of them into the market, and the other one would go to the meat house," she said.

"How could you do that? because I couldn't do that to an animal, I raised for the show, and it didn't make it in." I said.

"It's called don't get attached to it, and you won't have any problem," she said.

"Well, that's where I would mess up," I said.

"So, why are you up here for anyways?" she asked.

"Well, I'll show you if you'd come with me," I said, and she followed me back to my trailer. When we saw it there, she couldn't believe it was mine.

"Oh my, I never knew it was yours. Where did you get this idea?" Randall asked.

"I thought of it," I said.

"My, it looks good, and you even have a pit on the front of it. How do you take it off?" Randall asked.

"Well, if we were to push this button right here, a winch would let it slide right off the back and go down a ramp that I made for it because there is no way someone is going to lift four hundred pounds three feet off the ground to get it on here. So, I made it easier for anybody who wants to use it." I said.

"Well, I believe you will make the top of the selling list with this trailer," she said.

"Yeah, that's what I'm hoping will happen," I said.

"You hope. I think this thing should make it with flying colors." She said, and I looked around to see if Mom was there, and so was everybody else.

"Hey, Mom, I didn't know you wanted to be up here," I said.

"Well, I could go home if that's what you like," she said.

"No, that's okay. How do you like it?" I asked.

"I think with that pit up there, the judges will like it and put ahead of these other trailers out here," she said.

"Yeah, because the one closest to me is only about five feet shorter than mine, making the judges think twice about which one would go first," I said, and she walked closer to get a better look at it. Everyone looked around it and then walked off to see the others.

The next day was the judging of the projects, and we had to be there about an hour early to get our projects ready to go for the judges. However, I left the house with Kristen late and got there about thirty minutes before I needed to be there because Steve and Kyle were showing their table first thing that morning, and I wanted to make sure I got to see it.

When I got into the arena, I saw Steve next to their picnic, and then he saw me.

"Hey babe, wow! you dressed up for this." I said.

"Yeah, but don't get used to it. I only did it for the show today and might do the same when we sell the table." Steve said.

"Oh, okay. Well, I came early to watch you and see what the judges will be like this year." I said.

"What time do you show yours?" he asked.

"Oh, not for about an hour or so," I said.

"Well, lucky for you, but a least we don't have to wait and be nervous and then wonder if this is going to sell or not," he said.

"That's nice to know and hear, but I'm used to waiting because I have always built things out of metal, and you will see how good I am at making almost anything that I please," I said.

"Well, it's about time for me to show this thing, so I'll see you after the judging," he said and headed back to the table, waiting for the judge, who had just started on the wood section and was about four projects away from him.

As I watched the judge go from project to project and ask questions about the project, the students would say things about it and try to keep up with the judge on what to say back. Then, after about thirty minutes, he talked to Steve, looked at the table, and asked him about it. I couldn't hear what they were talking about, but he finished in about ten minutes. Then, Steve walked up to me after he walked off.

"Oh man, that was some intense stuff watching him just starting at the table and trying to find something wrong with it," he said.

"Well, how well did you think you did, or could you tell?" I asked.

"I'm not sure, he was asking this question, and I would answer some, and then Kyle would get the other ones that I didn't know an answer to, but I think we made it," he said.

"Well, that means I'm going to have a tough time convincing this judge about my trailer out there," I said.

After about another forty minutes, it was time for me to head out to the trailer and wait for the judge to come over and look at it.

"Good luck," Steve said.

"Thanks; I'm going to need all the luck I can get," I said as I walked out to the arena with Kristen not too far behind me.

As the judge made his round around the projects, Kristen was doing some last-minute touches on the trailer to get it looking as neat as possible. The guy next to us was doing the same thing, but he only had a little time because the judge just walked up to his project and started talking to him about it.

After he finished his, Kristen and I were the other ones left out there. I was nervous because I kept thinking I would mess up somewhere, but he walked up to me first and had another judge with him.

"Hi there, and your name is Kristen?" he asked.

"My name is Crystal. Kristen is over there." I said.

"Oh okay, well, let me take a look at this right quick," he said, and he looked at all of the little things that I did, and after he walked around the trailer, he returned to me.

"Okay, well, I saw a pit on the back and braced to where it can't fall off, and I also noticed it was on a rail system. Could you explain that to me?" the judge asked.

"Yes, sir," I said, and he followed me to the back.

"Right here is where I put in two extendable rails to let the pit slide off the back without somebody having to lift it off and putting it back on. Also, the pit is hooked up to a winch so it can be pulled forward and released to let it come to the back of the trailer." I said.

"Well, that's a good idea to have for this pit," he said, and he walked to the side and saw some other things too.

"I see you have side guards on here. Are they removable?" he asked.

"Yes, sir, they are, and this is how they come off," I said and showed him how easily they came off and how to put them back in. He looked for another five minutes, said thank you, and walked off.

I felt a significant weight lifted off of my shoulders as Steve walked back down there to me.

"Well, what do you think he is going to say about this?" he asked.

"Oh, I know it's going to make the sell, but I don't know if it's going to be the grand champion just yet," I said.

"Well, how about we go for a walk and see what else we can find is being judged," he said, and we walked down through the arena and out into a minor part of the place. I met Laura earlier that day and saw that she was showing her goat with about twenty other people, and all the goats were about the same size. I couldn't tell how they could tell them apart by just feeling them on their backs and down the side, but they were doing so, and at that same time, they were putting them in order from what seemed to be the best to worst and Laura was upfront with her goat and the judges came through for one more round of checking the goats out.

As he checked each one, he took them to the other side of the pen and placed them in their final order, and as the judge checked Laura's goat, the judge gently grabbed Laura's arm and put her in the front of the whole group, and he didn't put anyone else in front of her.

After he finished, he said that Laura had the grand champion of the male goats and that they were free to take the goats back.

"Hey, Laura," I said.

"Hey there, how did your judging go?" she asked.

"Oh, you don't want to know about it," I said.

"Sure, I do, but first, I need to go help out Randall with her other pig. Will you hold Buddy here," she asked.

"Yeah," I said, and she handed me the leash. I followed her to where the pigs were and saw Randall in her pen with the pigs.

"Hey there, when are you showing?" I asked.

"Oh, in about ten minutes. How did yours go anyways?" Randall asked.

"Oh, that? the judge was tough to figure out when he came to me because there were four goosenecks up there, and they were all close to the same size, mine being the longest of the bunch." I said.

"Well, it sounds like you have a challenge for that top spot," she said.

"Well, don't rub it in until I know for sure, girl," I said.

"So, Laura, do you know how to handle a pig?" she asked.

"Yeah, you showed me how and I still remember," she said.

"Okay, because the person I picked last year said the same thing, but the pig got away from them, and they couldn't control it until a couple of guys came in that way. They finally put it back in her hands, but I told them to let someone else do it because I knew it would get away from her again," she said.

"Oh, well, don't worry about it; I will have control of this pig. I was with this one almost all day yesterday so that we can get used to each other," she said.

"All right, because it's time to see if you have been with him since he is the feisty one of the two," she said. They took the pigs to a pen and put them through their routine because pigs are not a very easy animal to raise because you couldn't put a harness on them, and the only thing you had was a tiny little whip to keep them in line with what they were to do.

As the judge looked at them and felt them, he was deciding which one would be the grand champion of them all. Then, there were to be a few rounds because they had many pigs to go through before the judges decided on a grand champion.

As Randall's pigs made it to the last round, there were still about fifteen pigs that were still in the small arena, and every five minutes or so, the judge would make about three more pigs walk out of the pen, but Randall's was still in the hunt for the top spot.

After another fifteen minutes, the judge ended with Randall's two pigs taking the top two spots, making her grand and reserve champion of the pigs.

"Well, that's what I wanted to happen," she said.

"Why do you say that?" I said.

"Because I just have no room for either one of these in the freezer at the house," she said.

"You mean if the pigs didn't make it, you would have them for food?" I asked. "Yep, that's right," she said.

"Okay, well, I'm going back to the back to wait for my project results," I said, leaving Steve to talk to them.

"Take her pigs to the slaughterhouse. Oh, I couldn't do that, no matter what." I said to myself, which made me a little sick just thinking about it.

Then, Steve finally caught up to me.

"Hey, was there a problem back there?" He asked.

"Yeah, just a little bit when she said that she would have them killed. Anyway, only if they didn't make the sale." I said.

"How could that be a problem? You eat meat from the store," he said.

"Yeah, that's a little bit different. I could eat that stuff, but I wouldn't eat something I just killed if it didn't make the sale. I would keep it until something got it, or it just dies of natural causes." I said.

"Oh, okay, I see what you mean by that," he said.

"No, you don't; I know when you lie to me, babe," I said.

"Okay, I just said that to get your mind off that and on your project," he said. I said okay. Then, we kept going toward the back and waited for the judges to return.

As we waited for about thirty minutes, the judge returned and had the paper in his hands, which everyone walked up close to hear him.

"All right, it was tough to choose the winners this year, but we have decided; some didn't make it, and we will call them out. Please come up here and get one of these ribbons for the ones I call." He started calling on those who didn't make it.

As I was hearing some of them, they came to some that were from my school, which I was shocked that they would do that to some of the Henderson students, but he didn't call Steve to go up there, so that meant he made it but how far back is he going to be. As the judges called the last name, he started talking again.

"All right, anybody called now is in the show, and we will be starting from the fiftieth and start forward," he said, and the last person was from Henderson with a little shop table and so forth until he was getting close to the twentieth spot, and he called Steve's name. Then, he went up to get a ribbon, and so did Kyle, and they put it on the table while I was still waiting for Kristen and mine trailer placed.

"All right now, we are starting to get to the part where it was to the wire of picking who. So, don't panic if your project doesn't get what you thought it would," the judge said, calling out the reserved champion in wood and the grand champion in timber. Then, there was one for the combination, and he got to the last few.

"Okay, Brittany Snipes, you are the reserved champion in metal, and you will be fourth. Courtney Williams, you are in third with your grand champion in combination," he said, and I was getting nervous.

"Okay, now, the one who got reserved champion overall is-" I was thinking that was me "-Justin Williams with your thirty-five-foot gooseneck trailer and the grand champion in metal." He said, "Overall in grand champion is Crystal and Kristen Dawlson with your forty-foot gooseneck with a pit on the front equipped with a winch," he said. I was so happy that Kristen had to get the plague that they gave us, and she brought them back to me, and I finally snapped out of it.

"Good job, babe. Now, we get to see how much this thing will sell." Steve said.

"I guess we will have to find out tomorrow, baby," I said and ran to my family, who were by the wall of the project area.

"Good job, kiddo," Dad said.

"Thank you, wow! I didn't know that it would go for that." I said.

"Well, you still did good no matter where it ended." Mom said.

"They said it was a hard choice this year. I wonder how come?" Kristen asked.

"Well, if you noticed that the top four spots go to the gooseneck trailer, and then about five smaller trailers follow behind that, so that's why it was tougher," I spoke.

"Oh, okay, well, what do you want to do until tomorrow, girl?" she asked.

"I don't know, but I want it to be fun, if you know what I mean," I said.

"Okay, hon, you know how far to go on that fun part right." Mom said, "Mother." we both said simultaneously.

"Okay, well, there's your response to that. I believe there are smarter than that." Dad said.

"Well, I just want them to be safe," she said.

"Don't worry, Mom, we have Steve to look after us," I said.

"Whoa, did someone just drop you on your head, or did you say that I'm your babysitter," he said.

"Well, I guess we will see you at the house later tonight," Dad said, and they walked off.

"Well, what do you want to do?" I asked Kristen.

"I know just the place," she said, and we headed to the car with her driving.

Kristen took us to a place with plenty of dirt, and she was having fun just making the car do one eighties and things like that, but I thought she had something else in mind other than just spending time in the sand.

"Kristen, I thought we were going to do something fun," I said.

"We are having fun, are we not," she said.

"Yeah, you might. But this doesn't get me excited at all." I said.

"Well, what do you have in mind?" she asked.

"How about a movie? They are showing a movie I have wanted to see for a while but never went up there." I said.

"Okay, let's go watch a movie then," she said and turned the car around. Then, she was back on the road, leaving a dust trail behind us leading back to the sand pits. As she pulled into the theater parking lot, I saw that the movie was about to show in about twenty minutes.

"Oh good, we still have time," I said.

"What's the movie called?" she asked.

"Oh, it's Ghost Rider, and it has Nicholas Cage in it. He is a good actor." I said.

"Yeah, I heard about him," Steve said, and we got the tickets, went inside, got some popcorn and drinks, and walked into the theater where it was showing. I sat in the front, and the other two waited for the show to start.

After the show, we noticed that it was only about five o'clock, and I was still so happy to go home. So, we went to Mcdonalds and talked with Kyle because he called Steve and told him he was there. So, we went to see him.

When we got there and saw him in the back of the place, we went to where he was and sat down.

"Hey there, how's the fun coming along?" he asked. "Oh, you know, just fine. What about you?" I asked.

"Oh, I'm up here with Miranda, and she just went to the restroom. She'll be out soon," he said.

"Hey, I'm going to the front. Do you want anything?" I asked Steve.

"No, I'm fine for now," he said.

"Okay, I'll be back," I said, walking off.

As I waited in line, some guys were staring at me from the other side of the counter, which was starting to bug me a little. Then, it was my turn to order.

"I'll have the number six, and that would be all," I said, and he told me my total; then, I paid him, and he handed me my cup, and I walked off to fill it up.

When I stood there waiting for the food, the same guys were still looking at me, which was getting on my nerves, and I was about to tell one of the managers about it if they didn't stop, but then, a female worker came up to me.

"Hey, I'm sorry for doing this, but a guy wanted me to give you this," she said and handed me a piece of paper. I opened it, and it had a phone number and his name. When I looked up, he pointed himself out in the back, and I almost got sick. The guy was not even my type, but he must not have cared, and then Steve walked up to see if I was all right.

"Hey there, are you feeling okay?" he asked, and I just handed him the paper, and he read it.

"Who wrote this?" he asked.

"That guy right there, the one that's waving at me," I said, and I guess the guy didn't see Steve when he was waving, but Steve saw him, and he stopped and just gave him a mean look that I had never seen before from him. Then, he mouthed something to the guy that I couldn't hear.

"Excuse me, sir, but I believe this person works here," Steve said, handing over the paper. "Oh well, did you just get this?" he asked. "Oh no, sir, my girlfriend must have got it, and then she handed it to me," he said.

"Well, that explains a lot, he just got in trouble for doing this, and it happened not too long ago. Don't worry, he won't be working here again after tonight, so he should leave you alone," he said, and he went to the back and talked with the guy about it while I just got my food. So, we headed to where Kyle was and started eating.

After I finished and waited on Kyle to finish up, we headed out to the parking lot, where we parked the cars while talking. Suddenly, someone tapped me on my shoulder.

"Hey, you could have just called me instead of making me lose my job," he told me.

"Hey buddy, she has a boyfriend; you can get lost," Steve said.

"So, you are her boyfriend? Baby, why don't you dump this loser for me? You know he is dragging you down lower than you need to be. I have lots of money; I can get you whatever you want." he said.

"Okay, how much money will it take to make you get lost? I don't like being called 'baby' by strangers." I said.

"Why do you have to be so stubborn with me? You are going to date me," he said.

"And what if I don't?" I asked, and he grabbed me by my throat.

"I will make you hurt every time you deny me of anything like right here," he said, but he didn't hold me for long because as soon as he did that, Steve hit him right in the ribs under the arm that was holding me.

"Touch her again and see if I don't rearrange your face, boy," Steve said.

"Man, you just need to get out of my way before you get hurt," he said, and he swung at Steve, but he missed and popped him on the other side.

"As I said, she has a boyfriend and doesn't want to hang out with you," Steve said and swung again, but this time when he missed Steve, he hit me in the face. I stepped back a few times, but then I regained my balance.

"Oh man, now you are in some big trouble," Steve said and moved out of the way.

"What are you doing?" Kyle asked.

"Just watch her," he said.

"Oh, so you are going to let yourself get beat up, huh," he said.

255

"If that's what you think, then bring it on," I said, and he swung for me, but he was so slow to me that I could get around him and get behind him and hit him in the back, making him yell in pain.

"Have you had enough?" I asked, but he grabbed my throat this time; I just looked straight into his eyes.

"Big mistake," I told him. My leg went straight between his legs, and I flogged him so that he came off the ground about five feet and back like a sack of potatoes.

"Whoa, where did you learn that girl?" Kristen asked.

"Oh, umm, I took a self-defense class and six years of karate class," I said.

"Well, you are better than me at one thing that I know of," she said.

"Oh, whatever; you know I'm a better welder than you," I said.

"Yeah, for now, give me a little bit, and I'll be up there with you soon," she said.

"Well, let's get out of here before he gets back up," I said.

"How about we go to Walmart?" Kyle asked.

"Sounds like a good thing," I said; we got into the cars and headed over to talk some more and get away from that stupid boy.

As we headed to Walmart and parked, I stayed in the car and listened to the radio until Steve opened my door.

"Hey, are you going to get out or what?" he asked.

"Yeah, just give me a second," I said, and I turned my car off, got out, and went to where they were standing, and they were talking about the show and how it turned out.

"Yeah, I can't believe we made it to the sale. We started thinking we were not going because they were calling people from our school out of it." Steve said.

"Well, they must have liked it enough to accept it," I said.

"Well, I knew you would make it because of what you built," he said.

"Yeah, I knew that from the beginning, babe," I said.

"Well, I don't know about you, but I'm heading inside for a while," Kristen said.

"All right, we will be right behind you," I said, and she started to walk off.

Laura and I started walking down the store with Steve and Kyle talking behind us as she walked into the store. However, as Laura and I were walking down and crossing the drive, Laura looked to the left and saw something that made her stop talking.

"Laura, what's the matter?" I asked.

"Look out," she said. I looked and saw a car driving fast, and I just froze right there.

"Babe! I'm coming!" Steve shouted and ran, but he wasn't going to get there in time. Laura had no choice, and she pushed me out of the way. The car hit her, and she flew about twenty feet and returned to the ground.

"Laura, oh no, Laura," I said as I ran to her.

"Laura, are you okay?" I asked, and she looked at me.

"I don't think so," she said.

"Don't move, girl, okay? I'm going to get help." I said, but when I looked up, I saw that Steve was on the ground too.

"Oh no, not this. I'm coming; baby, hold on." I said and ran to his side, where he got hurt too.

"Oh baby, are you okay?" I asked.

"I'll be fine, babe, don't worry too much about me," he said.

"Don't say that because I will worry more, which I can't handle," I said.

"Go and check on Laura. She got hit harder than I was," he said.

"Okay, I'll go see about her," I said, and I wanted to see who was trying to hit me.

So, I looked for the car and saw that it hit another one and the driver was still in there, and as he got out and turned my way, I noticed that it was the same guy from Mcdonalds'.

"You are mine," I said, and this time, I could not stop my anger from getting out of hand, and I ran to knock him to the ground and just started hitting him.

I didn't stop until Kristen returned and pulled me off him.

"He's not worth it, girl," she said.

"I don't care! he deserves it at the moment," I said.

"I know, but let the police take care of that," she said.

"But he hit Ste-."

"Listen, I know you are angry at him, but you have a friend that needs you right now, and so does Steve. So why don't I make sure that he doesn't run away and you take care of them," she said.

"Okay," I said and walked over to Laura. She got worse than a minute before because I saw blood on the ground underneath her.

"Laura, are you still with us?" I asked, but I didn't get a response from her.

"Laura, are you okay?" I said, and I checked her pulse, but it seemed her heart was about to give up.

"Tell Randy that I love him very much, but I couldn't be here for him," she said, letting out her breath and never taking another one.

"Is she gone, Crystal?" Kyle asked.

"No, not yet," I said, and I turned to my crystal for the help that I needed and called for my dragon side; people were looking, but I didn't care.

When I finished transforming, I got my tail, put it right on her chest, and said "Abracathereba," which meant granting life back to someone in dragon language, and a bright light formed at the end of my tail. It made a beeline for her heart, and it started beating again, and she opened her eyes and saw me.

"Crystal, did you save me?" she asked, and I powered down.

"Yes, it was me," I said, and she sat up to look at me.

"But I thought I saved you," she said.

"Yes, you did, but I wanted to return the favor, and now we are equal," I said.

"Thank you for bringing me back," she said.

"That's what I do."

"Laura, is that you?" I turned around and saw that Randy was running to her.

"Oh! I thought you were dead by the looks of it," he said.

"Well, thanks to her, I'm okay now," she said, and he turned to me.

"Thank you so much for saving her life," he said, and he hugged me

"Not a problem," I said, and he turned back to her.

"Hey babe, I could use some help too," Steve said, and I walked over there.

"You know I could just leave you like this," I said.

"And how can I show my table at the show?" he asked.

"I'm only kidding, babe. Here, take my hand." I said, and as he held it, I was healing him from the inside out, and by the time he was on his feet, he was back to himself.

"Well, I think I should get hurt more," he said, and I looked at him.

"I'm just pulling your leg, don't freak out on me," he said, and we saw the cops taking that guy away as we were heading into the store for a while until I needed to get home and get ready for tomorrow.

As that night ended and the next day started, I got up and saw that I had overslept. I needed to get to the barn so I could get the trailer ready and run through what I needed to do and have Kristen do a few things because it was going to take both of us to do all of them, but she was not in the house.

"Where's Kristen at?" I asked Mom.

"Oh, she left for the barn show about an hour ago. She waited for you, but you never got up, so she just went ahead and left," she said.

"Okay, thanks," I said, and I ran out the door and drove up there to meet her. As I got there and went to the trailer, I saw her wiping it down and making it look like a seller.

"Hey, about time you got here," she said.

"Yeah, I kind of slept in," I said.

"I bet you did. The show will start in about three hours, and we need to get this thing up there about thirty minutes before it starts, so Dad is supposed to be here in about an hour to hook up his truck," she said.

"Hey, sleeping beauty," Steve said as he walked behind me.

"Hey babe, how are you doing?" I asked.

"Oh, you know, better than ever," he said.

"I bet you are. Did I do it too much last night?" I asked him.

"No, you didn't, hon; you had no choice because your one friend wouldn't have survived if you didn't, so don't grieve over it," Kristen said.

"Thanks for the comfort," I said.

"Hey, I would have done the same thing if it was me, okay babe," Steve said.

"I guess you're right about it," I said.

"Well, let's get the projects ready for a show," Kyle said.

"Yeah, let's do it to it," I said, and we got busy. After about two hours of getting them ready, Dad showed up with the truck, and as he backed up to it, his vehicle seemed higher than when we first picked it up.

"Umm, Kristen, we have a problem," I said.

"What is it?" she asked, and she saw what I was seeing.

"Okay, we will just have to pick up the trailer together," she said.

"All right, well, let's do it on three, one, two, three," I said, and we picked up on it.

"All right, Dad, back her up," I said, and he started to back up.

"Okay, keep it coming and stop," I said, and we sat it right on the hitch, and it clicked into place. As I locked it down and hopped out of the truck's bed, Dad got out to see it again.

"I'm so proud of what you have done over the past few months with your attitude with your friends and us, just keep it up, and you will do good in college as I did," he said.

"Thanks, Dad," I said.

"Well, let's get this trailer to the front of this thing," he said, and we drove out of the back of the barn, moved around to the front, and parked inside the building, waiting for the sale to begin.

As that happened, I got onto the trailer, got the pit off it, and let it on the ground to show how it works. The buyers were watching me doing that, making them more interested in my trailer than the one behind me, which was also a gooseneck.

The main guy walked to his seat and asked if we were ready. So, we said yes.

"All right, let's get this started. Let's start at $5,000," the announcer said, and he started talking fast. The buyers were taking the price up in no time as they saw what I did to the pit, and it never messed up once as it was making its way to the front of the trailer.

As the bid went past $8,000, I was getting happy about it because my last trailer went for nine grand, and that was the highest that I ever have heard of around my school, but then it went past that, and it just kept going, and as it was reaching $10,000, it was slowing down but not by much I would say.

After it reached a bid of $10,600, the guy started saying.

"Going once, going twice. Sold to the guy in the cowboy hat right over there," he said, and the guy came walking over there; his wife was there.

"Hi there," he said.

"Hi," I said back to him.

"All right, now, let's get next to the buyer." said the man taking the pictures, and I did so know that this trailer was the best-selling one I had done.

As everyone else went through and returned to where we were, we saw Steve and them coming back there, and they looked happy about it.

"Hey, how did it go?" I asked.

"Oh, we sold it for nine hundred dollars. How about you?" Steve asked.

"Oh, it went for $10,600," I said.

"Well, I'm impressed by that. You know that was the highest anything has gone around here before," Steve said.

"Well, that is something to be happy for, I guess," I said.

"Yeah, well, I would be too, but don't let anybody tell you differently," he said.

"Okay, I'll make sure," I said.

"Hey, you know that prom is not too far away from now, right?" he asked.

"I know that," I said.

"Well, do you still want to go to the dance with me or not," he asked.

"Let me think about it, and I'll tell you at school next Friday," I said and walked off to think about what to do.

Chapter 13

As I went back to school, everything was getting back to normal. I was trying to make it through the rest of the school year and make good grades to get into the college of my choice.

However, the one I wanted the most was still waiting to respond to me, and I kept sending them letters, but they never seemed to write back to me. As the weeks faded away and prom was not too far away, I was still thinking about taking Steve to the dance because I had heard rumors about him getting too close with other girls, but I am the type of person who doesn't believe in tales easily.

But as days went by, he was slowly drifting away from me, and I was trying to pull him back, but it was like we had a tug-of-war. It seemed like a game to him, and he was playing me, which I was not ready to do since it was so close to the end of the school year.

As April started and the prom drew near, Kristen walked with me one day, talking about it.

"Hey Crystal, have you bought your prom dress yet? I haven't, and I would like to go with you when you do," she asked.

"No, I haven't thought about it, but I was thinking this weekend would be a good time to go and get one since we just had our money back from the trailer," I said.

"All right, it's a deal," she said and walked into her classroom while I walked onto English class. When we were doing something about this book, I had no idea we were doing it because I wasn't the

English type. I was more the math type and could put numbers into my head and get an answer faster than a calculator.

When the class was over, and I made my way across the hall into Economics, the teacher made us solve some stuff about stocks and checked if we could make some money out of it. I was doing all right, seeing that I was not that good at it, but I was doing my best, which would help me later in life.

As Steve walked in and came close to me, he never once stopped to say hi to me, which was the first time he had ever done that to me. So, I turned to him.

"Hey babe, what's going on?" I asked him.

"Oh, hi, I didn't see you there," he said.

"It's hard not to see me sitting here and looking straight at you as you walk by me," I said.

"Well, I was thinking about something," he said.

"Yeah, like I'm that dumb?" I asked, and I turned back around and waited for the teacher to let us begin on our stuff.

As the class ended and we headed for lunch, Steve was trying to get close to me, but I kept pushing him away because I didn't particularly appreciate how he treated me in the classroom, and it was making him mad, which I didn't care about at the moment.

"What is your deal today, huh?" he asked as he got in front of me.

"That is none of your business," I said.

"Oh, it sure is, we are going out, and you will tell me what the problem is with you," he said.

"I don't have to tell you anything if I don't want to," I said and started walking off when he grabbed my arm and pulled me back.

"One way or another, you will tell me your problem," he said.

"Let go of my arm," I said.

"Oh, I will, just as soon as you tell me what is happening with you," he said, but I didn't answer him.

"I told you to let go of my arm," I said, and as he did, he pulled his arm out of my hand.

"That will remind you about this, and next time you will tell me, or it will be worse," he said and walked off without saying anything else.

I went to school the rest of that day wondering why he did that and hoping that he wouldn't do it again because next time he does that, I'm going to let him meet my leg very closely.

"Hey, what seems to be the problem?" Kristen asked as we were driving home from school, and her car was in the shop getting fixed. It would be ready in a few days.

"Oh, nothing," I said.

"Come on, tell me the truth now. It's your sister you are talking to here," she said.

"Well, for some reason, Steve didn't say anything to me during any of the classes, and at lunch, it seemed that he got aggressive with me and just walked off," I said.

"He did what to you again?" she asked.

"He got angry with me and walked away," I said.

"Was there a reason for it, or did he just feel like doing that?" she asked.

"Well, he didn't say anything to me during AG and then did the same thing during Economics. I asked him before the class started why he was not paying attention to me, and he said that he had other things on his mind. I guess he was trying to get my attention, and I made him mad, and he ignored me to tell him what his problem was." I said.

"Uh, sounds like someone is not happy here, or he is doing something bad on his end," she said.

"I don't know what it is, but I intend on finding out one way or another," I said, and we went on to the house and continued to talk about other things.

At school that next day, I was sitting in the same class where Steve didn't say anything and when he walked in, he went to Laura and whispered something to her that I couldn't hear all that well, but when I was able to, he got done talking to her and walked to his seat and waited on the teacher. Laura turned around and winked at him, and he did the same thing back to her, which made my stomach turn and make a knot.

When I finished what I was doing, I just waited for the bell and thought about what Steve and Laura were doing behind my back and what they were not telling me. I hoped he was not cheating because that was the last thing I needed.

As the bell rang, I got out before anyone else because I needed to get down there and talk with Kristen about what I just saw.

"Are you sure about that, Crystal?" she asked as we sat outside at a table.

"Yes, listen, I saw her wink at him, and he did the same thing back like I didn't see him do it or something like that," I said.

"Okay, let me get this straight, you think he is cheating on you with Laura, and you are sure that he is." she said, "Well, not really. I haven't seen them do anything bad just yet." I said.

"Okay, well, don't judge him until you see him kissing her or holding her passionately," she said.

"But I have heard from other people that he has been cheating on his previous girlfriends," I said.

"Is that Crystal talking, or is someone else talking for you? If I were you, I would not believe in rumors until you see them with your own eyes," she said, and I said okay to it. Then, the bell rang again for lunch to be over, and I headed off to my next class.

I couldn't wait for the weekend because I was going to Tyler to pick out my dress for the prom, and neither could Kristen. As we went there, we talked about what we would get and how we would look.

Sapphire wanted to come with us to see if she wanted to get something because I would buy her one if she found one she liked.

"Hey, let's go here," Kristen said.

"All right, let's see what they have," I said.

We pulled into the mall parking lot and walked in, and saw a store with some beautiful dresses that looked like something from one of my dreams.

"Hey, try this one on," Kristen said and handed me one.

"I don't think it's my style," I said.

"Well, you're not going to find out until you try it," she said, so I went into the dressing room and tried it on.

As I looked into the mirror, it didn't seem like me at all, and as I walked out and showed it to Kristen, we had the same thoughts.

"Oh, that may be a bit much," she said.

"Yeah, I agree. Oh, this one look nice." I said, and I pulled a blue one with a low back on it, and I took it inside and tried it on.

When I walked out and showed it off, Kristen was amazed.

"Wow, you look good in that. Put that to the side and try another one," Kristen said.

"All right, but that is still my number one pick for the time being," I said, picked another dress out, and kept doing that until I was out of choices.

"All right, I'll have this one here. It's your turn, Kristen." I said, and she went through some of the dresses until she found one that fit her perfectly.

It was dark pink and was about the same design as mine. Kristen wanted to get it so bad, so we bought the dresses, and Sapphire wanted to walk into a store she had been looking at ever since we walked in.

She got a dress also that she wanted to wear next year.

"Well, that should be able to fit you next year, girl," I said.

"Yeah, I don't think I'm getting any taller than this. You just got lucky to get that tall," Kristen said.

"What? are you saying that being almost six foot is tall?" I asked her.

"It is for a female," she said.

"Yeah, you are right about that, but I just took after Dad instead of Mom," I said.

"Well, you should be happy about your height, girl. I wish I were shorter; some guys prefer girls to be shorter than them; I'm taller than half of the seniors at school, so be thankful for it." Kristen said, and we drove to the house to show the dresses off to Mom and Dad to see what they thought about them.

"Oh, they are nice girls; you picked them out well." Mom said.

"Thanks," I said.

"I hope no one tries to do anything to ruin your night," Dad said.

"Oh, Dad, I'll be just fine," I said.

"All right, just as long as that Steve guy takes care of my daughter like he needs to," he said.

"Yeah, he will," I said, forcing a lie about him.

Afterward, I went to my room and put the dress over my bed. I was staring at it, then my door opened, and Kristen walked in.

"Hey, girl," I said.

"Are you going to tell them about Steve?" she asked.

"Not right now; I'm going to see what happens in the next few weeks before the prom gets here," I said.

"Well, you better let them know before then, or they will find out from somebody else sooner or later," she said.

"I may tell them sometime next week," I said.

"Don't go back on your word about it," she said and shut the door simultaneously.

When I was walking the hall the following week heading to my class, where I always met Steve, I was running a little later than usual and hoping that he was still waiting on me, but that wasn't the case this time. When I turned the corner, I saw him with Laura, holding each other. I stood there just wondering what they would do next, and that's when it happened. She leaned in and kissed him on the lips, and he returned the favor, and that's when he noticed me watching him.

"Laura, stop," he said, but it was too late; I was already sick and ran down the hall to AG while he was trying to catch up with me.

He could do that right outside the classroom, where he grabbed my arm and turned me around.

"Crystal, I didn't see you over there," he said.

"Oh, I'm supposed to pretend I didn't see you kiss Laura right before me?" I asked him.

"She came onto me," he said.

"Am I supposed to believe that too, huh? Well, I don't let stuff like that slide when some already told me of the students that you were cheating on me, and at first, I didn't believe them until I just saw you kissing Laura back there." I said.

"She just got dumped by her boyfriend and needed a friend to talk to," he said.

"And make out with her? even though you have a girlfriend, you don't seem to care about me; what will you do now? because I know what I'm going to do, you will not like it." I said.

"I do care about you; I didn't want to hurt you," he said.

"Oh, you're way past that. You have already torn my heart, and I cannot forgive you, even in the next life." I said.

"I'm sorry for what you just saw." He said. Then, I took off the ring and the necklace he gave me.

"Here you go." I placed them in his hands. "Go and spoil another girl, and they treat her like dirt afterward. I'm not going to be your girlfriend anymore." I said and walked into the classroom with Kristen standing right in the doorway, and she heard every word that Steve said.

"Come here, girl," she said, and I fell into her arms crying, and I couldn't stop it for anything.

"There, it's okay. I'm here for you." Kristen said, and Steve walked in and came towards me.

"Tell her I'm sorry for what I did," he said.

"You know, I think you have said enough to her already. Just let it go; you made a mistake. Now, you are going to pay for it from me." she said, and Steve just walked to his seat and sat down without saying anything else to me for the rest of the class.

The class went outside that day and worked around the shop; I wondered what and why Steve said that. I was too down to think about happy thoughts to cheer myself up from this fall and have someone to catch me.

As the teacher told us to come in and get ready to leave, Steve tried talking to me again. Still, Kristen just looked at him, and that made him leave me alone for a while until the class was over. I ran out the door and headed straight for my next class, where Laura would be, and I knew what would happen when I got there.

When I made it into the building, I saw that Laura was outside the classroom and looked like she was waiting on Steve to get there, but when she saw me.

"Oh no." that was all she said, and she ran down the hallway, and I went after her.

"Come back here, you little slut." I said. I finally caught up to her, grabbed her hair, and took her into the restroom where some girls were.

"Get out! NOW!" I told them, and they didn't hesitate to get out of there. I had her in the corner of the restroom, looking straight at her.

"What gives you the right to kiss my boyfriend in front of me, huh." I asked, "I thought you wouldn't mind." she said.

"Oh, you thought?" I said and slapped her a few times on the face. "You thought wrong bitch." I said.

"Well, I'm going through a rough time," she said.

"Don't we all? Thanks to you, I don't have a boyfriend now." I said.

"Well, he didn't like you in the first place," she said, and then I just looked right at her.

"What was that?" I asked, and I could feel my anger building up from what she said, and I was waiting for her to repeat it.

"He said that he never liked you in the fir-."

I hit her right in the mouth and put her to the ground, where I kept hitting on her until someone came in there and pulled me off, but I hit them, and they fell to the ground. I went back at hitting her until about three guys came in that way and finally pulled me off her and took me out of the restroom, where a cop was waiting for me.

"Hands where I can see them," he said.

"Yeah, I know," I said and turned to face the wall. Then the cop put the cuffs on me while the girl that I hit was helping Laura out of the restroom. As she walked off, I saw how much damage I had done to her, but I got my revenge back on her for what she did.

"All right, missy, this way." said the cop, and then he took me to the office where Laura was getting doctored up, and I could see where she was.

"Now, don't leave her alone, you got that?" the cop told another.

"I'll be right here," he said.

"I'm not playing when I said that because she can get out of those cuffs and go after her again, which we don't want," he said.

"Yes sir." the other one said, and the cop talked to the principal about what just happened.

The cop wasn't doing well in keeping an eye on me because my hands got uncuffed, which he didn't realize. I was waiting for the perfect time to go after Laura again because I didn't make her suffer enough the first time.

When he looked away and was staring at one of the girls walking by, I made my break for her which he overlooked until he heard a scream, and I was already on top of Laura. When I was running to where she was, she was in a room waiting for the nurse, and when she wasn't paying attention, I slipped in and shut the door. Then, I locked it and placed a wheelchair on the door to secure it more.

"Oh no, not you again! Help! Somebody help me!" she screamed, but they couldn't do much.

"Now, I'm going to make you suffer for what you have done to me," I said and knocked her to the ground. Then, I continued to hit her all over her body, and I could hear her bones starting to pop but not break; I wasn't ready for that yet.

I looked up to see what they were doing as she lay limp. When she hit me in the chin, she fell, and she was crawling to the door when I grabbed her legs and pulled her back to me.

"Oh no, you don't, not today. Today is when you feel my pain." I said, and I hit her in the leg, making sure that it was hard enough to break, which I did because she screamed about it. Then, the teachers were still trying to get in there to get me, but they couldn't.

I kept hitting her. Then, I broke her other leg, and then I was going for her arm when the window behind me was busted open, and a guy came in there and hit me in the head. I fell to the floor, but I wasn't out yet but gave him enough time to open the door and get Laura out of there. I was back on my feet and was going after her when that cop got some pepper spray and shot it right in my eye.

"Here, have some of that girl," he said, and I fell to the floor in pain. I had no choice but to be handcuffed, and they didn't play with me this time.

Before they got done restraining me, they had me cuffed three times behind my back this time and even had me strapped to the chair they had me in.

"This is your biggest mistake; you will regret doing this to me," I said.

"We will see about that; now, you just stay there and wait for the principal," he said, so I did.

Laura was still in the office area as I sat there and waited. I could see her, but this time, they had three cops watching her to ensure I couldn't reach her, but that wouldn't stop me from anything. I still need to break her arms, and then I'm done. As they were carrying her out of the office, my chains were tight on my arms and legs, but there was no way to break them like they were unless I had transformed, but I couldn't do that unless my crystal ball thought I needed it, but I wanted to get out of the chains so bad. I did the impossible, and somehow, I broke the chains and transformed.

Then, I went after her as they took her to the ambulance. When she saw me, it was too late to do anything as I swooped down, picked her up, and went up into the sky with her.

"I'm not done with you just yet," I said. Then, I tossed Laura into the sky and hit her like a piñata until another dragon girl came there to stop me.

"Crystal, stop this; this is nonsense." it was Kristen.

"Why do you care about this little piece of nothing anyways?" I asked.

"She was your friend at one time, don't do anything you will regret in the long run," she said.

"The only thing I'm going to like is when she feels the pain I had to go through while seeing her kissing Steve. He is also next on my list of people to hurt." I said, and then, another dragon appeared.

"Crystal, you are not supposed to be doing this. The crystal is not to be used to harm anybody unless it's an enemy." Randall said.

"Like you care!" I said and then felt another one, but this one was not coming from the school but from somewhere else.

"That cannot be her," I said, but out of nowhere, Silverie came flying towards me and was going to hit me, but I put Laura in front of me, making her stop before she hit her.

"I wonder when you will show up around here again," I said.

"Crystal, put her down, and we will talk about this," she said.

"You want me to put her down, and we will talk?" I said it back to her.

"Yes, put Laura down on the ground and stop this madness," she said.

"All right, I guess I'll put her down," I said, but I wasn't going to put her down quickly either. As I put her in a laid position, I hit both her arms, breaking them on contact, and then I let her fall to the ground where the medics could get her to the hospital.

"Now that was just wrong, Crystal; that is not the dragon girl way. Look how you tricked the crystal into giving you powers almost to kill her and how you turned your form into a dark one compared to ours. When I picked you to be a dragon girl, I didn't expect this behavior from you, so I left you with a choice, which I can do no matter what you say. You can put Laura back into a state before all of this happened, or I will do it and strip you of all your power and your memory about the dragon girls and let you become the kind of person that you are right now." she said, and I just looked back at her.

"I'm not playing with you; I'm serious about what I'm saying. Make a choice before I do," Silverie said, and since I didn't want to lose my powers, I stopped time, went down to Laura, picked her up, healed her up, and put her back onto the ground.

"There, I healed her back," I said.

"That was a good choice on your part. Now, power down," Silverie said, and I went back to the ground and powered down, and she was right there with me.

"Now you will have to pay the price for doing this but not this way. I'm going to erase their minds to where they don't know anything about what happened, and you will have to deal with me later," she said and did a magic spell, but it didn't affect me. Then, she said something as I had time stopped, and it was like everyone was walking backward before hurting Laura.

"Now, when time starts again, I want you just to leave her alone and walk to your classroom like nothing has happened, and don't try this again, or I'm going to do something bad to you," she said.

"Yes, but she broke Steve and me up today," I said.

"Don't think about that; if he is yours, then he will come back to you soon, okay," she said, and she let time go. Silverie walked with me back into the building and ensured it didn't happen again.

As the week of prom started, Steve and I were still not back together. He was trying his best to do anything to ask me back out, but I would say nothing to him because I didn't want the same thing happening again right before the dance.

"Crystal, listen to me, girl. I have been thinking about what I have done, and I am kicking myself and beating myself up for being the kind of fool you have dated in your past. Please don't push me away from you," he said.

"I'm still not taking any reason from you saying that you messed up with me," I said.

"Okay, I know that already, but you have been ignoring me for the past few weeks. The dance is already this weekend, and I want to take you to prom, then go after hours to have some fun while we can, please?" Steve begged, but I kept walking down the hall while he was still behind me.

"I miss you, baby," he said, and I stopped to turn around.

"What did you say?" I asked.

"I said that I miss you, baby," he said.

"Oh, okay, well, I figured that was something you would say to me to get back to me," I said. I turned back around and kept walking.

"I still love you, and I don't want to let you go; I know that I was an ass about three weeks ago, but I have learned that from you by you not paying any attention to me," he said, and I stopped once more and turned around.

"You still love me, is that actually true, or are you just saying that to me?" I asked.

"I do, baby; I just don't want to lose you again," he said.

"Well, let me think about it but don't ask me again, or I'll just not go with you to the dance," I said.

"All right, just let me know," he said. I just walked off to the class where Kristen was waiting for me and talking to me about what the prom theme was going to be.

"Hey, I just found out that the prom theme was going to be Paris," she said.

"Oh, that should be lovely, huh?" I said.

"Hey, what about Steve? Are you going to take him to the dance or not?" she asked.

"I'm not for sure just yet. I don't trust Steve as I did before; it's still in the air about him." I said.

"Well, don't wait too long, or he is going to find someone to dance with him up there, and that someone might be Laura," she said.

"Oh, don't remind me about her. I'm not in the mood to hear that because I had to listen to Steve the whole way down the hall, and I'm getting exhausted about it," I said.

"Well, I'm thinking about going by myself to the dance," she said.

"Why is that for?" I asked.

"Well, these guys around here that have girlfriends are asking me. I could tell that they had girlfriends because they came around at the wrong time, and I would catch them talking; of course, they were lying, saying that I came up to them but when I said that, he came to me. The girl believed me over them and slapped them across the face and walked off, and they get mad and want to hit me, but I put my hand up, and they back down and walk the other way." she said.

"That must be some interesting stuff to get into, huh?" I said.

"Yep, you should try it," she said.

"Umm, no, I'll just stay the person I already am to people," I said, and we kept talking as the teacher was busy doing something else that he told us to stay in the classroom for the time being.

As that Friday was halfway over, Steve was waiting for me to tell him my answer. However, I still didn't know just yet, but at lunch that day, when I was sitting down with Kristen and talking about some things, Silverie came over.

"Hey there, what are you doing over here and not over there," she said, pointing over to where Steve was.

"Oh, because we are not going out now, that's why," I said.

"Well, you know that he called it off with Laura, and he is waiting for you to return to him." she said, "How do you know this?" I asked her.

"I have been watching him for the past few weeks, and he doesn't talk with her anymore," she said.

"So, you are saying that he I-" "s waiting for you to ask him to take him to the dance." she finished my sentence for me.

"So, go over there and talk to him and see what he would say to you," she said, and I got up and walked over to where Steve was sitting at a table by himself, and I sat by him.

"Hey there," I said.

"Hey," Steve said.

"I was thinking about what you said, and I came up with an answer," I said, and he looked at me.

"I accept your offer to the dance," I said.

"You mean you will go to prom with me?" he asked.

"Yes, I will go with you under one thing, you are to never cheat on me again, or it is over for good between us. You got that?" I asked.

"Yes, I do, Crystal," he hugged me.

"Well, would you like to go out to eat before we good up there?" he asked.

"Yeah, I would love to eat out," I said.

"Well, I'll be at your house tomorrow at five to pick you up," he said.

"All right, see you then," I said, and I walked back over to Kristen and them to talk to them about what he said, and this time, if he messed up, I would not return to him again.

As Saturday was starting, I was getting ready from that morning up to where I needed to get my dress on and get ready for Steve, and when I was upstairs changing, the doorbell rang. Dad answered it, and he opened the door. I could hear Steve's voice and Dad telling me that Steve had arrived, and I said okay. I was putting the last touch on myself and walked out of my room and down the stairs to the living room where Steve was; he saw me in my dress and couldn't say anything for a minute or two.

"Wow, you look beautiful, Crystal," he finally said.

"Thank you," I said back to him.

"Wow, dear, you look just so beautiful. I need to take a picture." Mom said, but before she was able to, Kristen walked into the living room, and Mom saw her too.

"Oh, now that's what I call something you don't see every day around here," she said, taking a picture of Kristen and me and then one with Steve. Then, I told her that we needed to go before we were late getting there, and she said okay, and we were out the door.

We went out to eat before the prom, but as we were there, I couldn't eat. Not because I didn't like it, it was just that I was nervous and didn't know what the students would say about me up there at the dance, and I told Steve, but he wasn't mad about it. He assured me that it would happen to some people anyways, so there was no need to worry about it.

As Steve parked the car in the parking lot and we walked up to the front doors, we discovered we were a little on the early side. So, we just walked in with no one to talk about that, but the teachers there complimented the dress and how beautiful it was. Then, we walked over to where they were taking pictures, and we all took one together, then Steve and I took one, and then Steve got out to let Kristen and me take one.

Afterward, we walked to the dance floor and waited for the crowd to get there; it didn't take long. In about ten minutes of us being there, everyone else was slowly showing up and doing the same thing that we were doing, and then I saw Miranda in a dress like mine, but it was a darker blue, but it was about the same design.

After the crowd was making their way to the dance floor and the DJ went to work with his job and was playing music that people were dancing to, a few girls asked Steve, and he looked at me to ensure it was okay.

"As long as you don't kiss her," I said, and he walked off with her, and they danced a few songs. He was having a good time, but I also wanted to get out there to dance.

"Would you like to dance?" I saw that Scott was there and had his hand out to me.

"Sure, I'll dance with you," I said, and I went with him to the dance floor; a slow song came on, and he took control of the dance as I followed him and he was telling me that he was there by himself and didn't have anyone to take to the prom.

"Hey, did you ask my sister?" I asked.

"No, I didn't. Why is Kristen here?" Scott asked.

"Yeah, she's right over there with nobody also?" I said.

"Well, I guess after this, I'll ask her if she would want to dance with me," he said.

"She would love that very much," I said, and we kept talking about what we would do after we got out of high school. Scott said he would go to college and play football, and I told him that I would do the same thing, but I would go to a different one than his, which he didn't like, but that was where we chose to go.

As the song ended, I returned to where Steve was waiting for me and wondered where I had gone. I told him that Scott had asked me to dance, and he agreed. Then, he wanted to dance with me, and so I did for the following two songs until a fast song came along; he said that he didn't do fast beat songs, but he stayed up there to dance with them because it was one of those things that you do what the DJ says. It was fun for me to do for about ten minutes until I needed to sit down and take a break from dancing to catch my breath and relax a little bit with Steve beside me.

We danced on and off during the night, and we were having fun at the same time. I wasn't complaining about the girl that he was dancing with, and he didn't care which guys danced with me either, and that was how I wanted my relationship to be with him, with us trusting each other and knowing that we wouldn't hurt each other for some dumb or stupid reason.

As prom went on, I saw Laura, but she wasn't with anybody, and she was sitting by herself in the corner; I had forgiven her in my mind, and I decided to go over and talk to her.

"Hey there," I said, but she only looked at me and then turned back to what she was doing, so I sat beside her.

"Hey, I know that I was a bitch when it came to when you were trying to take Steve from me, but I have gotten over that, and I hope that we can be friends again," I said, and she turned to me.

"Well, at the time, I didn't have anybody, so that's why I turned to him for someone to talk to, and we just got a little too close, and it got too far out of hand," she said.

"Yeah, well, everyone makes mistakes, and if I had done the same to you, you would have tried to get your revenge on me also. Am I right?" I asked, "Yeah, you are, but as I said, I'm sorry for causing you too much pain. Can you forgive me." she asked.

"I forgive you, and I'll be your friend again but don't do it again, please, or I'll just have to do it back to you, but I'll make you want to kill me," I said.

"Deal. Hey, where is Steve anyways?" she asked when he walked over and saw that I was talking to Laura.

"Hey there, girl, are you two friends again, or am I just seeing things?" he asked.

"Yeah, we are. Would it be too much to ask Steve to dance with me?" she asked me.

"No, go ahead and have some fun, girl. Tonight, he can do things to a certain extent." I said, and they went and danced a few songs while I watched them; after a while, it was getting close for the prom to end and after hours to begin.

As we were heading out to the car, we had about thirty minutes to change out of our clothes and into something that we didn't mind getting dirty in by playing games and stuff. It took me only a short time because I had already prepared what I would put on when I got to the house, but Kristen didn't do as I did, so it took her about ten minutes longer than me.

Steve was ready in about five minutes because all he had to do was change his shirt and shoes, and he was waiting on us to get back downstairs and head to the after-hours party. We arrived right on time as some of the students were slowly showing up, and we took Steve's truck because it was raining, and we didn't want to risk getting our car stuck in the mud if we parked it in the grass.

As they let us through, they told us where to park. Then, we got out and headed out to the door. They saw who we were and allowed us to come in with a ticket we had to walk in.

It seemed like we were going to have a lot of fun in there that night because when we walked in, they gave us some fake money to gamble with, and at the end of the night, we could bid on certain things, and whoever bid the highest would get the item. However, I was more interested in the ring they had set up and wanted to play.

I wanted Steve to get in there so I could throw punches with the big gloves they had, and of course, he beat me a couple of times, and in the end, I finally beat him. I was tired and wanted to try something else. As I looked around, I saw another game where you had a bungee cord on a harness and a bag that would stick to the middle wall. Then, you must run as fast as possible and see who could get theirs the farthest. I played it against all my friends. I beat them a few times, and they would beat me, also. After that, I saw one where you were on a pedestal, and you had to knock your opponent off the other one without being knocked off yourself, which I was not good at, but I still had fun playing anyways.

After about forty minutes of doing all of that, I got very thirsty and went to get a drink, and then we sat down to rest up before I would pass myself because if I played too hard without resting, I would make myself pass out due to too much energy loss. My body couldn't cope because I had the same problem as a kid. So, my doctor warned me about it.

"Hey girl, what are you doing over here?" Steve said.

"Oh, I just trying to catch my breath for a minute," I said.

"Well, are you having fun? Because I know that I am," he said.

"Yeah, I just have to rest every once in a while, or I'll pass myself out if I don't," I said.

"Oh, is that a problem you have had since you were born?" he asked.

"Huh, oh yeah. When I was a kid, I would play all the time, and my parents would let me until after a while; I would pass out for no reason, so they took me to the doctor. Then, they found out about my condition and told me that I had to rest because my body couldn't keep up with the demand for a ton of energy. So, I had to cut back on the fun, but it didn't stop me from having fun." I said.

"Oh, okay, at least you are having fun, are you not?" he said.

"Yes, I'm having fun up here with you," I said, and after that, I was ready to go back out there and continue my fun.

As the night ended, they were coming close to the part where they were giving away a few things. I didn't get anything because everyone seemed to overbid me, so I didn't get anything, but it didn't matter to me. All that mattered was that I had fun up there.

As we walked out to the truck, it was raining while we were inside, and the ground was soaked. I knew that my car could not handle this at all, which was a good thing that Steve brought his truck to my house, and we rode in it. It took us about five minutes to get out, but we did okay by not spinning any tires and slinging any mud anywhere because there were some cops up there, and they were telling the kids that were doing it to stop, or they would get into trouble.

I told Steve that I didn't want to go home right after we left because I wanted to spend some time with him before we split off when high school was over. So, I told him to go to my favorite spot, and he said okay. Kristen was with us also, and she had Scott following us to my location so that she would have someone there with her.

It took us about ten minutes to get there, but since no one knew about it, it was empty, and we parked the cars. I got out, and the moon was coming out, and it was a full moon. Then, Steve came right beside me and held me.

"You know that I will keep in contact with you. You know that, right?" Steve said.

"Yeah, I know that, but I will still miss you not being there with me," I said.

"Well, I'll try to come and see you when I can. Is that all right with you?" Steve asked.

"That would be okay with me. Oh, the moon is so beautiful tonight." I said.

"Yep, it sure is. People said that a full moon makes some people fall in romantic love with the person they love the most," he said.

"That's what I have heard also, but I have never seen it happen," I said.

"Well, only certain people get that feeling," Steve said.

"Well, I'm just not feeling that right now," I said.

"Don't worry, you will just keep looking at the moon, and you will," he said, and I looked at the night sky. I saw all the stars that I could see, and there were a lot of them, and I wish I could be one of those stars up there so that I could see what it's like being one.

As the hour went by, I saw that Kristen and Scott were talking to each other. I went for a walk and Steve went with me.

"Are you okay?" he asked.

"Yeah, everything is okay," I said, but my face was saying otherwise.

"No, something is bothering you, and it's showing," he said.

"Well, when I was out that night and almost made myself die, I had a vision, and you were in it. I saw myself, and we were in a field just playing around, and I saw a little girl also out there with us, and I was always wondering if that was going to happen or not." I said.

"Well, I mean, it should happen since you've seen it," he said.

"Yeah, but that's what I can do. I can envision the future before they happen; sometimes, they don't happen for a while. One of them took a year for it to happen." I said.

"Well, it should be true then, girl. So, do you want to keep walking or what?" he asked.

"Yeah, let's walk back to the car," I said, and as I did, I started to feel a little romantic. When we got to the car, I was in love with Steve, and I turned to him and kissed him.

"Well, that would tell me something," he said, and we got close to each other. We stayed at the spot until morning came, and we went home. That was the best time I would have for a while with Steve because graduation was coming up after that night, and I needed to make extensive preparations for it.

Chapter 14

As I went to school after prom and the end of the year were nearing, I was thinking about what I had done over the year and wondered if I had enough fun during it with friends I had made over the year.

I want to make more in Tyler because the college that I picked gave their response and accepted me. I would also play football for their team, making my family much prouder.

When I got into AG class and saw that Steve and company were there, they wanted to tell me something.

"Hey girl, what are you during this summer?" he asked.

"I don't know just yet except having fun before I start college," I said.

"Well, how about you go with me to South Padre Island for one week and just have fun," he said.

"Oh, that would be lovely," I said.

"Laura and Kyle are going with us, and I think Kristen said she would go too," he said.

"Yep, I'll go with you," she said as she walked in the door.

"Okay, I'll go too. But I'm taking my car with me." I said.

"Well, I was going to ask you to take it anyways because there is no way we all can fit into my truck and make it down there," he said.

"All right, so when is the trip going to happen?" I asked.

"Well, I haven't thought of it yet," he said.

"Well, you'll think of something when the time comes," I said.

"Okay, class, let's head outside and do some work." Mr. Ingram said as he walked into the door, and we headed out to where the other classes were.

When I got there, I saw that Laura and Randall were out there, and they were helping with some chickens that didn't make it to the sale. So, they gave them to us.

"Hey, Crystal, did you hear about Steve's trip?" Laura asked.

"Yeah, and I'm also going," I said.

"You should know it's going to be great down there," I said and picked up a chicken, then continued plucking off the feathers. While doing that, some guys were watching me.

"Man, you know how to work with that chicken; how about you and I hook up after school, and you can work me?" he asked.

"How about 'no' blondie?" I responded.

"Whoa, you are an aggressive one. Come on now, don't do this to me," the guy said.

"Boy, I can do whatever I want to, so why don't you walk off and bother someone else instead," I said.

"No, I don't want to do that and leave you here alone," he said.

"You have about ten seconds to leave me alone, or you will have no choice," I said.

"Oh, are you going to fight me now? Well, I think I can handle you since you look so thin. I can slap you, and you would cry to someone." he said.

"What did you say about me?" I asked.

"Didn't I make myself clear to you? Okay. Let me repeat it; you are one puny little girl I could barely hit. Then, you would do as I say." he said.

"All right, does that bite of yours huge like your bark, or are you just all talk but no walk?" I challenged him.

"All right, I will show you," he said, and as he walked to me, I just cut the chicken and was getting the inside of it out, and I got a handful of them and waited for the right time to throw them.

"Come on, blondie, show me what you can do then," I said; he was about five feet from me and got closer.

"Here comes the kiss of death," he said, and he swung with his fist but missed, and I threw the guts at him and got him right in the chest, and he went to whining about it.

"Oh no, my shirt, you ruined it! You are going to pay for that." he shrieked.

"Is she now? Well, you must go through me to get to her." Steve said, and he walked in front of me.

"And who might you just be?" he asked.

"Well, I'm her boyfriend, and I'm not allowing you to hit her," Steve said.

"Well, we will see about that," he said, and he swung at Steve, but Steve caught his fist and turned it up, then made him drop to his knees.

"Have you had enough for one day, or do you need more?" Steve asked.

"Nope, I'm still going to hit her," he said, and he used his other fist, but Steve caught that one and did the same thing as the other one.

"Now, do you give up, or do you need more pain?" he asked.

"All right, I'll leave her alone," he said, and Steve released him. Then, he ran off and didn't bother me for the rest of the class.

As the week went on and everyone was finally getting ready to get out of school for the summer, I was getting ready for a little show I would do at the graduations with Kristen and Randall. I needed to be prepared for it because we would sing a song that would tell all about our class and what we would do with our lives and things like that.

"Hey Crystal, are you doing anything tonight?" Randall asked.

"No, why do you ask?" I said.

"Well, I was hoping that you could join Kristen and me to sing the song and get it down right and know what we are going to do," she said.

"Okay, I have to go to the house for about thirty minutes, then I can come by your house," I said.

"Okay, see you then," she said, and she was off just like that, so I headed for my sixth-period class, which was my favorite of all my types since it dealt with building things, and the teacher liked the things that I create out of everyday items that we use at the house.

"Hey Crystal, how is your day going?" he asked as I walked into the door.

"Oh, it's going well as of the moment," I said.

"Well, today, we will combine all your building skills and make a bridge. We'll see if it can hold more weight than the others," the teacher said.

"Well, that sounds like fun," I said and sat down in my chair, waiting for everyone else to get in there so the lesson could start.

After he told us what to do, he let us go to work on making some drawings on paper. I knew how to build mine, but the bell rang before I could start putting wood down on it. I had to get cleaned up and go to my next class and heard the guy wanting to meet my mother, which I would have to keep telling him that she couldn't do because she had other things to take care of first.

As the class ended, I ran out the door to my car, got in, and waited for Kristen. Kyle came by to tell me something.

"Hey, you need to come with me to meet my new girlfriend," he said.

"What? happened to the other one?" I asked.

"Ohh, we decided to break it off for the time being. Miranda's parents didn't like me very much," he said.

"Oh, who is this new one that I must see?" I asked.

"Oh, just follow me, and you can meet her," he said, and I told him okay. Then, we went to his truck and followed him to her house.

It took about ten minutes to get there, but as we pulled into her place, I thought she was living in some apartments on the outskirts of town, and she lived in the back of the site, which I didn't like because of the way it felt to me.

"Is this the place?" I asked as I got out of the car.

"Yeah, she just lives right up here," he said, and he walked to the door and knocked, and she answered.

"Hey there, come on in," she said, and then she saw me.

"And who is this?" she asked, looking at me.

"Oh, she's my friend," he said.

"Well, you didn't tell me your friend was a girl," she said.

"Kelly, can she come in?" he asked. Then, we went inside the house. I saw that she had a couple of kids also like me, and they saw me and just ran to me.

"Oh, well, that's nice of them," I said.

"Yeah, they do that to all the new guests they meet," he said.

"Okay, well, I'm just going to sit down," I said, and Kelly looked at me with evil eyes like she didn't want me there.

After a while, she stopped staring at me and talked to Kyle, and she would look at me and give me an exact look I didn't like before.

"I have a question for you, Crystal. Do you ever see yourself with Kyle in the future?" she asked.

"No, I'm dating Steve right now, and that shouldn't change the fact that Kyle and I are friends and only going to be friends. You shouldn't worry about that." I said.

"Well, don't do anything to make us fight, or you won't be able to see him anymore," she said, and then my phone rang.

"Hello," I said.

"Hey babe, what are you doing?" Steve asked.

"Oh, I'm at Kyle's girlfriend's house now," I said.

"Yeah, that's right, he told me about that. Kyle just wanted me to ask you if you wanted to come with me over there, but you already are," he said.

"Well, how close are you?" I asked.

"Oh, I just pulled into the parking lot and parking right by your car and got out, so I'll see you in about a minute," he said.

"All right, love you, babe," I said.

"You too," he said and hung the phone up.

About a minute later, there was a knock at the door, and Kyle answered it. It was Steve.

"Hey there," he said.

"What's up?" Steve asked.

"Come on in and join the party," Kyle said.

"Don't you mind if I do?" Steve said. He walked over to me, kissed me on the cheek, and sat beside me. Kelly was still looking at me, which I tried to ignore, but it wasn't helping, so I just got fed up with it.

"I'm sorry to ask this, but what is your problem with me, Kelly?" I asked.

"Oh, nothing; I don't have a problem," she said.

"Oh yeah, you do; now, what is it?" I asked her again.

"There is nothing wrong at all," she said, and the kids did something they weren't supposed to do. She got on to them, but it didn't work because they returned to do the same thing.

Another thirty minutes went by, and the kids were still doing the same thing but were not listening.

"Can you do anything about them? or am I going to have to," I asked her.

"What did you say about them?" she asked.

"I said are you going to stop them, or am I?" I asked.

"You are not to touch them at all," she said.

"I'm not going to do anything of the sort; just show you how to punish young kids," I said and walked over to them.

"You two play nice with each other, or the toys go up, and you get to sit on your beds until I say to get off of them; you got me," I said, and they started sharing the toys, and I sat back down.

But it didn't last long, and I got back up and walked over to them.

"Now, what did I tell you earlier? Give me the toys and sit on the beds until I say so." I said, but they didn't listen to me.

"Don't make me take them because then you will be in the corner, which I know you don't want now, do you," I said. I was looking mad at them to make them give me the toys, and they did. Then, they went to sit down on their beds until I told them to get up.

"Now that's how to discipline; learn on this," I said.

"I told you not to do anything with my kids, now didn't I?" she asked.

"Kelly, you have you get mean with them, or they are just going to keep pushing your buttons until you give up, and I should know that," I said.

"How can you? I know you don't have kids because you always boss around other people's kids like you just did, and I would have to see your kids and how they act with you punishing them," she said.

"I may not have kids, but I had to take care of my little sister as she was growing up to help out with my Mom as she was having health issues at the time," I said,

"But I told you to leave my kids alone, and you didn't." I want you out of my house and never come back," she said.

"All right, fine then, I will leave," I said, and I was walking to her door when I shook Kyle's hand. She got mad and grabbed my hand and pulled it away.

"I told you not to come between Kyle and me," she said.

"That is your first mistake," I said, and I pulled my arm out of her hand and wanted to hit her but not with her kids nearby.

As I opened the door and was getting out, she pushed me out of the door, and I tripped as I went outside.

"I don't want you back in this house ever," she said, but I got up, grabbed her by the arm, and started pulling her outside.

"That would be the last mistake you would ever make to me," I said, pulling her away from her house. I wanted to do something to her, but it wouldn't be right unless she hit me; then I would.

"Kelly, just let her be and come back in here," Kyle said; he got my attention, and Kelly slapped me across the face and was starting to walk away from me, and Steve was coming out there.

"Are you okay?" he asked.

"Yeah, I'll be fine for now, I guess," I said, and she looked at me one more time. I just gave her a sign that she knew all too well what it meant, and she slammed the door shut. Then, I walked to my car with Steve by my side.

It wasn't long after I left that two cop car was going by me on the road back to Kelly's house, maybe to talk to her about what just happened while I headed off to Randall's house to get ready for the show coming up.

When I knocked on the door, she answered it.

"Well, it's about time you show up here," she said.

"Well, can I come inside right quick?" I asked.

"Why? Is someone after you?" she asked.

"I'm not sure, but I don't want to be out here when they show up," I said.

"All right, come on inside." She said, and Steve was right behind me. Then, she went to her room, and the house seemed empty.

"Where are your parents tonight?" I asked.

"Oh, they are out of town for the weekend and won't be back until sometime Sunday afternoon," she said.

"Ohh, okay, well, let's get busy with what we need to do," I said, and we listened to the song we were going to sing. After I heard it the first time, the second time that they played it, I sang to it, and the others followed me in the song after about ten minutes of it. I needed a break from it to get some water.

"Well, you are doing great, Crystal," Randall said.

"Thank you for that; I'm taking a break right now to rest my voice," I said.

"You know, that new show that they have called American Idol, you should go on there and see if you make it," she said.

"Yeah, I heard about it last week, and they said that they were going to be in Austin in May, and I want to go down there when it happens, but if my parents didn't let me go, that would be the problem there," I said.

291

"They should let you; I mean, you are a good singer by the looks of it," she said. "Yeah, but try saying that to them and convincing them about it," I said.

"Don't worry about it, Sis; I'll take care of it for you, okay?" Kristen said. "All right, let's get back to singing before the night slips away," Randall said, and we went back to singing. We were getting better by the minute, but after about an hour of singing, my voice gave up. I told them that I needed to go home and rest my voice.

"Okay, I guess we will see you later," Randall said, and I drove off and then went to the house. As I got there and parked the car, I noticed that there was a cop car sitting down the road, but I couldn't tell if he was watching me or not. So, I walked up to the house and was about to unlock the door and go inside when a light was shined on me, and a cop came from behind, pushed me up against the wall, and told me not to move but to do as he said as he put handcuffs on me and took me back to his car and put me on his hood and then he talked to me.

"Okay, miss, were you at the Hawkins residence earlier this evening?" he asked,

"Who are you talking about, sir?" I asked.

"Were you at Kelly's house or not?" he asked.

"Yes, I was for about an hour or so," I said.

"And did you not hit her anywhere on her body?" he asked.

"No, I didn't, sir," I said.

"Well, it appears that you did, and she has the bruises to prove that you did," he said.

"I never even touched her, but she hit me instead, sir," I said, showing him my face where she slapped me.

"I believe that you told somebody to do that to you so that you can get out of this little thing that you have done to her," he said.

"Sir, I never touched her with my hands, let alone wanted to," I said.

"Well, you have to come down to the station with me and stay the night in jail," he said, putting me in the back and driving off to the station.

As he was driving, it didn't seem like he was going to the station like the officer said he was going to do, so I questioned him, "Sir, where are you taking me?"

"We are going to the station," he said.

"But the station was back there," I said.

"Oh, I'm sorry, I meant my station at my house," he said, and then I knew that he was not a cop, being a kidnapper, and he was taking me somewhere I didn't know.

"Let me out of the car now," I said.

"I don't think that would be a possibility right now, my dear," he said, and so I was looking for a way out myself, but when I looked at the door, there was no handle for the door or for the window of that matter, and the other side was the same way.

"This is not happening to me right now," I said.

"Oh yes, it is," he said, and he kept driving.

He stopped at a light. He turned to me, hit me in the temple, and knocked me out, and all I heard were these words, "This will keep you quiet until we get there, my dear." I passed out.

When I finally woke up, I noticed that I got handcuffed to a pole that looked like it was in a basement but was very dark. I tried to move my hand but didn't have much wiggle room to move them.

The door opened, and the guy came walking down; he had something in his hand and saw that I was up.

"Well, I see you finally woke up from your nap," he said.

"Where am I? and who are you?" I asked.

"Well, if I told you that, then I would have to kill you," he said.

"You know you won't get away with this," I said.

"You know, you are the seventh girl that has said that and they still haven't got me yet, and I'm about tired of that and this-" he slapped me across the face.

"-will remind you not to repeat it, you got that?" he shouted.

"No, I don't get it at all," I said, and he slapped me again.

"You are a fighter, and I like that in a girl. Well, I'll keep you down here until I want you out of here," he said, and he walked up the stairs and didn't say anything else, then shut the door.

After he left, I looked around to see what I could use to get myself out of the cuffs, but there was nothing for me to use, but I knew that I could break them just with my strength, but with my hands behind me, it was going to be more complicated.

After about two minutes, I broke them and got freed for a moment. I walked up the stairs and opened the door and saw that I was in a big house and I could hear him on the second floor of the house, and another girl was screaming, which meant that he was doing something to her, but I didn't want to find out. So, I made my way to the door of the place and saw that he had locked it, and before I could do anything, I saw a girl sitting in the corner. I knew her from school but didn't know her name, so I went to her.

"Hey, are you okay?" I asked.

"I'll be fine; just get out of here and tell the police about this place before he hurts anyone else," I said, and I saw the guy coming. I needed to get her out, but she told me to leave. So, I went back to the door and opened it.

However, as I walked out of the door, I felt my hair get pulled back inside, and he was the one doing it.

"Oh no, you don't; you are coming with me first," he said.

"Oh no, help me!" I yelled as loud as I could, but he shut me up by hitting me in the head; it didn't knock me out; it just gave me a severe headache. Then he threw me down on a bed, tied me up, and looked at me for a few seconds before hitting me in various spots until he grew tired of it because I wasn't yelling in pain. He leaves me there on the bed as he leaves the room.

He came back after about ten minutes, and he had one thing in mind, and I knew what it was. I waited for him to get close to me as he told me, "You're going to love what I do." but as he reached for me, I kicked him in the face knocking him off the bed, which gave me time to break the rope he used. I ran out of the room but not before he kicked me in the back, making me go down the stairs. I rested at the bottom as I still heard him yelling in pain.

As I got on my feet, I felt pain all over, but when I looked up, I saw him coming down the stairs toward me, "You're going to pay for that." he said, so I darted for the front door, but he grabbed my hair and tried to pull me back. I turned around and punched him twice in the face, which made him let go of me, and I opened the door and ran out of the house. He was right behind me, but my legs kept me ahead until I ran into some woods and hid while he searched for me. After about ten minutes of trying to look for me, he gave up and returned to his house.

Then, I continued going through the woods until, after about thirty minutes, I finally came up to a highway I knew and could recognize.

I was on Hwy 64 and was about twelve miles from town from what I could see around me. So, I started walking to town, keeping an eye out for him in case he was coming after me to kill me. It took me about twenty minutes to reach the city, and I went straight to Steve's house and told him what had just happened to me, and when I walked up to his house, I saw that the lights were still on, and so I knock on the door, and he answered the door.

"Oh, my goodness, Crystal, what happened?" he asked.

"I was kidnapped, taken to this guy's house, and assaulted by him," I said.

"Well, need to get you to the hospital," he said, and he grabbed his keys, and then he got me into the car, and we left for the hospital.

When we got there, they saw me, rushed me to the back of the ER, and put me into a room. They were checking me out to see if there were any problems.

After they did what they needed to do, they let Steve in to sit with me.

"Hey, they have the police on the way. I want to let you know," he said.

"Okay," I said, and he started to walk off, but I grabbed his arm.

"Stay right here, please, babe," I said. I didn't want him to leave my side for anything.

"All right, I'll stay right here with you." He said, and then the police came in to talk with me.

"Are you Miss Dawson?" he asked.

"Yes, sir," I said.

"Okay, I'm going to need to talk to you privately," he said.

"Oh no, I want Steve to stay with me," I said.

"Miss, I'm not going to hurt you," he said.

"You don't understand, sir; my boyfriend is staying here with me no matter what you say," I said.

"But, ma'am, I'm not like that crook," he said.

"Listen, Sir, I'm not leaving this room because a so-called officer just assaulted her, so I'm going to have to be in here with her whether you like it or not, and that's the bottom line," Steve said.

"Okay, I see your point." Miss, tell us what happened," he said, and I told him everything. After I finished talking, he knew who it was and knew where to find him. Then, he told us he would go to his house and get him. He left after that.

"Are you okay for about five minutes in here?" Steve asked.

"Yeah, I think so," I said.

"Okay, I'm going to the restroom, and I'll be back," he said and left me in the room alone.

The next day, I got discharged, and Kristen was up there with Randall waiting for me outside.

"Hey girl, I heard what happened to you. That must have been an awful experience for you." Randall said.

"What do you think? how about you go through the same thing that I did and then tell me about it because it's ten times as bad as it sounds." I said.

"You have to excuse her, she's still a little skittish around people, and she is not herself right now," he said.

"Yeah, and anything else they want to know about me?" I asked, but they didn't say anything else to me. As I walked to Steve's car and got in, I waited for him to get in and get me home.

When I got home, a cop was waiting there, and I was getting a little nervous because I didn't know who he was, nor was Steve. He came to my side and opened the door; I hopped right out, went right by his side, and didn't want to be close to him.

"Hi there, can I help you?" Steve asked him.

"Oh, we just want to ask Miss Dawlson here if this picture is the guy that took her front right up there last night," he said. I saw the picture; true enough, it was him, and I turned my head away.

"Ma'am, is it him or not?" he asked me again, and I turned back to him and put the picture back up.

"Yup, that is him," I said.

"That's what I figured since you told me about him a little bit. He was a cop at one time until he got caught taking young girls to his house and charged with a few counts of sexual assaults, but the cops never could get him because he would have just left when we got there. But last night, we were able to get him, and he sits in jail looking at life in prison." he said.

"Well, that's some good news. That guy didn't get a chance to do that with me just decided to assault me." I said.

"No, it doesn't, and I'm sorry that you had to go through it. I had a sister have the same problem happen to her, and I know how badly it affects a family and know that your life will never be the same again," he said.

"Well, thank you for telling us, and you have a good day, sir," Steve said, and the officer walked to his car and left. I didn't let go of Steve until the vehicle was out of sight.

"What was it with that cop anyways, girl?" Randall asked.

"Well, if you were listening, he said that the guy that kidnapped me was a cop at one time," I said.

"Oh, so that's why you were so close to Steve," she said.

"Yeah, and I will be more mindful about people after that. "I said.

"Well, how about we go inside and see what is happening here," Steve said, and he walked me to the door. It was unlocked, which meant that Mom and Dad were home. I was hoping that they would be back by now. I told them not to say a word to them until I did, and it would take me a while before I could get the nerve to say anything to them until I could find myself again and get the courage to say anything.

As May was approaching and American Idol was going to be in Austin that weekend, I told Mom and Dad that I wanted to go, but they still didn't give me an answer.

I told them that I was going with Kristen and Randall and that they would also try out. They wanted me to go so badly, but then my Mom said something that made me stop, "And there is another thing, what is this about you going to the hospital while we were gone one night and you didn't tell us?" she asked.

"Well, I didn't want to tell you until I was ready to say anything about it," I said.

"What happened?" she asked.

"I got trapped by an ex-cop, which he is now in jail for it, and he won't be getting out anytime in the next eighty years or so." I said, and my mother couldn't say a word, but my Dad could, "What do you mean sport?" he asked.

"A guy tried to have fun with me, but I was able to stop him from touching me, so instead, he assaulted me, Dad," I said, and he walked over to me.

"Baby, it's not good holding that stuff inside of you for that long period," he said.

"I know, but if you were me, you would have done the same thing because now, I'm looking behind me in school just to make sure that no one is sneaking up on me, and every time that I see Steve, I'm right there next to him because I know he will protect me from anybody that wants to hurt me," I said. I started crying, and my Mom held me.

I was about an inch taller than her, but she still had me, and my Dad did the same.

"Well, at least you told us the truth because your sister Kristen already told us the whole story. We just wanted to hear it from you, and we were giving you time to think about and to answer your question about going to Austin; you can go," she said.

"Oh, thank you, Mom; you won't regret this not one bit," I said.

"That's what I'm afraid of, my dear," she said. My sister walked out, and Sapphire and David followed; Kevin and Susan hugged me.

"And don't worry about anybody bothering you; you will have us behind you wherever you go, girl," Kristen said, and I hugged them all.

"Thanks for caring about me," I said.

"Now go and make us proud, dear. Go to Austin and make it through that American Idol thing," she said. So, Kristen and I went to get ready for it, and we were to head out that next day when we got in from school. I phoned Randall to let her know about it, and she was excited too.

But as I headed out the front door, I saw smoke in the distance. So, I morphed and flew to where it was and saw a house on fire and that they were yelling about a kid stuck on the house's second floor. I went in to see if I could find the child.

After about five minutes of searching, I found him, but Tasha was there; she kicked me out of the house, came out right behind me with the child, and held him by his foot.

"Don't hurt him," I said, and she let go of him, and I dove for him catching him in time and putting him back onto the ground safely. Then, Tasha wrapped a whip around me to pull me back to her, and as I returned to her, I hit her in the face. Then finally, she went back to the future and left everything alone, which didn't seem like her at all because she usually always tries to kill me, but she didn't this time.

As we got out of school that next day, we all got into my car and headed straight for Austin to beat a line of people before it was too late because we knew that the place was going to be packed full of people.

I wanted to avoid getting stuck out of the world's biggest show, and anyone I knew would be on it.

So, I didn't stop anywhere until we got on the interstate that went straight to Austin. Then, I stopped so that we could take a break from driving and stretched our legs out, and then after we finished what we had to do, we continued down the road until we arrived at Austin.

We found out the exact location because Randall had the map to find the place, but we needed help because Austin was such a prominent place, and it would take us a long time to see if we needed to know where to go. But luckily, the new car I got had GPS navigation. It took us right to where we needed to be, and when I found out where it was, I had to find the hotel and check-in.

I went to the main desk to check in as we arrived at the hotel.

"Hi there, I have a reservation for Crystal Dawlson," I said.

"Okay, one moment," she said, looking at the computer.

After about two minutes, she turned back to me, "Okay, I have one for you for two nights, is that correct?" she asked.

"Yes, that would be mine," I said.

"Okay, here is your key, and you have a nice stay with us," she said, and I walked off to the elevator, and the others followed me up to the seventh floor.

I walked out of the elevator, looked left, and saw our room at the end of the hall. As I entered, it was excellent, and they placed an extra small bed for one of us for those two nights; it was going to be me on it because I knew the other two would take the big ones, which didn't bother me.

"Hey Crystal, are you ready to go and eat?" Randall asked.

"Yeah, give me about a minute to get ready here, and I'll be right there," I said.

Since I drove the whole way here, I needed to make at least myself look better than this.

After about three minutes, I was ready and followed them to the car, and we went to eat at a place I didn't know they had down here until I saw it with my eyes.

"Hey Crystal, let's go there," Randall said.

"All right, let's go and see what they have," I said, pulling into the parking lot to park my car. It was a nice restaurant, and the host asked about how many.

"Three for nonsmoking," I said.

"Okay, right this way, misses," he said, and we followed him to a booth in the back of the place where they had a fish tank in the wall and a few TVs around the room. I was able to see them all from where I was sitting.

After about three minutes of waiting, our waitress came by, "Hi there, my name is Tessa, and what would you like to drink tonight?" she asked.

"Umm, what do you two want?" I asked.

"I'll have tea," Randall said.

"And me also," Kristen said.

"And make mine the same," I said.

"Okay, I'll be back with them," she said, walking off, and we looked at the menus. Then, my phone rang, and I looked at it, and it was Steve.

"Hey baby, how are you doing?" I asked.

"Oh, I'm doing okay. Where are you at right now?" Steve asked.

"Oh, I'm in Austin; why do you ask?" I said.

"Oh, I was just at your house, and your Mom told me you were going there; I guess I don't remember you saying that to me; I'm sorry," he said.

"Oh no, that's okay, dear. I should have told you about it during school today, but I just never said anything about it." I said.

"Okay, well, let me know how you're doing and hurry back home because it's not the same without you here with me," he said.

"Okay, babe, I'll be home as soon as this is over," I said, and he told me he loved me, and I did the same and hung up the phone. Then, the waitress was back.

"Here you go, miss," she said.

"Thank you," I said.

"Now, are you ready to order?" she asked.

"We are," said Randall.

"Okay, go ahead and take their order and then come back to me,"
I said.

"Okay, now what is your order?" she asked, and they told her. I
saw what they were getting, and it looked pretty good, but I needed
something else. So, I looked for something else that I liked.

"Okay, I'll have the grilled chicken but don't put any peppers on
them, and then I'll have a salad on the side," I said.

"Okay, I'll be back with your food," she said, picked up the menus,
and then walked off.

As she did, Randall looked at me, "Why don't you like peppers?"
she asked.

"Because I'm allergic to them, and I found that out when I was
about four years old when my mother put it in my mouth to try, and I
broke out with this rash all over my face, and she panicked. She rushed
me to the hospital, and they told her that I'm allergic to them." I said.

"Oh, okay, well, I didn't know that," she said. "Well, you should,
you're my cousin, and my mother told your mother about it," I said.

"Well, she never told me about it," she said.

"Well, now you know," I said, and I heard someone screaming
outside, I got up to see what was going on and saw that someone was
chasing a female down the road, so I went after him. He was running
fast but not faster than me, but he caught the girl he was chasing but
didn't know I was behind him, so I grabbed him by the neck and
pulled him back.

"Let her go now, or I'll break your neck," I said, and he did, and
the girl looked behind him and saw that I was a female.

"Now, I want you to get on before I call the cops; you got that,"
I said. "Okay, whatever you say," he said, and I let him go, and he ran
off. I started walking back to the restaurant when the girl stopped me.

"Thank you for stopping that, guy," she said.

"You're welcome; I had the same problem before," I said.

"Well, I best get going home," she said, leaving me there.

As I made my way back into the restaurant, the girls looked at me, "Oh, there you are; why is it that whenever someone is in trouble, you go running after them?" Randall reprimanded me.

"Because I don't like that kind of stuff." I said, and we stayed there for about forty minutes eating our food, and then I paid for it and walked out the door to see that it was still daylight, "Hey, what do you want to do." I asked, "Well, let's find the mall." Randall said.

"Okay, let's go," I said, and we got into the car and left.

As we drove to the mall, the sky was slowly getting darker, and I needed to find it because that's where the tryouts would be. However, as I looked everywhere, I almost gave up when Randall pointed to it, so I pulled in and parked the car. Then, we went inside the mall and saw it was big.

After about forty minutes of walking around, I saw where they were, and I told the girls that we needed to get back to the hotel and rest. So, they followed me, but we weren't going to leave because when I walked out the door, I saw everyone outside running around, and I looked up to see that Tasha was back.

"Oh, it has to be you to ruin the show, huh?" I growled.

"Well, I have always loved to crash parties that no one wants me at," she said, and she came after me, but I dodged and then morphed.

"You two get back to the hotel; I'll take care of her," I told the other two, and they went to the car and got out of there.

"Oh, come on, I wanted them to fight," Tasha said.

"This is only between you and me, and I'm going to end it," I said.

"Oh, you are, huh? We will see about that," she said, and she sent Sapphire's clone after me. I had to fight her and take her down without a problem. Then, she sent her clone after me, which was a little bit harder to fight, but after about ten minutes, I threw her to the ground, and then with my swords, I stabbed them both in the stomach, destroying them forever.

"Oh no! my creation. You are going to pay for that!" Tasha exclaimed.

"Bring it on then," I told her, and she came after me and had her swords out, too, and we went to fight in the sky and had people watching as we did.

Then out of nowhere, she hit me and knocked me to the ground where about fifty people were standing. They had to move, but one of them didn't, and I landed right on them, but I only knocked him down to the ground.

After I snapped out of it, I went back after her, but Laura got in the way of it, and I had to fight her, but it didn't take me long before I stabbed her in the stomach, making her fall from the sky and Tasha was next in line for me.

"How can this be?" she said shockingly.

"I have grown stronger over the past few months," I said.

"I'll guess I'll see you later," she said and flew off. Then, she disappeared into the distance, and the others were gone too.

As I looked down at the ground and saw all the people who witnessed what happened, I didn't want them to see who I was. So, I flew off to the hotel, and the girls were already there when I got there. So, I flew up to our room and knocked on the window, and they opened it.

"Oh, there you are, Crystal," Randall said, and she helped me in. I de-morphed and sat on the bed.

"Are you okay?" she asked.

"Yeah, but about two hundred people just saw me take out three girls," I said.

"Hey, that's okay. You just had to do that, or it could have been you instead," Kristen said.

"Yeah, but I even saw little kids watching it, too," I said.

"Well, at least you are still with us," she said.

"Yeah, that's something to be proud of, girl," Kristen said.

"Yeah, I guess you're right," I said.

"Well, let's sleep because tomorrow will be a big day," Randall said.

"Okay," I said, and I lay on the bed and went to sleep, hoping tomorrow would bring a better day for me.

As the next day came, we headed to the mall and waited. We had to stay in a long line of people already there. Most of them did not make it through the first two sets of judges, and only about twenty of them got through to the last set of judges, which didn't surprise me at all because I know this is a tough competition to go through.

As I made my way up to the sign-up desk, they asked for my name, and I did; they gave me a number to put on my chest so that they knew who I was when it came down to it, and then I sat back down until they called for me to go inside the place and sing in front of them.

It took them about forty minutes before they called my number. I walked inside the first room and saw three judges sitting in there. They asked for my name, so I did, then I started singing my favorite song. They told me to stop after about a minute, and they told me that I was going to the next set of judges, so I walked back out of the door and waited again. The other two also went inside the first room on my way back.

But as they walked back out of the room, I was walking into the next one, and they asked for my name, and I told them. Then, they told me to sing, so I did, and they liked it. And so, they told me I was the best so far that they had heard the whole day. So, they informed me when to go into the next room.

I was getting excited by the minute because I was probably going to make it all the way, and when I met up with the other two, they told me they were going to the next room.

I was happy for them and everything. After they went through and finished with what they needed to do, they went to the last judges. They were ready for them, but they called for them before me, which needed clarification. However, I didn't say anything.

They went in one at a time, and both came out but were unhappy.

"What happened?" I asked.

"Oh, we would have to come back next year and do this again," Randall said.

"Why is that for?" I asked.

"Because our voices are right there, but they want to give us another year to get them ready for them," she said.

"Well, I think they just called for me," I said; they called me again, and I told them I'd see if I made it. As I walked into the door, I saw them behind a table.

"Hi there, you must be Crystal." the guy in the middle said.

"Yes, that would be me," I said.

"Are you sure? Because we had the same girl, just like you walked in before you," he said.

"Oh, that would be my sister Kristen you are talking about," I said.

"Oh, okay, well, go ahead and sing for us," he said.

"Okay," I said and got the beat in my head, and I went singing. After about a minute of singing, the guy stops me.

"Well, I like your voice and how you can catch a pitch like that." said the guy to the left.

"Thank you," I said.

"I like how you just went to singing like the singer of that song, and I think you do have the talent needed for this show." the lady said that was on the other side of the guy in the middle.

"Thank you," I said again.

"Now, I hate to say this, but you do have a beautiful voice, don't get me wrong, but I think the show needs somebody with better singing," he said, and I was ready for the worst when he told me that I wasn't going to cut.

"But Crystal, you are going to Hollywood with us," he said.

"What? are you serious? Oh, my goodness! I can't believe it. Thank you for all of this." I said, and I went up to them and then gave them hugs, handshakes, and things like that.

Then, the guy gave me a paper saying where to go to Hollywood later in the summer, and I walked to the door. When I opened the door and saw Kristen and Randall outside, they saw the paper and were happy too.

"I'm going to Hollywood!" I told them excitedly.

"Are you kidding us?" Randall asked. I handed her the paper, and she saw it.

"You are going, girl; I knew you could do it for us," she said.

"Oh my, now I can't breathe," I said.

"Okay, let's get you to the hotel and get ready to leave tomorrow," she said, then she walked me out to the car and went to the hotel.

As the weeks passed and the end of school was nearing, I told my family that I had made it and told Steve about it. He was happy that I went that far into the competition and told me we'd see how far I could go in it, and I told him okay.

As the week of graduation came, and I had to be at the expo center for the graduation thing, I had to turn in my book and at the same time pick up my gown. Then, I had to go to where we were to practice, and we had to be there, or we weren't going to walk down the one that night. I ensured I was there; Randall talked to the principal about what she wanted to do for the whole class of 20 and said that Kristen and I would be singing with her.

"Well, you can do that just don't get carried away about it," she said.

"Oh, don't worry about it; we will keep it reasonable," Randall said, and we went to the stage to get ready for what was going to happen tonight and where we were going to stand and stuff like that.

After we finished everything, we had to go to the front of the place to meet up with the rest of the class and find out where we would sit during the event. I knew I would not be at the front with Randall and Kristen because I didn't do much during school. Still, I was about in the first twenty-five percent of my class because of where I was sitting, and after everyone sat down, the principal was in front of was, and she went to talk.

"All right, class, this is how this will work right here. The way you are sitting right now, this is how you are sitting in the other room tonight; now, during the whole time that we are doing this, you are to be quiet and not to do any funny business, or you will go home. You will have to wait till after graduation to get your diploma." She kept talking about other things. Then, she told us to return at six o'clock to prepare for the graduation. I left with Kristen and the gang.

We decided to head to my house and have a party; my parents had invited everybody to our house so that we could celebrate our graduation and begin our lives out in the real world, which I didn't prepare for yet.

After the party, I saw that we had about forty minutes to get back up there, so everybody got into my and Kristen's car. Then, we went to the expo center and waited until it was time to get out and head into the building.

At six o'clock, I got out of the car and walked into the building; half of the class was sitting. So, I took a seat where I was supposed to, and the other students slowly walked in and sat down, which I didn't know about, but Tasha was sitting about three spots down from me, which I didn't worry about at all.

As the time came for us to walk to where we were supposed to be, we got up row by row and started walking outside the building and down to the other part of the place. Then, we had to wait for about ten minutes until they were ready for us to walk on through.

As I made my way through, I saw it got packed with parents, friends, and things like that. Then, I finally got to my seat and sat down, and we waited for everyone else to get seated, and I saw Steve walk by, and I waved to him, and he did the same and walked behind me and sat about four rows back with Kyle behind him.

As everyone was in their seat, the place got quiet. The principal came up to the mic and talked for about fifteen minutes about how we are full of potential, how we could change the world we live in, and stuff like that. Then, it came time to name the Valedictorian and the Salutatorian, Randall was the first one, and the other one was a girl I didn't know, but her name was Lauren. They were up there, and

Randall talked to the class about how we have changed over the past few years to become better people since we started high school. Then, she wanted to sing a song and called for Kristen and me to come up there, so we did. Everyone saw me walking up there, and they were talking about me.

As I got up there, they handed me a mic, and they started the song; Randall was to do her part, then I would take over, and then Kristen was to sing her role, which we had all figured out before we got up there.

As she was singing, the students listened to her, and the chorus came. Then, they all sang and came to my part of the song; the students liked my singing because of what they said to me.

Then, in the last part, Kristen sang, and after she finished, we did the chorus one more time, and then the song ended. They clapped their hands again and stood up. I was amazed and then went back down and waited for the main part to start.

As they enumerated the students' names, they grabbed their diplomas, walked back to their seats, and called me, "Crystal Dawlson took the football team to the championship game and won Texas Scholar." I walked up to the front, got my diploma, returned to my seat, and waited for everyone else to do the same.

After everyone got their diploma, the principal came back to the stage and held the mic to say,

"Congratulations to the class of 2020," she said, and everyone threw up their hat, and then all the parents came down from the stands.

"Hey babe, that was some good singing. Can you sing for me tonight?" Steve said.

"Well, I'll think about it," I said.

"Good going, sport; now you are going put a dent into my spending for you?" Dad asked.

"Dad, how can you say that?" I asked.

"Ahh, you know I'm just playing around with you, and you know it," he said.

"Well, your grandpa would be proud of you, girl, and you know it." Mom said.

"Yeah, it's just not right that he is not here with me right now," I said.

"You know he is watching you from above," she said.

"Yeah, I know he is," I said.

"Hey girl, what are you doing this summer?" Laura asked.

"I don't know, maybe just have tons of fun," I said.

"Well, let's get started," she said and went outside the place.

As I was heading outside, I saw Silverie enter the gates and drive up to me.

"Hey, there you are. Listen, I need your help, and I mean big-time girl," she said. "What is it?" I asked.

"Tasha's back, and she is not in a good mood, and I think she has found someone else to use against you," she said.

"What are you saying?" I said.

"Someone you are going to meet in college," she said.

"Well, let me go to the others real quick," I said, but they were already waiting behind me.

"Let's go get her," Kristen said, and we morphed and flew off to try and stop her.

www.ingramcontent.com/pod-product-compliance
Lightning Source LLC
Chambersburg PA
CBHW071108250626
47159CB00002B/656